STEEL

BRACKEN RIDGE REBELS MC

MACKENZY FOX

Cover by: Mayhem cover creations
Formatting by: @peachykeenas (Savannah Richey)
Editing and proofreading by: Laura M Wilkinson (Fiverr)

AUTHOR'S NOTE

CONTENT WARNING: Steel is a steamy romance for readers 18+ it contains mature themes that may make some readers uncomfortable. It includes violence, possible triggers including domestic violence and a hostage situation, and LOTS of steamy love scenes!

BRACKEN RIDGE REBELS M.C. – Enter at own risk……..

Bracken Ridge Arizona, where the Rebels M.C. rule and the only thing they ride or die for more than their club is their women, this is Steel's story

Steel:

I didn't mean to get involved. Really it wasn't my fault. I'm the Sergeant at Arms and it's my job; to look out for the club, ensure ongoing safety and above all else refrain from violence where possible. I don't do anything by halves. But that was before Sienna Morgan waltzed into town acting like she owns the place, and now she does, well the clubhouse at least. One minute I'm sent to extract an offer to give us back what's rightfully ours, the next she's on the back of my sled and I'm about to lose my mind. I don't do romance and I'm not looking for an ol' lady, but that's all about to change.

I didn't mean to make her mine, but then again, rules are meant to be broken and I'm the right side of wrong.

Sienna

He's bad. He's mean. He's kind of hot in a *don't mess with me* kind of way. But I'm no fool, I know this town's run by bikers and I have something they want, something they need. I just never thought it would come to this and I'd be in the middle of a mess I may not be able to get out of. The more I try to run the closer he gets. I don't know if I can keep resisting but my own haunted past lurks in the shadows, ready to pounce if I let it. I fear Steel may become an addiction but I can't let that happen, I can't let him get too close because if I do, he may just break me in half for good.

SIENNA

I HAVEN'T BEEN in Bracken Ridge Arizona for very long, but I've been around long enough to know that nice girls don't belong in this bar.

The Stone Crow. It's an eclectic mixture of all the pitfalls of society dregs.

Some are here for a good time, some for a wild time, but mainly they're all drunks. There's of course the usual suspects that you'd expect in any hard liquor serving establishment; the regulars with their own seat at the bar, creepers who came to hook up with random strangers and chat up anything that moved, and the after-work 9-5'ers escaping for a while before they got home to the wife and kids. Predominantly however, it's filled with all the men your mother warned you about and to stay away from.

Oh, and then there's the bikers.

I've taken this job for the easy money plus it's not exactly rocket science. Bar tending's something I've done in college, though that was a million years ago now and not exactly something that I thought I'd see myself doing at almost thirty years old, that is until I found myself in Bracken Ridge.

Its not lost on me that this feels like failure, that somehow I am really just hiding out from all of the baggage that I thought I'd left behind in California, left for good along with a whole boat load of painful memories.

The only good thing about a Friday night at the Stone Crow is the time goes fast; you're too busy to think or question your life's choices, just keep the drinks flowing, don't make too much eye contact oh yeah, and stay away from the bikers. Hence the reason I'm here.

The Bracken Ridge Rebels MC.

A motorcycle club who own half of this place as well as a lot of the businesses across town. They hang out here sometimes and I'm sure that's just to scare some of the unruly patrons away.

I've been here two weeks, six hours and counting. My estranged Father Max passed away suddenly and left me in his will. That would be sad if I'd known him or even liked him, but I didn't, and now he's left me everything he owns.

He'd lived in this dreary little blue collar town for more than half my life. My parents divorced when I was small, he'd always been a big drinker and a bad gambler, he also wasn't very forthcoming with child support or *any* kind of support for that matter. I'm only here now to clean up his mess.

I'm aware he has a string of bad debts, unpaid loans and an even worse reputation of being a first class A-hole.

So this is where I find myself, in this strange little town run by bikers with even stranger people I don't know, in a bar that smells like stale beer and fish fry.

I live in the apartment upstairs; the co-owner Stef doesn't use it and she's taken a liking to me, plus the rents cheap and no-frills. I'd prefer that than having to rent a house I can't afford or worse share with a stranger.

Despite my complaints it's been a good thing to get away from Cali and all the bad memories there including a psycho ex-boyfriend and a restraining order. I never thought I'd be one of *those* women but sadly I'd put up with way too much, and when things turned physical I was lucky to get out when I did.

Now this is where I exile myself, a zillion miles from anywhere.

My main goal; to sort Max's affairs before the nasty lawyers and bank foreclosure step in to do it for me. Once I clear it all up there may be some cash at the end of it, if I'm lucky, and then I can escape this god forsaken place and start afresh somewhere new.

Dear old dad owns a farmhouse in the country, a couple of shops in the main street that are leased, and the bikers clubhouse out of town.

I try not to shudder at the thought.

The motorcycle club own the building to their headquarters but not the land, they'd been leasing it from Max for years. Subsequently they now want to buy it, and while it's a cut and dry transaction, I don't exactly relish the thought of having to go to that meeting.

"Yo beautiful, buy yourself one." The guy I've just laid a couple beers down for yells at me, distracting me from my thoughts. I smile sweetly and put the tip in my jar, which overflows most nights, it's only because I'm fresh meat and disengaged from reality; a lot like my current surroundings which I try to blot out, still, I move on up the bar without a second glance to the next customer who can't keep their gaze at my eye level. It's nothing to brag about; a simple Ramones tank-top and skinny black jeans was all it took to get the guys around here excited, which just goes to show the level of intellect, god help me. I try all night not to roll my eyes at every second person ogling or slurring incoherently like they don't have a drinking problem. I try in equal measures not to throw in the towel, because this is better than what I could be doing. This is better than my actual reality, one I refuse to go back to.

In all honesty I need this, the anonymity, I can do what I want, I get to be someone else for a while, *anybody* else, that's freedom, that's my source of power. And this ridiculous town called Bracken Ridge is just the place to do it.

*

We pull up outside the devils lair, although for all intents and purposes the gnarly skull and cross bones sign out the front declares it as the Bracken Ridge MC Headquarters. Subtle.

My attorney Laney Locket isn't from around here. I figure its best to hire someone out of town who isn't influenced by this notorious motorcycle club, plus I've watched Sons of Anarchy, I kind of know how things work and I'd prefer them to work in my favor. I have to be smart about this.

I've done some research and gotten valuations on what property is selling for around here, and while it isn't a boat load of cash it will still be enough to pay back all of the bad checks Max wrote, plus put a couple of months on the mortgage payment to get ahead. I don't need the bank foreclosing on me, that would be a disaster. There's a for sale sign in the front yard being banged in as we speak, it'll be listed online by the weekend.

I look at the building in front of us and cringe at the thought of going in there; I mean it isn't exactly welcoming with the skull and crossbones winking menacingly at you. That aside, today should be straight forward, a quick deal; the price is fair and at market value. There's nothing but a set of stupid iron doors stopping me from going in there signing the papers and walking away less a motorcycle club and a spring in my step.

I can do this. I just have to breathe.

"Are you sure this is a good idea?" Laney says from the car seat next to me, eyeing the clubhouse with a pained look on her face, that is not reassuring. She's brought along an assistant whose name I've already forgotten, but he isn't any help, in fact he looks like he couldn't fight his way out of a paper bag.

This isn't what I need. I need a ball busting lawyer and her fearless assistant ready to take on the world.

The club president is a notoriously hard man, from what I've heard, his name is Richie Hutchinson and he's been at the helm for over twenty-five years.

"It doesn't really matter if it's good or bad, it has to be done." I remind them, unaware until now that I am apparently the voice of reason. Neither of them however are making any moves to get out of the car.

It's going to be fine. I tell myself again. *Breathe in, breathe out, now is not the time to panic.*

Unfortunately, I can't meditate my way through this meeting; I have to get out of the car.

I bravely make the first move and step out of Laney's SUV and straighten the loose bow on my blouse and then I flatten out the front of my pants. I've decided to dress as business-like as possible in a sheer grey floaty blouse with built in camisole, the best black pants I own and a pair of patent pumps.

I've even gone to the lengths of using one of those donut buns, the thing that keeps your hair in place in a tight knot while doing all kinds of crazy things like windsurfing, horse riding and meeting with a biker club in their notorious clubhouse.

Laney follows suit holding her brief case and a large file stuffed under her arm which her assistant quickly takes from her, he then proceeds to drop it awkwardly on the sidewalk while attempting to tuck his shirt in at the same time. I internally face palm myself; I hope to god they don't have hidden security cameras out the front watching our clumsy exchange, they're probably all laughing at us right at this very moment. Seriously, this is all I need.

I also never knew a set of doors could be intimidating, but up close the heavy metal seems even more over the top, it dawns on me for real that we're not in Kansas anymore. The same skull and cross bones logo is etched into the framework, the kind that reminds you that you're about to potentially step into hell, you know, just in case you forgot where you were.

Above it was a plaque that read:

Ride or Die – Bracken Ridge Rebels Motorcycle Club.

I sigh a loud, noisy breath and wonder if it's too late to go get my brown paper bag from the car for breathing purposes. I refrain and pull the doors open with force, amazingly I'm greeted by a large, clean foyer and not what I initially thought; something crossed between a sleazy nightclub and a dungeon.

It's clean, bright and airy, the floors are polished concrete, good for party clean-up, I can also see now that the tinted windows are two-way, so you can't see inside from the front but you can see out.

It's predominantly black and white but has a huge red backsplash set behind the bar which look like it holds every hard liquor known to man, along with black leather couches, a huge projector screen, pool tables, a couple of dart boards, the usual things you would expect a biker club to have minus the stripper poles. The only thing missing was a mud wrestling pit and girls in skimpy bikinis, maybe they only worked the night shift since it was empty and quiet right now.

Before we go anywhere fast a pretty girl with dark hair appears out of nowhere.

"Hi!" She says brightly coming toward us like she's been expecting our arrival. "I'm Liliana….you must be…" she trails off expectantly.

"Sienna," I reply shaking her outstretched hand, she couldn't be older than about twenty-one. Realizing I only know one of my companion's names I smile awkwardly. "And these are my associates."

I internally slap myself for not paying attention. This is a very bad start.

"Laney." She also shakes Liliana's hand.

"Jarrod," says Jarrod. *Phew.* Okay. *Jarrod.* I have to try and remember that but I'm so bad with names and even worse with inconsequential people.

"Well, the guys are all looking forward to meeting you," she says brightly, like this is the best thing since sliced bread.

She ushers us forward.

Guys. *Guys?*

"Umm, aren't we just meeting with Mr. Hutchinson?" I at least remember *his* name; I look over my shoulder to Laney in panic.

Liliana's heels click clack across the shiny floor as we follow behind. She has a short skirt on, a Harley Davidson t shirt knotted at the front and sky-scraper heels. I wonder who she is and what she's doing here, not that it's any of my business, but she seems too pretty and sweet to be hanging out here.

"Oh no, all the patched members who hold a position are required to attend a meeting like this," she tells me as if we're discussing how lovely the taste of cotton candy is.

I have no idea what 'patched members who hold posi-tions' are and I'm afraid to find out.

"Can I get you guys a coffee, tea, water, hard liquor?" She laughs, giving me a wink.

At least she seems to have a sense of humor, that's strangely comforting.

"Are we going to need hard liquor?" I reply dead-pan.

She laughs again like I'm hilarious but doesn't answer; instead we stop at some heavy set closed wooden doors and she proceeds to knock, she waits a few moments then pushes one of the doors open.

"Hutch, your guests have arrived," she announces.

Guests? It sounds like she's just let the pack of wolves know their dinners ready.

I hide my apprehension as I hear a booming male voice say something and Liliana turns back to us.

"Please go ahead." She turns to us with a smile, motioning for us to go inside.

"Thanks," I reply, hoping that the beat in my chest cannot be heard because that's all I can hear and it's loud.

"Good luck," she adds with a wink as we proceed to enter the room, seemingly at our peril, into the depths of hell as the door closes behind us with a thud.

*

There's a large wooden table in the center of the room and around it sit six men, each one clad in leather vests and jackets. The one at the head facing me, I can only assume by his authority, is the club President, Richie Hutchinson, he looks kind of important.

There are three men to his left and two to the right, and they are all staring at us.

I'm completely blindsided and I momentarily consider turning back around and running out, back to the safety of the car and you know, daylight. I'm so glad I haven't come here alone, that would be just a little bit too much right now. I swallow hard and steel myself.

"Mr. Hutchinson?" I start, realizing my trusty counterparts are standing safely behind me and are completely still and mute, fat lot of good these two have been.

He's an older guy, maybe mid-fifties, with broad shoulders, he's not bad looking in a rough and tumble kind of way, he has a handsome, unshaven face with greying stubble and is wearing a black bandana wrapped around his forehead in your usual bad-ass biker way, he also has a sleeveless leather jacket on with words "President" stitched to the left breast pocket. The patch is worn and tattered like he's been wearing it a long time.

He nods from his chair and gestures us to the table before him.

"Miss Morgan," he says in a deep rumbling voice. I can tell immediately he's a man of presence just by those few words alone, some people just have that knack and it's slightly terrifying. "We've been expecting you. Please have a seat."

Polite enough, but why's it so dark in here? There are only a couple of small windows around the top of the far wall that hardly let any light in. This room definitely needs a woman's touch and it smells like smoke.

I avoid the other pairs of eyes on us and take a seat at the end of the table where three chairs have been set out. How they knew there would be three of us I don't want to think about, they've probably all been watching us sit in the car for fifteen minutes arguing about who was going to get out first. I'm probably right about the surveillance cameras.

"Thank you," I reply. "Please call me Sienna, this is my attorney Laney and her assistant….." *Shit, umm….. Jesus H Christ…..*"Jarrod," I finally spit out.

I glance momentarily around the table and see a mixed variation of men. It's hard to take it all in at first, a lot like when you stare at the sun for too long and start seeing spots.

Tattoos. Bandanas. Chunky jewelry. The smell of leather.

The taste of cigarettes. There's enough testosterone in this room to fill an entire village, it's almost palpable. Weren't bikers meant to be old, cruddy, beer-bellied fat guys? These dudes are pretty damn hot and the only old one is Mr. Hutchinson, though he's not exactly ancient himself.

The others in my posse follow suit and any minute now Laney's going to launch into lawyer mode and bowl us all over with her smart and witty well thought out plan of attack…..*any minute now……*

Instead Mr. Hutchinson decides to get the ball rolling by getting the formalities out of the way. He's eyeing me curiously and has an amused look on his face.

"These are the guys, they'll be witnesses for the meetings proceedings, this here is my Vice President Brock." He thumbs the guy to his left with the widest shoulders and largest chest I've ever seen, he obviously lifts weights, he has long, wild hair and a beard and piercing blue eyes, yeah he could cut glass with his eyeballs. Mr. Hutchinson continues before I can linger too long. "Then there's Gunner, Rubble, Bones and Steel."

As my eyes fell on each of them, I take them all in one by one.

Gunner looks like the youngest, he's blonde and blue eyed with floppy hair hanging around past his ears, Rubble has dark hair and tattoos running up his neck, he's also got more jewelry on his fingers and up his wrists than I've ever seen on a guy ever. The one named Bones has a freshly shaved Mohawk and a fairly applaud worthy beard, he grins at me tipping his head, and lastly there's Steel, he just stares at me with these piercing dark green almost grey eyes and his jaw ticks like he's clenching his teeth. He's the biggest out of all of them and has tattoos scattered and completely covering both his arms and hands so you can't see any actual skin, his fingers are linked together as he assess us at the end of the table, or rather, *me*. I don't know what he sees but he doesn't look happy.

Why was it that all bikers have weird nicknames? Well it's true when you think about it; their mom's probably gave them perfectly good, normal names at birth. I'm sure nobody in their right minds would choose to call their new-born bundle of joy Rubble.

The one named Gunner grins at me, *ooh he's cute*. My heart rate kicks up a notch as he assesses me head to toe quite obviously with a smirk plastered across his face. He has a baby-face, golden blonde hair and striking light blue eyes, he's very good looking and he looks like he knows it. As he smirks his eyes twinkle suggestively. *Unnerving and slightly awkward.*

They all give a chin lift as they're introduced, all except the one named Steel, I don't know why my eyes linger on him, maybe it's the bad-ass look he's giving me or maybe he just got out of bed on the wrong side and I'm imagining it.

"Sergeant at Arms." The blonde one, Gunner helpfully pipes up. *Awesome, I've been caught staring.* "Steel's the clubs enforcer; he not only takes care of security issues but also rounds up cute, little lost girls from out of town who appear to be on the wrong side of the tracks."

Some of the guys snicker. My eyes go wide.

"Just kidding," he laughs giving me a wink. I don't know which part he's kidding about.

Steel doesn't laugh, oh no, he just watches me with a blank expression that's completely composed, he's got that down pat, at least Gunner seems friendly.

"Excuse the hostility," Mr. Hutchinson cuts in giving Steel the side eye. "We don't usually have bit…. uh…..*Women* in the meeting room." He flashes a grin, he has perfect white teeth but it's more like the grin of a wolf before it devours its prey, that does nothing to settle my nerves.

I gulp and question what I've walked into, and was he about to say….. *Bitches?* Rude.

I smile back sweetly like the intimidation going on here isn't affecting me one bit. No, I hang out at biker clubhouses all the time and embroil myself in biker business.

I realize they probably think being a woman ultimately makes you stupid and therefore unable to partake in negotiations, like the one in progress, therefore it's probably beyond my mental capabilities, but little do they know; they're messing with the wrong bitch.

Finally, with relief so palpable you could bottle it, Laney decides to speak, hoorah! I try not to blow out a full lungs load of air as she takes over.

"We have drawn up the proposed agreement for the purchase of the property." She begins as I listen on with silent intention. That was Jarrod's que to fish the documents out from the manila file.

"My client wishes for a quick and simple transaction, and we feel the price is reflective of the current market value, everything is in the paperwork attached."

I hand the file to the one closest to me, Bones I think, the one with the Mohawk.

I don't want to think about how he got his nickname and hope it didn't involve breaking any.

He's not as chunky as that Brock guy or Steel but he's still muscly, he has a tattoo of a naked woman on his forearm with a snake wrapped around her and an apple in her mouth, I glance down at it wondering why anyone would get that much ink and of a naked woman right there for all to see, or the pain one would go through in order to get it.

Bad-ass bikers that's who. I want to shudder, I hate pain, I'll never get a tattoo.

He winks as he catches me looking. "Ex-girlfriend," he tells me as my eyes blink rapidly in succession.

I look away embarrassed as he takes the papers and passes them to Steel; he's still watching me with frosty regard throughout the whole exchange. I stare back, I don't know where this sudden bravery has sprung from but I refrain from giving him the middle finger.

Okay I'm a woman and you hate me, whatever.

Mr. Hutchinson fishes out some reading glasses, if you can believe it, from his top pocket and flicks open the file and begins to study the papers as soon as they land in front of him.

I can feel the one named Gunner looking at me, my eyes inadvertently move to his and he purses his lips like he's about to say something. *Jeez he's easy on the eyes.* I'll bet he gets any girl he wants without even having to open his mouth, and what a beautiful mouth….

"I think everything should be to your satisfaction," Laney adds after a few moments of uncomfortable silence as we all wait for him to finish reading.

Mr. Hutchinson holds up one hand to presumably stop her speaking and he keeps on studying the documents like it's the most interesting thing he's ever read. This goes on for quite some time.

Maybe it's time to break the ice a little bit. I mean, I'm not exactly shy and this just feels kind of weird with nobody saying anything, you could hear a pin drop in here.

Do not talk about the weather.

"How come you don't have women in this room?" I ask referring to Mr. Hutchinson's earlier comment, directing my question at the cute one, Gunner. He seems like the most friendly and approachable of the bunch. I feel Mr. Hutchinson look up momentarily from over the top of his glasses but he doesn't say anything, he goes straight back to reading like I'm not even there.

I feel my useless colleagues look at me sharply like I've

gone insane. Well, it doesn't say anywhere that I can see that 'bitches' can't speak. If this is some kind of 'secrets men's' club then they shouldn't have invited women into it.

Gunner bites his lip, fighting a smile as Brock grunts and shakes his head, like it's the most outrageous question he's ever heard. Maybe women weren't allowed to even think in their presence let alone talk?

I smile sweetly just to get my point across, hoping I appear as ditzy as they believe I am, I'm sure that kind of impression can only help me where they are concerned.

Gunner leans his arms on the table; his mid-length hair falls about his face as he brushes it off with one hand. "Because women don't make decisions here sweetheart." His eyes drop to my lips very obviously. *No shit, I kind of got the memo on that one.* "But we sure as hell love 'em visitin'," he adds mischievously.

I don't know if I've taken a shot of adrenaline alongside my coffee this morning, but it's such a sexist statement about women not making decisions that I just can't help myself. *Who cares?* I'm never going to see any of them again.

"So this must be a very intriguing scenario for you then?" I reply. "What with me owning the place and everything." I want to add that they are a sexist bunch of ass holes but I somehow refrain, I'm sure it's obvious by my sarcastic tone.

I mean honestly, do they even hear themselves? *Women don't make decisions here sweetheart. Barf.*

I feel all eyes on me but I hold my head high.

It's possible that they hate Max just as much as I do, but my reasons are entirely different.

"It's certainly a new experience," he replies with a laugh, sitting back in his chair relaxed, at least he's enjoying himself, nobody else seems to be. It kind of feels tense in here.

Maybe it's another of their tac-tics. Get the cute one to flirt with me and because I'm a woman with no brain cells or free will -who knows- they may just be able to pull a fast one over me by intimidation and hostility. Well, little do they know, I have nothing to lose.

With a thrumming heart we sit and wait for Mr. Hutchinson, ruler of the world, to finish reading every single word on every single line of the contract, the very same one that was emailed to him weeks ago that he's probably read a hundred times already.

Well, I will not be intimidated, I refuse.

He looks up eventually, taking his glasses off and chews on the end of one of the arms, the look on his face is thoughtful but gives nothing away.

I'm trying to gauge it here, usually I'm good at that and at reading people and I can usually decipher someone's general mood, but for the first time in a long time I'm actually totally unsure of what he's going to say. He doesn't look mad, he doesn't look entirely happy either, if only I could be a mind reader, oh yeah, *and not a woman.*

Everyone turns to look at me and I wait, very patiently, for deliverance.

2

STEEL

I DON'T KNOW why she's picking me to have a stare down with. She shouldn't take it personally; I look like this at everyone. It's my job to be a cold son-of-a-bitch. It comes with the territory, and right now she's in *my* territory, in *my* clubhouse.

It's almost comical that she's technically our new land-lord; I've never seen a landlord who looks like that. Still, she wants out and we want in. We've been eyeing this land for years, so on the surface, things should be cut and dry... a done deal... if only things were that simple.

I watch as she fiddles nervously with her hands on her knees. Her body language gives her away. Every now and then she looks around, being careful not to linger anywhere too long, and she's avoiding looking at me, which is smart.

She's pretty. Fucking beautiful actually. Her hair is a soft honey blonde, and for some god awful reason it's tied up in a bun. I imagine my hand pulling it down to wrap around my fist. *Jesus.* Even though her unsure blue-green eyes dart around, she has the grace to keep looking hopeful, like things in this room might get better before they get worse. Boy, do we have news for her, and it's all bad.

I continue my silent, mindless observation. She's tan because she's from California, well dressed... a neat and tidy package, not like the girls around here. I can tell she's got a tight, hot little body under those clothes and tits that would make you sit up and weep. She shouldn't wear anything sheer like that. Ever.

That fucker Gunner is giving her a full-on fuck-me grin, but that's typical of him. God's gift to women, he's got the kind of look that works on women of any age, color, or creed. He has a way with the chicks because of how he looks and his charm, but he's too obvious with it. Then again, some chicks like that I guess. I wonder what little Miss Sienna Morgan likes.

Unbeknownst to her, I know all about her. Unlike some of my brothers, I haven't just come into this meeting to check out some new piece of ass and hopefully sign the deed to the clubhouse. No, I've done my research like any upstanding Sergeant of Arms of an MC would. I've come prepared.

My training in special ops in the military means I can do background work quickly and thoroughly, and even though there was quite a bit to sift through, I guess old habits die hard. I know more about pretty little Sienna Clare Morgan than I have a right to.

I know she's twenty-nine and from southern California. She majored in Business Management, and until recently she worked as a senior associate at a bank. She's not married, no brats, was raised by a single mom, and has no siblings. I don't know much about her financial status, but obviously she's inherited good ole Max Morgan's investment portfolio, or should I say *debts*. She has no criminal record, and judging by the looks of her, she's probably never even gotten a parking ticket.

17

I stare at her as she taps one of her light pink nails on the table absent-mindedly, trying to pretend that none of this is getting to her.

"How long are you in town for?" Gunner has the audacity to ask. *Is he actually crazy?* We're in the middle of a business deal, and here he is chasing pussy right in front of everybody, which is just his style: he doesn't care, as long as he gets in first.

I'm not sure if I'm buying this whole sweet, innocent act she's got going on yet though, and I can't stop thinking about bending her over the end of the table and giving it to her hard and fast.

For fuck's sake. I need to get my head in the game. I also try to zone Gunner out, which is never easy.

The Stone Crow. Oh yeah, I know all about that too. Where she works, where she lives, where she goes; I had to get a bead on her before the meeting, and it's not stalking behavior exactly... It's for the club. One thing's for sure, though; Sienna Morgan isn't the type of girl you hook up with and screw once. Hell, you'd have to get past her best friend, her advisors, and her tennis coach to even get a look in; and even then, she'd want a contract drawn up. I hope not by her useless lawyer, though, or there'd be no chase at all.

As far as the club is concerned, Hutch would much rather the bank foreclose so he can snap up Church super, super cheap, and that's the plan, she just doesn't know it yet. So, this little charade is exactly that, a charade, going through the motions. It's shitty, but that's how business works. She's in our town now, and these are our rules.

I cross my feet at the ankles and wonder idly if she has it in her. The fight. 'Cause she's about to be on the ride of her life, whether she knows that right now or not.

Of course, having a deadbeat like Max Morgan as your

dad would make anyone tough, estranged or not, so I kind of hope she has some fight in her.

I glance at Hutch; he's still reading the papers like he doesn't already know what's in there. We all do; nothing's changed.

I risk another look at sweet Sienna's face and catch her exchanging a glance with her attorney. It's a *"what the fuck is going on?"* kind of look.

I glance at Gunner, who, I can tell, is about to go in for the kill. I subtly kick his chair leg with my boot before the words escape him. He glances over at me. I shake my head once at his questioning frown.

Keep it in your pants, big boy. We don't want to scare her off.

If everyone around here would just let me do my job and didn't try to screw things up every five minutes, then my life would be a hell of a lot simpler. The last thing I need is him screwing with the club's new landlord. Then again, maybe it would do her some good. Gunner can do some pretty wild shit.

"…There are some things to discuss with my brothers here," Hutch begins as he removes his reading glasses. "So, we will review the terms set out here amongst ourselves and get back to you in due course."

He's going to draw this out for her. I glance her way again. She looks just slightly stunned, and her forehead creases in confusion. I hope to god she kicks up a fight.

I wonder if she's a spitfire in the bedroom, too. Suddenly, a range of positions that I'd like to see her in come to mind, and I wish Gunner would kick me back under the table so I'd get my mind out of the gutter. I can't help it: she's perfect, but she's way too sweet to be here.

"I was hoping that we could discuss it today, we're happy

to wait outside," she counters, clearly desperate to get this deal done.

Hutch looks down the table at her long and hard. He's one tough motherfucker. He definitely isn't used to "negotiating" with a woman. Not that we're total Neanderthals, but in his eyes, old school ways still rule. Women have their place, and it isn't in meeting rooms discussing business, especially his clubhouse. Even though his ol' lady works in real estate and is a ball buster herself, she doesn't come in here. Hell no. Club business is between men, which Gunner already pointed out, and I saw how well that went down with her. She thinks we're total assholes.

But this is different. Miss Morgan now owns this joint, and if she's smart she'll realize she has us by the balls.

Hutch always has to be right. Always. And he isn't going to let a woman come into *his* Church that he's spent over half his life running and keeping legit and tell him what to do, especially a beautiful, twenty-something-year-old beauty queen from the golden state. Not going to happen.

I almost feel sorry for her. If I didn't want to bone her so bad I might, actually, but I can't stop looking at her. Picturing her hair loose and my mouth at her neck is rendering me speechless... and rock hard.

"That just isn't going to be possible," Hutch mutters. "We will discuss the counteroffer, and once we've done that, Steel will deliver it and our terms in person."

She blinks a couple of times as if digesting what he's just said. Surprisingly, she doesn't move to leave as most people would after that blunt dismissal. She just stares back.

"Counteroffer?" She fires back, repeating his words.

Hutch sits back in his chair and studies her. He's a fairly big man, not bigger than me, but intimidating enough. To emphasize his point, he crosses his arms over his chest and narrows his eyes as if he's not understanding why she's still sitting here.

"That's what this is, Miss Morgan, a negotiation."

She doesn't let up. "I'm confused. When you say, 'delivering your terms', what terms would those be exactly?"

Hutch doesn't miss a beat.

"Well, given the fact that the club has built this building from the ground up with our own funds from its previously dilapidated state, no depreciation, for example, has been taken into account for what we've put in."

She clasps her hands together tightly.

"Depreciation is claimed on your taxes though, right? It's not something that would be reflected in the price of land or its value. In fact, it has nothing to do with it. If you chose to use money of your own to rebuild and renovate this building, that was between you and Max. So, I don't see how it's relevant, to be frank."

Fuck. She's smart. I have to bite the inside of my mouth to keep from smirking. We all stare and can't quite believe the words that just came out of her mouth. She has no idea who she's dealing with, and she doesn't seem to care.

Hutch's jaw twitches. He isn't used to anyone, especially a woman from out of town, firing back at him like that or posing any kind of challenge.

I try not to stare at her chest as her breathing becomes more rapid. This is getting more delicious by the second, and I don't like where my thoughts are going but I can't help it. She's hot.

"Like I said, we'll be in touch," he says with finality, frost in his tone.

"Right," she counters, then glances at the woman next to her, completely ignoring the dude on the other side. "Well, we'll see ourselves out then. Thank you, Mr. Hutchinson, for your....*time.*"

I like the sarcasm, but *Mr. Hutchinson* sounds so wrong. I like her. She's got spunk.

He gives her a curt nod.

"See you around," Gunner calls after her. Bones snickers across the table, shaking his head.

The assistant gathers the remaining contents of the paperwork together messily while I stare at Miss Morgan's perfect ass as she disappears.

I glance over to Brock, who just sits there shaking his head and running a hand through his hair, an amused look plastered on his face.

"Nice piece of pussy," Gunner remarks before anyone can cut in. "Wouldn't mind getting me some of that."

"Didn't know you did redheads," says Bones, referring to the lawyer lady, whatever her name was. More laughs ensue.

Gunner rolls his eyes and sits back in his chair. "Funny fucker," he mutters.

"Keep it in your pants," Hutch replies. He sounds exasperated and definitely not pleased. "We don't need sexual harassment charges on us. She doesn't even realize she's got us by the balls, and I'd like to keep it that way. She might be a sweet piece of ass, but that doesn't mean I'm going to let you charm the pants off her and blow this whole thing. The last thing I need is some crazy bitch disgruntled because you wanted to chase some tail and didn't call her in the morning."

"Gunner hasn't charmed anyone in his entire life," says Rubble. "Let's be real here."

"I think what I have in mind might actually sweeten the deal, for everyone concerned," Gunner laughs like he'd be doing this poor, unsuspecting chick a favor. "She might be a little bit more flexible about things when I'm done with her."

I don't know why I want to punch his face right now. Maybe it's because I like her... or maybe it's because someone should fuck up Gunner's face just so he'll give it a rest for a while. He can't rely on personality alone; he needs his looks.

"Not with this girl," I mutter.

All eyes fall on me.

"She's too smart for you anyway, brother," I add. "A woman like that won't jump into bed with you or anybody, that I can guarantee. She's too prim and proper, she's a ball buster, and she ain't gonna go down without a fight. I know her type."

"I'd like to see her prim and proper on the end of my…"

"Steel's right," Hutch cuts in before we all get an unwanted visual of what Gunner's about to describe. "She's not exactly stupid, which is a shame because it would make life a hell of a lot easier. If she's inherited Max's pig-headedness this could be a long, drawn out process."

Groans roam around the table. He's right.

"What's the plan of attack?" Bones asks. "What's the offer?"

"More than we should pay," Hutch grumbles. "We're better off riding this out, getting the bank to foreclose, and moving in with a dirt cheap offer. What she's asking is more than fair in this current economic climate, but I don't feel like playing fair right now. Max fucked with me for too long, and someone has to pay. It's a pity that it has to be his pretty daughter, but life isn't fair… plus, I don't really give a shit."

"Should we be riding this out?" Brock asks, concerned. "I mean, prime real estate in this town doesn't come around too often."

Hutch gives him a pointed look that says everything. "Who is honestly going to dare to outbid the Rebels?"

That is an extremely good point. Nobody in this town is going to go in and undercut Bracken Ridge MC, or Richie Hutchinson for that matter. They'd have to be demented… or suicidal. While the club is completely legitimate, there is still an element of fear around the MC where outsiders are concerned. Although, they don't seem to mind too much when donations are needed for charity events or town projects. Oh yeah, they are happy for the Rebels help then.

The club has been established in Bracken Ridge for over thirty years, but it had taken Hutch a good ten years to drag the club's name out of the dirt and stop all the illegal shit going down. This meant other members had come and gone; some were locked up and some just dropped off the radar. Now we all have businesses and work, no illegal shit and definitely no drugs. Too many brothers over the years had been into guns and drugs and ended up in a concrete box or six feet under. No one sitting around this table wants any of that shit going down again. It just isn't worth it.

"You got intel on her?" Hutch asks me.

"Yeah," I reply, offended he even has to ask. "Not much to tell, she's an ex-banker or some shit from Cali, an only child, single, no kids, and she's got a fucking degree in business management. So she knows money and obviously has some smarts, not your average blow in, lord knows why she's bartending."

"She was definitely well put together," Rubble remarks.

I leave out the intel on her personal life that I'd stumbled upon. I wish I'd left the single part out, too, on Gunner's account.

Ever since I first laid eyes on her ten days ago, I haven't been able to get her off my mind. One thing is for sure though, I sincerely doubt she wants any biker action.

Brock sighs. "So, what's next?"

"We send back a ridiculous counter," Hutch retorts, like it's obvious. "And if she refuses, then we won't budge. If it's a war she wants, then she's got one. Max owes this club, and we're going to get our dues, brothers, that I can promise you."

Agreement goes around the table. Hutch pounds the gavel and sits back, satisfied.

Then he turns and points at me. "You're going to deliver the new counteroffer." He turns just as swiftly to Gunner and then points at him. "And you're going to keep it in your pants at least for the moment, you got me?"

"This sucks," Gunner mutters like a little girl.

"Until the deal is done," Hutch grunts. "Then I don't give a flying fuck where your dick lands. Chase her out of town for all I care."

I bite back my bark at that thought. What do I give a shit what Gunner does anyway? I mean she is just another piece of ass, a challenge for him, another notch on his belt. That shouldn't bother me at all; I was the same at his age. She probably found him attractive; most women do.

"You got that?" I say as we stand, glancing at Gunner. He's not amused, but I like winding him up; it keeps him on his toes. "What little Miss Morgan doesn't realize is she needs a real man to soften the blow, not some pretty boy hotshot who can't even grow a decent amount of facial hair and has nipple piercings."

"I know what she'll be blowing," he counters, smiling sarcastically. "Just because we're not all mountain men doesn't mean we're useless."

"You're too fuckin' pretty. That's your problem. Chicks want a bit of rough, not Keanu fuckin' Reeves."

"Bite me."

Then I grab my junk for good measure. "They don't call me Steel for nothing, bro."

"Shut the fuck up, the pair of you," Hutch bellows. He crosses out the amount typed neatly on the purchase offer and scribbles some stupid amount that even I balk at, then shoves the papers at me. "Nobody's sticking nothing nowhere, got me? Now get out of my sight and go bicker like little schoolgirls somewhere else. And Steel, when you've got her answer, call me. Until then, I don't want to see or hear from either of you."

We shove each other around until we get to the door, and he insists I go first because of "age before beauty". I elbow him hard in the stomach, winding him as he curses me under his breath. Pussy boy.

"Good thing you got looks, brother," Rubble grunts, barging past Gunner and shoving him into the door too, injuring his shin and causing him to curse some more. "Cause you're shit at comebacks and even worse at growing a beard."

I laugh, leaving Gunner cursing both our names and wander to the lot out back to retrieve my Harley and get home to my baby.

3

STEEL

THE WORKSHOP IS LOCKED up by the time I get home. Steelman's Mechanics is my own business, one I started a couple of years ago after investing in Rubble's tow truck shop in the adjoining building. We'd both worked every shitty shift in the universe to make his business viable, and then in turn he'd helped me build the workshop from the ground up. Now we share the lease on both the buildings. Fixing cars and bikes is my day job, but restoration is my real love --- my passion --- although I don't get to do a lot of custom jobs around here.

My other love is my dog Lola, my baby. She looks up from where she lies between the office door and the couple of steps down into the workshop. She has a good vantage point from there and can see everything. Her tail wags wildly when she sees me, but she's too lazy to get up. I sigh as I see the pink headband around her head with a flower attached. My sister Lily or one of the other club girls has clearly been here today. This is what they do: replace the skull bandanas I put on her with frilly, girly shit, just to annoy me.

My dog's a rescue, a pit bull ex-bait dog that I'd taken in

some years back as a foster, but she'd never left. She wasn't a fighter, which was why she had half the side of her face ripped open and had to be rushed to emergency surgery after she was dumped on the side of the road. Her sack of shit owner had deemed her useless and too costly to fix. Subsequently, she lost one ear and almost an eye on the same side, yet somehow the vet had managed to save her, which was basically a miracle. They'd literally sewn her face back together, when any other vet probably would have put her down.

I didn't mean to keep her. I've fostered quite a few dogs over the years with the local shelter in town I help, Faux Paws. I just prefer a dog's company to that of humans'. They don't judge you; they just accept all your flaws. She's helped with my night terrors, something I used to get every damn night after returning from my tour in Afghanistan. Without her, I probably would've had a gun down my throat at that period of my life; things were bleak back then.

I tracked down the dog fighting ring she'd belonged to with a bunch of other keen dog lovers, including my club brother Rubble, and we'd gone at the perpetrators with a baseball bat. They wouldn't be harming anybody again, that's for sure, and the illegal dog-fighting ring was shut down.

Sometimes the club likes to dish out their own form of punishment to those who deserve it, and most of the time it isn't pretty. I never harm anybody innocent or anybody who doesn't deserve it, but jail is too good for those sons of bitches or anyone that can knowingly inflict that kind of torture on a living being. It boils my blood like nothing else can.

"Hey, baby," I say. I take the four steps up to the office level, kneel, and rub behind her good ear as she rolls her head into my hand. I continue this daily ritual under her neck too, just how she likes it. "How's my little angel?"

She whimpers in response, licking my hand as her tail whips around madly. I don't know what she sees in me, but I'm grateful every day to have her.

She's the most perfect dog I've ever seen: white with a bit of black around her face and a dark patch over her good eye that makes her look like a badass. She does look kind of mean, but she's like me; her bark is way worse than her bite, not that I'd admit that to anyone. Despite her distrust of humans, she took to me right away. Maybe we clicked because we were so similar. We were both broken back then.

I rip the pink thing off her head, pull a skull bandana out of my back pocket, and place it around her head. She likes something around her noggin where her scars are. She'd had to wear a compression headband bandage for six months after her operation, then whined when we took it off. I guess she's just gotten used to having something there, and it's now like a comfort thing for her. I just don't like the soft, pink, pretty shit. We've been doing this for years with the headbands, and so far neither me or the club girls have backed down. I'm determined to make her a biker bitch, and they're determined to make her a princess.

I live above the workshop in the small, adjoining apartment. It's convenient, and it has all I need. Plus, I save on rent.

"Come on, girl," I say, heading to the flight of stairs that leads to the apartment. "You hungry?"

Her head whips up, and she suddenly jumps up like a spring chicken and flies past me up the stairs. She always acts so lazy and useless, until it's dinner time, then she's a puppy again.

I sigh, thinking about going to the Stone Crow later, although I've had worse jobs to deal with and this by comparison is a piece of cake.

I switch the lights on when I get upstairs and Lola is

already at her empty bowl, moving up and down the kitchen impatiently, growling and snuffing at me to hurry up. I snort a laugh, toss my phone, wallet, and keys on the countertop, and reach for the fridge handle to pull out a beer and the container of dog food at the same time. I eye some lasagna in a glass dish that somebody left in there; I don't cook very often so it was definitely not me. I flip the lid off my beer using the edge of the countertop and take a swig. Lola brushes up against my legs, looking up at me like she's never been fed in her entire life.

I can smell strong disinfectant, meaning one of the girls or sweet butts has been in today to clean too while they were at it. A few things are out of place in the living room.

Sweet butts, the girls who hang around the club hoping for more, take turns cleaning my joint. It's always neat and orderly to begin with, though, something I'll never grow out of from being in the military. But I don't clean shit like bathrooms and kitchens; that's women's work, and anyway, they do a much better job than any prospect could ever do. I shudder at the thought of one of those turds being up here in my place, no thanks.

I pick the enormous empty dog bowl off the floor and even though it appears clean, I wash it again, just to be sure. Then I pile in shitloads of the meaty concoction I bought in bulk from some lady in town who makes organic fuckin' dog food that Lola loves. I mean, I wouldn't eat shit that comes in a can, so why should she? I put the bowl down, and she automatically sits and looks up at me, waiting for my command.

"Okay, baby girl," I say as she devours her food in record time.

My apartment is pretty small; it has the kitchen, a living room with a TV so big it's obscene, two bedrooms, a tiny laundry, a bathroom, and a balcony... not that there's much to look out on except a deserted street at this time of night.

I walk into the living room, switch the TV on for some background noise. I then straighten up the remote controls back in the correct order, right the coffee table that's been moved to vacuum, and then place the TV guide back to the left of everything, where it belongs. Yeah, I have slight OCD where belongings are concerned. I remove my cut and place it on the back of one of the kitchen chairs, undress, and saunter naked to the shower.

I turn the taps to full blast; the hot water feels good on my skin as I climb over the tub and get under the hot spray to wash the day away. I have no use for the actual tub itself since I don't fit in it horizontally.

My mind wanders to Sienna. When I'd first seen her in action at the Stone Crow a couple of nights ago, she was completely unaware of my existence. There's no mistaking she's drop dead gorgeous, I had eyes. That night she'd had on a black body suit that made her tits look big, but her ass was small and petite, and didn't every guy in that place know it. I'd certainly paid attention. She didn't make much small talk with the punters, just did her job, kept to herself, and smiled when necessary. The tip jar, I'd noticed, was overflowing with cash.

My hand slides to my dick, imagining her and that smart little mouth, and what it would be like to be with her gets me going. I get hard just thinking about it. Shit, am I really going to jerk off to this chick? What the hell's gotten into me?

Well, it has been a while, so who can blame me. The old has-beens around the club are getting a little tiresome, and doing club sisters ---the respectable girls of the M.C.--- is something you don't do unless you plan on making her an ol' lady. Plus, half the girls are either siblings of club members, daughters, wives, or just girls I don't want to have hanging around. And I don't do relationships. Haven't done one in a long time. I like things uncomplicated and I like my space, and where women are concerned that means complications. You have to be careful even with sweet butts, they hang around the club primarily for sex but they are known to get too clingy given half a chance.

There's something different about Sienna, though, and not just because she's new in town and looks as sweet as pie. It's true; good girls like her don't fall for bad boys in an M.C. Not that I'd ever want that to happen, but I'd like to take her for a ride, and not on my sled. Hell, it could be quite convenient, after closing hours on the bar for example. I imagine her legs wrapped around me as I do her and she tells me she wants more... *Hell fire.* I have to stop thinking like this; it's never going to happen. Especially not after she sees the counter Hutch scribbled over the original offer.

She's probably going to throw daggers at me, literally, I guess I'll know in about an hours' time. My gut feeling, which is rarely ever wrong, tells me she's going to be a bit of a spitfire, like, seriously pissed. I stop rubbing myself; this won't do. I shut the water off abruptly before I can finish.

I glance down as I step out over the tub; Lola has made herself at home on the bathmat waiting for me. I bend and pat her head as I step over her and reach for a towel.

"Dad's got to go out for a while," I say. She looks up at me, then puts her head back down almost immediately. She's used to my comings and goings; she doesn't care as long as I come home.

I'm the Sergeant at Arms, the protector and enforcer of the club and all its members, including the girls and the lowlife prospects. I also oversee the security of "Church", our clubhouse headquarters. There's no room for weakness. Weakness only makes you vulnerable, and that's something I can't allow. So, no matter how this turns out, I have my role to play, we all do, and I know how to do it and do it well.

I get dressed swiftly in a fresh pair of jeans, my black

henley, boots, and my cut. I throw on a bandana too, to keep my hair back, and slide out of my apartment in record time with my Harley keys in my hand. Lola has moved again and is already asleep on her bed on the floor next to mine, snoring. It's the last sound I hear before locking the door behind me and tucking the papers into my inside pocket. I hope that Sienna isn't wearing anything even remotely sexy tonight, although she'd look good in a paper bag.

Thank god Gunner won't be there. He may be horny, but he isn't going to go against Hutch's wishes. No woman is ever more important than the club, and even though he often acts like a fool, he knows the deal. He just enjoys the chase. I'm too old for it, or I can't be bothered ...maybe a little of both.

Fuck. I have to stop these wayward thoughts about screwing around with her and keep my mind on the job.

Not that the job is going to take very long once she takes a look at the contract. I chuckle low to myself. I really hope she gets fucking mad. I bet she turns a beautiful shade of crimson when she's pissed. I can see it now, and while it is a tad misogynistic, I can afford the luxury of being a complete asshole. It's what's expected, and it's a role I play really well and have for years.

I leave the lights on in the workshop for later and start my engine as the roller door slides up. My sled roars to life and I rev it up, the straight pipes sending out rumbling into the night like I own the world. And I do when I'm on her, cruising to wherever it is I'm going. It's magic time. Nothing compares to it.

I pull on my helmet, and a few moments later I rev again before roaring off into the night like a bat out of hell, leaving a trail of dust in my wake.

4

SIENNA

WEEKENDS at the Stone Crow are next level crazy. There's live music tonight, and the bar is jam packed. I like being busy, though, so I don't mind. It takes my mind off today's proceedings and the way asshole club President Richie Hutchinson had just dismissed me like some dumb bimbo who was beneath him.

Women don't make important decisions around here. Who the heck did he think he was? Like seriously. So archaic. They probably thought I'd just sign the papers then and there and scuttle out of town with my tail between my legs. Well, I didn't come all the way to this godforsaken place to be run out of town before I've even sorted out any of Max's shit.

When we've reached some kind of agreement and negotiation Steel will deliver the counteroffer and our terms in person. Pass me a bucket. I want to choke him with his stupid bandana.

Cocky sons of bitches.

As annoyed as I am, I keep the drinks flowing and try not to take it out on the customers. It isn't their fault I'm pissed off. *Goddamn bikers.* Why was Max doing business with these guys in the first place?

It's somewhere between that unpleasant thought and stuffing another tip into my jar that I meet eyes with someone that shouldn't be so familiar.

No, I definitely could never mistake eyes like that, as if his towering, overbearing presence isn't enough.

Steel.

The big, brooding man at arms or whatever he's called is leaning against the end of the bar like he owns the joint. He's kind of hard to miss, and he frowns when I catch his eye. I take a few moments to observe him from afar as I keep serving.

He's huge, tall in stature and in bulk. His arms bulge as he leans against the top of the bar, and he's wearing the same leather vest as earlier. It has dirty patches on it that are filthy and worn.

He's a handsome devil, even I can admit that. I don't even mind the beard; it's short and neat. I didn't think I even liked facial hair on a man until this very moment. His hair is long too, something I didn't notice earlier because it was slung back in a messy kind of man-bun. The black bandana around his forehead makes him look badass. You definitely wouldn't mess with him in a dark alley... or anywhere else for that matter.

I don't miss the subtle chin lift he gives me when I finally work my way towards him. Ignoring him would've only proven futile because he has something I need, that contract.

"What'll it be?" I say, sashaying up to him. He'd have to be a good lip reader, though, because it's almost impossible to hear me above the pounding music. I'm only five-four, so stepping up on the bottom rail and leaning toward people so I can hear them is something I've perfected. I bet he's a whiskey or Corona type of guy; you can tell.

I'm standing waiting for an answer when he beckons me with the crook of his finger. Something about the gesture lurches in my stomach, and if I'm honest… somewhere else. I have no idea what that's all about, but it feels kind of foreign. It's been a while since someone gave me butterflies. I roll my eyes, step up, and lean toward him.

Even though it smells like a brewery in here, along with the sweat of about two hundred people, I can't mistake his aftershave. He smells freaking amazing: a mixture of cigarettes, soap, and something dark and musky. Again, I chastise myself for noticing.

"Corona," he mouths in a gravelly voice near my ear.

I resist another eye roll. My body betrays me though, and I feel goosebumps rise on my skin at the masculine tone of his voice. Thank god I have the bar to hang on to. His voice is sexy, like him and his damn aftershave, but that's where the niceties end.

I don't know what I ever did to him in a former life to piss him off, but he doesn't smile and he definitely doesn't look impressed.

Sorry that I'm breathing the same air as you, you big ass biker. Can't exactly help that.

His eyes don't leave me, though, as I turn to the cooler and grab a Corona by the neck, knock the lid off noisily, grab the metal tongs, and shove a wedge of lemon down into the bottle with force, making a big song and dance about the whole production. I slide it on the bar, and it skids across towards him. Not my finest hour, but I'm annoyed by him and his stupid club.

He shoves five dollars at me, sits down on a stool, and tells me to keep the change. *Big spender.* Then he takes a long swig with his eyes still on me. He looks a little dangerous, in fact, I think he hates me.

I serve a few more people, but since it's almost 10pm and I haven't had my break yet, I ask Leroy, one of the regular bartenders, if I can step out for a dinner break. I need to get this over with. I make my way back down toward Steel. He takes brooding biker to a whole new level.

"Do you have the papers?" I yell over the music. My hands automatically rest on my hips.

His eyes make their way slowly, very deliberately, down my body as I stand in front of him, and they stop at my hips where my hands are planted. It's hard to understand if he likes what he sees because he clearly gives nothing away. Then again, why would I care?

His chin lifts once, like that's an answer, then he nods his head behind him. I assume that's caveman talk for "this way."

I lift the side latch on the bar and move into the patrons' side, a very scary place to be on a packed Saturday night, and an even scarier place to be when I crane my neck to look up at him. I lead the way through the crowd to the adjoining restaurant; they aren't serving food anymore, but the waitresses are still cleaning up. We can talk in private here without having to bellow.

I slide into one of the booths, and he scoots into the seat opposite me.

Jesus Christ, he's cute up close, and very large; he barely fits onto the seat and doesn't look comfortable. If your face met with his fist, I know without a doubt you'd be dead. I notice chunky metal rings on most of his fingers, which also have tattoos on them. He's still holding the beer bottle as he reaches his other hand into the pocket inside his jacket.

My eyes drift south; he's wearing a chain around his neck with some embellishment, but it's tucked into his shirt. His henley hugs every muscle on his very fine body; that's a sight to behold. I curse myself for being attracted to him. I don't know what's gotten into me, but he's making me equally aroused and nervous all at the same time. I blame the close proximity and the fact that he's a biker and this is a little thrilling, the most exciting thing that's happened to me in months.

Not. Going. To. Happen. Ever.

I need to keep telling myself that. Maybe I've finally lost my marbles? Yes, that definitely explains it.

I've been nothing but perfectly polite to him, yet he continues to act like I've done him a disservice by even existing. Like don't smile or anything, it may kill you.

"So?" I blurt out, impatiently rapping my nails on the table. It feels like he might even be enjoying dragging this out. He's the club's "enforcer," right? So he obviously likes punishment. He probably gets off on it.

We glare at each other as he shifts in his seat. He takes another long sip of his beer, as if he has all the time in the world, which just makes me all the more furious.

"So?" He hits back, mocking me. He's got a death grip on the papers, so there's no way I'm going to wrestle him for them.

I nod to his hand and lean forward. "What you got for me?"

He cocks an eyebrow, and I can't control feeling it somewhere I shouldn't. The man is the epitome of gorgeous, but he's dangerous. I just can't help the fact that my pulse is racing, betraying me. His eyes look green now, instead of the gray from earlier, which is not something I should be noticing. It's flat out wrong.

A biker, I remind myself. *A dirty, lowdown biker. He's probably a criminal.*

I let out a slow breath, hoping counting to ten will keep me from flipping out. I'm not exactly known for my patience, but in this moment, he's becoming quite intimidating, even though he's just sitting there holding the papers and saying nothing. He's probably enjoying this, the sadistic son of a bitch.

"Sweetheart, you shouldn't lean forward like that." His voice is deep and gravely. It's the first time I've heard him address me properly, you know, like a human being, and it's a proper sentence, so he isn't a mute like I first thought.

There I go again. I'm like a freaking White Snake song on repeat.

When I open my mouth to respond, his eyes drop to my lips, and even though his expression doesn't change, something in his eyes does. As I try to figure that out for a moment, I have a realization that he might be right; I suddenly glance down at myself and realize what he's referring to. My v neck tank top is gaping open at the front, and he's getting a good ol' eyeful of my cleavage. Well, good for him. I hope he has a good memory because a glimpse is all he'll ever be getting.

"Dinner and a show," he smirks as the corners of his lips turn up slightly like he's fighting a smile, obviously enjoying my discomfort a little too much. *Asshole.*

Well, I won't give him the satisfaction of being embarrassed. I grasp the fabric of my shirt, shove it to my chest, and sit back in my seat, heat rising in my face.

"Nice of you to notice," I shoot back. "Can I have the counteroffer please? This isn't an all-night break. I have to get back to work."

I have to hand it to him, he has it under control. I imagine he's the type to interrogate someone just using the right stare, frightening them into submission without any words needed, but I'm not going to let him intimidate me. I'm in a public place and I have every right to tell him to go shove it up his ass or anywhere else for that matter.

"Is this a Sergeant at Arms thing?" I snort, remembering his "title" just as he's about to flip me the papers. A puzzled look comes over his face as he leans closer to me across the table. His forearms bulge, and I instinctively move back further, even though I have nowhere to go.

"Is what a Sergeant at Arms thing?" He replies in a low voice.

I whirl my hand around in front of me, gesturing between us. "The death glare, three-word answers, and keeping me in suspense this whole time when you could just tell me what's going on and put me out of my misery."

He grunts. *Great, he's a caveman too.* "Yeah, Sweetheart, you have me all figured out."

The way "Sweetheart" rolls off his tongue shouldn't sound that good.

No. It. Should. Not.

Even though I know he said it with complete sarcasm, I'm now thinking about his mouth again. I'm obviously deprived; there's no other explanation for it. It's been a year since I've been with anybody, but I've never been the type of girl to do hook-ups. After my last asshole boyfriend, I sort of swore off men forever. I don't know why this hairy, hot biker is doing things to me, because that isn't normal.

"Whatever," I huff. Then he lets go of the papers, and I swiftly grab them, flipping the pages till I get to the dotted line where the offer is neatly typed, or should I say *was.* It's now crossed out with an angry slash and a new figure is scribbled over it.

I glance at it, blink, then bring the papers closer to my eyes like I'm perhaps seeing things... or rather, *not* seeing things.

"There seem to be some zeros missing off this," I say unsteadily. My eyes slide to Steel's, then back to the paper in front of me, then back to Steel's again. My confusion and impending mood swing to violence isn't just palpable; it's volcanic. "I mean, this *is* some kind of joke, isn't it?"

He sits back, his hands clasped together now on the table.

"I'm just the messenger," he informs me, ever so coolly. "Just doin' my job."

I make a loud scoffing noise in the back of my throat.

"Right. The beef, the muscle, the brawn, right? That's why he sent you. To intimidate me. Is this how your club normally does things?" I can't hold back the snark in my tone. "I'm surprised you haven't come to give me my last rites if I don't comply. Is that what you bikers get off on? Scaring people?"

He gives me a long, cold glare. "Do you find me intimidating?" He replies eventually, one eyebrow raised.

I feel the pounding of blood in my ears, and that isn't good. "Not at all, actually." I lie.

He grunts again.

"So, this really isn't a joke?" I stammer, just to clarify. "You actually expect me to sign this?"

He takes another long swig of beer, his eyes never leaving mine. "Sweetheart, we both know I didn't come all the way here tonight for a joke. I'm sensing from your response that you're not happy with the counter?"

He's gonna get a flipping response alright, when I beat him over the head with the contract and anything else I can use as a weapon.

He steadies me with a level gaze.

I gape at him, realizing this is not a sick joke after all; it's all very real. "You're all completely out of your minds if you think I'm agreeing to this ridiculous, *no*, downright insulting, lousy, lame ass offer!"

He doesn't seem shocked by my outburst, far from it. But who am I kidding? He's heard way worse than my ridiculous taunts. He might even be enjoying my outrage. Some guys like that kind of thing.

"So, I'll leave it with you then?" He cocks his head,

goading me. That volcanic energy inside me now feels nuclear; I could explode at any moment.

"No," I say haughtily as I fling the papers right back at him. He looks momentarily stunned, which gives me about two seconds of satisfaction. "You can tell your precious *Prez* to go jam this up his..."

He cuts me off with a raised palm before I can finish. "Don't go spouting things you'll regret," he warns.

"Or what?" I fire back. I feel a little bit more satisfaction mixed with a tiny bit of fear as his nostrils flair at my tone. "And who says I'm going to regret it? Or are you just here to teach me a lesson not to mess with you?"

He might be a badass biker and maybe I've gone too far in the yelling department, but I don't care, they can't do this to me.

He doesn't look impressed, not one bit. Oh, that's right, these bikers are Neanderthals, not to mention sexist assholes; I can't expect them to reason.

Women don't make decisions around here. God, are they living in the Dark Ages? Do they go around pounding their chests and treating all women like total idiots? Or is it just me? These dudes need to get a grip on the reality of the times.

He leans forward again. "I'd like to teach you a lesson." His tone is low, his eyes dark.

I open my mouth and then quickly close it again. Trying to calm my rage, I bite back another feisty comeback. *Umm, what?*

His eyes are smoldering as we glare at one another. I don't do this; I don't swoon over guys, especially sexist pigs who clearly think that women are stupid.

"Well, that's certainly not going to happen," I assure him after a moment too long. I fold my arms over my chest with finality. *Who does he think he is, talking to me like that?*

For the first time, a smile almost crosses his face. *Almost.* I can only tell by the crinkle of his eyes. It fades as quickly as it appeared. I've never come across anybody like this: someone who's so hot and cold and zero to a hundred in two seconds. Now the look in his eyes tells me he might be enjoying this after all, just as I suspected. He doesn't say anything; he just looks back at me totally unmoved, and for once in my life I am totally speechless. I've got nothing.

I go to get up. "When your *Prez* decides to come back with an offer that doesn't insult my intelligence, then I'll think about re-negotiating. For the moment, the offer is off the table, I'll keep the clubhouse for the time being." There. Take that, assholes.

I see his jaw tighten. Not the outcome he was expecting. Good. If I were him, I would've gone with flattery.

The sting that lingers after that pathetic counteroffer makes me want to tear the contract up, make confetti, and throw it in the air, preferably in his face. I refrain from doing that, obviously, but he's declared war.

I think about what they could do to me if they really want to shut me up, and I realize that they aren't very good things. I've always had a feisty temper, though, and now I've let him get under my skin. Anyway, Stef wouldn't let anything happen to me, *would she?*

"As you wish," he says darkly, watching me get up from the table as he stays seated.

I whirl around. He has the good grace to be taken aback by my sudden movement. Maybe he thinks I'm unhinged. Maybe I am.

"And just in case any of you get any funny ideas, there are people who know I'm here by the way, you know, should any 'accidents' happen."

He cocks a brow again; hopefully I've hit a nerve. "What's that supposed to mean?" He barks. *Like he doesn't know.*

I wave my hand in the air. "Biker gangs," I blurt out. "In case I get knocked off or mysteriously disappear or something, there are people that would come looking for me. Just so you know."

He stares at me unblinking for a few moments. Maybe I've gone a step too far.

He seems to sense the panic in my eyes. I turn to leave, but before I can even take a step, he's up out of the seat behind me and grabbing onto my arm. I jerk out of it and step back wildly.

He holds his hands up in front of him, palms facing me, as if in surrender. Then, he towers over me as he cages me in against the wall. His hands rest on the frosted glass on either side of my head as I look up at him in shock. His eyes are ablaze, and not in a good way. He actually looks really pissed.

"*One,*" he says as I back up against the wall with nowhere to go. "We're not a *biker gang*, and we're not one percenters. The club is completely legitimate, and we all work for a living, so whatever's whirling around in that head of yours is completely off base."

I have no idea what that lingo means, but his growly tone tells me all I need to know.

"*Two.* Nobody is going to knock anybody off. This isn't the movies, Princess. This isn't a cabaret. We're civilized people, believe it or not, and we settle things above board, fairly. And *three.* Do you really think we'd do something like that?"

Above board? He has some nerve if that crummy offer is anything to go by.

"I don't know," I say honestly. I feel my heart hammering wildly.

Something flashes behind his eyes, and his brow furrows again. "I'm not going to hurt you," he says, as if suddenly registering my concern.

I nod, but I know I must look scared because he backs off, pushing away from the wall.

"We're not boy scouts, but we're not into hurting women or making them disappear," he goes on, like I've slapped him. "But I wouldn't expect you to understand that since we're just a bunch of dirty bikers, right?"

He stares down at me and runs an exasperated hand through his messy hair, like he doesn't know what to do with me. I'm too stunned to feel smug.

I nod again, hoping he'll leave. Even though he's a monster in size and clearly agitated, I don't feel afraid. Still, *I know I should*, especially where angry men are concerned. Maybe I'm just naïve, or maybe I just need a strong shot of something.

"My job as enforcer is to avoid violence and only use it when absolutely necessary, and before you jump in, I don't use violence against women, period. You're judging the club because of what you *think* you know, and you don't know shit."

I stare at him. "Enlighten me then," I hear myself say.

He raises a brow. "Seriously?"

"Seriously." I nod. *Clearly I've lost my mind.*

"What would you like to know?"

I flatten my hands on the wall behind me. "What's a 'one percenter'?"

His dark eyes seem to get frostier. "Outlaws. Clubs who do illegal shit."

"Oh," I whisper quietly.

"That it?"

I swallow hard. "Did you really think I'd just sign that contract?"

He purses his lips. "Honestly? No."

I frown. "Then why'd you do it?"

"I don't get to pick and choose, princess. I've got orders, and I follow them."

"Like all good club enforcers?" I challenge.

His eyes crease again at the corners. "You got spunk. I'll give you that."

My eyes go slightly wide. "I'd say thanks, but I'm not sure that's a compliment."

"We done?"

I huff out a slow breath.

"Please tell your boss I don't accept the offer... I need time to think... and... and I need to get back to work."

"It's Prez."

"What?" I stammer.

"It's Prez, not boss to you, Sweetheart."

"*Prez,* then," I say with a roll of my eyes.

He regards me with an almost bemused expression. "Thought you said for him to go shove it up his ass?"

Somehow my bravado has suddenly left the building. "Yes, that too."

He crosses his arms over his chest but doesn't move. We stare at each other, and I don't know if I'm the only one who feels the strange electricity buzzing between us, but I don't think it's healthy.

He's a complete alpha male, and I cannot fathom what he's thinking. But there's something strangely sexy about that. My eyes drop to his mouth as I wonder what it would be like to kiss a man with a beard. Before I linger there too long, he speaks.

"If you were mine, princess, trust me, I'd find more interesting and productive things to do with that smart mouth of yours."

I gape as he smirks at me, satisfied it seems now that he's got the upper hand. Then he turns and stalks off across the room, heading back into the bar and clutching the crumpled papers in his fist as he leaves.

I stare after him. *What the hell was that?*

With a jolt of adrenaline, I wonder if he will actually tell his precious Prez to go shove it up his ass, courtesy of me. Well, if I've just pissed off the entire club, then there's not much I can do about it now. I'm not going to tuck my tail and run away. I've got nothing to lose.

It crosses my mind that it may not be the smartest idea in the world to pick a fight with a motorcycle club. I also don't want to be stuck here in Bracken Ridge for any longer than I have to be, but they're the ones drawing this out, not me. They're the ones making it complicated.

If you were mine, princess, I'd find more interesting and productive things to do with that smart mouth of yours.

I scoff at his boldness, but I know my protest is half-hearted. My mind whirls instead at my body's reaction to him. The fierceness in his eyes and the dark and dangerous cloud around him spell trouble, and I have no idea why that appeals to me on some level. Like he said, they're no boy scouts, and I definitely believe that. Maybe I need a lobotomy.

I'm not going to hurt you. We're not boy scouts, but we're not into hurting women or making them disappear. I push my stupid thoughts away and stomp back to the bar. If there's one thing I'm good at, it's putting on a brave face and slinging beers while I do it.

5

STEEL

I ROAR HOME a little ticked off. I'm definitely not used to being spoken to in that way by anybody, much less someone I don't know, and especially not a woman. Though you have to expect some lip from non-club girls who don't know their place. Yes, that is completely sexist and misogynistic, but I come from a long line of them. Not that it's any excuse, but serving in the military and now being a part of the Bracken Ridge Rebels MC means that kind of shit is ingrained into you.

I love women, and I meant what I said; I don't treat them badly. I don't even mind a little bit of lip, but not in front of my brothers, that won't do. And I definitely don't enjoy insinuations being thrown at me by this woman who knows nothing about me or the club. That's only asking for trouble. The only place I allow myself to be even remotely dominated is in the bedroom, and even then those moments are rare. I take control in all things, and this hot little chick from Cali is driving me crazy.

Sienna Morgan is trouble with a capital T. She's clearly tough, to stand up to me like that; the woman has balls. I'd scared her, though, and that wasn't my intention, which is why I backed off immediately. Maybe she has men issues, or maybe it's just me.

Her lips. Jesus fuckin' Christ, her lips are beautiful. If only she didn't have such a smart mouth.

The cold wind on my face feels good as I ride home in a fury. I've only had one beer and I rarely get drunk, but right now I need a shot... or three.

I also have the joyful task of letting Hutch know the outcome, which I'm sure he saw coming, though a part of me thinks he was actually convinced she'd go for it. Another strange part of me feels a little bit smug that she's hell on wheels. She turns a beautiful color when she's mad. I don't really like her rage being aimed at me, but still.

It doesn't matter how pretty or hot Sienna is, though. The scowl on her face shows she clearly doesn't like me, that's abundantly obvious. That kind of comes with the territory of being Sergeant at Arms and part of the M.C., but she definitely isn't like other girls. Most chicks usually like how I look, or the ones at the club do anyway. They like the tats, the brawn, and perhaps the power that my position holds at the club, but few actually dare to come over to me, only the brave ones. Something about wearing a cut and being the guy I am tends to keep them at bay. They're not really sure if they should approach or run a mile. I like how Sienna didn't run.

I always attract the wrong girls, though. There's always easy chicks going around Church, sweet butts that would do anything to be part of the club and get in with a brother. Most of them that hang around there are all pretty easy.

Sienna's a good girl. It's written all over her. She definitely isn't the type of chick you take home for a one-night stand, and she definitely isn't looking for a bad boy to tame or whatever it is chicks try to do. Not this girl. Unobtainable.

Christ, that does nothing for the hard on I'm sporting just thinking about her pretty little mouth on me that I'll never have. Or her on the back of my sled – hellfire. The thought is equally arousing and depressing. The things we could do, the things I could do to her if she'd let me. I'd make it good; I'm not selfish in the bedroom. I'd take my time and worship her like she truly deserves.

I haven't been with a good girl since college... I should stop thinking thoughts like this; they won't do me any good. I have nobody to go home to and relieve the tension, just me and my palm again, which is not an appealing thought.

I park in the garage next to the workshop and lock up. I text Hutch that the deal was a no-go, and I can't help but grin. She has gumption, that's for sure, but Prez is sure to be pissed. He likes things to go his way, in all areas, so this little spitfire is sure to be an unexpected surprise.

I switch the lights off in the workshop and head upstairs to my vacant, except-for-a-snoring-dog, apartment and kick my boots off. I reach for the top shelf in the kitchen and pull out the bottle of Jack that has been calling my name all the way home. I don't even bother with a glass, and I don't feel the sting as it glides down my throat with ease. I wait about ten seconds before I sigh and pick my stray boots up off the floor and place them in my closet again next to my old ones. I can't leave anything scattered around. Habits like order are hard to break. When I have order, I have a clear mind.

I glance at my bed, and though it's calling me with fresh new sheets that smell inviting, I don't crawl into it just yet. My baby is asleep in her bed below my feet, and she doesn't even raise her head. Her light snore is like warmth to my heart.

I leave her and go back into the living room to switch the

television on, thinking maybe there's a game on or something murderous like Game of Thrones that I can fall asleep to while chasing away all thoughts of Sienna fucking Morgan.

*

I'm an early riser by nature. If I do happen to sleep in, which is mainly on the weekends when the garage is closed, I still wake up at the same time. It's like a curse. If I don't, Lola will come and lick my face and try to play with me until I give up and drag my ass out of bed so she can be fed.

I ended up downing almost a full bottle of Jack, not that it really has any effect anymore. I spend all of Sunday working on my project in the garage, a custom Fat Boy; it's a work in progress. Monday rolls around fast, and I have a shitload of paperwork to do, which reminds me again that I need to hire a new office girl. Unlike my neat and orderly apartment and workshop, the office is a complete wreck. None of the club girls will work for me because apparently I'm not nice to work for. Really, they just don't like to work so they whine about everything. Lily helps me when she can, but now that she has a beauty salon in town, she's always booked and can't get by to help me as often. I know I'm behind on invoicing, which is my least favorite thing to do because I don't know shit about computers.

I make a mental note to text Lucy, Rubble's ol' lady, to see if she can come in and help me clean up. Rubble's wife is the best bookkeeper this side of Bracken Ridge, and thankfully I haven't pissed her off enough to tell me to shove it. The downside is she's always busy with the tow truck biz and doing the books for Brock's junkyard. At least Rubble's paperwork is under control; he's one lucky son of a bitch. Maybe if I had an ol' lady she'd be able to get my books in order too, but that's hardly a good enough excuse to do something ridiculously stupid like get tied down. I'm not that desperate.

I glance at the clock. 5:55am – right before my alarm - like clockwork. I sigh and throw the top sheet off. I pull on a fresh pair of boxer briefs out of my nightstand and stretch my arms out wide with a growly yawn. I quickly make the bed and tuck the edges in nice and tight, fluffing the pillows up so they don't keep the indentation of my head.

Lola is nowhere to be seen. I go to the bathroom, take a leak, and wash my face with cold water – hoping that will help with the dark circles. It doesn't. They're always there, like battle scars, a reminder that I'm not invincible and that same son of a bitch stares back at me. My sleep is a lot better now that I have Lola, but I still don't get enough.

I spray some deodorant on, brush my teeth, and comb my hair up into a messy ponytail. After that I go to the Keurig that sits proudly on my countertop, a gift from my mother at Christmas. The one woman who knows the key to my heart.

My mom is the most beautiful person on the planet, she's a nurse at the local hospital.

I switch the thing on and grab the milk out of the fridge. If I don't have a decent cup of coffee first thing in the morning, it sometimes sways my mood for the rest of the day. I'm a pretty moody person at the best of times, so I don't like to chance it.

I pull out the drawer that stores all my coffee pods and select donut caramel. I shove it into the pod contraption and put my clear thermal cup below the spout before pushing the button.

While it's doing its thing, I look around for Lola. I find her curled up on the couch, but she's awake and watching me. It's a little early for her breakfast, so I place some fresh dog biscuits in her bowl and top up her water as she yawns. She looks how I feel. Thank fuck she's a good dog and not needy, not that I would mind anyway. That's probably why we get along so well.

"Gotta go down and sort some shit out, baby girl," I say, dreading the pile of papers waiting for me. Now I know why people hate Mondays; it's paperwork day.

I don't usually eat until later, so I reach for my coffee, add some milk, and dump two heaped sugars in before taking a sip. Satisfied, I screw the lid on and head down the stairs. It's too early for anyone else to be at work yet, which is good because I need time to concentrate. When the boys clatter around, it's nearly impossible to get anything important done, so I utilize the quiet time while I can. Nothing starts around here till about 8 o'clock.

I flick the lights on in the workshop and then head up to the office. It makes me nervous just looking at the mountain of paperwork I have sitting there, not even in a neat orderly fashion at all. I run my hand over my head and take deep breaths. I pull out my phone and send Lucy a text, even though it's early, because if I don't get her in here to help me, I may just pass out. Nobody wants that on their hands.

I begin by switching the computer on, that I do know how to do. The lights blink and it makes several disgruntled noises as if I've woken it from a deep slumber. I know I need a new computer system that works and does everything for me, but just thinking about anything that advanced gives me an instant headache.

Most of my invoicing is done by hand in duplicate copy books, which is not the way Lucy thinks I should do it, but it's all I know. The business is getting busier and constantly growing, and I know I need to upgrade, but I'm digging my heels in. I have months and months' worth of paperwork that I've neglected, which translates to thousands and thousands of dollars that are owed to me that I can't get on top of. Something drastic has to happen.

Admittedly, I'm not the easiest person in the universe to get along with, or probably to work for, but I don't think I'm *that* bad. I only yell at the guys when they goof off. All the businesses of the club bring money in respectively and all members share a percentage of their profits. It's how things continue to grow strong, and it's how we all live so well. The club is acquiring more and more businesses, land, and investment properties, and with Hutch's ol' lady being in real estate, we know about all the bargains when they come around.

I sip my coffee and glance around the busy desk; I have no idea where to actually start. Perhaps the overflowing tray of papers is a good place. Smaller jobs, car servicing, and tires are paid up front with cash or on pick up, but larger businesses, companies, and corporate clients get billed and then pay by check or bank transfer. I don't have a credit card machine, and I don't have an overdue system in place except for another tray of piled up papers with a red stamp on them. Usually one phone call is all it takes to get money, but I barely get around to doing that.

I hold my head in my hands and then grab the first tray of overflowing papers and begin to sift through them. Any distraction would be a good one, but it's so early that even my dog is still asleep. I manage to get through about three invoices using my unique one finger typing method, which takes forever, then I send them to the printer and glance at the clock. Damn that took me forty-five minutes, not very productive. I sit back in the chair and glance at my phone on the desk as it buzzes. It's Lucy. Thank God.

Lucy: Why have you not hired somebody yet?

No salutation or good morning or anything, typical Lucy, straight to the point.

Me: Cuz apparently I suck.

My phone beeps an instant reply.

Lucy: So, you need my help, huh? What's in it for me?

Typical woman; can't just come help me out of the goodness of her heart, oh no.

Me: My continued reassurance of security

I could almost hear her laughing from across town.

Lucy: Ha! I get that anyway!

I think for a moment, knowing this is gonna cost me.

Me: Remember that concert you wanted to go to?

Bribery is the best way to get to Lucy; I learned this a very long time ago.

She's typing as I sit back and wait.

Lucy: What concert?

I pull the top drawer open and take out the envelope with the tickets in it for Carrie Underwood. I got them a while back knowing they'd come in handy at some point in time. I'd planned on giving them to Lily for her birthday but whatever. I take a photo and send it to her.

Me: There's four tickets. Take your girlfriends.

She's typing back.

Lucy: OMFG!! Are you kidding me right now? I don't know how you pull this shit off, Steel, seriously. I'd be waiting until dooms day for Rubble to get me tickets to anything

Me: So that's a yes?

Lucy: Wait. How do I know that you really have those in your possession?

I sigh loudly.

Me: What? You want proof?

She sends back a smiley face with a thumbs up.

Fuckin' Lucy. I grab the tickets, hold them next to my head, grimace like I'm really pissed off, take the selfie, and press send.

Me: Happy?

Lucy: I love you. When do you want me?

I smile broadly. Lucy is like a sister to me. I've known her that long. She takes no shit from anybody, but she's a good ol' lady. I know she has Rubble by the shorts, but she acts the part of the good wife in public. Behind closed doors I have no doubt who wears the pants. It makes me smile.

Me: 'Bout 8?

Lucy: K. See u then.

Me: Roger that. Bring food.

I just saved myself a long, horrible day, even though technically it cost me a bomb. Feeling pleased with myself, I finish my coffee with a sigh of relief.

*

I let Lucy chastise me for most of the morning over my lack of bookkeeping skills, and I let her get away with it only because I need her and don't want her to go. She had the good sense to bring a bag of blueberry muffins with her. I like a woman who listens.

I don't hover around while she rapidly gets through some of the paperwork, best to leave the woman be. I don't work on the tools every day, I have guys to do that, I only help when things get really busy or there's a particular job that needs my expertise. Although I've served in the military, mechanics has been my trade since I left school as an apprentice; it's what I always go back to.

My restoration shed is the separate locked garage next to the workshop with a security alarm. That's where I work on custom bikes and cars when given the opportunity. Like the Fat Boy, which is my own project, I get to it when I can. I have no pressing jobs at the moment, but occasionally a good pay dirt will come in and I'll throw myself and a couple of my guys into it. My portfolio is legendary; however, I have neither the time nor the energy to concentrate on promoting that side of the business. Maybe in time, when I get on top of things here and have someone reliable to man the phones and do office shit. I certainly have no customer rapport, so I don't go anywhere near the damn phone.

About halfway through the morning, Hutch rings my cell. About time, he's been ignoring me all weekend.

"Maybe I should send Gunner in," he says immediately, an exasperated tone in his voice. That irritates me more than it should; jealousy isn't a trait I usually possess, but knowing she's no pushover helps with my annoyance. She's also so fucking hot that it's off the charts. I've spent all weekend trying to forget her blue-green eyes and pouty little mouth, and I admit I may have jerked off last night imagining that mouth and her hands on me.

*If you were mine, I'd find more productive and interesting things to do with your smart mouth?...*Oh brother, what was I thinking? I can't even blame the booze for that comment.

"Perhaps a less chilly offer could sway her," I suggest. "It was pretty lowball, even for us. You didn't really expect her to actually take it. I told you she wasn't stupid." I know deep down I don't want Gunner going near her. If anybody is going to show her a good time between the sheets, I want it to be me. I wrestle with that illicit thought, not for the first time today, and wait for his response.

"You have any other bright suggestions?" He barks, clearly not liking that one.

"Yes. We wait it out, let her come to us. She probably needs the dough, so I'm sure it won't be long before she's rethinking her options. Chicks like to mull things over, you know what they're like, plus it's like you said, worst case scenario the bank will foreclose."

He grunts. "She probably just needs a good lay to loosen her up a bit. I wouldn't say Gunner's the best, but he's got the goods and could charm honey from a bee... unless you'd like to volunteer."

I just about spit my coffee out. I'm not exactly known to

be the club member with the most notches on his belt, and I'm certainly not known for my subtlety or charm, but there are some healthy rumors about my size and stamina. That I don't mind, but this? I know from Saturday night's conversation that she isn't gonna be persuaded by pillow talk. Girls like her never are; she's too smart.

"I don't think it will come to that, Prez," I say, pinching the bridge of my nose with my thumb and forefinger, trying to keep my temper in check and my voice at a normal octave.

I don't know why I'm suddenly feeling like this every time there's a mention of sending Gunner in. Probably because I know she won't look twice at me now. I'd backed her up against the wall after making her furious enough to hurl fireballs from her eyes. I shake my head at the memory, at her big eyes looking up at me like that.

"Keep Gunner away from her. She just needs to cool off. I'll deal with this."

I don't exactly know what my plan of attack is, but unless I come up with the goods soon, he'll send his best man in. Something about the challenge makes me want to sit back and see what would happen, if she'd actually fall for someone like Gunner, if even for the night. Anyway, just because she may be up for a bit of a good time for a night did not mean she'd decide to give her assets away at cost price and forget her money troubles, something tells me that she has a lot more gumption than that.

I push the thought out of my head. I don't like drama, which is why I live with a dog and not a freaking woman. I was married briefly a long time ago, but that fizzled out quickly, so instead of settling down I instead threw myself into my business and the M.C.

Chicks were trouble; I will do well to remember that. I like simple. No ties, no strings, and besides there is no shortage of willing pussy at Church to be had. Even if things do get monotonous at least nobody has me by the balls.

Maybe I just need a quick hard and fast lay myself. *Yes.* That's all I need, then perhaps I will get Sienna out of my thoughts once and for all. It feels futile. She doesn't like me, not like the girls at Church do, and that only appeals to me all the more….. The way she sashayed towards me when I leaned on the bar, those hips had some moves, her tits looked fantastic in that top that she had on with a sexy lace black bra, it got me instantly hard. I'd love to have those beautiful things in my face all night, sucking her, making her moan….*shit.*

The problem being now if I am to try and get back in her good graces that may prove to be difficult. I'm not exactly known for my verbose and friendly banter, funnily enough.

I think Hutch and the crew are kind of forgetting I'm used to dealing with bikers and man to man problems, not whiney little girls who were hard to control, I've got enough of that with my little sister. Not that I have any trouble controlling women, ones that want to be controlled that is, ones that knew how it works.

When it came to Sienna; if looks could kill I'd be dead about fifteen times over.

Hutch barks something else incoherent at me and hangs up. I tuned out when he started yelling.

It seems I'm about to have me one hell of another day, rubbing my temples I drop the phone onto the desk and go hunt for more muffins. I'll go to the gym soon to work off some frustration and in the meantime work out a plan of attack, I get my best ideas when lifting weights and working out.

Yeah, she's definitely a little pain in the ass, one I need to forget.

I just wish to god I could get her out of my head.

6

SIENNA

I DON'T SLEEP WELL after my spat with Steel. Truth be told I'm furious. While admittedly he is super-hot and smelled like a brut advert, that's certainly no excuse for his 'I'm just the messenger,' act and to man-handle me by back me up against a wall. On the other hand; I really have no idea or excuse as to why I can't stop thinking about him and it's making me crazy.

I have Monday through Wednesday off, as those are the quiet nights at the Stone Crow, so I decide to do something nice for myself and the first port of call is a hot yoga class. It's just what I need to get my mind clear and off dirty bikers and all the other crap going on in my life.

I own a bikers' clubhouse. I shudder. I mean, how more bizarre and surreal could my life actually get? And now I'm warring with the club and everyone in it, maybe I do have a death wish after all.

Breathe Sienna, just breathe.

I feel good after the class, all my annoyance and pent up rage seems to have dissipated.

I'm on such a high that I decide then and there I'm going

to go to the nearest department store, wherever that is, to buy myself some new linen and a comfy set of pillows, I'm fearless like that and new sheets always makes me feel better.

I swing my gym bag over my shoulder and sling my sweat towel around my neck, as I pass by the clear window that looks into the gym I come to an abrupt halt as my eyes lock with a frowning, grey-green eyed monster using one of the arm weight machines.

Goddamn it. It's *him*. I know Bracken Ridge is small, but this is ridiculous.

I do not want to run into *him* today, or ever, thank you very much.

Steel's half-way through pulling some very heavy weights down in front of him when our eyes lock. He stops midway, his biceps bulge so huge that I'm sure they're about to explode, I've never seen muscles that big.

He's wearing a black Metallica singlet and it's hanging off his body, leaving little to the imagination, in fact one would argue why you'd even wear it. He's completely covered in tatt's too, they're everywhere. I don't gawk because of his glorious, sweaty, muscled body, no, no, I gawk because I've never seen anything so damn hot in my life.

A thrill runs through me and its then I realize I've stopped walking and I'm now staring, clutching onto my water bottle and yoga mat for dear life.

I watch as his eyes travel down my body lazily, then when he's finished ravishing me, he raises an eyebrow as if to question what the hell I'm staring at.

Move your feet Sienna, get out of there.

I practically sprint out to the parking lot. Only when I'm safely inside my car with the doors locked I take a few calming breaths then curse myself. He saw me gawking at him, great, that's all I need, something else to use against me. His body is so ridiculous that I can't imagine anyone not being moved by such a majestic sight, his ink is almost too much to take in, his tattoos are all black and basically cover every spare inch of his skin. I grasp the steering wheel and internally slap myself. I need to get a grip.

My phone rings suddenly making me jump.

It's a number I don't recognize.

"Hello," I answer rubbing my temple with my free hand.

"Hello, is this Sienna Morgan?" I don't recognize the caller.

"Yes," I reply.

"It's Kirsty from Bracken Ridge real estate."

Oh, it's the lady I've been dealing with about the sale of Max's house, what a relief, she said she'd call me this week and touch base with an appraisal, we've been corresponding via email.

"Oh, hi Kirsty, thanks for calling."

"Is now a good time?"

"Yes, sure now's perfect," I reply, welcoming the distraction.

"I've been going over the numbers for the estate and I think that what we discussed via email is a good starting price, it has a large lot and while the property needs a lot of work it's still got good bones, a renovators dream and it has that large garage at the back and is fully fenced."

Ah yes, the garage I have to clean out by the weekend, don't remind me.

"That's wonderful." *Maybe my luck is starting to change?*

"If you're happy to drop in later today or tomorrow to sign the paperwork, I can get the photographers out there this week once you give me the all clear and it can be listed as early as the weekend." My heart soars at her words.

What a relief! This is great news.

"That sounds perfect, I'm going out there tomorrow with

the removalists to get rid of all the furniture and do some cleaning, so I can drop by before that."

"Excellent," she replies brightly.

"Thank you, Kirsty I really appreciate this, it's a load off my mind."

She's been a godsend, I've literally not had to do anything.

"Well now, you're welcome," she says, kindly. "And I hope this isn't a conflict of interest, I can assure you that whatever happens with the club it will not affect our working relationship."

I frown.

What is she talking about? I suddenly have a very bad feeling in my gut, and this was all going so well….

"Umm, I'm sorry Kirsty I'm not following." My heart rate picks up about seven hundred notches.

"Well it's a small town and being Hutch's wife things get around."

My eyes go wide, and I literally hold my breath. *Is she freaking kidding me right now? Hutch's wife?*

I've inadvertently hired that awful man's old freaking lady?

Not for the first time I'm starting to question what I did in my former life to deserve this.

"Sorry, I'm not sure I heard you right, you're Hutch's wife?" I try out the words like they're not poison spluttering from my mouth.

"Yes, my husband is Richie Hutchinson, President of the Bracken Ridge Rebels," she tells me it like it should be obvious.

I swallow hard. I don't understand how a person like me can be this unlucky.

"I….I had no idea," I admit, but really, am I surprised? *Don't they own everything in this stupid town?*

"Well as I say, I'm happy to take the listing and run with it, it's a really great property and while the market is slow I don't think we'll have a problem getting close to asking, and I also just wanted to assure you whatever we discuss is strictly confidential."

I press the bridge of my nose with my thumb and forefinger to try and stop the oncoming headache.

It's not like I can fire her ass now. I kick myself for not doing my research more thoroughly.

I mean, I guess there is only one real estate broker's office in town, so it's not like I have much of a choice regardless, but the way my lucks going I dread to think who I'm going to run into next.

"I'll drop by tomorrow," I say defeated, I rest my head on the steering wheel and contemplate what this means, I feel a nuclear migraine coming on.

"Perfect, and don't worry, as I say the property has a lot of pluses, I'll get the photographer out early next week, I'm going to get you the very best price I can." At least she seems chirpy.

"Appreciate that." I manage, defeated, wanting this conversation to be over.

"See you tomorrow." She sing-songs as if my life hasn't just been run over repeatedly by a freight train.

I toss my phone on the seat next to me and then bang my head repeatedly on the wheel, anyone watching me will think I'm insane but I don't care, seriously.

Fuck my life.

*

Steel

A whole week's gone by and I've not come up with any solution to the Sienna situation, other than give her space. Space I'm finding difficult after seeing her in that hot pink yoga outfit the other day. Some things should be illegal.

If she were my ol' lady I wouldn't let her out the house looking like that, she'd stop traffic. I've even thought about just propositioning her once and for all, screw Gunner. The way she'd looked at me at the gym was sinful, she couldn't take her eyes off my body.

There's nothing quite like a beautiful woman appreciating the goods to make my gym sessions all worthwhile. She may still hate me, that is actually very probable, but she can't deny the sexual chemistry going on.

I don't want to see her again because I may just do exactly what I shouldn't, given half the chance, and that's a very bad idea. That's why tonight I plan on checking out the smorgasbord at Church, it's Friday night after all.

Hutch has organized a band this weekend so everybody will be there. I don't have to think about work, bills, or piled up invoices, *or her.* Maybe I'll find some strange to sink my aching dick into and forget about life for a while. *Yeah.* That's what I need, and that's exactly what I'm going to get.

I still keep a room at Church where I could sleep if I need, or as I plan on tonight; to use a bed and drive it home when I nail some hot chick to the mattress, there'll be very little sleeping going on.

The bars pumping when I arrive, some of the crowd aren't part of the club but hang here on the weekends, or they're friends of friends, and that ultimately brought in new chicks.

The band are regulars and played all different kinds of rock and some country music, nothing too hard core, they're in full swing. During the winter we usually have a bonfire lit when it's cold out, but tonight there's a couple of large fire pits outside, someone's ordered in the wood-fire pizza guy and the drinks are flowing.

Behind the bar is Summer, Gunner's sister, who is just as pretty as he is, and Ginger one of the ol' ladies belonging to Knuckles, and yeah he got his name because he used to fight, bare-fisted. He's retired now but Ginger still helps out at club functions and important events because she can sling drinks like nobody's business, and she keeps us boys in line.

"Hey beautiful," I say as Ginger winks at me when I stroll up to the bar. She puts a large glass of whiskey in front of me before I can blink. That's my kind of woman.

"You look rough," she remarks, eyeing me in a motherly way.

"Thanks," I grunt but I know it's true. It's been a long drawn out week, and though Lucy helped a lot with my bookwork, I've still got shitloads to do. I'll give myself tonight.

"Anytime sweetheart."

Next to me Brock turns and tells me I look like shit too. One thing about this crowd; they won't lie to you.

"Nice to see you too, brother," I mutter and throw the whiskey back, it's top shelf, none of that cheap shit. I give Ginger a wink as she turns to leave.

"Does this have anything to do with that little golden haired Cali chick?" He asks, cocking a brow at me. He's only just shorter than me at six-five, all muscle, he boxed in high school and turned professional for six or seven years.

"Don't even say her name." I warn.

He has the audacity to chuckle.

"Prez told me, sure you can handle her?"

His mocking tone does nothing for my temper. She's making me look like a god damned fool. I have a certain stature and reputation to uphold around here, I get shit done, that's my whole purpose of existence of the club, as well as security and recruiting and keeping the prospects in line. Speaking of which, some of them may need a reminder tonight who they're leering at.

Just because I'm drinking doesn't mean I don't see everything that goes on around here. Club sisters are out of bounds, as are ol' ladies; they obviously belong only to fully patched members, but the regulars, sweet butts and chicks that aren't officially claimed are fair game on the pick up stakes. Chicks don't come here unless they want to have a good time, they know the deal, and by the looks of Gunner, who has two girls on each side of the couch and one on his knee, the party's in full swing, greedy bastard should leave some for the rest of us.

"Of course I can handle her." I grimace at the thought, my eyes flick to Colt, one of the prospects talking to a chick I haven't seen before. "Nothin' I haven't handled before, what is this anyway fifty fuckin' questions?"

He holds up his hands in surrender. "No need to bite my head off."

I give him a sideways glance. "Been a long week brother, I got shit up to my eyeballs."

"You been on that computer again?"

Everyone knew how useless I am when it came to technology. I hate it.

I grunt. "Whoever invented those stupid machines has a lot to answer for."

"So why don't you hire someone?"

"In this town?" I bark, like it's his fault I can't hold down a permanent receptionist.

"There's plenty of trustworthy people, perhaps you should leave the interviewing to somebody less intimidating, and someone who doesn't just hire chicks depending on how big their cup size is."

He had a good point. The last one did have huge knockers; pity she couldn't actually do any book work or know anything about mechanics.

"I'm fucked," I declare, downing the rest of the whiskey and turning around to put my glass on the edge of the bar, its quickly refilled.

"That we can agree on," he says as we clink glasses.

"Good crowd," I mutter as Hutch walks toward us; he has his arm slung around his ol' lady Kirsty. She's still looking good for her age, nothing a bit of botox and silicone hasn't fixed but she's still foxy at fifty-something. She's got bottle blonde hair and wears a lot of makeup, but she looks after herself, you gotta admire that. She puts twenty somethings to shame in her patent leather pants and leather biker jacket.

I imagine Sienna wearing my cut and almost choke on my own thoughts. Ol' ladies don't have to wear your cut, your club colors, but some of the ladies like to, like Kirsty.

"Hey boys," she says, then looks as me and narrows her eyes. "You not sleeping honey?"

I shake my head, muttering.

"I worry about my boys," she goes on, looking concerned. "What's keeping you up? Girl troubles?" She gives me a conspiring wink.

"Nothing I can't handle," I reply as Hutch rolls his eyes at me.

"No news then." He assumes gruffly. He's still not happy with my lack of progress. Everyone just needs to stop hassling me, Rome wasn't built in a day and all that shit.

"I've got a plan." I assure him, though I have no clue right now what that is.

Hutch gives me the side eye. "Fuckin' women."

"She actually seems very nice," Kirsty pipes up giving Hutch a look which he ignores. "If you took the time to get to know her better, she's very sweet, a little naïve, but sweet all the same, so you just be nice Steel and not your usual self."

Oh how I love being told off by someone other than my mother.

"Well, maybe I should send my wife in to sort her out," Hutch snorts. "She seems to have done a better job getting to know her than my own guys, perhaps I should bring her into the meeting room while I'm at it, kick your sorry asses out."

Kirsty shakes her head but pats a hand on his cut affectionately. These two are so lovey dovey it's almost sickening. He kisses her chastely.

I wonder if I'll ever find someone I'll actually want to be monogamous with. I have no idea why that thought just crept into my head. I don't want a steady, I don't need anything permanent and I sure as hell don't need no ol' lady.

"Deanna here tonight?" I ask, trying to divert my thoughts. Deanna is their daughter and a couple of years older than Lily.

"She had to work late," Kirsty explains. "With school finishing up she never stops, I barely ever see her these days."

Deanna's hot like her mama but dark haired like Hutch, and though sweet on the outside, she packs a mean punch. She takes no shit from any of us and is what you'd call a wild child.

"She works too much," Hutch grumbles as they move on to work the crowd.

Prez is fiercely protective of his girls, of all the women in the club, that's something I do respect. He has no time for men who treated women badly, he might be a sexist asshole and commands respect, but he doesn't condone violence against women, none of us do.

Lee, one of the other prospects, passes by picking up empty glasses.

"Hey, pencil dick," I call to him as he turns to look at me.

"Hey Steel."

"Who's that chick talking to Colt?"

She's not a hang around. She looks a little bit out of place, but the conversation seems like it's going a little bit too good in Colt's favor. She laughs at something he says and tosses her hair over her shoulder like girls do when they like something. She's pretty enough; has long brown hair, a bit on the skinny side but her ass is perky. Maybe she'll do.

"Dunno," he replies with a shrug and goes back to his duty.

I sip my drink, watching her. Her eyes flick to mine suddenly from across the room and she gives me a little smile. She was prettier when she smiled. I don't like her hair though, it's not long enough, and her tits are too small. That isn't a turn on, not like somebody else I know.

I blow out a breath. I'm a man and extremely frustrated right now, I'm not ashamed to admit I jerked off over Sienna in that yoga outfit, I seem to be doing that a lot lately.

I take another long gulp of my drink without flinching at the sting as I watch the girl flirt with Colt. Every now and again she looks over at me, it kind of irritates me to be honest, there's no loyalty anymore, she shouldn't be laughing and joking with one guy and making eyes with another. Of course, he's a prospect, whether she realizes this and his insignificance is beyond me and I really don't care, and it also doesn't stop me from going over there. I push off the bar and stride over like a man on a mission to where they're sitting. Why Colt is sitting down enjoying himself is a mystery.

"Hey Steel...." Colt begins, when he sees my face and where I'm bee-lining towards his face drops with annoyance, but he wisely refrains from saying anything. As a prospect you are the bottom-dweller of the club, the only thing higher than you is dog turd, so Colt will watch on as I take who-ever-she-is away from him so he can get back to work. He won't question me, not if he wants a fist in his face and his ass beaten.

"You're meant to be working." I point at him then turn my attention to the girl. She's not as pretty up close but it's not her face I want to see.

"What's your name?" I ask her as she looks up at me

blinking, she's slightly astonished at me standing over her. Yeah, I get that a lot.

"Melanie," she says a little shyly. Yep she's definitely new around here.

"Has this weasel dick even gotten you a drink?" I ask, disgust in my tone.

"Hey, I got her a drink…" He begins, but shuts up as I glance at him again, I haven't given him permission to speak and I'm losing patience here, I need to know if she's in or out.

I lean closer and whisper in her ear. "Want to come out the back and see what a real biker looks like up against the wall?"

Her eyes go wide as she glances down my body, lingering on my crotch, she looks back up at me. I'm not a pretty boy like Gunner but I can tell she likes what she sees.

"Answer me," I say harshly. "Yes or no?"

She's not drunk, thank god, I don't do inebriated chicks.

"Ye….yes," she stutters, Colt's long forgotten.

"You get back to work," I bark at Colt as he watches us.

I grab her by the hand and yank her off the chair, ignoring Colt's very pissed off look as I practically drag her across the room.

Summer gives me a serious eye roll and shakes her head as I pass and make my way down the corridor toward the back store cupboard, very classy. Nailing her against a keg won't be the worst thing I can do tonight, though I don't exactly have a hard on yet and hopefully she'll do something about that.

Maybe if I imagine it's Sienna…… I punch myself in the face internally for about the hundredth time today. All Sienna has to do is glance my way and I'm standing to attention, ready and able. Maybe I could picture her in that yoga outfit again, that might help me get it up.

We get to the end of the hallway and I pull her into the room, she's looking at me with a little bit of trepidation all of a sudden, now we're alone this seems a lot more real. I'm six-foot six so I can appear to be slightly intimidating, or so I've been told.

I don't think she's very smart, but if she wants to go, I'll obviously let her, I'm not a total caveman.

"You sure you wanna do this?" I say, grazing her body with my eyes. "You wanna back out the doors behind me..." I thumb towards her pending escape as she takes me in.

She licks her lips and then before my very eyes she pulls her tube dress down and stands there in her black underwear. She's nicer without clothes on. At least my dick seems to have woken up a bit, though still at half-mast, it's better than nothing.

"I've always wanted to do a biker," she admits excitedly, though she could be saying her hail Mary's for all I care, I've tuned out, she reaches for my belt buckle, eager little thing. It's a pity her lips aren't full and luscious like......*fuck*, why can't I just give it a rest?

If I could stop picturing Sienna doing this and my dick in her mouth then I would, I wouldn't put myself through the torture on purpose now would I?

She tugs to remove my shirt and cut but that's not happening, only the jeans and the boxer briefs have to drop slightly to get this done, nothing else. No need to get carried away.

"You have a dirty mouth Melanie, how old are you?" I ask quickly, though she has to be over twenty-one, I hope.

"Twenty-three and a half," she replies. Wow, like that whole half a year really makes a difference.

That's quite a bit younger than me by twelve years but I don't ponder that too closely. I back her up against the wall and lift her by the ass as she squeals as I sit her on one of the Kegs.

Jesus. I wish she was Sienna.

"Are you gonna get my dick out or just fuckin' fumble around for half an hour?" I bark.

I'm being an absolute ass, but it's clear she doesn't expect anything less because she doesn't balk at my tone. She also doesn't get time to answer because at that exact moment my phone buzzes in my back pocket. She's barely got the zipper down.

I ignore it completely, even though I know it's Lily because she's set the ring tone to some stupid song that I can't fathom how to get rid of.

Not a good time Lil. Kinda busy here.

I go to kiss her, hoping that a bit of tongue action might get me more in the mood, but the phone goes off again before I even reach her.

I sigh out loud, at least the buckle's undone, she's now unbuttoning the top button and going for the zipper, hallelujah. I reach in my back pocket for my phone and glance at the screen.

I read the text, then read it again.

"Jesus fuckin' Christ," I mutter as the girl stops and looks up at me. I run my hand through my hair as I instantly turn away and press send to call Lily immediately, I hope this is some kind of joke. The phone rings but she doesn't pick up. I try again. It does the exact same thing.

"Is something wrong?" says Melissa or Melanie or whatever the fuck her name is.

I reach down and chuck her dress at her. "Sorry sweetheart, parties over, get dressed, I gotta go."

I leave her standing there staring after me, it looks like Colt is going to get lucky after all, just as well because I could barely even get it up. I stride back into the bar and search for Brock and Bones. *Shit.* Lily's in trouble, I need my guys.

"Back so soon?" Brock hollers as I spot him by the pool table and march over in a couple of strides, he's rubbing one of the sweet butts Chelsea's ass with his hand as she tries to take her shot. He sees my face and immediately stops and straightens.

"It's Lil," I say, striding past him and making for the clubhouse doors. "Find Bones and anyone else sober, somethings going down at the Crow."

I race out to the parking lot trying her phone once more and it now goes straight to message and doesn't even ring. Jesus Christ.

Lily where the fuck are you?

I'm all the way across town but that won't matter, my bike is a hellcat when she wants to be with straight pipes and a throttle like no other. I grasp the handle-bars with ferocity. If someone is about to hurt my sister, they better be ready to die. There are very few people I would be willing to go to prison for and Lily is one of them.

Help, I think my drinks been spiked.... Those were her words in the text, now she's not answering her phone. My baby sister's in trouble and I may be about to commit blue murder.

7

SIENNA

I NOTICE the girl from the other day at the clubhouse talking to a guy at the bar.

Liliana; I think that's her name.

She seems like she can't handle her booze well, even though I've only served her two drinks. The guy with her gives me an eye roll as he escorts her from the bar a short time later. She also leaves her phone next to her empty glass, so I grab it and walk up to Leroy.

"Be back in a second," I yell over the music. "A girl I know just left her phone."

He gives me a chin lift as I make my way out of the bar area and push my way through the crowd. Oddly, they don't make their way to the front to leave but to the back, where there's only the restrooms and the emergency exit.

I keep working my way through the busy hustle of people, avoiding grabby hands as bodies sway and dance to the music. Being Friday night, the party is in full swing and the band is rocking hard, it's a crazy crowd tonight, as wild as they come.

By the time I get through, they've gone out of the back exit, so I push the metal bar on the door when I reach it.

"Hey!" I call, but they are already behind the dumpster. "You forgot your phone!"

The guy turns to look at me, he's a little startled. The exit door shuts behind me with a loud bang, drowning out the noise from inside. He's parked behind the dumpster. My hackles instantly rise on the back of my neck. There's something off with this situation. He gives me a huge grin and waves his hand.

"Oh, thanks," he says, coming towards me, then rolls his eyes as if to say, 'silly me'.

"She seems pretty wasted on two drinks," I reply, looking over at the back door of his car where Liliana has just been loaded into.

"She's a lightweight," he smirks. "She's got a drinking problem, had a few before she got here, I'm always hauling her ass home."

He seems like a blue-collar kind of guy, smartly dressed, freshly shaven, and good looking. But I can't put my finger on why my gut is telling me something different… it's telling me to get the hell out of there.

"I'm new in town, she's Sarah, right?" I blurt out.

He glances at me. "Yeah, that's right. She knows not to drink tequila, I guess some people just can't handle their liquor." He smiles, hoping he's convincing me.

Sarah? Goddamn it. He doesn't even know her, and now I'm damned sure he's just spiked her drink. Oh, holy fucking crap, I'm out here alone.

I hold onto the phone. "Well, that's true; I see it all in here." I nod back to the exit door and make my way closer to try to escape and get help.

"Hey, where you going?" He moves toward me and tries to snake an arm around my waist, I recoil at his touch.

"Don't touch me," I say, whirling around. My heart is beating so fast in my chest, I'm sure he can hear it.

"Oh, come on, my girlfriend is out of it and you're mighty fine yourself, you sure you just wanna give me the phone or something else? There's no reason why we can't have a little bit of fun out here, nobody's watching, you look like a girl who knows how to have fun."

I literally want to vomit. I also took a self-defense class after Ewan, my ex-boyfriend. You want to hit a guy where it hurts them the most, so I turn in his arms and smile sweetly as if I'm enjoying his revolting touch, he lets his grip loosen slightly, smiling back at me… oh, he likes compliant girls, does he? I think he only likes unconscious ones though, ones who can't fight back, what a pig. In my peripheral, I see Liliana's body half hanging out of the car, he's attempted to drag her onto the back seat but her legs are still hanging out, touching the pavement. My stomach twists at this sick son of a bitch.

Before he can man-handle me for another disgusting moment longer, I bring my leg up fast and knee him in the balls hard, then I quickly turn and lunge for the door, getting a good grip on the handle and yank it open. I can hear him groaning behind me. The weird thing is, I don't make it inside because I run right into a large, concrete brick wall of a chest and I'm swiftly pushed back out the door.

I glance up and almost cry with relief. I never thought I'd be as happy to see the son of a bitch in front of me as I am right now. Steel looks down at me, enraged, and then grabs my shoulders and hauls me behind him.

"What the fuck's happening?" he demands, looking from me to the guy on the ground holding his junk. "Tell me fast."

"He took this girl from the bar and she left her phone, I'm pretty sure he slipped something in her drink, he said her name was Sarah, now he's trying to man-handle me, so I kicked him in the balls." It all comes out so fast that I don't even know if he caught it all. I point to his car on the other side of the dumpster.

Before I even know what's happening, I turn around and he king hits the guy so hard, he flies backward and hits his head on the pavement as he lands awkwardly. I wince and jump back. He rushes over to the car and I watch as he lifts Liliana's lifeless body up, checks her pulse, then steadies her back onto the seat gently. The guy, who's now flat on the ground moaning in pain, has blood gushing out of his nose, he won't be getting up for a while. Steel turns back to face me. I hear the unmistakable rumble of motorbikes in the distance. The cavalry is on its way, why am I not surprised?

Steel's dark eyes look more menacing than usual as he walks back over and kicks the guy in the ribs. He kicks again, then holds him up by the lapels of his shirt and punches him in the face again and again and again. He only stops when I call his name, but it's more of a shriek.

He glances up, dumps the guy's body down, he could be dead for all I know, and moves toward me quickly.

"Did he hurt you?" he barks at me, pointing in my face.

I shake my head because I can't speak but I flinch at his ferocity.

"Jesus, woman, I'm not going to hurt you," he states, looking over his shoulder toward the car. "That girl he took from the bar… Lily, she's my sister, she sent me this weird text…"

But before he can finish his sentence, I hear the sirens. Someone must have seen the kafuffle and called the cops because the patrol car is turning off the main street and making its way up the alleyway toward us, the blue and red lights flashing wildly.

I close my eyes and steel myself to stand up straight.

"You're Lily's brother?" I say slowly, I don't know why I'm

shocked, maybe because she is so tiny and fragile and he's like a monster.

He doesn't answer.

I watch on as he does the unthinkable. The cops get out and immediately start yelling at us, Steel's face is an unreadable mask of coldness, and his eyes—that striking green-grey that hold mine—are fierce as he backs away slowly from me, then drops to his knees, one by one, nice and slowly with his hands behind his head.

What the hell is he doing?

Before he gets all the way down, he slides something towards me and says, "Put this in your jeans, they won't search you."

I realize, as it skitters towards me, that it's a large knife wrapped in a pouch. I grab it quickly and do as he says, shoving it into the back of my jeans as I pull my shirt out to cover it.

When I glance up, he's facing me, waiting to be handcuffed as his dangerous and beautiful eyes never leave mine.

"You need to explain to them exactly what happened," he says calmly, too calmly, like he's been here before.

"Okay." I nod. The only thing I can do is tell the truth here anyway.

I look from him to the cop car at about the same time as two officers run our way, telling him to freeze and put his hands up, which he's already doing anyway.

"Miss…" the lady officer yells, looking from me to Steel, then to the guy on the ground trying to work out what's going on. Her gun is held out. "Are you hurt?"

"No," I say shakily, "but he didn't do anything." I point at the guy rolling around on the ground noisily, "It's that asshole there, he drugged Lily at the bar, she's over in the back of that car…"

The male officer comes behind Steel and, unnecessarily,

he pushes his knees wider with his boot, roughly frisking him, then cuffs him swiftly at the wrists so his arms are pulled all the way back behind him.

"Talk to me, Steel," the officer says urgently.

So, they know each other. He looks like a navy seal— short hair, not tall but thick and bulky and wears his uniform well. He glances at me then shoves at Steel again to make him talk. "What the hell's going on?"

"Lily needs an ambulance," Steel replies, nodding over toward the dude's car. "She's been drugged."

The officer nods to the lady cop and she makes the call, then he looks towards me. "What's your name?"

"Sienna Morgan," I stammer. "I work here, I followed her out because she left her phone on the bar and then he tried to attack me too."

Steel's eyes go wide and he actually turns a shade of purple right before my eyes, he looks so angry he may combust, in fact, he begins to rise again but the cop shoves him back down with his boot. The female officer is checking on Lily now, she comes back into view a few moments later.

"This true, Steel? Talk to me," the male cop barks. *Why isn't Steel defending himself?*

"You know that's Lily," he gruffs angrily. "Check her phone if you must, Sienna has it. Better still, mine's in my back pocket, she sent me a text about bein' in trouble and I came to find her."

The cop does just that. Clearly, they know each other but have trust issues.

"You gonna uncuff me?" Steel barks at him.

Satisfied with what he reads, the officer reluctantly uncuffs him. *Steel has done nothing wrong!* I want to yell at him.

The guy on the ground begins to roll over suddenly, I honestly don't know how he can even be breathing, his face is covered in blood and swelling fast. Although he doesn't stand or even get to his knees, he reaches toward me helplessly like I'm going to help him! He's a mess and he's a glutton for punishment. I give him another swift kick in the balls since he won't be using them for a while, and the officer yells at us to freeze. I don't know if it's to him or me.

"Sick son of a bitch!" I yell at him as he drops down again, clutching his crotch.

I look up to find Steel's hand on my elbow, he begins steering me backward away from the commotion. "I'm glad that boot isn't aimed at me," he says quietly, a smirk dashing across his lips.

He moves me aside, his hand still at my elbow as the cops do their job and haul the guy to his feet, or rather, drag him toward the police car. A crowd has formed behind the vehicle as people strain their necks to see what's going on, the sound of rumbling motorbikes has stopped. Two of the guys from the meeting—I can't remember their names, but the one who has the Mohawk and the other large guy with long hair, Brock, I think—come skidding on foot into the alleyway as the female cop tells them to get back.

"We don't need any more trouble," the male officer adds with authority.

"Hand him over to us, Jenkins," Steel says calmly, turning to face them head-on. "Then there won't need to be any trouble."

He still holds me with one hand, it snakes firmly around my arm, I'm now facing his back so I can't see, it's as if he's shielding me. Unfathomably, I clutch onto the back of his leather vest so I don't fall, shock suddenly setting in.

"Just step aside," the officer called Jenkins replies, "don't make this any harder than it already is, Steel, I'm warning you. This is now a police matter and we will deal with it."

More police cars arrive and I can tell from the looks on

the other biker's faces that they are bummed they're too late. I can only imagine what they had in store for the guy if the cops hadn't got here so quickly.

He turns back to look down at me. "You okay?"

I nod. He lets go of me once the dude is safely in the back of the patrol car and then races back over to the other car and picks up Liliana in his arms. An ambulance comes screaming down the other end of the alleyway a few moments later, and she swiftly gets loaded in the back on a stretcher, it's awful seeing her limp, lifeless body like that. I feel so sick just watching it.

"Steel?" Brock says, then some silent communication goes on between them.

"I'm going with Lil to the hospital," Steel replies, then points at me. "She's coming with me; she may have been hurt, so she needs to get checked out too."

They nod as Jenkins comes back toward us after closing the doors of the patrol car, two other male officers come up behind him, backup has arrived.

"We need you to come down and give us a statement," Jenkins states, then nods to Steel.

"After she gets seen by a doctor." Steel has authority in his tone. When I try to object and say I haven't been injured, he just gives me a look of disapproval, so I keep my mouth shut.

Jenkins reluctantly agrees. "Drop by the station immediately after she gets the all-clear." He shifts his eyes back to Steel. "I hope Lily is okay."

The concern on his face is very kind; he seems like a good guy.

Steel nods and reaches his hand toward me, beckoning me to him. As if I were a fragile deer, the mohawked biker gently steers me by my elbow and escorts me toward Steel. When I reach him, he takes me by the hand.

"I'll go and let the bouncers know what happened, Stef here?" he asks me.

I shake my head. "She went to a funeral out of town."

"Okay, honey," he replies and disappears through the exit door after Brock.

Steel helps me into the back of the ambulance.

"Are you sure you're okay?" he asks as we sit opposite each other in between Lily's stretcher.

I nod. "Just shaken up, that shit was pretty heavy."

I glance down at his bloodied hands, but he does not seem fazed by it and shrugs off one of the paramedics who offers to take a look. I notice the other hand bears knuckle dusters and I shudder at the thought of the damage he's done to that guy's face; he'll probably be drinking from a straw for the rest of his life. That piece of shit deserves it though.

"Are your hands hurt?" I whisper.

He runs the knuckle dusted one through his hair then glances over at me, taking his time to respond. "Not as much as his face," he mutters as if just taking in the severity of the situation. "What the fuck just happened?"

The paramedic has Lily stable and a blanket is wrapped around her. "It's likely Rohypnol," he says. "It'll wear off in about six or eight hours."

"The date rape drug," Steel confirms.

The paramedic nods. "We need to give her fluids, monitor her, let it run its course."

I stare at her lifeless body and feel sick all over again. Relief, however, swiftly replaces that, the fact she's okay is all that matters now. I'm so glad Steel arrived; I don't want to think about what could have happened… what *almost* happened.

We ride all the way downtown to the hospital in complete and utter silence.

*

I hate the smell of hospitals. They are extremely depressing places but Steel refuses to let me go home, and frankly, I don't actually know how to get back to the Stone Crow from here.

We're seated in the emergency room, waiting for word on Lily.

Suddenly, from behind a curtain, an older woman comes rushing towards us in scrubs and then she does a very strange thing; she looks up at Steel, then he bends and gives her a hug followed by a kiss on the cheek.

"Mom, this is Sienna," he says as my eyes go wide. *Their mom.* She's so tiny. "Sienna, this is my mom."

"Helen," she replies, then instead of shaking hands, she pulls me into a tight embrace. "The ambulance officers told me what happened; I don't even know where to begin or how to thank you."

I look up at Steel leaning against the wall, he makes no attempt to save me.

"It all happened so fast," I admit. "Can we see her?"

She pulls back and smiles at me kindly, she has Steel's eyes.

"Yes, of course. Follow me."

She starts up the hallway and we follow behind. I feel his hand at my elbow again; it seems he likes doing that.

"She needs to be checked out," he says to his mom and I presume he means me.

"Speak for yourself," I retort, pointing at his bloodied hands.

We follow her into a room and see Lily hooked up to a monitor, she has a clear bag of fluid on a drip attached to her arm. Helen sits on the end of the bed looking at her.

"The cops get him?" she asks as Steel closes the door quietly behind us.

He nods. "Yes, unfortunately."

"Well, it's for the best," she mutters, but her tone indicates she doesn't mean that. She looks at me. "Were you hurt, Sienna?"

I shake my head. "No, but I did knee him hard, I've got pretty hard kneecaps, though I may have a bruise tomorrow."

Her eyes go watery. "I can never thank you enough for your quick thinking, this is my baby." She pulls out a tissue from her sleeve and wipes her eyes; I feel a lump in my throat.

"I'm just so glad she's going to be okay," I say in a small voice, looking over at Steel. He likes to lean a lot, somehow, he makes it look cool. He moves over to the closed bathroom door and goes in, I hear the water running and he comes back a few moments later with clean hands.

"She'll be fine; I just don't even want to think about what could have happened," Helen sniffs. "I'll be here tonight anyway on shift, so don't worry yourself." She looks up at Steel. "Jayson, make sure she gets home safe now, won't you?"

Jayson?

Steel's jaw tightens at the mention of his name and he gives her a very obvious eye roll.

Maybe if I stay here a bit longer, I'll find out some more details about her larger than life son who can't fit through a doorframe without ducking. I wonder if his mom is in the club too, is she an old lady? She also doesn't seem concerned about his bloodied knuckles, she barely glanced at them.

"Pigs want us to go make a statement," he grunts.

"Which you'll be sure to do," she tells him in no uncertain terms. It's odd seeing his mom boss him around in front of me. It's very normal and un-biker-like, I think I like her.

He pulls out a cigarette and puts it behind his ear, then pulls his phone out and dials.

"Patch? Yeah, I'm at the hospital. No, she's fine. I got there in time and so did the cops, yeah, I know, let Hutch know and I'll be back soon. Get pencil dick or whoever is sober enough to drop my sled off at the pig shop, gotta make a statement… yeah, no a half-hour or so. Thanks, brother."

He ends the call and nods up at me.

What the hell is a sled?

"We have to go," he says to his mom. "Text me when she's awake."

His mom still has her arm around me. "Don't be a stranger now, little miss," she tells me with a kind smile. "And don't you worry, Lily is in safe hands now." She kisses me on the head and I almost lose it.

"It was nice meeting you," I reply, my voice unsteady.

"Likewise."

"Later, mom."

She nods. "I'll talk to you soon, son."

I get following Steel's hasty retreat, he grabs my hand as we leave and links his fingers with mine, I have to walk super-fast to keep up with him.

He looks down at me as we walk. "You wear steel caps, princess?"

I realize he's referring to my knee-high boots.

"No, just the regular kind."

He snorts and I realize he's making a joke.

We step outside and I breathe in the late-night air with a rush of relief. The last time I visited a hospital, I was getting fixed up myself, I don't like to think of that time, it's just too hard.

As soon as we're outside, he releases my hand and proceeds to light up the cigarette, cupping his hand around the flame as he takes a long drag.

We keep walking and I see the police station lights up ahead.

"Are you really alright?" he asks, not looking at me, he blows a cloud of smoke out in front of him. He's asked me this about five hundred times already. "Shock does things to people."

"I'm not in shock," I reply. "I feel fine."

"How do you know you're not in shock? And anyway, it was a really dangerous move going out there alone in the alleyway, Sienna, what were you thinking?"

I look up at him with wide eyes… wait, is he mad at me?

"What the hell?" I reply.

"Well, it was a dangerous situation," he gruffs, the cigarette dangles from his lips as he speaks. "One that could have ended a lot differently if I didn't get there in time."

"Well, I subdued him, you showed up and she's fine, so that's all that matters. I didn't know he'd drugged her at the time, I just went to give her the phone back."

He gives me an uncertain side glance but it softens when he sees my face. He stubs his cigarette out with his boot as we approach the station doors.

"What will the guy get for doing that?"

"I don't know," he says with a sigh, "but Hutch is not gonna be happy the pigs got to him before we did."

I don't have time to think about that too closely as he opens the door and lets me under his arm. Giving my statement doesn't take that long, and Steel lets the Jenkins officer know they can come by and get the security footage from the bar tomorrow. It may help when convicting him. Steel seems very agitated through the whole exchange, like he can't wait to be gone.

"I'll take you home," he says finally.

"Thank you, that would be great." I smile gratefully.

We walk toward the curb and it's then I realize we're moving towards a motorbike that has mysteriously turned up right outside.

I turn to him.

"You aren't expecting me to get on that thing, are you?" I frown.

He rolls his eyes to the heavens and huffs a long outward breath.

"Can you be compliant for just one evening?"

He doesn't wait for an answer as he swings one leg over the bike and kicks the stand up, starts the beast, roars it with one hand on the throttle, and then turns to me and hands me a helmet. "Put this on, princess, you're gonna need it."

8

STEEL

A MILLION THINGS run through my head as I watch Sienna stare at me as I hold the brain bucket out to her. What I'm gonna do to this guy when he gets free is at the top of that list.

"You cold?" I ask her.

She is, I can see her shaking.

I don't wait for an answer, I shrug my cut off and, fuck me if I don't also lean forward and wrap it around her shoulders. She looks good in it, damn fine, a little too clean-cut, but damn sexy.

Chicks always dig the leather but I'm the one in awe.

"I've never been on a motorbike," she admits as she shrugs her arms into my jacket, it's huge on her. Resigned to the fact that she's got no choice, she pulls the grey helmet down and I help her fasten the buckle.

"All you gotta do is hop on, hold on tight, and scream if you want to." I shrug like it's easy.

My hard-on kicks in my jeans at her standing there in my colors, I just wish she'd be more compliant and do as I say; I'm trying to get her home safe for Christ's sake. Hopefully, with her virtue intact, but then again, maybe not. I know for a fact I've never thought about a woman wearing my cut. Ever.

As she climbs aboard, I quickly adjust myself so I'm more comfortable, and once her thighs are wedged behind mine, I turn and call over my shoulder.

"You gonna hang onto me, princess, or you wanna fall off?"

I light another cigarette as she wraps her arms around my waist, her forearms rest at my belt buckle—a little too close to home but I won't complain, it just makes it all the more exhilarating.

My sled rumbles beneath me like the badass she is, it could wake the dead. I feel powerful when I'm straddling her, when I'm on the open road and the end is nowhere in sight.

I know it's morbid, but I thank Max for kicking the bucket. If not for him, she wouldn't be here right now. She's a fucking angel, and she just saved my sister from being raped and probably herself too if that guy's track record was anything to go by. Jenkins told me he was wanted in a couple of other states and they think he has links to human trafficking. My blood is literally still running cold at that information. I've got some shit to report back to Hutch.

One thing's for sure, there's gonna be no more beef with the club going forward. Sienna will get whatever she wants, and the club will be in her debt because of this. She's gonna learn how loyalty really works and she'll see we're not all big, dirty-assed bikers.

I feel very protective over her, it overwhelms me because sickos like this guy can just prey on innocent people and there ain't nothing you can do about it, especially when you've been drugged. Poor Lily, she's going to be really suffering tomorrow. Then she has my wrath to deal with.

I take off from the curb and my tires squeal from the

sheer power of the throttle. I hear Sienna scream behind me and I laugh, it only makes me go faster.

Her hands grip me tighter around the waist and I have to physically restrain myself from moving at least one of her hands south of the border so she can see what she's done to me. My hard-on is ridiculous now, hardly containable. I imagine her hand working me; I'd love to watch her jacking me off. I let out a low grumble in my throat at the thought, she can't hear me, my sled's too loud.

Having her legs and arms wrapped around me makes me want her so bad, I want to take her home to my bed, worship her, and kiss every fucking inch of her. I wonder if she likes it gentle or rough or a little bit of both, I really hope I get to find out soon.

She also has no idea I'm taking the scenic route back to downtown, just so I get a few more minutes of her body pressed against mine. I'm gonna keep her safe, she just doesn't know it yet.

When we reach the back of the Crow, I park next to her dark blue Datsun, I know it's her car because I've seen her driving it around all week. As I park up, I will myself to not switch the engine off… I'm not staying. I kick the stand down and tell her to climb off.

She releases her hands from me and uses my shoulders to help herself climb down, immediately, she yanks the helmet from her head and shakes her long, honey-colored hair out and I swear I've never seen anything so beautiful in my life. It's a wonder she doesn't grow wings and fly.

"How was it?" I ask, raising a brow.

"Amazing." Her cheeks are flushed and my lips twitch. It's a delicious sight.

I shut my mouth, climb off, and for once, I purposely don't reach for her, it's dangerous if I do, I take the helmet back from her hands and put it under the seat.

"You have your key for the back door?"

She pats her jeans pocket and nods. "Yes."

She shrugs my cut off and hands it back to me. Our fingers touch as I take it and throw it back on; I don't think it's just my imagination that I can smell her vanilla-scented perfume on her neckline.

I swing my leg back over and mount my bike with total ease. The bar's quiet but I still don't like the thought of her going in there alone.

"Go get inside, it's late," I tell her. "You gonna be okay?"

She's still looking at me.

Fuck. This. Is. Not. Good.

I turn away because, if I don't, she's gonna feel the wrath of my kiss and a whole lot more. She looks at me like she wants more, like she's disappointed that I'm dumping her off, but she has to know it's for the best. I can't get involved with her.

"Answer me," I bark.

She nods again; she probably thinks I'm a fucking prick. Me pummeling that guy was probably pretty scary for her, whether he deserved it or not, maybe she thinks I'm a thug.

Then I have an idea… I dig out my phone from inside my jacket pocket.

"Give me your number," I demand.

She hesitates for a fraction of a second then calls it out to me. I type it into my phone and call her, then I hang up.

"Now you have my number too, call me if you have any… security concerns, I'll be up for a while."

I can't believe I actually just said that. But yeah, I'll be up all night now and it's all her fault. I do not add that I can do booty calls as well at a moment's notice, right now I have to get to Church as the guys are waiting for a debrief.

"Okay." Her voice is quiet. "Thanks again for coming to the rescue."

I swallow hard, "Get gone inside," I tell her again. "Make sure the door locks properly behind you, I'll wait until you get in."

"Steel…" she tries but I ignore her.

Christ, my name sounds good on her lips.

"Later, babe," I say, not wanting her to finish because we won't make it to the backdoor if she keeps looking at me like that.

She bites her lip then nods and I watch as she walks to the backdoor and unlocks it, disappearing inside without a backward glance.

I sit there for a few moments until I see the upstairs light go on at her window. I don't like her being here alone, it doesn't feel right. I need to talk to Stef about upping the security after what happened tonight, this won't do. I know a guy from the New Orleans chapter who owes me a favor.

I run a hand down my face, and with a resigned sigh, I rev the engine louder than necessary and take off back to Church. I've got shit to do, and that's all that stops me from turning the bike around and banging on the back door for Sienna to let me in.

*

A few things happen on Sunday that changes the course of the Bracken Ridge Rebels M.C. that nobody could see coming. As expected, Hutch is not happy that the pigs were called and got to the scene before we had the chance to string up that coward and bleed him out. His fate at the moment lies with the county, but if he gets off, he's a dead man. After what Jenkins revealed, mainly to shut me up, it doesn't sound like he's getting out anytime soon.

Secondly, Hutch called a meeting with Sienna tomorrow, not with the whole club this time, just with him. There are things to be said and contracts to be ironed out. She won't say no to the offer this time and she won't be throwing anything in my face.

Thirdly, Linc, my right-hand man in the 'hacking information land', got back to me last night after I'd asked him days ago to get more information on Sienna, not that she has any kind of criminal record, the girl probably doesn't even have a parking ticket. What she does have is a restraining order on someone called Ewan Reynolds; subsequently, he'd been done for battery and assault and did time, only six lousy months. It explains a lot but I'd never pick her for a battered girlfriend. Linc said she's been assaulted by this guy, her ex-boyfriend no less.

I don't even know the guy and I want to kill him. I'd get pleasure in it.

I called Sienna earlier and told her to meet me at Church on Monday night, something I'm not sure she'd do after the last time she came here, but things are different now.

She's apprehensive, of course, but nothing bad is going to happen to her, not while I'm around.

At eight sharp, I lounge against my sled as she rolls her beat-up car into the lot, I watch as she kills the engine and reapplies lip gloss in the rearview mirror. She doesn't know I'm here. Car parks are bad places for girls to be at night-time, she should know that after the other night.

"You own a pepper spray?" I ask when she gets out. She squeals and jumps back, pressing one palm to her heart, startled. She had no idea I was even there, not good.

"Jesus, Steel, you almost gave me a heart attack."

"That's a no then?"

Just as I thought.

I uncross my feet at the ankle and stand slowly. She's so small compared to me, another thing I like about her.

She breathes in a couple more times as if to steady herself, then shakes her head.

"You should always have a pepper spray, after the other night's incident, it should be a lesson to take more care," I scold.

"Thanks for the pep talk, dad."

I give her a pointed look which she ignores with a scowl. "Not funny."

"How's Lily?" She's also good at changin' the subject.

"She'll be fine," I grunt. "She's asking for you, wants to have lunch or some shit, she's taking it pretty hard."

She bites her lip. "I'm sure she is, it's pretty frightening what went down, I can't stop thinking about it."

I kick the gravel with my boot.

"How've you been?"

She looks up a little surprised… what? I can't make small talk and ask how a woman is? She's been on my mind for two whole freaking days; I can't seem to get her off it.

"I've been okay." She shrugs, her voice is small, I don't think she's okay.

"You wanna talk about it?"

Please say no.

She shakes her head. "Is the guy still locked up?"

I nod. "Yeah, he'll be there for a long time, he's wanted for other really bad shit, trust me when I say you don't wanna know."

She gulps and my mind runs to that restraining order and the battery and assault charges, my blood boils at the thought of anyone hurting her. I'd kill them.

"Best not keep Prez waiting," she says with a small smile. "He isn't going to chew my head off again, is he?"

I shake my head, resisting the urge to touch the small of her back, I like touching her.

"No, sweetheart, he isn't."

I lead the way through the front doors. Summer is tidying

up the bar and mopping the floors. Gunner's also there, playing pool with Patch and Colt.

"Well, well, well," Gunner whistles low, leaning against his cue, giving Sienna the once over. "What do we have here?"

"Hi, Gunner," she says and gives him a small wave.

I turn and look at her, shocked. She remembers *his* name alright, of course she does. He grins at my annoyance.

"Hey yourself, sweetheart, this is Patch, Colt, and that little ray of sunshine over there's my little sister, Summer."

Why would she care?

She gives them a small wave too. Summer approaches, still holding the mop. She's just like Gunner in looks; blonde, pretty, turns every head in the room, but that's where the similarity ends. Unlike him, she keeps to herself and doesn't have a whole lot to say to anyone. I think the damage of her childhood took a hold; they had a rough and violent upbringing. She never dates, I've never even seen her with a guy, she's damaged goods. Every time I see her, I feel pity, she could have any guy she wants just on looks alone, a lot like her brother, but she doesn't go there, not ever.

I clear my throat.

She hugs Sienna with one arm. "We all appreciate what you did for Lily," she says softly. "Like really, that was amazing."

Sienna looks taken aback but holds her own. "It was nothing; I did what anyone would do."

"Nothing?" Gunner laughs ."You kicked the dude in the nuts twice and disabled him before the cavalry arrived, pretty fuckin' great if you ask me."

"I took self-defense classes," Sienna says, earning a side-ways glance from me. She looks from me to Gunner and shrugs.

"He claimin' you now?" Gunner chirps; he's all smiles

tonight. "Can't say I blame you, Steel, she's definitely no sweet butt, that's for sure."

Sienna looks up at me, startled. "I've no idea what that means but it doesn't sound good."

"Fuck off," I bark at him as he laughs. "See you later."

I don't let Sienna hear any more profanity as I grab her hand and steer her in the direction of Hutch's office.

I'm not claiming her, she isn't mine to do so. When a member does that officially, it means your woman is a no-go zone, she is yours. I don't think we are quite at that point.

"What does he mean?" Sienna asks from behind me. "What's a sweet butt?"

"He's being a dick," I retort.

"Claiming women sounds very archaic."

I turn to her with a frown. "Once you belong to a patched member, you're like their wife, that's all it means, it's no different to a marriage, nobody can go near your ol' lady or try their luck with her, so it isn't an insult."

"What's a sweet butt then?"

That, on the other hand…

Do I answer that or pretend I hadn't heard?

I sigh. "It's someone at the club who sleeps around with the guys."

I don't need to turn to realize that she's probably got steam coming out of her ears.

"What the hell?" She looks mad, really fuckin' mad.

"He said you're *not* that," I remind her. "Which you're not and will never be, obviously."

"You have girls that do that kind of thing?" she whispers, shocked. I don't know why.

"No different to people hooking up on a Friday night at the Stone Crow or any bar in the world for that matter."

She doesn't loosen her grasp on my hand, that's a relief.

"Do you always talk to people like that?" she asks after a moment. "Telling them to 'eff off?"

I roll my eyes. "It's Gunner, trust me, he deserves it."

We reach Hutch's office; the door is ajar and I knock loudly. He bellows us to come in. I turn and gesture for Sienna to go in ahead of me.

"Miss Morgan," he declares as we enter, he's sitting in his massive black leather chair, a laptop screen in front of him, he moves it aside. "Please take a seat." He motions at the chair in front of him. I stay standing but close the door behind us.

"Please, call me Sienna." She sits down crossing one leg over the other.

"It seems I underestimated you," he says, looking over to her. "Steel told me what happened on Saturday with Lily at the Crow, you showed remarkable bravery doing what you did."

A few uncomfortable moments of silence pass.

"It wasn't great," she admits, I can tell she's wondering where he's going with this. "I don't know about bravery, I'm just glad that Lily's okay, that's all."

He looks right at her, his business face on. He's a hard man but he ain't goin' in for the kill tonight. "Thanks to your quick thinking, no less, I knew you had the smarts that very first day. My wife says you're a woman with spirit, there's nothin' wrong with a woman with a bit of grit in this town."

She seems confused by the comment, stumbling on her words, "I'm not sure how to answer that," she says quietly. "I didn't do anything really, in fact, if Steel didn't turn up…" She trails off as he appraises her with a deep frown that closes her mouth quickly.

"You have to understand that where we come from, Sienna, loyalty is everything, it's the core, the very foundation of this club. We stick together not just by our motto but it's in our blood." He bangs against his heart with one fist. "I built this club up from the ground with my bare hands, when other clubs changed tact and went over to the dark side selling drugs, guns, you name it, I could have folded, I could have gone down that very same path as many others have done, it's easy to take that road for the money, for the fast life it gives you, but that's all it is, you spend every day lookin' over your shoulder, wonderin' if you're gonna be the next one in a concrete box, or worse, a wooden box permanently, but it always catches up with you, which is why I turned this club around, it's why what you see around you now still stands."

He wants her to know we ain't one-percenters; outlaws.

"I respect that," she says. "But I'm not sure what this has to do with me."

"Anyone new to the club or not involved in an M.C. won't understand it," he explains. But I want you to know where I'm coming from, that the decisions I make aren't just for me, they're for everyone involved with this club, and sometimes those decisions aren't easy. Liliana, for example, is like a daughter to me, I've known her since she was born, practically raised her, she's precious, and she could have been violated in the most offensive and degrading of ways that could happen to a woman. Our job is to protect our women first and foremost... as men, that's our job, it's simple, there's no two ways about it, and we look after our own, all the brothers that belong to the Rebels, and when you stand with the club and not against us, we'll protect you too."

I would give a penny for her thoughts.

"Alright," she replies, sounding a little unsure.

Hutch regards her with a long look, then he slides the contract across the desk, it's been flattened back out, but still bears the creases of where she screwed it up that night and threw it at me. I hold back a grin.

He then slides a check over with it. "You'll take this, and we'll shake on it, and that will be the end of the negotiations."

She slowly looks at the check, ignoring the contract, then looks back up to Hutch.

"Umm, there seems to be some mistake."

Hutch raises an eyebrow. "There's no mistake, it's yours, all of it." His voice is firm.

"That's more than it's worth, I really can't accept this," she protests.

Hutch ignores her, picks up his glass of half-filled whiskey, and takes a long-assed swig.

"Well, you can and you will, not that there's a price on Lily's safety and security, she's priceless, and before you go thinking you're now somehow indebted to the club… *don't*, it's yours free and clear, no strings."

She just stares at him as he continues. "Now that we're on the subject of security, while you're here in town, you'll be under the club's protection from now on. If you have a problem, you call Steel or one of the boys, you got me?"

She doesn't say anything but watches as he pours himself another whiskey. "Now, you go on and bank that check tomorrow and we won't hear any more about it."

"I… it's…"

"No lip," he tells her sternly. "Now give me your hand and we'll shake on it."

He stands and holds his hand out. I watch as she slowly rises and shakes his hand. His eyes flick over to me.

"I really don't know what to say," she mutters her stance rigid.

"Steel," he says, ignoring her. "A minute."

I open the door and Sienna steps outside. "Wait here," I tell her.

I turn back to Hutch and close the door again. "Boss?"

"See she gets home safe, and that the check gets banked."

"On it."

"Steel?" he calls before I can leave. I know that tone. "You got somethin' goin' on with her?"

"No," I reply because I don't… not *yet* anyway.

"Girls like that are hard work."

"Thanks for the tip, dad."

He smiles. "You know what I mean, she ain't from around here, she'd have expectations, a woman like that, she's crossing onto the wrong side of the tracks."

"The wrong side is lookin' pretty good from where I'm standing," I retort with a shake of my head.

"Just don't fuck it up."

I snort. "Getting a bit ahead of yourself, aren't you?"

He gives me a pointed look. "Make sure she's safe."

I nod. "Will do."

"Now, get out of here."

"Night, Hutch," I call over my shoulder, making for the door. She looks up at me as I close it behind me, her eyes are a little wide and slightly bewildered.

"You alright?"

"Can I get a shot please?"

Of all the things I expect to come out of her mouth, that isn't it.

"You really think that's a good idea?"

"Probably not," she admits.

We head over to the bar.

"What's your poison?" I turn to face her and find two shot glasses.

"Southern Comfort please," she replies.

I pour us both a shot, hold my glass out to hers, and we clink. I sling it back with my eyes on her. She's so goddamn beautiful. She coughs as she comes up for air and I smirk.

"Better?" I ask, giving her a chin lift.

She nods. I'm not giving her anymore when she's driving.

We go out to the parking lot and I admit, I don't want her to go.

I stop at my sled and she doesn't make for her car.

"Let's go for a ride." She nods to my sled.

The pulse in my pants speeds up.

"Isn't it past your bedtime?" I mock.

She rolls her eyes.

"You rollin' your eyes at me, princess?"

"What if I am?" she retorts.

I shake my head. "You like the adrenaline rush that much?"

She smiles shakily, I wonder if the shot has just gone straight to her head.

"Maybe I do."

I am so going to hell.

I look down at her skirt and rub my beard. "Not really dressed for it," my eyes linger on her legs for far too long.

"I'm a girl, I can improvise."

I balk. "You asked for it, princess. Get on."

9

STEEL

I TAKE her out of town, down the 101 onto the deserted highway, and ride south into the mountains, there's nothing around us for miles, just the rugged landscape, darkness, and the freedom only a bike brings you. This is where I feel most alive and her clutching onto me, wrapped around me, her chin resting on my shoulder is the best feeling in the whole entire world.

I know that if I stop at the lookout, I'll want to kiss her, and kissing her will lead to me wanting her in every single way. I use it as a turnaround point and do not stop.

I reach around and pat her leg. "You good?"

I feel her nod. I like how she seems to enjoy this; she's been on my sled twice now and I can tell she's enjoying herself. I smile to myself and take off from the top of the mountain and head back down. It feels like I'm the king of the world.

She squeezes me tightly, I look down quickly at her small hands wrapped around me and I get it now. This feeling. I'm falling for her big time and I've no fucking clue what to do about it. Her holding me like this, no, it definitely doesn't help. I look back at the road, there's no way in hell I can get off this bike once I drop her back because she's going to see what she does to me every time she touches me... and it's burning a hole in my jeans. I wobble the handlebars suddenly as I feel one of her hands snake its way south, over my belt buckle, and yeah... right there. At first, I think my imagination has gotten the better of me. But no.

Holy Jesus, what the hell is she doing?

I jerk, almost crashing the bike as she finds my throbbing length—not like she could miss it.

Holy Mother of God. She holds her hand there and fuck me if she doesn't start to rub me through my jeans. My cock is so hard, it's painful against my zipper.

I look down and seeing her hand there makes me want to pull over and bang her hard and fast over my sled or against the nearest tree, it wouldn't matter.

I can't take it. I dive for her hand, grab it, and move it north, back to my stomach where it's safe and I hold it there so she doesn't try anything else. We're no good to each other banged up or dead on the side of the road, which is what will happen if she keeps going.

I don't know how I make it to the back lot of the Stone Crow without crashing, but I do. I park my sled, wordlessly, and kick the stand down. My breathing is ragged like I've just jogged a marathon, and I realize I'm still holding her hand. My heart is racing.

I let it go and she pushes off my back instantly and I hear her dismount, she tugs the helmet off and shakes her hair the way I like it. I'm still staring ahead, trying to compose myself.

"Sorry about that," she says as I turn to look at her. I turn the keys and my bike hums to a stop.

"*Sorry about that?*" I mimic her voice.

"It was just so exhilarating; I was lost in the moment."

"More like that shot went straight to your head," I mutter.

I stare at her. I have no reason to stay away from her—none at all now that club business is sorted. As if we could ever be just friends.

I swing my leg over the bike and put my hands on my hips and stare down at her.

"What am I going to do with you?" I wonder.

Be gentle with her, I tell myself. I'm so rock hard, it's not even funny.

"You shouldn't have done that, princess."

"Why not?" she asks in a whisper.

"You playin' games with me?" It sounds harsher than I mean it to.

She blinks as if she's misheard me. "No, I'm not suicidal."

Good answer. I snort a laugh.

I move toward her. "You wanna play, princess?" I cock a brow.

I look down at her heaving ample chest; her breathing is as ragged as mine. I want to touch her, so I don't wait for an answer.

"Get your keys."

She listens, for once, and fishes them out of the small bag she has slung over her body.

I walk behind her to the back door and she unlocks it. We move in silently and I shut the door behind me and secure it with the locks. That act alone says I'm not planning on leaving anytime soon, oh, hell no. There's a set of stairs just off to the left, I follow her up them, my eyes on her sweet little ass all the way. We don't touch, we don't speak, and my body is literally throbbing for her.

"This is me," she sing-songs when we get to the top. I want to laugh.

"I should go," I say, but make no attempt to move and I don't really mean it but it gives her an out, if she really wants one. I don't want to go, I want to come inside and sink myself into her sweet body and take my time.

She looks up at me with those big blue eyes, "I'm not sorry," she states suddenly, flooring me, there's a fire in her eyes. "I meant to do that."

I cock an eyebrow. "Did that one shot really do all of this to you?"

She rolls her eyes at me.

"Did you just roll your eyes at me again?" I say, my voice is hoarse and we both know it.

"What if I did?" she says quickly, brave little thing.

I fold my arms against my chest like that can help me. "You know, grabbing someone's junk while riding a very fast motorcycle isn't exactly the brightest way to get a man's attention," I inform her, my eyes flick to her lips. "You could have killed us."

"Junk?" she says with a laugh. Now she's laughing at me. I really need to teach her a lesson.

"So, tell me, Steel, exactly what is the best way to get a man's attention?"

She's got some nerve, making all the moves. If I wasn't so horny, I'd be impressed.

"This," I grunt, dipping my head as I take her lips. She's soft, delectable, everything I thought she would be as I kiss her hard, I feel her hands move to my biceps as I walk her backwards until she hits the door, I cage her in with my hands on either side of her head against the wooden frame.

My tongue seeks entry and she makes a noise in the back of her throat that goes straight to my groin. Her hands squeeze my muscles and I press my hard-on against her hip as she literally moans into my mouth, it's the most beautiful sound.

It's hot, so freaking hot, I could unzip right now and fuck her against the door.

"You feel that?" I growl, pulling back.

"Uh-huh," she gasps.

"This is what you do to me, you get me so rock hard," I say in her ear.

I breathe hard, watching her. Her hands snake down my chest then they reach my hips and move around the back to my ass, she grabs it and presses me hard, encouraging me. *Jesus, woman,* she'll be the death of me.

I kiss her again as she gasps, it's all tongue. I move my hands and hitch up her skirt and lift her by the hips as I hold her against the door, she wraps her legs around me. She's as light as a feather and I love her hands on me; I want them everywhere.

"Door key." I manage as she pulls on my neck to get me back to her mouth. I realize she's still clutching them in her hand. I move my lips to her neck and trail kisses there. When I get to her pulse, I bite down gently.

She squeezes me harder and groans, that noise again gets me all worked up, as if I need any more amps, *ahh shit, woman.* I take the keys from her and, without looking, I fiddle around with the lock until I somehow get it inside. Thank fuck for that.

"You feel so good against me," I tell her as I get the door open and I carry her inside. "I want you so bad, babe."

"*Steel...*" she breaths, it sounds more like she's begging, and she will be soon.

"Call me Jayson when we're like this," I say suddenly, though I can hardly believe the words have left my mouth. I could cut my tongue out. But I want to hear her say it in the throes of passion. I kick the door shut with my boot and she drops her bag to the floor. I let her down as she slides down my body, I spin her around, move her hair to one side, and kiss down her neck. She rolls her body so it presses back into me. I pull her against my chest as she snakes her arms around me and squeezes my ass.

"I can't wait to taste you," I whisper, skimming kisses up her neck. She smells like vanilla and sex. "I want to hear you scream my name; I promise you'll like every minute of it."

"Don't stop," she moans breathlessly. I like how I'm affecting her.

"Not gonna stop, babe, I'm not gonna stop until you're begging me to take you."

Looming over her, I look down at her perfect tits through the material of her shirt as she breathes heavily. I cup them and squeeze hard; she pushes them out further into my hands.

"Fuck, you're beautiful," I mutter in her ear.

Her nipples are rock hard as I play with them with my fingers through the material, my mouth still at her neck, teasing her. I tug gently and she calls my name breathlessly— my real one—and I just about lose it in my pants.

"You've got such a beautiful body." She feels all-woman beneath me, all curves; she has the softest, sweetest smelling skin I've ever encountered. "I can't wait to taste your honey but right now I need to be inside you."

She grinds her ass into my junk and I close my eyes. I yank her tank top up and throw it, then I unhook her lacy bra and throw that too. I look down at her naked breasts; she's goddamn perfect. I squeeze her glorious tits together and it takes all of my resolve not to lose control. She grasps my hands with hers over the top and flexes them, she moans as I continue to please her.

I whirl her around and remove my hands, looking down at her gorgeous body and I curse a string of profanities as I look at her. Her skirt is still hitched around her waist, time for her to lose that. I unzip it and let it fall; she steps out of it and reaches for her shoes.

"No, leave those on," I bark. The lacy thin scrap of material covering her pussy won't be there for very long either.

I drop to my knees and pull her closer, my mouth going to one of her succulent breasts and I suck hard on her nipple, pulling and palming the other one at the same time. She tips her head back and moans. *Oh yeah, babe, I can do this all night, my specialty.* I move to the other one and do the same, lapping her with my tongue.

"Tell me what you like," I mutter into her flesh.

She moves her hands into my hair as I watch her enjoying my movements, but she doesn't speak.

"Answer me," I demand, taking her hands in mine and linking our fingers.

She opens her eyes as I bring my mouth up her body and back to her neck, her lips are bruised and swollen from our illicit kisses. I want those lips all over my body, I want them everywhere. Just imagining her on her knees before me makes me want to explode; I won't last, so that can't happen tonight.

"What was the question?" she asks in a low, breathy voice.

I smirk. "You're so hot for me, you can't remember."

"Take your clothes off," she retorts, ignoring me. It almost sounds like a demand.

I cock an eyebrow, but secretly, I love this kind of bossiness in the bedroom, when it's coming from her that is.

"Yes, ma'am."

I shrug my cut off, tempted to throw it, but I don't, I hang it over the nearest chair. She takes over and lifts my shirt up and I pull it the rest of the way over my head.

She stares at my body, her hands at my pecs.

I smirk. "What do you like?" I remind her of my question.

"I like your tattoos," she whispers, surprising me.

I grunt, moving back to her. "You like my tats, babe?"

"Yes, they're sexy on you."

"What do you like in bed?" I ask because she's not getting the hint. I need to know.

"I… I don't know," she stammers, suddenly embarrassed.

"Don't be shy around me, princess." I pull one of her hands down to my dick that's so hard in my jeans it may never come down, it presses against my zipper like it's in prison and in dire need to be let out. I hold onto her hand as I rub it up and down, showing her how I like it.

"That's what you do to me," I grit out. "This is what I've been living with since I first saw you."

"Since the clubhouse?" she whispers as I kiss her neck and behind her ear.

"No, I saw you long before that."

She squeezes me hard and I groan.

"Fucking Sienna," I curse into her neck. "I'm gonna do you all night, babe, so I hope you don't plan on getting any sleep…"

"I like whatever you want to do," she moans, almost bashfully, her words muffled in my hair. "But, it's… it's been a while."

I glance at her and it's like music to my ears—every man's dream. I resist a cocky smirk.

"How long?" I ask, kissing her gently.

She buries her head into my neck, trying to hide.

"Don't be shy, babe, you can tell me."

I feel her breathe hard on my skin.

"A year," she mutters.

My eyes go wide though she can't see me. *A year? She hasn't had sex with anyone in a whole year? Goddamn.*

"That sounds pretty fuckin' great," I admit, I can't help it. Imagining that just spurs me on even more.

I rub my hands down her back to her ass and up again, repeating the motion.

I glance over her shoulder at the bed and frown. Jesus, it's small, I'm never going to fit.

She doesn't stop stroking me, squeezing me harder as I fight to stay in control. It feels so good.

I reach one hand into the back of her hair and I grasp it gently, pulling her to me. I snake a hand down south to the rim of her sheer panties. I dip my hand inside and one of her hands follows mine, holding me at the wrist, halting me.

I stop. *Is she telling me no?*

"I won't hurt you." I assure her, looking up at her big round eyes. With her man troubles that I'm not supposed to know about, I don't want to risk scaring her. She gulps and closes her eyes, removes her hand from my wrist, and I continue gently, cautiously, rubbing her sweet spot, she's so wet and slick. I want to take her hard and fast but I know I can't. She's nervous.

A whole year? How is that even possible?

I rub, pinch, and flick her back and forth through her folds as I hold her head in place so she has to look at me.

"Let go, babe," I command, and on queue as I keep moving at a slow and steady pace, she comes all over my hand, it's such a glorious sight as her skin pinkens delightfully from the rush. The noise of her moans drives me over the edge.

I plunge my tongue into her mouth as she contracts around my fingers and I slow down. I want in, I want in so bad.

"Gonna let me in?" I ask, she's panting so rapidly and holds onto my neck as I back her toward the bed.

"Yes," she stammers. I stop, and with my hand still in her pants, our eyes lock. I dip a finger inside and she moans, she's so tight, Jesus Christ. I move my finger in and out and I know it won't take long until she's having a second orgasm. I insert a second finger and she gasps.

"You're so beautiful," I tell her again. "So fuckin' tight

around me, I wanna hear you scream my name all night, baby."

She moans into my neck but it's incoherent. I smile into her hair as my thumb dances over her nub and I'm delighted when she explodes again so quickly, loudly this time. Jesus, it sounds good. Her hands move suddenly to my belt buckle shakily, I glance down to watch.

She releases the button and unzips me, her fingers brushing my hard-on, making a rumble tremble through me. I can't remember when I've wanted somebody this much before or been this excited… maybe never.

She caresses me through my boxer briefs and swears under her breath looking down at my bulge.

"What's up, Sienna?" I manage, my eyes still watching her fondle me.

"You're so… *umm…*"

"What?" I encourage, though I know what she's going to say because I've heard it before, many, many times.

"*Big,*" she states. I sense she may be a little bit afraid.

"It's alright," I tell her softly. "I won't hurt you. I'll go slow, it'll feel tight because it's been a while but I'll make sure you're ready and wet for me." I brush the hair back off her face and hold my hands there until she looks at me. "You trust me, don't you?"

Her big eyes blink and she looks so good post-orgasm that I lean in for a chaste kiss.

"Y-yes," she stammers.

I feel her hand go under the elastic of my briefs that I'm bobbing out of and she rubs her hand all the way along my shaft. I make a noise that's foreign to me and there is literally no room left inside my jeans to house what I have going on in there. It's like pure paradise; there's a party going on and I'm making a mess.

"Take my dick out," I tell her. *For fuck's sake.* I can't take much more of this sweet torture. "Touch me, baby, play with me."

She does just that, yanking my briefs down to my knees and my dick bobs free, finally. She grasps me with one hand and I wince at the contact, her eyes staring down south. I so want to push her down to her knees so she can suck me off but I don't want our first time to be me ramrodding down her throat. This is about her, not me. I watch as she pulls me off slowly at first, I move a hand over hers and quicken it a little bit.

"Like this." I show her and as I watch her take over, it's almost my undoing, it's so damn good.

"You like that?" she whispers. I open my eyes, and when I look down, she's looking at me with a very sexy, sly grin, using my words back at me.

"Yeah, I like it, princess, gonna do you so fuckin' good."

She bites her lip and I lose the rest of my composure, I yank my jeans and briefs down the rest of the way.

I push her down onto the bed and she scrambles backwards. I remember somewhere in the small part of my brain that I need a wrap, so I reach down to my jeans and find my wallet and take one out. She watches me in awe.

"Jayson..." she begs, holding her arms out to me. "Hurry up."

"I'm comin', babe." My voice is gravelly and raw. I move towards the bed and crawl onto it, I reach for her and snag her panties by the hips and rip them down her legs. No need for those anymore.

I'm delighted to see she has no tattoo's, I can't remember the last time I've been with someone who has no ink. But it's perfect, she's perfect. Her skin's so beautifully unmarked, it's how it's supposed to be with her.

I know just looking at her that it won't only be a one-night thing. I know I can't, I know I won't. I'll want more.

Once won't be enough.

I rip the foil with my teeth.

"Put it on me." Her eyes go wide again and I laugh out loud. I can't help it.

"Really?" she says, squirming as I loom over her.

"Really," I repeat.

She astonishes me by complying, pleasing me even more. She takes the wrap from me and rolls it over my length as I whistle through my teeth at her touch.

"Jesus, Steel, you're so big, you're not gonna fit…"

I groan at her words, the head nudging at her thigh. Her dirty talk has me wanting to take her so bad.

"I'm gonna fit, babe, and you're gonna love every minute of it."

She reaches for me and I move over her, I know now that if this is it, then I'll die a happy man.

Nothing and nobody will ever compare to this moment. I want to savor it forever and never let her go.

SIENNA

I SHOULD BE TERRIFIED, he's massive—and not just his appendage—yet he's treating my body like it's a temple and I cannot get enough of it. I watch as he sheaths himself a few times with his fist and then moves his mouth to mine and kisses me like he's a dying man. It's like I'm having an out of body experience. His beard is soft and a little bit prickly but I like it… no, *I love it.*

His body is like a temple. Hard, muscled, his abs a sight from heaven, dark tattoos cover his entire body, even his legs, not that I'm looking there because he's all front and center.

"Talk to me," he says again, hovering over me. He seems to like that, the dirty talk, but I'm no good at it.

"Jayson…." It comes out like a whisper; it's all I can say to not come undone at the very sight of him.

"Yeah, baby, talk to me."

He holds himself over me, his forearms next to my head and I feel the heat radiating from his body.

"Please," I beg him.

"Please what?" He nibbles my neck as I clutch him,

thrusting my hips up. I've never been so aroused in my entire life. He's so open about sex and all about what I like that I don't know how to answer, I've never had this kind of experience before. I didn't know it could be like this.

I reach up to grab his ass and he groans again. I can feel the head of his very large manhood nudging at my entrance.

"If you could see how beautiful you look…" he murmurs in my ear. "I can't wait to be inside you, Sienna."

I moan again at his words, I don't know who taught him to talk like this but it's freaking turning me on. He takes a nipple into his mouth and sucks again, I feel his hand move between us but he doesn't penetrate, he rubs me very deliberately with his hard length up and down my slick center. I came so fast the first time, it's embarrassing, but who can blame me? My body is on fire. I barely have time to register when another orgasm builds just as quickly then rips through my body as I cling to him, panting his name, his mouth sucking on my nipple as he rides me through it. *Number three done and dusted.*

He groans, moving to my entrance. He nudges me once, then twice, then slides in slightly. I've never been with anyone so big before, he feels tight, but so damned hot. He mutters how good it feels and a string of profanities follow.

He moves the tip in and out slowly, then goes a little further on each thrust. I close my eyes to the pain, it's like the first time all over again, my nails dig into his ass as he pumps into me with a beautiful rhythm. He's a fine specimen and he's all mine, at least for tonight.

"You're so tight," he grunts roughly in my ear. He works me in and out and slowly goes deeper. He's everywhere, all my senses are so tuned in, I can barely breathe. "Let me in, babe."

He's so much gentler than I imagined he'd be, not a barbarian at all, but I want more, my body aches for him. I cling to him, digging into his ass cheeks and on the next thrust he goes full tilt. We both moan and he stills, letting me adjust.

Shit, he's big. My heart drums so fast in my ears, I can't even hear anything else.

"You okay, princess?" He looks down at me and I meet his eyes.

"Yes," I breathe.

"You've no idea how this feels for me, babe. No, don't close your eyes, look at me."

I do and I run my hands over his back and smile.

"So beautiful, this pussy is mine, babe. You got me? All mine."

Our eyes lock as we stare at one another.

He moves slowly out of me then back in again, I can feel every single nerve ending in my body light up. He leans in and kisses me, his tongue finding mine.

"I knew you could take me, tell me how good you feel," he whispers, he thrusts a little harder at the end, the pace is picking up but it's still slow and controlled. *Out, in, thrust. Repeat.*

"So good," I mutter. He grins at me—actually grins—I've never seen him smile this whole time, he should smile more, it suits him. His arms completely surround me as I hang on for dear life.

"Wrap your legs around me," he commands. I do and he tilts my hips a little bit, going deeper, thrusting on every return, hitting the end of me.

"*Yes!*" I call out.

"Come for me," he whispers. It's my undoing, I spiral around him again, for the third… or is it the fourth time? He watches me, drinking me in, feasting on me.

The pace, the thrust, the slowness, the contact, it makes

my pleasure go on and on, I don't ever remember sex being this good. It's complete ecstasy.

He whispers dirty stuff in my ear as my hands travel all over his body, feeling him, encouraging him as he pumps me again and again with control over my entire body.

"You weren't lying," I say breathlessly. "Fuck me harder, please, Steel."

A look of pure lust comes over him as he quickens the pace, honestly, I don't know how he's lasted this long. The bed hits the wall with such force, it's a wonder it doesn't break, the sound is as erotic as hell.

"Oh, fuck, babe, gonna come, can't hold on anymore, feels too good, *fuck...*"

I go over the edge with him as he groans and makes noises I've never heard a man make, banging me hard and fast as his hands grip the sheets and I feel him pulse between my legs and then he stills. A few seconds later, he collapses on top of me. We're both covered in sweat.

He completely crushes me and I squeal under him. He lifts up suddenly, kisses my sweaty forehead, and rolls off to lie next to me.

"Princess," he mutters, lying beside me as we gasp for breath together.

"I know." I can't seem to form words.

"Holy shit."

"Yes, that too," I pant in agreement.

"That was fucking fantastic, I came so hard," he states to the ceiling.

Satisfaction fills my every being. "You and me both."

I feel the bed move as he chuckles. I think I like this Steel, he's softer like this, no way near as harsh or scary as he is when he's in biker mode.

It's silent as we both catch our breaths.

"I want to do that again," he declares a few moments

later, his breathing is so fast and hard, I feel quite proud of myself. "After a breather," he adds as I turn to gaze up at him.

I pull the duvet around me, covering myself as he looks at me sideways, I suddenly feel a little exposed.

"As long as you liked it? I got a bit rough there at the end." He looks at me with a frown.

"Of course, I liked it," I tut, my hand roams his chest as I trace a finger around the swirling patterns of his tats. "Didn't you hear me?"

He sits up on one elbow. "Yeah, I heard you, but you need to talk to me more though, I like hearing what you want me to do to you."

He likes dirty talk, how can one man be so freaking hot?

"What?" he nudges me with his elbow as a grin breaks across my face, I can't help it.

I bite my lip for what I'm about to say. "You're way more talkative in bed than in real life."

A ghost of a smile traces his lips. He's gorgeous when he smiles.

"In real life?"

"Well, you know what I mean; our track record with conversation hasn't been that good."

He bends to kiss me.

"We're gonna do that again." His hand moves to my hip.

"So soon?" I say with wide eyes.

"Oh, yeah."

"This isn't a thing." I reassure him.

He snorts. "Oh, yeah, babe, it's a thing."

I drop my eyes. "I've never had a one-night stand." It sounds foreign to my ears.

He tilts my chin up with his hand. "This isn't that."

"No? What is it then?"

He brushes my hair off one shoulder. "I don't know,

haven't figured it out yet, but while you're here, this body is mine and mine only, got me?"

I stare at him unblinking. "That's a little demanding, isn't it?"

He does not seem fazed. "Yeah, well, I'm just saying."

My heart races. *Great, now he thinks I'm cheap.*

"I don't sleep around, I just told you that it's been a year. I'm not going to go off and share myself around like some… like some *sweet butt!*" I hurl at him. Of all the nerve!

His eyes darken. "You know that's not what I meant, I told you before you'd never be that, ever."

"You may as well pound your chest while saying what you really think."

"Didn't hear you complainin'."

I glare at him. "You really are something."

He bends down and kisses me. "Don't get mad, save that rage for our next round." He rolls off the bed and I watch his bare ass cross the room as he disappears into my bathroom. It's easy to find, my apartment is tiny. I hear the toilet flush a few moments later and the faucet run.

When he returns, I watch as he picks up my clothes and lays them over the back of a nearby chair. I have no idea what his obsession with picking up clothes and folding them is. He strolls back to the bed in all his naked glory. He really is one very fit and fine man.

"What about you?" I say, watching him, hardly believing what we just did. It's cold without his body heat near me.

"What about me what?" he replies without looking up.

"What if I don't want you with anybody else while I'm here?"

He turns to stare down at me, amusement crosses his face.

"You don't like sharing either, sweetheart?"

I shake my head. "Nope."

"Bossy little thing, aren't you?"

"What's good for the goose and all of that." I tilt my head to smile sweetly at him. "Right?"

"You tellin' me what to do, princess?"

"Why, don't biker babes do that?"

He comes down on me and I yelp as he flips me over so I'm straddling him.

"Biker babes?" he grunts as our mouths find each other again.

"Well, I'm not a sweet butt apparently."

He balks as we kiss.

"No, babe, although your butt is very nice, but if you keep sayin' that, I'll spank your little ass red-raw."

My eyes go wide as he pulls me back down to him and he works my mouth with his tongue, he's such a good kisser. Our bodies melt together and I feel the heat below starting all over again.

"You ready so soon?" he mutters when I grind against him and he breaks the kiss.

I move my mouth to his neck, he smells so good, so masculine. "Yes," I giggle, unashamed.

He grunts and his hands move down my body as I sit up. He cups my breasts, pushing them together, then moves his hands down to my hips and runs them back up my stomach and around to my ass, and whispers, "This is mine."

I close my eyes at his touch. "Yes, yours," I agree. His hand begins to rub me again as he watches me come undone. I'd agree to anything right about now; the man is insatiable.

He relaxes back onto the pillows, watching me with a look of pure lust on his face. I ride his hand and he inserts two fingers into me, his thumb working my clit, his other hand reaches up to pinch my nipple as I tip my head back.

"I want to watch you ride me," he says, I've never heard anything so sexy in my life.

His words are my undoing and I fall shamelessly into a long, never-ending spiral as I groan out incoherently. When I come down from my high, he removes his fingers and I move over him, rubbing myself against his bobbing dick, it's hard again though I don't think it ever came down.

I love what I do to him so easily.

"Wrap," he grunts.

"Where's your wallet?" I breathe.

"You don't have any?"

I roll my eyes in the dark. "No."

"Good, let's keep it that way. In the back of my jeans hanging on the chair."

I scoot off the bed and find them easily and bring the foil packet back with me.

"Why do you fold everything?" I ask, straddling him again.

"It's a habit," he replies.

I tear the packet as he watches me. Without being told, I roll it down over him and he hisses, his dick bobbing again at my touch.

"Come here, babe."

He pulls me to him and sits up, we kiss long and hard.

I lift my hips, and holding him at the base, I sink down slowly. I don't take him all the way at first. He hisses my name as he looks down to where we're joined.

"Fuck," he whispers.

"I think I like being on top," I tell him with a smirk of my own.

His eyes come to me and he grabs my hair and kisses me with such ferocity, all I can do is hold on for dear life.

He lifts me by the hips and I sink back down. "Take me," he moans. "Fuck, Sienna."

I love watching him come undone; it's so sexy.

All I manage in return are incoherent moans as I move up

and down faster; his fingers dig into my hips as he watches me bounce up and down.

"You have a beautiful body, I love how you show it off to me, your tits look so fuckin' good bouncing like that. Touch yourself for me."

I do as he says and cup my breasts and push them together as I ride him faster. He moves a hand between us to find my sweet center, and within seconds, I explode around him, my orgasm so hard that I'm seeing stars. I realize he's all the way in. He moves his hands to my ass.

"You're beautiful when you come," he says against my lips. "Push your tits together so I can suck them both."

My mouth is so dry from his dirty talk and the dirty sex, I may never come down from this high. I do as he says and I watch as he sucks one nipple then goes to the other then back again, repeating the rhythm. Moving my hips as he does so, groaning so erotically, it pushes all of my buttons, moving me up and down as he sucks and licks. He's a freaking expert when it comes to sex, and he seems to know exactly what to do.

"You like your tits being sucked?" he growls.

"Yes." I close my eyes because I can't watch him anymore, it's too much.

"Did you imagine this when you saw me at the gym that day?" he asks out of nowhere.

My hands are in his hair as we move up and down, I'm so lost in the sensation, I can barely breathe.

"Yes," I admit.

"Yeah, babe? I saw you looking at me; I wanted you then and there, wanted to do you so bad."

His hands squeeze my ass cheeks, he tongues one nipple, sucks, then licks it again, then does the same to the other one. I'm so pent-up with need, I could explode any second just watching him tease me.

"What did you want to do to me?" he breathes in between sucks and licks.

"This," I say, squeezing him between my legs, "and this." I rub myself against him again and he hisses.

"I went home and jerked off," he tells me openly, his breathing ragged and fast. That knowledge goes straight to my core and kind of shocks me at the same time.

"Oh, God," I moan.

"What did you do?" he pulls back to look at me. He gets off on this.

My breathing goes up ten notches imagining him doing *that* over little old me.

"Don't be shy, tell me what you did."

"Touched myself," I whisper in his ear. He bucks again, his hands on my ass grip tighter. He moves back to my breasts and starts sucking again, he pulls my nipple with his mouth and tugs gently. He isn't finished with me yet.

"Did you, baby? Did you imagine it was me? Doing this to you?"

"Yes," I say, nipping his ear.

"Fucking you?"

"Yes, doing everything to me."

"I *am* going to do everything," he reassures me. "You like your tits being played with?"

"Babe..." is all I can say, the sensations on my breasts are so sensitive, I can't even deal. Nobody has ever paid my body this much attention, it's almost too much.

I tug his hair and I feel him laugh into my skin. He knows that's a yes.

"Say my name," he tells me gently. "Next time you come, say my real name, you look so good riding me."

Yeah, it's safe to say he likes me on top. He sits back and watches me; his eyes shift to where we're joined and he thrusts up to meet me as I slam back down on him.

"I love it," I say, the ripples starting again.

"I can tell you love it babe, I'm gonna keep doing this all night so that tomorrow you can't even walk and all you'll be thinking about is when I'm gonna do it again."

"Jayson..." I say as I spiral out of control, I moan out an incoherent string of curses along with his name several times.

He follows moments later, calling my name violently, he pulses so hard between my legs, I look down at him in wonder.

Who the hell is this man? I collapse on top of him and we both cling to each other as we try to catch our breaths.

"You'll be the death of me," he says, he's panting and breathing hard. "But you need a bigger bed."

I don't move, I'm tired, sated, orgasmed-out. I rest my head on his chest and mutter something incoherent. He's drawn every pleasure possible from my body and now I'm spent.

"Sleep well, princess." I'm sure I hear him say as I drift off but I can't be sure. "You are fucking amazing."

11

STEEL

"If you can't get it loose then we'll have to get bolt cutters," Rubble says, handing me a wrench. I'm under a family sedan and it's hoisted above me in the air. I'm trying to get the axel free, but it's being a little bitch. It's not my day for tools but I'm lending a hand to keep my mind off a certain little blonde I'd left warm in her bed.

Admittedly, it was hard leaving her this morning after the long night we'd had, and what a night it was—blew my mind. I knew we'd be good together, I knew it since the first day I laid eyes on her. She's soft in all the right places and tough where she needs to be, perfect, the whole package, and I can't get enough of her. If she thinks this is a one-time thing then she's sadly mistaken, her being wrapped around me is oh so good. Terrifyingly good.

I let out a string of curse words as I wrestle with the wrench, using all my might to loosen the bitch. "She ain't playin' nice," I grunt through gritted teeth, wondering why I didn't just stay in bed with Sienna all day. "But she's gonna play nice when I'm done with her."

"You okay under there, boss?" Jaxon asks, he's another

one of the prospects with the club and also my apprentice.

"I'm confused about why I'm under here like a grease monkey and not you."

"Because you're stronger than two of me put together," he answers wisely.

I snort a grunt.

I hear the little doorbell jingle as someone comes in the shop, I know because of the low wolf-whistle that it's a female. Then I hear muffled voices. Great, I'm under here sweating my nuts off and some babe just walked in and I'm stuck fixing this bitch of a thing. It ain't my day.

I can hear Rubble saying something, she's asking about second-hand cars and used car parts. I roll my eyes. She probably has one of those cheap and nasty made-in-China pieces of junk.

I hear the voices get closer and then Jaxon quite distinctly clears his throat. Rubble then proceeds to kick my foot with his boot.

"Deal with it," I grumble. *Where's Gunner when you need him?* Seriously, boys, were we bikers or bitches?

I hear the clickety-clack of heels just as I get the stupid part free, heaving with all my might, and declaring that it's a motherfucker when I hear a familiar voice and stop what I'm doing.

"I don't know what it's worth, I think it's just scrap metal, but I really need the parts gone as soon as possible," she says.

What the fuck is Sienna doing here?

She doesn't know my place of work, I never told her.

Jaxon is saying something back and Rubble kicks me again, he moves around the side of the car I'm working on.

I drop the spanner to the ground and keep the wrench in my hand as I slide myself out from under the car on the roller. Of course, I'm covered in fucking oil and grease and shit, but at least I have overalls on.

I lay there looking up at her, I watch the unbelievable sight of Rubble and Jaxon looking over her shoulder at something on a tablet, *what the hell's going on?*

I don't know why their eyes are so wide but I'm ready to punch someone in the face for standing so close to her like that. Yeah, I'm a jealous son of a bitch all of a sudden.

"Is that an Aston Martin?" I hear Jaxon declare. *Idiot.* What would he know about anything?

I clear my throat. They all look down at me in unison.

Sienna gasps when she sees me. Clearly, she didn't get the Steelman's Garage memo. I haul myself up and wipe my dirty hands on the front of my overalls. I'm a stinking mess.

We look at each other for a few awkward moments. She's wearing a camo skirt with a black tank top and black heels. She doesn't dress like no girl around here, she's a Cali girl through and through and I like it a lot.

Her eyes are wide. *"Steel?"* she says, shocked to see me, and I'm thrown back to last night when I made her come over and over again, except she said my name with a lot more reverence and a heck of a lot of *ahhhs.*

"Morning, princess, you sellin' that hunk of junk Datsun?" I grab a rag from the hood and wipe my face and then my hands.

"I… umm… no, I'm not. Wait, my car is not a hunk of junk!" she declares. Her face has gone red, I wonder if she's secretly having flashbacks too.

Jaxon and Rubble look from her to me again.

"You sure about that?"

She looks only slightly insulted. "You work here?" she looks around the workshop.

I toss the rag back on the hood. "No, I own the joint. *Steelman's.*"

"Oh." She ponders that. "Your last name is Steelman?"

I don't get to answer.

"Yeah, we prospects all thought he was nicknamed because we heard that when you hit him, it's like seriously hitting a chunk of fuckin' metal," Jaxon helpfully informs her.

I give him a glacial stare and he immediately shuts his mouth.

"What are you doing here?" I ask, I don't take my eyes off her. I have a chub in the making at her in a skirt. I love her in skirts.

Rubble is fighting a knowing smile; he's put two and two together pretty fast.

"I… umm, I had some errands to run this morning and I have these cars here that Max had locked up in a shed at his house," she tells me in a rush, she looks anxious to be outta here. "Just want them gone, the guy at the scrapyard said he'd give me a few hundred bucks for them and he'd come and get them today."

Jaxon is shaking his head, Rubble just leans back against the car and rubs his chin, his smile is about to get wiped off by my fist if he keeps it up.

"A few hundred bucks?" Jaxon says like he might fall over. She darts her eyes to his.

"Is that a good or bad deal?"

Rubble is now shaking his head, his forefinger and thumb pressed against the bridge of his nose and he's muttering to himself.

I ignore Jaxon, "What's she got?" I ask Rubble.

She hands me the tablet, but before I can look, Rubble says, "Fuckin' vintage Mustang and a red Aston Martin convertible."

I almost drop the tablet.

Without words, I look at the photos she's taken and scroll across. They aren't great quality because of the lighting but I see enough to look back up at her.

"Jack offered you two hundred bucks?" I say. The piece of

shit, I want to go over there right now and smash the crap out of him. Okay, she doesn't know anything about cars, but that is daylight robbery, just because she's a girl and won't know any better.

"Yeah," she says hesitantly with a shrug. "He's doing me a favor he said; nobody wants cars like this anymore. Oh, and that's for the whole lot, there's like four more I can't get to that aren't pictured."

"Here we go," Rubble says in a low murmur.

"Shit, Steel," Jaxon is still shaking his head.

I grip the tablet and hope I can reign my temper in.

"Get fuckin' Jack on the phone," I bark.

"*Steel,*" Rubble says like I should know better. "You know what it's like, she's a girl, he's a wheeler and dealer, no offense, sweetheart," he gives Sienna a wink, "but Jack would sell his own grandmother if he made a profit."

She narrows her eyes at him, and I refrain from barking out a laugh. There's my little spitfire.

"So, he's ripping me off?" she surmises, unimpressed.

"Umm, yeah, just a little bit," Jaxon says like she should know this. "You probably got quite a few k on your hands there, what you think, Steel?"

I twitch my lips as she watches me. "She's got a gold mine and he fuckin' knows it."

"Well, I'd love to stay and chat," Rubble seems to find something amusing, "but I've got shit to do. Sayonara, bitches, See ya, Sienna."

"Bye, Rubble," she replies sweetly. She is sweet as pie in every sense of the word, delectable, and I want her again right here, right now.

I look at Jaxon. "Time you went on an extended lunch break."

When I look back at Sienna, her eyes have gone wide and she looks a little startled.

"But it's only eleven," he starts, then he sees my icy glare and snaps his mouth shut.

"Take the scenic route," I add.

I wait until he's gone before I move right in front of her. She's so pretty in the light of day. Her hair is in a low ponytail, great for grabbing onto. She looks out of place here, too pure.

"You okay? You didn't reply to my text."

I'm pretty sure it was good for her; maybe she's had a change of heart?

I sent her a text in the wee hours telling her I'd gone home, I didn't want to appear like an asshole when she woke up and found me not there, but I have to sleep in my own bed.

"Do people always do what you tell them to?" she wonders.

I shrug. "If they want to keep their jobs and get paid, then yes, he works for me and he's a prospect, he does as I say."

She holds the tablet to her chest and assesses me. "Nice overalls." Her lips twitch, fighting a smile.

"You're nice," I tell her.

She blushes a little and drops her head. I lift her chin to look at me.

"You sore?"

Her mouth drops open and I drop my eyes to her pouty lips. They seem a little swollen, I hope it's because of me last night, I can't wait for her to blow me with that hot little mouth.

"A little," she shrugs, embarrassed.

I smirk. Good, it means I did my job properly.

I lower my head and take her mouth gently; she reciprocates, *okay, good sign, she's kissing me back.*

"I had a fuckin' fantastic time last night," I say against her lips. "I wanna do it again."

Her breathing is accelerated, she smells like a ball of cotton candy.

"I'd like that."

It's like music to my ears.

"Still not a thing?" I cock my head to the side.

She smiles up at me. "I don't know but I like your overalls."

I hold her chin and run my thumb over her bottom lip and think about biting it, but instead, I go over to the front door and lock it, then turn the sign around to 'closed'. I grab her hand and pull her with me as I approach my office door.

Lola is lying on the floor; she looks up as we approach. Since Sienna's a girl, she isn't fazed one bit and just looks up, bored.

"That's Lola," I tell her. "Don't worry, she's a pussy cat."

She's wearing her skull bandana, she flops her head back down as we step over her and go up the stairs into my office.

"I didn't know you were a mechanic," she says. "Do you fix bikes too or just cars?"

I've no idea why it matters or why she's interested but I go with it.

"I fix everything. You name it, I fix it, I restore shit too."

She looks around my office; I hate how messy it is. This isn't how I operate.

"What did you bring me in here for?" she asks, turning back to face me.

"To tidy my office, of course."

She smiles. "Really? I'm not very domesticated."

"You'll learn."

Her eyebrows rise. "You want to pound your chest while saying that, Tarzan?"

I purse my lips because of her cheek, she'll have to learn to not talk back but I like her spunk, it's refreshing. Most women don't say shit to me.

"Someone's cheeky this morning."

"I had a wild night, some badass biker kept me up all night and I didn't get any sleep."

I watch as she puts her hands on her hips, challenging me, not a good move but sexy as hell.

"Yeah, well, he's about to keep you up again, against the back of this door."

She bites her lip and looks down at the bulge clearly showing in my pants. She walks over to me and slides her hands inside, pulling the stud buttons open roughly. *Holy Christ.*

"You naked under there?" she breathes as her hot little hands run up my chest to my pecs.

My voice is husky with want. "Why don't you find out?"

I watch as she dips one hand lower and finds my dick through my boxer briefs and

begins fondling it right there in the middle of my office. She is gonna make me die, I swear it.

I shrug half out of the overalls and the arms flop down to my waist as she takes me in.

"Your tatts are amazing," she says as I can't take my eyes off her hand, she moves under the elastic and rubs her palm over my length. I hiss as I watch her.

"Did they hurt?"

"Not as much as you're gonna be hurtin' when I'm done pounding you against my door."

Her breath hitches.

"You know how to sweet talk a woman." She's good with sarcasm too.

"Nothin' sweet about it."

"I don't know; last night was pretty sweet. You've got some moves… and stamina."

"At last we can agree on something," I murmur.

She shakes her head playfully, I think I like playful Sienna.

"I've always had this fantasy about doing it in my office," I close my eyes at her hand still working me.

She looks over her shoulder toward the door. "I'm not *doing it* in your office."

I fall against my door and bring her with me. "Why not?"

"Someone could walk in."

"Nobody here but you, me, and my dog... and she's asleep."

"It's the middle of the day." She actually has the good grace to look slightly horrified.

I bark a laugh. "Shock horror, people can have sex during daylight hours."

"In respectable workplaces?"

"Ain't nothin' respectable about this joint, babe."

She laughs; it's a sweet, sweet sound.

"And anyway," I go on. "You shouldn't have your hand down my pants if you don't want any of this."

She doesn't get time to answer, I shut her up with a kiss and it feels just as sweet as last night, it feels like she's always been here and that is a very scary place to be.

What the hell is happening to me?

I want her on her knees, oh, yeah, I do, but that's selfish. As if reading my mind, she pushes my overalls down and my boxer briefs go with them.

"You're so hot, Steel," she says, a little smile on her face, her words confound me.

"Yeah, you like me naked?"

She nods.

"You wanna go on your knees, baby girl?"

Her eyes go wide, can't say I blame her; I'm not exactly small in that department. To my astonishment, she drops down and takes the tip of me into her mouth, it happens so fast, I let out a hiss as I look down at her, then she looks up at me and takes me further. She is the most beautiful thing I've ever seen. I have to close my eyes because while I've got stamina, I won't last two seconds watching her take me like this. I move my hand over hers and help her sheath me the way I like it.

"Like that, baby, yeah, that feels good." I don't thrust, I don't want to choke the girl, I just let her take me—most of me, not all of me—and when I open my eyes again, I can't let her continue or I'll blow my load right down her throat. I yank her to her feet and lift her by the hips, she squeals at the sudden movement but wraps her legs around me. Her skirt has helpfully hitched up all by itself. I reach a hand into her panties as I hold her against the door with my other arm.

"Ever done it against a door, princess?"

"Absolutely not," she says, her eyes closing at my touch.

She's wet already as I rub her with my fingers gently, finding her sensitive spot.

"How sore are you again?" I cock an eyebrow.

"A little, not too much."

"Not gonna take you rough, you good with that?"

"Yes," she breathes. *So much for worrying about people barging in on us.*

I plunge my tongue into her mouth and she gasps. It's a wonderful sound, everything about her is wonderful. She clutches my shoulders, squeezing me.

"Wrap your arms around my neck," I say, my breathing ragged. She does as she's told, good girl, and I reach down into the pocket of my overalls, take my wallet out, and get out a wrap. I make quick work of it and move my hands back to her hips.

I pull her panties aside and nudge her entrance. I know for a fact I'm not gonna last long after seeing her on her knees, that was heaven.

"Next time we do this, it'll be in my bed," I tell her before I can stop myself, "and I'm gonna taste your honey until you're begging me to take you."

"Steel," she murmurs, her hands in my hair. Her lips find mine and, at the same time, my tongue goes into her mouth and I slide in slowly, making sure not to go too fast or too deep. She winces a little. Normally, I'd warm her up with a couple of orgasms but we ain't got all day.

"You're such a badass," she tells me in a whisper. I slide in deeper and pull out slowly.

"You know it."

"I thought about you all morning," she says out of nowhere.

I smile into her neck, nibbling her with my teeth as she clings to me. God, being buried in her is like fucking heaven, I never wanna leave.

"Yeah, babe?"

"Yeah."

I suck the base of her throat hard, it'll probably leave a mark but I don't care, I thrust in and out nice and slow but firm, giving it to her like she deserves.

"Not gonna last, not with you in that skirt," I growl into her neck, "you got me all wound up, babe."

"Steel..." she cries.

"What's my name when I'm buried inside you?"

"Jayson..." she says quickly as she lets go right then and there; I feel her pulsating around my dick, "oh, God, yes."

I smirk again but that's it, my resolve is gone and time is limited, I pump once, twice, then lose my load as I grunt her name in her ear. I still for a few moments, enjoying the feeling.

"That was too quick," I mutter into her hair.

"You're a really bad influence," she giggles, out of breath, her cheeks are pink and luscious.

"Don't you know it." I kiss her gently then pull out, let her down, discard the wrap, tie it, and drop it in the trashcan under my desk. She's still smoothing her skirt down when I pull my overalls up.

"Your office really is a mess," she tells me again as she continues to fluff herself back together. I realize I'm turning her to the dark side, but seeing her like this— disheveled and just fucked against my door—I don't really care.

"Tell me about it," I grumble. "I got no office girl."

"That explains the mountain," she nods at one of the overflowing trays.

"I got no invoicing system on the computer," I admit, "tryin' but paperwork ain't exactly my forte."

"Can't you hire someone who knows what to do?"

I didn't want to get into this with her because now she's gonna think I'm an asshole when she hears how many girls I've managed to piss off and then fire.

"Hard to believe, princess," I say, slumping down into my seat as she leans her butt on the edge of the desk, "but apparently, I'm not the easiest person to get along with, nor am I the nicest person to work for."

"Surprise, surprise," she mumbles.

"And anyway, I did have Lucy helping, that's Rubble's ol' lady, but she's too busy now with the tow truck and doing Brock's bookwork, Lily helps too but everyone's busy."

A little smile creeps on her face. "I could help you."

I narrow my eyes. "You don't have to be polite around me."

"I'm not," she shrugs, "I worked in the financial department at a bank in my last job, I'm sure I could get my head around it."

I look at her and she's totally serious.

What the hell?

"You don't wanna work for me, trust me," I tell her.

"And there's that little ditty that I'd never get any work done and everyone would be on extended lunch breaks every day."

She bites her lip, laughing. "Well, I could help you out, not work for you, that means no funny business in the office."

I lean forward, clasping my hands on the desk. "Long as you work under me," I say as she throws me a look.

"Well, looks like you'll be here until doomsday otherwise."

This is true.

"What about the Stone Crow?"

"I only work four nights a week."

I really don't like her working there. If she sticks around, which I plan on trying to make happen for a while longer, then she's gonna have to quit that shit. I'm all for women's independence, but not when it comes at the expense of other dudes checking out my woman.

My woman?

Oh my, how the mighty have fallen, I have to get a grip and fast.

She looks toward the tray. "May I?"

I nod. "Go ahead."

She picks up a stack and runs through the pages quickly. "Some of these date back three months ago."

"Yeah, no shit."

She frowns again. "Why do they say COD or check?"

I shrug. "Because that's how they pay."

"No credit card machine? They all get invoiced?"

"The smaller jobs pay cash and the bigger jobs and corporate shit gets invoiced."

"You need to have a decent payment system, it would clear up a lot of unnecessary work."

"Too complicated," I mutter, it gives me a headache thinking about it.

"It's not that hard, Steel," she says, eyeing me. She may be getting the picture that I don't like change. "Honestly, I could help you set it up."

I like that she wants to help me, even if she doesn't want to work for me.

"You'd do that for me?" I stare at her. *Why would she wanna help me? She barely knows me.*

She nods, she actually looks a bit excited about the prospect. "As long as I don't have to start calling you boss," she stifles a laugh.

"Only in the bedroom," I grunt.

"Ha-ha."

"But we haven't discussed the terms yet."

"Terms?"

"Yes, starting with appropriate office attire," I pull at her singlet top with my finger.

"You're not seriously going to tell me what I can and can't wear, are you?"

Shit. Yes, I am, then I remember she's not part of the Rebels, she's not a club girl, and she sure as hell ain't my ol' lady. Remembering her in my cut from the other night has me stirring in my overalls again. Five minutes ago, I didn't want a permanent piece, now I'm imagining her in my club colors.

"We'll discuss this later," I say, wanting to deliberately change the subject. "First, I wanna go and see what Max has in that shed, then I'm gonna go smash Jack in the teeth for trying to rip you off."

"Are you always this brash?"

When it comes to Bracken Ridge Rebels property, yes. She doesn't realize it yet, but the protection order means that she is part of the club, even if Hutch means temporarily. And I don't mind the sound of that, not one bit.

"Yes, babe," I say, giving her a quick peck, "so you better get used to it."

SIENNA

CLEARLY, I've lost my mind. I just had sex in Steel's office. I don't even know who I am anymore or what's come over me. To top it off, he insisted on going to Max's on his bike, which he calls a sled… I have no idea why, and I end up on the back.

Maybe I've lost all of my sense and sensibility, or maybe I never had any.

Being with him complicates things, I mean, I know it's just sex and I shouldn't get ahead of myself, but it feels different to anyone I've been with before. Him being a biker though, that isn't something I'm sure about, but this isn't a long-term thing. My brain is telling me to run, my body is telling me to shut the hell up and go with it, my heart; well, it can't keep up with any of it, it is just along for the ride.

He's probably been with boatloads of women, he's clearly very experienced, what's more, he probably told them all the nice things too. So, there's really no use getting all attached, all I am right now is the new shiny toy in town, something new to play with—nothing more.

When we get to the shed, he digs out a large torch from the saddle bag of his bike, I unlock the padlock and he shines it while I follow behind, he peels the covers all the way back, muttering under his breath at each one as he makes his way deeper into the back.

He has a good look at the black Mustang. "All the interior is original," he says almost in wonder, ducking his head through the door as it creaks open. "Looks to be in good condition considering it's been here for so long, at least there's no water damage because it's been kept undercover."

The cherry red Alfa Romeo is in a similar condition, though the paint has faded severely. Then he tells me there's a 1954 silver Mercedes-Benz, a 1957 Chevy Bel Air that used to be green, now it just looks murky, a beat-up Cadillac Series 62, and a gold Chevy Camaro. They all just look old to me but it seems Max was an avid collector.

"Seems dear old dad had a few projects he never got around to," he muses when he's finished his inspection; he lets out a low whistle.

"Are they worth anything?"

He glances at me. "Yeah, princess, they are."

He seems pleased. I remember him saying something earlier about restoring cars and bikes.

I decide to probe a little. "Do you like these kinds of cars?"

He smirks. "Oh yeah."

"I guess that old saying is true; they don't make them like they used to."

He grunts in response. "I'll get them moved into storage until you decide what you wanna do with them, or if you want, I can see what auctions are happening around the city, that's gonna be your best selling point, unless you get an avid collector from Craig's list or somewhere."

"That's kind of you," I say, really, it's one less headache too because I need these cars gone.

He stares at me blankly. "You offered to help me, so I'm helping you."

"Is that how you operate? Mr. Nice Guy?"

"Nothin' nice about me," he leans against the back of the Cadillac looking at me. "Why'd you come here, Sienna, to Bracken Ridge?"

The question throws me, just out of the blue like that... no warm-up or anything.

"You know why, Max's estate."

"That the only reason?"

What the hell is he talking about?

"Yes."

"Why have you been single for over a year?"

Wow. This is getting really personal really, really fast.

"Well, if you must know, I was having a break, not that that's really any of your business."

He snorts again then folds his arms over his chest because, now that we've slept together, he probably thinks he has some biker claim over me.

"I just don't understand it, you're beautiful."

He seems like he is being sincere, he's looking at me like he's trying to comprehend it.

"A year isn't as bad as it sounds," I mutter, "and I chose to be single."

He cracks his neck at the thought. "It would kill me, or rather, I'd literally want to be dead, I'd put myself out of my misery."

No, he definitely isn't the sort of person that can go without sex—typical male. After my ex, I've been sworn off men forever.

"And anyway," I go on haphazardly, "there's all this talk about me but I know nothing at all about you."

He levels my gaze as I lean against the car opposite him.

"What you wanna know?"

My eyebrows shoot up, is he really going to give me information about himself?

"What's the longest you've ever gone?"

He cocks an eyebrow. "All the questions in the world and you ask me that?"

I shrug. "Well, you asked me what I want to know, so that's it."

He lets out a disagreeable sigh. "Three or four weeks."

I literally gape at him.

"Longer when I was deployed," he goes on.

Deployed?

I'm stunned. "Did you serve in the military?"

He looks down at his boots then back up at me. "I trained in the army, worked in special ops, went to Afghanistan, Iraq, I got discharged six years ago, came home, went back to my trade, prospected for the club, and here we are."

I literally have no words, though I can imagine him as some big, tough, army dude.

"What does special ops involve?"

He rubs his chin with one hand. "All the shit you don't wanna know about, stuff of nightmares."

"Have you ever killed someone?" I almost whisper.

"Yes."

"Holy shit." I ponder that for a moment. I've never even held a gun, much less shot one.

"There are bad people out there, princess," he adds, seeing my apprehension. "The worst of the worst."

I look at the ground then back up again. "Why did you quit?"

He looks past me. "Because I suffered from PTSD, a lot of shit went down on my last mission, I had a lot going on at home too, none of that shit is good for you mentally. I had severe night tremors, really bad, had to take sleeping pills for years, then I got Lola and everything changed. She helps a lot, it's not so bad now and I'm happy here, I found my place, found my club, I don't wake up every day and wish I was somewhere else."

Wow. I envy him. I wish I felt happy somewhere, grounded, secure. To have that would be the ultimate luxury. I'm stunned at his admission.

"Tell me about your ex," he says before I can say anything.

"Tell me about yours."

He narrows his eyes. "I was married once."

My eyes go wide. *What the hell?* I cannot imagine him tied down to anybody, much less married!

"Are you serious?"

"She's ancient history or more like a big mistake, we were young and I was an idiot, didn't know any better, but that's enough about me." He cocks a brow.

I look at my feet again, he's really pushing it.

"I don't really want to talk about it, if it's all the same with you."

"That good, huh?" He hooks both thumbs into his belt loop as he assesses me.

I keep my eyes on the ground. I can't go there. I don't know him well enough to blurt out my sorry, sad tale, and I don't want to discuss exes. It brings back too many bad memories.

I've just gotten to the point where I don't feel so afraid anymore... that's when he doesn't try to call, oh yeah, he finds me, he always finds me. I change numbers all the time but he always calls or texts me, I don't know how he does it and the police do nothing about it. Restraining orders are just a piece of paper. They won't stop him.

He doesn't know about Bracken Ridge, so he won't know where I am, I can be me for a while, I don't have to hide.

"Let's just say I've been sworn off men for quite some time."

He looks like he wants to say a whole lot more but doesn't.

"Fair enough, some people just shouldn't be allowed oxygen."

"You can say that again."

His phone rings but the signal out here is crap, so he walks out of the shed and toward the front yard. A few moments later, he comes back.

"I gotta go, we'll lock up here and I'll get the cars sorted out for you."

"Thanks so much." I feel a weight has been lifted off my shoulders, the removalists have been and all the furniture has been donated to goodwill, so things are finally moving. "It's a relief to be getting rid of all this stuff."

His eyes trail down my body. "I got a situation, babe, I help at the Faux Paws stray dog rescue, they call me when they can't get a dog safely or it's a little dangerous, you can tag along if you want because it's closer from here than from town. Lily's gonna bring Lola to help."

"Okay," I say as I lock the shed behind us.

"The rescue is where I got Lola from," he says, "she was an ex-bait dog."

I follow behind him as we get back to the motorcycle.

"What's an ex-bait dog?"

He hands me the helmet and I pull it on.

"A dog used to attack in illegal dog fighting rings. She's a pitbull but not a fighter, in fact, most pitties aren't, they're usually not the aggressor, they're actually very submissive dogs. I got her when she had half her face ripped open, they left her for dead on the side of the road after they were done with her."

I stare at him, shocked. Clearly, he has a love for animals.

"I'm so sorry, that's awful, I can't believe people do that."

"She's a survivor."

"And she trusted humans after that?"

He shrugs. "It took time, *a lot* of time, and patience, she's wary of people she doesn't know, but she's resilient."

"She's an angel," I smile.

He flicks his eyes to me as he swings a leg over his bike. "Anybody who survives being hurt physically or emotionally deserves that title."

I can't help but feel there's an underlining meaning behind his words, but he doesn't know anything about my Ewan situation, so that's stupid.

I thought, at first, it was a case of what you see is what you get with Steel, with no in between. I never would have guessed when I first laid eyes on him that he has this side to him, even though I'd only been with him last night, he definitely has a softer side behind closed doors. I guess I did judge a book by its cover, but behind all the tattoos and the club, he seems like a good guy. A *decent* guy. He loves dogs for heaven's sake.

"Jump on," he commands, breaking me out of my reverie. There's another thing I've done with Steel that I never imagined myself doing; riding on a motorcycle, it really is kind of fun and I'm really not a thrill-seeking kind of girl.

We take off down the street but it doesn't take long to get to the location, and when we do, I see Lily pull up in a canary yellow shiny car. She has Lola on the passenger seat beside her.

Steel guns the engine, kicks the stand down, and I climb off.

"Hi!" she says as we approach.

"Hi, Lily."

She bites her lip as she studies me. "Thank you for the other night, I've been meaning to call but I didn't know what to say."

She hugs me, and for a little thing, she sure does knock the wind out of my sails. Guess it runs in the family.

"It's alright, I'm just glad you left your phone on the bar, I had no idea that he wasn't actually your boyfriend," I say when she lets go of me.

"Yeah, let that be a lesson to you," Steel barks.

Lily's eyes narrow on her brother, she rests both hands on her hips. "That reminds me, I've got a bone to pick with you."

"Well, it's gonna have to wait, I've got shit to do," he lets Lola out of the car and begins scratching her head, then he turns to Lily, "you put this pink shit on her?"

She has a thick baby pink elastic headband on her head with a bright sequined heart on the side. It looks adorable.

Lily shrugs.

Steel grumbles and kisses his dog's head. "Sorry, baby girl, I don't have another one."

"If he takes it off, Lola whines," Lily whispers to me.

"He doesn't like the girlie shit?" I whisper back.

She giggles. "Oh, hell no."

A van with Faux Paws on the side arrives too and we all turn to look.

"Wait here," he tells us as he stalks off with Lola by his side following him.

Lily rolls her eyes.

"You okay?" I ask, she seems like she might need an unbiased friend to offload to, I know what that can be like.

"No, well, *yes,* physically, but it's been rough, and now Steel's got a prospect following me everywhere I go."

She nods to the far end of the yard; I've only just noticed the figure sitting on a bike under a tree.

"What's a prospect again?"

"It's when you try out for the club, you get all the shitty, horrible, worst jobs in the world, if you last a year or prove your worth, then you get patched in, which means you get the club colors and the respect of Pres and the members, and of course, the women and all the other perks."

"Oh," I say, thinking about that for a second.

"Not women like *club girls*," she assures me quickly, "that's girls like me, Deanna; Hutch's daughter, Summer, we don't sleep around but the sluts that hang around the club for the boys do, some of them are hanger-onners and want to be more or hope to be more."

I look at her, dumbfounded. "Sounds just a tad bit misogynistic."

I think about Steel with another woman and a surge of jealousy runs through me.

"You have no idea," she agrees. "It's pretty gross, some girls have no self-respect and definitely no class, like seriously."

"So, they're the sweet butts right?"

"Yes, and they think by sucking off a biker whenever they ask for it will get them to ol' lady status. An ol' lady is your regular piece, wife, or girlfriend who is off-limits, and it gets you a certain amount of respect, not that it's much, but it isn't that easy for a sweet butt and it rarely ever happens. Nobody wants an ol' lady who everyone's been with."

I glance back at Steel. I remember him saying I'd never be a sweet butt, I wouldn't sleep with anyone else anyway, much less any old biker at the club, but does he think I'm easy now? My blood runs a little chilly.

"Why would they do that if it rarely ever happens?" I whisper.

"Well, it *could* happen, sometimes, but in the meantime; they get good dick basically, so they don't complain."

My eyes go wide. She's certainly not backwards in going forwards in her explanations.

She laughs. "Don't look so horrified."

"It's all new to me," I admit. I feel kind of grossed out if

I'm honest. I wonder how many women Steel usually hooks up with and if he's going to keep sleeping around while I'm here, even though he said he's not, I just met him though; he could be full of shit for all I know.

A few moments later, an Animal Control van rolls up and more people get out.

"My brother likes you," she says, watching Steel.

I glance at her again. *Did he say something to her?* Now may be an opportune time to get some dirt off his chatty little sister.

"He does?"

"Yes," she giggles again. "For one, he never lets any woman on the back of his sled, this has to be a first, that tells you everything."

Hmm. Interesting.

Now is definitely the time to make friends with her, I feel like if I stand here for long enough, she will just give me his life story without any probing whatsoever.

"Is that a big thing?" I frown. "I mean, they're bikers."

She turns to me again. "Yes, they're bikers, but having a female on the back means something, it's a statement, no girl ever just jumps on the back of your ride, like ever."

I feel my mouth going dry.

"A statement to what?" I don't know if I want to know this information.

"Well, that he likes you, that he's claiming territory; he doesn't want any of the other guys to get a look in."

Claiming territory? I remember Steel's brief explanation the night I went into the clubhouse to meet with Hutch about how all of that worked.

"I don't think he's doing that, we just met."

It all sounds very chauvinistic. *What kind of people are these bikers?*

"Still. Steel has always known what he wants and he isn't

149

afraid to go and get it. And don't look so worried, he's really not that bad and the club are a family, we all look out for one another."

Claiming. Ol' ladies. Sweet butts. Sleds. Goddamn bikers. It is a possibility that these people may actually be insane. I close my eyes, wondering if I've made a mistake sleeping with Steel so quickly.

I feel embarrassed all of a sudden. *Is it obvious we're screwing?*

I didn't come here to get tied down to a motorcycle club or to somebody like Steel, even if he has surprised me by some of his admissions and how good he is in the bedroom.

It's just sex, Sienna, and you haven't had any in a while. That's what I tell myself, and that may be so, but I'd be wise to keep my guard up, I can't let him get under my skin. I'm not going to be claimed or paraded around like some trophy. Is that his end game? Another notch on his belt, see who gets to screw the new girl first? Maybe that's it. Maybe everybody knows.

I shouldn't feel this hurt but it stings.

"Don't worry," I assure her. "I'm only here for a couple more weeks; once Max's house sells, I'm gone."

I see her smirk out of the corner of my eye. "We'll see," she laughs, "you don't know my brother."

I decide to ignore that comment as the man in question turns and looks back towards us and gives me a chin lift. I look away quickly.

It's just sex. Yeah, I need to keep telling myself that and maybe I'll actually start to believe it.

13

STEEL

"Is he hurt?" I ask the animal control guy, Kevin. He's been out here since earlier today and couldn't catch the dog, now the little guy is hiding under the house.

"Not that I can see, just very underweight, poor thing probably hasn't had a decent meal in weeks."

"No signs of aggression?"

"None. He was whimpering and crying when we almost got him the first time, so terrified he peed himself, the neighbors say they think he was abandoned. They tried to catch him but had no luck, that's why they called me."

A lump forms in my throat. Despite my size and what some would call an unfriendly exterior, when it comes to animals, they have my heart—they have me hook, line, and sinker.

Ever since I started helping out at Faux Paws, long before I got Lola, it helped me a lot being around the dogs. I'd go and clean out the cages, take the dogs for walks, and keep them company. Faux Paws rehomes all kinds of strays that have had a hard life, most have either been abandoned, can no longer be cared for, or abused in some way. It's something

I am very passionate about. I can't stand animal abuse or cruelty, some of the cases are general neglect, some are downright barbaric, and like my baby, Lola, just plain cruel. When we get cases like that, they have to restrain me and I've been known to take matters into my own hands on quite a few occasions.

We've placed a water bowl and some food outside the small opening where the dog has managed to get under the house.

I move over toward the porch and get down on my knees. I bend low and turn the torch on and try to see where he is, it's pretty dark under there, I can't see a damn thing.

I reach into my jacket pocket and grab a couple of long meaty dog sticks out and throw them in, then I break another one and place some little pieces just inside the entryway and outside it. If the dog is hungry, he'll come out, he may not like it but he'll come.

I don't know if this will work, but sometimes it isn't about treats and commanding words, it's about presence. It's about patience, and I have it in some things, just not *all* things.

I glance up and over to where Sienna is standing... nah, I don't have patience when it comes to her. I fuckin' hope Liliana isn't filling her head full of shit either, they seem to be in deep conversation. It was a very bad move asking her to bring Lola out here but I needed her, Lola is good with other scared dogs, she does what I can't sometimes. I'd never put her in danger but Kevin says the other dog isn't aggressive, only scared, so that gives me some hope. Lola comes and lies down in front of me as I sit with my back against the bricks of the house. She's a special dog, I've fostered lots over the years, but she was my foster fail, we bonded and I just couldn't let her go. I look at her now and I sometimes wonder how anybody could do something like that to another living being and how terrified she would have been as a bait dog. I still can't get over it, it's the only thing to date that's ever made me weep.

I lay the catcher's pole next to me, which has the slip lead attached to the end. This may be risky but it could be better than a cage. It takes some time, but eventually, he sticks his little head out, and when he does, Lola just moves her eyes, nothing else. She's so smart.

I start talking to him in a low voice and I don't go to touch him or do anything. He ducks his head back inside, then a few minutes later, he pops back out again, eating the treats. He's hungry. When his little body comes all the way out, even I am shocked. He's skin and bone, his little ribs poking out. It's safe to say his state is the worst I've seen a dog in for a while. His fur is very matted and clumpy and he stinks to high heaven. I make a mental note to call my man, Linc, later to find these people so I can pay them a visit. How you can leave a dog by itself and move is beyond me, and here he is, still waiting for them to come back. *Loyal*, it could make a grown man cry. They don't deserve him, the fucking bastards.

He looks up at Lola and his tail wags. Not aggressive, not at all, he makes a little whimpering sound at her. She just looks on, unaffected.

"You wanna come for a ride with me and Lola?" I say in a fake happy voice. "Do ya, boy?"

I scruff Lola on the head and she makes a mewling sound. He bows his head, totally submissive, and I know this ain't gonna be hard, I won't even need the pole.

He sniffs over to me and I let him smell my hands. I scruff under his jaw gently, careful not to approach him from over the top, and he lifts his head up, tail wagging. I can't believe this dog is so skinny, so small and fragile, neglected and unloved by his humans and he instantly gives me love without a second thought. Dogs are so fuckin' amazing, *unlike people.*

"You wanna come in Uncle Steel's jacket?" I ask him as he comes closer to my lap; Lola studies him but still has her head down low in an equally submissive stance. She nudges his hind leg with her head and he licks her. Jesus, she's a good girl, my angel.

"Little guy, this is Lola, we're gonna take you and get you cleaned up." I know he doesn't know what I'm saying, but still, I think he likes the sound of my voice since he puts two paws on my leg as I break a beef stick in half and feed it to him. "You like these, do ya?"

He gobbles it and I pick him up gently without any qualm or struggle. "That's it, little guy, it's all gonna be okay from now on, I promise."

I get up and walk over to the Faux Paw's van holding him and nod to Sally, one of the volunteers. "He's gonna be okay."

"Good work, Steel," says Kevin taking the unused pole from me.

"Thanks for coming out," I say to him. "We got it from here, gonna get him cleaned up."

"No problems at all, happy to help."

Thank God that was easy; no dog wants to end up at the pound, though, thanks to Faux Paw's, we keep it empty for the most part.

"That was good going, Steel, I'm gonna take him and bathe him, give him a haircut and get him checked out, he's very underweight, might need fluids and some medicine," Sally says.

"You want me to call Stacey?"

Stacey is the vet we use, she hangs around the club sometimes with the sisters but I haven't seen her in forever, we've never hooked up or anything but she's great, always helps us out.

"Nah, I got it," she replies.

"I wanna come and help," I tell her. "I just gotta take care of a few things, drop by in a bit."

She takes the little guy from me and wraps him in a blanket. "Roger that, you know where I'll be."

I nod and make my way back towards Lily and Sienna, who are leaning against Lily's car. I restored it for her as a twenty-first birthday present, she loves it. It took me about three or four months working on it by myself and about twenty thousand dollars, not that she'd appreciate that.

They both quieten as I approach, which makes me think they've been talking about me. Sienna is looking at me with a mixture of uncertainty and awe. I wonder what the hell she's thinking.

"That was so cool!" Lily says. "I told her you were the dog whisperer."

"What else did you tell her?" I grumble.

Sienna shifts on her feet. "He's safe now, you did great, that was amazing," she says, but the sentiment doesn't touch her eyes. *Fuckin' Lily.*

I look pointedly at Lily and she shrugs. I'll deal with her later.

"Lil, take my baby home, I've got to drop Sienna off and go down to Faux Paws and help Sally."

That's where we leave it, the girls say their goodbyes and I drive back to town, pulling up behind the Stone Crow.

"You alright?" I ask as Sienna climbs off and hands me the brain bucket.

"Yes, why wouldn't I be?"

Not the kind of answer I wanted. I want her to kiss me goodbye but she's standing further away from me, clearly not in the kissing kind of mood.

"Just wonderin' what my big mouth sister said to you?"

She bites her lip. *Shit.* She has said something then.

"Nothing, just chatted about this and that, passing the time."

"This and that, huh?"

"Yes."

She offers nothing more. I run a hand through my beard; I don't have time for this. I gotta go sort this shit out and comfort the little dude, but she'll be seeing me later tonight, that's for damn sure.

"Later," I say.

She nods without reaching to kiss me or anything, much to my disappointment. I purse my lips annoyed but drop it. I got bigger fish to fry at the moment. She gives me a wave and walks to the back door and lets herself in without a backward glance, just like the first night.

Fuckin' Liliana.

IT's late as I stand by the back door. I sent Sienna a text to tell her I was coming over. She doesn't appear to be ignoring me but said something about being tired. Fuck that shit.

I pound on her back door. A few moments later, I hear the locks unbolt and she appears before me in pink silk pajamas. She's a sight for sore eyes, and after the day I've had, it's a welcome sight.

I went home and showered before showing up, I even washed my hair, it's still wet.

"You good?" I ask.

"I'm fine," she lies, not letting me in.

We have a moment where we just stare at each other and she doesn't move one inch, blocking my path.

"Am I not invited in?" I ask, raising my eyebrows.

"Steel, I don't know if that's such a good idea," she says as

I stare at her, dumbfounded. I remind myself to call my sister and go strangle her later.

"I see."

"Things are… getting complicated."

"Complicated?" I say like the words are foreign. It's sex. She's hot, we had a good time, what the fuck is complicated about that? Of course, I know that when girls get together they talk.

I should have known better than to let leave her alone with Lily but you'd think my own sister would be sticking up for me, not throwing me under the bus.

"Do I get to defend myself here or do you just get to kick my ass out before I even know what I did?"

"You didn't do anything," she says with a sigh, "but the motorcycle club thing…"

I roll my eyes and put my hands on my hips and part my legs wider, taking up all the room in the doorway.

"Can't help I'm a biker, you knew that and didn't have a problem with it last night and you sure as hell didn't have a problem with it wrapped around me earlier in my office."

She bites her bottom lip and it takes all my patience not to take her mouth and claim it. She doesn't get to just end this thing, not like this, I won't let her.

"I'm not going until you tell me what's really up." I cross my arms over my chest like a five-year-old.

She sighs. "Come up, it's freezing out here."

She turns and begins to mount the stairs, I bolt the door behind me and follow behind, my steps are heavy. I reign in my annoyance as best as I can.

Something is very wrong. Lily didn't tell me shit, the little bitch.

I mean, seriously, what the fuck have I done now? She's letting me in so it can't be *that* bad, maybe it's just to kick me back out again, or maybe it's just PMS but I'm obviously not gonna say that out loud.

We get inside the apartment and I lock that door too, just to let her know I'm staying.

She turns to face me. "How did it go with the little guy?"

I look down at her, my anger at whatever Lily's said forgotten for the moment. "He's better, shaved all the matted fur off him, he's had a good wash, and he's gotta stay at the vet for at least a few days. He needs antibiotics and a lot of fluids, the bastard has moved and left him there, he was still waiting, breaks your heart."

She blinks; she has her arms crossed defensively across her chest. "How can people be so cruel?"

I ask myself this all the time and never get an answer.

"Because having a pet is an inconvenience to some people, they just spit them out like garbage the minute it doesn't suit them or their lifestyle."

"What will happen to him?" At least she's worried about the dog… me, I'm not so sure about.

"He'll get better; we'll find a home for him when he's well again."

"It's a wonderful thing that you do."

"Glad you think so," I say as I move toward her, she takes a step back. "What I'm curious about though, is why you've had a change of heart."

She looks down then bites her lip like she does. This chick can't lie for shit, not to me.

"I haven't, I just don't want things to get messy."

At least she's talking to me, that's something, chicks have a way of assuming you're a mind reader so you can't do right for doing wrong half the time.

"What did my sister say to change things?"

She looks guilty. "Nothing, she didn't say anything bad,

but things just seem to be going so fast, and I don't know... I don't know if this is a mistake," she trails off.

I keep walking her backwards until her legs hit the couch.

A mistake? She's gotta be shittin' me.

"What if I say I don't believe you?"

"Steel, don't."

"Talk to me, Sienna, I want to know. If I don't know then I can't fix it, if it's because I'm part of an M.C. then I can't change that."

Maybe she doesn't want me to fix it? That makes me feel strange.

I stand over her and give her a brow lift for good measure. "We had a good time last night, and an even better one this morning, and I want more of that, now you've gone all cold on me and acting weird, what's the deal?"

Her eyes go wide. "I don't know what to say."

"Spit it out, angel, I ain't got all night."

Now is not the time for me to act like a Neanderthal but I can hardly help it, I don't like games, just tell me what the fuck I did and I'll try and fix it. Simple.

"It's nothing, but Lily was just saying..."

I blow out a rush of air as I wait.

"That me being on the back of your bike is a statement."

Okay, not so bad. *"And?"*

"And that it means you were sending a message to the others in the club."

Okay, *not* great from her point of view, but still not *that* bad.

"And that it meant you're putting a claim on me."

Why can't Lily just keep her nose out of my business? Can't a man get a goddamned break around here?

I shake my head. "My fuckin' sister can't keep her mouth shut."

"Is that true, Steel? Are you doing those things?"

I don't want to lie to her and I won't. "I do like you on the back of my sled and, yes, that does send a message to the other guys because it means you're off-limits, trust me when I say they'd all be swarming around you if I didn't and I know you don't want that. But I ain't claimin' you, babe, it's a little bit early to get into all of that, we're just fucking, right?"

She gulps as she grips onto the back of the couch.

"Claiming me? That whole statement in itself is so misogynistic, Steel, nobody talks like that. It's not normal."

"We do, it's how we are and it's not a bad thing. I told you that we don't treat women like shit but we have certain rules in the club, we all have our position and women are a big part of it, and I like you, so sue me for not wanting someone like Gunner to try to get into your pants."

Her eyes go wide.

"I would never let him do that." She looks disgusted, that pleases me for a second.

"I know that."

"I'm not anyone's property," she adds.

Oh, here we go.

"You're overthinking this," I say again, shaking my head.

"Am I, Steel? Am I really?"

"Yeah, you are, you can't just take it for what it is and go with it."

She looks up at me, trying to gauge if I'm being genuine or not.

This guy, whoever he is, really did a number on her. I want to hurt him.

"I just don't want you to think I'm easy," she whispers, "that I'd sleep with just anybody."

And there we have it, the root of the problem. As if I would care, I'd want her anyway, but the fact she doesn't is a huge turn on.

I rub a hand down my face slowly. "Is that what this is about?" *Oh, thank fuck.*

She nods. "That you'll think I'm just another sweet butt who'll do anyone. I don't do that, I don't even like most men…" she trails off, her eyes glaze over.

My face softens, she's just so damn gorgeous. As if she'd ever be like that, she's got too much class. She's too good for me and I know it.

"Babe." I brush a lock of her hair from her shoulder and then cup her face with one hand. "I would never think that about you, you don't act like one, you don't look like one, I don't treat you like one, and you sure as hell won't ever be one, so get that shit out of your mind."

"I don't sleep around."

"I know that, caught it the first time."

"I'm not going to."

"Know it."

"I'm not anyone's property to own."

Yeah, we'll see about that.

"Listen and listen good, princess, I'm the type of guy who ain't gonna lie to you and sometimes that gets me in more trouble than it's worth. With you, I'm in unchartered territory, I like you more than I should, I admit it, I don't deserve what you're offering but you seem to want it and I want it too, so let's not get crazy, let's just enjoy it. I won't hurt you, I already told you that before, I don't hurt women and I'll only be honest with you even if you don't wanna hear it."

She almost breathes a sigh of relief.

"Got me?"

She nods.

"If you don't want this, babe, all you gotta do is say and I'll leave."

I mean it, I will go, reluctantly, but if it's what she wants…

"I don't," she says, moving towards me. "I just got scared, I don't know how it works with your club, I don't want you to think I'm just some floozy who waltzes into town and sleeps with the first biker she sees, I haven't been with anyone in a year like I told you, so it all feels very foreign, I've never done anything like this."

She's so innocent looking up at me, I contemplate leaving her alone but it's only for a fleeting second, the devil in me knows I could never do that. I've had a slice of heaven and I want more because I'm a greedy son of a bitch.

"Good to hear that," I gruff. "Know that I'm not takin' what you're offering for granted."

She seems to relax. "I just wanted to get that off my chest, it was bothering me a little."

"Then, next time, just tell me," I say, shrugging. "You can't offend me, babe, I'm not a mind reader, and I'll be telling Lily to—"

She shuts me up with a kiss I don't see coming and she presses her hot little body up to mine and against my eagerly waiting hard-on.

"You know what I like better than you in silk pajamas?" I ask when we come up for air.

She shakes her head.

"You out of silk pajamas."

She laughs, pulling me down by my shirt, wrapping her arms around my neck and we devour each other. I kiss her like she's the only one I'll ever want.

I don't tell her all of it. That I'm feeling shit I shouldn't be feeling on day two of us hooking up and I don't know what to do about that. I push those thoughts down for the moment, there's more pressing things to attend to, like the uncomfortableness forming in my jeans.

I glance over her shoulder. "That bed has gotta go."

"Or we can improvise?" she gives me a sexy smirk.

I grin into her neck, sucking on the skin as she moans.

"Gonna do you so good you won't know what hit you and I got all night, sweetheart, not going anywhere."

I hear her breath hitch at my words, I wish she'd talk dirty to me.

"Yes, I want that too," she says into my hair as I move over to her other pulse and nip her with my teeth, my hands squeeze her ass, encouraging me.

"Yes, what?"

"Yes, *Jayson*," she accentuates my name sarcastically and I buck her with my hips.

Fuck, I love her saying my name. I reach down and pick her up by the hips and she wraps around me, I move toward the kitchenette with her in my arms.

"Where are we going?" she stammers.

"The kitchen ain't just for cooking, babe."

14

SIENNA

HE'S STILL cold as I wrap my arms around his shoulders. He kisses me hard; his short beard feels sensual against my skin. I want his mouth everywhere. He places me on the kitchen counter and I pant just watching him. He reaches over and peels my pajama top off, and seeing my bare breasts, he rubs his junk through his jeans and adjusts himself.

"Touch yourself," he says hoarsely.

I cup my breasts as he watches me.

"Fuck, you're beautiful," he almost snarls, but he still doesn't touch me. He loosens the top button and moves his hand into the front of his jeans and continues to rub himself, I want to replace his hand with mine but I'm enjoying watching him too much. "Squeeze them, thumb your nipples, let me see."

I do as he says and his eyes look even hungrier as he watches me play with myself.

He removes his hand from his jeans and shrugs his shirt off, placing it neatly on the stool behind him. My eyes dip to his body; it's so hard, muscled, and perfect. He could be in any tattooed ink magazine, he's that pimped up. His tatts up close are even more dazzling. A large skull face greets me on his chest, there's patterns dancing all over his arms, swirls and intricate detail, the end of what I think is a dragon's tail; it wraps around his body, an Indian-type feather is down the side of one arm, a woman's face on his other bicep, there's so much to look at, I could get lost for hours.

"Like what you see, baby?"

I nod, biting my lip as I undress him with my eyes.

"You have so many tattoos," I breathe in wonder.

He smirks, unclips his buckle, and unzips his jeans. I watch as he does it, so turned on I can barely breathe.

"Take your pants off," he says, his voice is low and husky.

Again, I want *him* to do that, but I do as he says and scramble to pull them off. I leave my black thong on that I put on for him because I want him to see it.

He dips his eyes and then he stops for a second. Before I know what's happening, he pulls me forwards by the shoulders and looks over to the back to see my ass.

He swears in a low, sexy voice as I hold onto his forearms. "You wear this for me, angel?"

I nod because I can't even speak.

"Me and only me?" he grunts.

"Yes," I say, "only you."

He sets me back and I keep my arms on his biceps, squeezing them. He deliberately moves one of his hands back down into the front of his jeans again and I can see his bulge sticking out through his black boxer briefs. He is rock hard.

His eyes are on mine as he rubs himself again through his boxers, then he ever so slowly moves his hand into the top of them, under the elastic. It's so hot, he could be on fire.

"Pull my jeans down," he demands. I do, leaving his boxers in place. His large hand in his pants covers his bulge and watching him touch himself makes me want to lose it.

I'm so desperately ready for him, I could jump him right now, "This is what you do to me, day in, day out."

He moves his free hand up to cup my breast, I feel so sensitive all over, I may combust right then and there. He squeezes it and caresses me at the same time.

I don't wait for him to tell me, I reach down and pull his boxer briefs down to his thighs, his package springs free. I watch with fascination as he jerks himself off with one hand right there in front of me, it's so ridiculously hot I can't look away.

I know he's watching my reaction, reveling in it.

"You want this bad boy?" he asks as if he even has to.

I flip my eyes to his; they are like a storm—fierce and unyielding.

"Jesus, yes," I reply, my throat dry.

He reaches out and pulls my hand down and I continue to pleasure him instead. His eyes dip to watch what I'm doing. He swallows hard and adds a bit of a hip thrust as I pull him off on my kitchen bench.

"I need to taste your honey first," he says in a low breath. He pulls me forward so I'm right on the edge of the bench, then dips to his knees looking up at me. I close my legs instinctively as I look down at him.

"Open up, princess, don't be shy."

My heart is racing as I watch him.

"*Steel*, I don't know…"

"You don't like it, babe?"

Oh, I'm sure I'd like him doing it.

He watches me silently. "You're gonna like it, I promise."

He moves his hands to my knees and parts them, his breath hitches as his gaze drops to me.

"So fuckin' sweet," he mutters, pulling the scrap of fabric to the side.

I lean back on my hands and push my body forward, I

want all of him and I want his mouth on me. He moves between my legs and bites the inside of my thigh as I squeal. Everything he does is so erotic. I do not want to think about him doing this to any other woman.

Then he moves and swipes his tongue through my heat, I just about convulse. He makes a very satisfied noise at the back of his throat. He finds my nub and licks it with his tongue, then he sucks gently and I do convulse this time, long and hard, how embarrassing, that took like three seconds. I feel him chuckle beneath me. When I finally come back from heaven, I look down and he's looking up at me, he pulls my legs over his shoulders and really goes to town, eating me alive, then he puts a finger inside and pumps me ever so gently, then replaces it with two fingers as I look up to the ceiling wondering if it's possible to have an out of body experience. His touch is torture, so good, his bristly beard scraping me just adding to the thrill. I lose control of myself again in seconds.

"Steel, *please…*" I beg.

He glances up, his eyes crinkle. "You forget my name, babe?"

"Why do you like me calling you Jayson?" I pant.

He stands up; his appendage is so huge I stare at it wondering how that thing is going to fit inside me.

"I just do, do you always ask so many questions post-orgasm?"

"That's when I get my best ideas."

He snorts. I watch as he bends down to his ankles and finds his jeans, goes into his wallet, and pulls out a wrap. After biting the foil wrapper away with his teeth, he slides it over his length.

"You taste beautiful by the way."

I feel myself blushing. "You weren't kidding about the kitchen bench," I stammer.

"Perfect height for everything." He kicks his boots off, pulls his jeans off the rest of the way, and nudges at my entrance.

He slowly slides in and we both moan in unison.

"You feel so good," I tell him.

"So tight for me, angel," he leans down and kisses me, his tongue in my mouth. "I could eat you all night but I can't hold off, the sight of you, fuck me, it's like nothing else."

"We're going to screw ourselves to death," I pant, hanging on for dear life, unable to believe I'm having sex where I made lunch today.

"One can only hope," he moves in and out slowly then pumps me harder, "not gonna last this time, babe, I'll make it up to you later though… like I said, I'm not going anywhere."

I stare at him in wonder, *make it up to me?* He just gave me two huge, earth-shattering orgasms with his mouth. The man is a machine.

"You're beautiful," I tell him before I can stop myself.

He grips my hip hard and his other hand holds the back of my neck and he increases the pace. "And you're fuckin' perfect, princess."

I feel it building. *"Jayson…"*

"Let go, babe, let me feel you, say my name," he pumps his hips harder, banging me literally on the bench and I do let go very noisily, a few moments later, he does too and swears like a man possessed, panting my name in several grunts as I feel a shudder run through him.

I've never had any experience like this. I'm not even sure what 'this' is but I'm not going to complain. I cling to him as our sweaty bodies press together; his breathing is just as out of control as mine is.

"Babe," I say into his shoulder as he kisses my head.

"Need to move to the bed, I want you on top."

"Can you give me five seconds to recover?" I say as he

picks me up and carries me from the kitchen to the bed in all of five strides.

"One, two, three, four, five…" he looks over my shoulders and frowns. "So need a bigger bed, and pronto."

"Maybe I don't want a bigger bed, maybe I like the bench."

I feel him chuckle into my hair. "Touché, princess, touché."

THE NEXT DAY, I find myself at Steel's office—big surprise. I'm like honey to a bee, but this time I'm not up against his door or doing anything untoward; I'm sitting at his desk trying to make sense of the hand grenade that went off in here. I spent most of yesterday afternoon googling the best office system for a small business that is also user-friendly. After seeing Steel's current invoicing system, it can't be too complicated if he's to learn it too. He also needs a credit card machine for instant payments.

Steel introduces me properly to Jaxon, Dalton, Patch—who I already met at the club—and a little tiny buxom blonde woman called Lucy, who introduces herself as Rubble's wife.

She shakes my hand with force.

I hand Jaxon a box of donuts I picked up on the way, the boys seem very happy about that, all except Steel, who frowns at me.

"Thought you might like them, a kind of office-warming present," I smile but Steel just rolls his eyes.

"Thanks, Sienna," Jaxon says.

"That's very thoughtful," Lucy agrees, shoving Steel in the ribs, "let's get ourselves a coffee and we'll get cracking."

We do just that and I follow Lucy as she shuts the office door behind us.

"Alone at last," she says with a smile.

She's smaller than me, probably five-foot with bottle-blonde big-hair, which she tells me is due to the fact she's from Texas and big hair is practically an Olympic sport. What she lacks in height, she makes up for in personality and sky-high stilettos.

I can't believe how nice all the club girls seem; I realize they probably would have hated me in the beginning or at the least regarded me with suspicion if not for the Lily incident.

"You're one tough nut to put up with his array of shit," she says, grabbing the chair from the other side of the desk so we can sit together and work this new system out.

"I'm not… we're not…" I begin but she just gives me a knowing smile.

"That's what I said when I met Rubble, I didn't want to be caught either. I was over men, let me tell you, honey, over with a capital 'O', then I met my big-badass Barney."

Barney? I almost laugh. Oh. *Barney Rubble*, I got it.

"That is kind of sweet," I say, blowing into my coffee cup. They at least have a decent coffee machine here which is a welcome surprise. "How did you two meet?"

She taps a long fingernail on her chin and grins. "He was getting a lame-ass lap dance at a club for his birthday, the chick was doing a horrible job, it hardly seemed fair, and he was so dang cute, so I took over. He said it was the best lap dance he'd ever had and the rest they say is history."

I stare at her, unable to understand if she's kidding or not, I don't think she is.

The door bangs open and Steel appears larger than life in the doorway.

"You two okay in here?" He's looking at me.

"Yes," Lucy answers.

"Why is the door shut?"

She lets out a noisy sigh. "We need quiet, we can't think

with you lot clattering around out there being noisy, we need to concentrate, this is important stuff."

He points at her. "No club talk."

"Wouldn't dream of it."

She blows a kiss as he disappears again and slams the door behind him.

She turns to me.

"How long have you guys been bangin'?"

I want to slam my head against the desk.

"Umm, we haven't…"

She gives me an eye roll; there is no point in lying. Her bullshit radar is probably as high as her hair.

"Is it that obvious?" I sigh.

"No judgement, I can see why, you're gorgeous, and he's not so bad once you get to know him and peel back all the layers."

I snort. "Sounds about right."

"They're all like that, big macho men on the outside, you just gotta find their Kryptonite and then go to work on it."

"I thought all women were Kryptonite to them?"

She smiles, giving me the nod. "Don't believe the B.S. they spout. Oh, they can be sexist assholes, that kind of comes with the territory of being in the M.C. like a rite of passage, but despite what they think or say about us keeping out of club business, they need us, and don't ever think otherwise, no matter what they say."

I start the software download as we wait for it to run.

"What does he mean no club talk?"

She rolls her eyes again, the girls all seem to do this a lot where the boys and the club are concerned.

"They think we're all stupid dumb idiots and we don't know what's going on, it's their lame-ass archaic way of keeping us girls out of *club business,* shit we apparently don't need to know about what's going down with this and that, trouble is, there's a thing called pillow talk, honey… one good blow job and they sing like a canary, though I can only speak for Rubble, of course; so who are the stupid, dumb idiots now?"

I laugh, almost choking on my coffee. I think I like Lucy.

"That's actually pretty accurate."

She nods. "They'll make you scream like you're having a body wax, but don't run away too soon, Sienna, he's a good guy deep down, even if he doesn't know how to show it, he's just misunderstood. Beneath that brawn, he's really a big teddy bear."

I don't know why everyone keeps acting like I'm sticking around, I mean, this is just sex… *isn't it?*

"I'm really not here for long enough, just sorting some stuff out of Max's."

"You don't plan on sticking around?" She seems surprised.

It may have something to do with Steel but Bracken Ridge is growing on me.

"Wasn't planning on it."

She seems thoughtful. "Well, I can see how Cali would be very enticing, but you know there's good things about small towns too, the community for one, and there's less crime, cost of living's lower, job security…"

"You planning on going into broking?" I laugh. "You'd make a good salesperson."

She laughs. "You know I've thought about it."

Suddenly, we hear a commotion coming from the workshop. Lucy jumps up and goes to the door, when she opens it, Rubble is belly laughing so hard, he's doubled over, holding his sides, and the rest of the guys are no better off, all except Steel who is standing there with a confused look on his face. He's looking over at Gunner, who's very animated about whatever it is he's telling them.

"Come on," she says to me. "We gotta see what this is about."

I follow her out. Rubble slaps Gunner on the back and he can't even get the words out, he's laughing so hard.

"What's going on?" Lucy asks, staring at her husband who cannot get his breath.

Between laughs, Jaxon fills us in, "You'll never believe it. He's been asked to pose for a *ladies* magazine as their monthly pin-up." He wipes his eyes on the back of his sleeve.

"He's what?" Steel looks at Gunner like he has grown two heads. "People pay money for that shit?"

"No, no, no," Patch, the wide-set, wrestler-looking dude says, pinching the bridge of his nose as if trying to ward off the very thought. "Please say it ain't so, I don't need that kind of vision first thing in the morning."

Me and Lucy exchange a look that says we don't mind.

"What kind of magazine is Sizzle exactly?" Lucy asks, cocking an eyebrow, folding her arms over her chest.

"The naughty kind," Gunner says, unperturbed by the guys' mocking. "Sizzle magazine is the highest-selling women's mag of its kind since Playgirl shut down, it's what I call tasteful nudity, plus it's the easiest ten grand I ever made."

"Are you for fuckin' real?" Steel barks.

"Yep. I also get more for chargeable downloads at Gunner after dark, that's where people pay a subscription on Instagram to see exclusive images of me."

My eyes go round as more laughter ensues.

"Are you like… fully nude?" Lucy gasps, putting a hand over her mouth to stifle a giggle.

"I said tasteful nudity, Luce, please, this isn't porn, it's a very classy and professional shoot." He grins as he raises his eyebrows encouragingly.

"Who the fuck would pay you ten grand to get your junk

out?" Rubble says, slinging his arm around Lucy's shoulders. He's still chuckling away to himself.

Gunner is one seriously hot dude; I can imagine that any red-blooded female wouldn't mind getting a gander at him in the buff. He's the ultimate bad-boy with a pretty face, colorful tattoos run up both arms and disappear under his cut sleeves, he's tall, lanky but with muscle, blonde hair, blue eyes, and so good looking it almost hurts. Oh, yeah, I can see why he'd get paid to strip alright. His degree of beauty could open many windows, of that I'm sure.

"I don't get my junk out," he corrects, sweeping his hands toward me and Lucy, "please, assholes, there are ladies present."

He grins at me and gives Lucy a wink.

"Oh, give it a break," Dalton, the older, grey-haired dude says shaking his head, "for ten grand, they're gonna want a little more than your bare ass."

He rolls his eyes like they're all stupid. "I don't have to take it all off, dummy, they have different outfits and props and stuff. Shame you boys have to slug it out here every day working hard like grease monkeys and all I have to do is show up and take my cut off and get paid for it."

"Shouldn't take much to hide it though if you did pose naked," Dalton goes on, rubbing his eyes with his palms to stop the tears. I've never seen grown men cry, especially not bikers.

"Yeah, just his pinky finger oughta do it." Rubble laughs out loud again.

Steel is the only one taking any of it seriously. "What does Hutch say about that?" he barks, still looking dumbfounded by the prospect. "We don't wanna be a laughing stock."

"Let's not worry about that right now," Gunner says quickly, "as long as I'm bringing in the coin for the club coffers, it shouldn't matter, plus I'm not gonna wear club colors or mention the chapter, this is just pay dirt for very little work, plus it's just skin, dude, don't be too offended when every chick in town is lining up to get some action."

Steel crosses his arms over his chest. "The hell it doesn't matter."

"I'm still having trouble understanding that women would actually *pay* to see you without clothes on," Patch just can't get over it.

"Well, alright, since you are all obviously jealous of my new-found fame, let's settle the score, shall we?" He waves his arm over to me and Lucy. "Let's ask the panel here, they're women of the world and know what's hot and what's not, let's find out if they'd pay to see me in compromising positions without clothes on."

All eyes fall on us. I bite my lip to refrain from laughing, there's something very wrong with this picture and I'm not sure I want to be involved.

"Come on," Rubble prompts Lucy with a shake. "Spit it out, we wanna know."

"For fuck's sake," Steel mutters, shaking his head.

"Well, my angels?" He turns to us and lifts his t-shirt up to show us an up-close and personal shot of his abdomen and chest. He has a large eagle spread across his pecs, his abdomen is ripped, there's a light, blonde trail of hair that leads from his belly button down into his jeans which I follow with my eye. Then he gives us a hip roll and then a thrust for good measure, laughing all the while. "What's the verdict?"

Lucy and I look at each other. "Hell yeah," we say in unison.

Gunner throws his head back and laughs, Rubble groans, and Steel just shakes his head like he is not happy at all with our answer. He isn't laughing, oh no he is not.

"Fuckin' women." Rubble kisses Lucy on the head affectionately. Gunner looks over at Steel then comes toward me and slings his arm around my shoulder, lazily pulling me into his side, I can tell by his demeanor that he's just trying to piss Steel off and it looks like he's doing a good job of it.

"I don't know, I think they've got pretty good taste."

He's an irresistible but harmless flirt, and he smells fricking good too. It's a fresh scent though, not musky like Steel.

"You're asking for trouble," Dalton mutters under his breath, a couple of the guys snort with laughter.

Steel comes towards Gunner and removes his arm from around me and pulls me to him instead. Gunner just smirks like he knew that was going to happen.

"You don't have to sexually harass the new office girl on her first day," he says, his tone clipped though his lips are twitching like he secretly finds this amusing but won't laugh to save himself.

"Sounds like a challenge." Gunner gives me a wink. I'm starting to think he has a death wish.

"Best not to poke the bear," I whisper as Gunner smirks and I feel Steel look down at me.

"I think we've all seen enough profanity for one morning," he huffs, "but I can only speak for myself obviously."

I glance at Lucy and she gives me an eyebrow raise. I roll my eyes. *Macho men.* Yep, she's totally right.

Steel leans close to my ear. "Don't you got work to do?"

"Yes, but this is way more fun."

He lowers his voice. "We're not here to have fun, fun is for later when you're wrapped up around me in bed."

I look around but nobody is listening, Gunner's shoving Jaxon around.

I look up at him. "I think I'm going to fit right in here."

He nudges me with his hip. "Don't get too used to it."

"Famous last words," I say and waltz back to the office; I

know his eyes are on my ass as I walk away, so I put a little more sass into it.

"Get back to work, all of you," I hear him bark as I smirk to myself, liking the fact that he's a little bit jealous over Gunner and I got to him. I think we just went way past complicated.

15

STEEL

SIENNA AND LUCY get a lot done on the first day, then Sienna threw herself into it like a woman on a mission. By Friday, she has so much done I can't even believe it. I like that she's got a brain… it's not just looks on her side but she's got smarts as well. I have no idea what she sees in me, aside from the fact I know I'm good in bed, but I know I'm all wrong for her and I shouldn't pursue her, but the more she's around, the more I'm convinced we could be a good thing.

It's been a big week. I brought the little guy home after spending four days at the vets, I gotta feed him slowly to get used to actual food again. Sienna named him Rocky because she said he looked like an underdog, which I think is pretty fitting. I think about bringing her up to my apartment tonight. We got a party at Church tomorrow to celebrate the clubhouse HQ being officially ours and, what's worse, Hutch wants me to invite Sienna.

I imagine what she'll think of our partying and shudder, I don't think she'd appreciate some of our customs as she's already been very vocal about our misogynistic ways.

But first, we discuss the real order of business around the gavel.

"Couple of guys from the New Orleans Chapter will be coming through on business," Hutch says at the helm, "be here for the party as well, Jett handles all the security down there so he'll set it all up, Steel's gonna talk to Stef about upping security at the Crow on a permanent basis, thinkin' of trying to set somethin' up for Colt to run, maybe Patch too, he's lookin' for extra work, there's a call for it, even more so now that Bracken Ridge has expanded over the years. I got people askin' for protection and we got the manpower."

Aye's of agreement roll around the table.

"Get Summer or Ginger to make up some rooms for the boys," he looks at Gunner, "and we gettin' that wood fire pizza guy again?"

"Already arranged," he replies, he's always thinking about his next meal.

Hutch turns to me. "Colt all set for tomorrow?"

His first shift as security detail at the Stone Crow is tonight, and if that goes well, he'll be getting patched in tomorrow at the bonfire. It's been a year, he's earned his colors, he's loyal and trustworthy, he'll make a good brother, and now he gets to have any sweet butt he wants. He'll be a happy boy this time tomorrow night. No more hauling shit, no more taking orders, no more being an ass licker. Which reminds me, I've only got today to give him as much shit as possible.

"Think he's just happy I finally released him from Lily duty," I mutter.

Hutch frowns. "How's she doing?"

"Back to bitchin' and doing what girls do, so I'd say she's back to normal."

A few snorts go around the table.

Hutch swings his eyes to his V.P. "You got the cut organized?"

Brock nods. "Already done."

"Who'd you find to sew? My mom has been on night shift all week," I say to Brock across the table suspiciously, I can't imagine Chelsea, his latest sweet butt, sewing shit. Mom does a lot of mending for the boys in the club since most of them don't have ol' ladies to do that shit for them.

"Angel," he says like it's obvious.

Angel is the best ink slinger and piercer in town, she hangs around the club a little bit now and again but she, like the rest of us, is always busy at her shop. Angel's done a lot of my work. Even though she's a chick, she puts any dude through his paces, chicks are also a lot gentler with a needle, so I've found out.

I grunt. "Angel? Since when does she fuckin' sew?"

"She sews, I picked up Rawlings from daycare the other afternoon, she owed me one."

Rawlings is Angel's kid to some loser she'd dated a while back. She's a good girl but doesn't know how to pick them. She had an on-off thing with Brock years ago when we were kids but now they're just friends, it's not unusual for the club to help out but normally it's one of the girls helpin' with the kid. I wonder if Brock has got something secretly going on again with Angel, he doesn't normally get involved with the kid stuff even though Rawlings adores him.

"You back on?" Bones asks before I get the words out.

"Nope," he says, sitting back in his chair, running his hands through his hair. His body language is all wrong though. "That was years ago, just friends, bro."

"Since when are you *just friends* with anyone?" Gunner pipes up, like he'd know shit.

"Since I met her," he says nonchalantly.

"You goin' soft in your old age?" I smirk.

He meets my eye across the table. "Nah, brother, just don't wanna be tied down. Rawlings is great and all but I like my freedom." *Right.* It's no secret he'd been hung up on Angel for years but never did anything about it aside from a couple of hook-ups. He also made sure not to be all over anyone at Church when she was around, I notice these things. I notice everything, it's my job.

"Rubble, you got anything?" Hutch says as we all turn to look at him. "You're unusually quiet."

Come to think of it, he does look a little lost if not a bit pale.

"I can help out at the Crow if needed," he says out of nowhere. *Huh?* Even if Colt is about to be patched in, he is *newly* patched so it's still expected he'll pull his weight, nobody expects any of *us* to actually do the security work and shit-kicking ourselves. We've all got full-time jobs. I'd help Jett do what he needed with the cameras and shit but this was Colt's baby to run from there on in, he would report to me weekly but that's where it ended.

"What the fuck, bro?" Bones slaps him on the back. "You in trouble with the ol' ball and chain or somethin'?"

He holds up a hand. "Don't even." He then runs his other, shaking hand through his hair that has me leaning forward to look at him, waiting for him to spill his guts.

"Surely, it can't be that bad," Bones shrugs, not understanding where the issue is, "you two having problems? Is Lucy okay?"

"What is this, group therapy?" I bark, annoyed.

"Shut up, *Romeo*, we're not all gifted with the art of caveman ministrations," Gunner chuckles. "That's how you snagged Sienna, isn't it? Yanked her off by the hair with your club, beating your chest, dragging her into your lair."

All eyes hit me, then more laughs ensue which I do not appreciate.

I shoot him a look that says it all. As usual, it isn't enough to deter him from shutting the hell up.

"Come on, let us all in on it, you're doin' her, aren't you? Does she squeal, yelp, or moan?"

I sigh heavily. He knows how to push my buttons, and though we usually talk like sexist assholes, this time it's different. I don't want to talk about Sienna like that with them; she's no sweet butt or piece of ass to be pawed over by him or by any of them.

"All of the above because I'm just that good," I say, looking him right in the eye.

"Fuck," says Brock, "way to go, brother."

"Sweet," Bones agrees, knocking his knuckles on the table.

"That's old news," says Rubble.

"Proud of you, son," Hutch slaps me on the back, it's like I've won Olympic Gold or something.

I'm sure Sienna would not appreciate being discussed like a piece of meat around the gavel meeting table. In fact, I know she wouldn't, she'd be pissed.

"She's fuckin' hot, dude," Bones admits as I turn to look at him. "Nobody blames you, bro, hell, if I'd had half a chance…"

I sock him in the arm. "Don't go there, brother."

More laughter and snickers. It seems everyone is in high spirits today at pissin' me the hell off.

"I don't know how you did it," Gunner continues just to rile me, "Sienna's high class, a top-shelf broad, Steel, never thought I'd be asking for tips from you, big guy."

"I'll give you a tip, brother, my fist down your throat, with knuckle dusters."

"Ouch." He laughs, rubbing his throat with his hand.

I have to shift the subject quickly. "Weren't we discussing Rubble?"

The best thing to do is not encourage any of them.

"This isn't group therapy," Gunner chuckles in a high-pitched voice, repeating my earlier statement. More laughter erupts. I could honestly sock him one, he hasn't had a good roughing up for a while and we usually get into tussles now and then. It's all harmless fun.

"What's going on, Rubble?" Hutch says, ignoring all of us. "Lucy okay?"

He sighs then runs his hands through his hair again, he's acting really weird.

"Shit, dude, is it something serious?" I'm worried now about Lucy but she's not said anything, I just saw her yesterday and she seemed like her usual self.

"I didn't wanna bring this up here, but, sometimes you know... you just gotta vent."

I lean on the table. *Shit, something may be really wrong with Lucy the way he's acting.* She's everything he cares about most in the world—that and his custom sled.

Everyone is silent, waiting for the revelation.

"She won't leave me alone," he states eventually, lighting up a cigarette, "the woman is insatiable and I mean, a man-eater, it's like she's taken crazy woman whore pills."

We all look at each other like we've misheard.

"What do you mean?" Bones asks in confusion.

"Is Lucy physically fucking okay?" Hutch barks out, clearly, he's had just about enough.

Rubble shifts in his chair and blows smoke up into the air. "Yes, she's okay, she's driving me nuts though, the hormone injections are doing funny things to her; the mood swings, the cravings, she's just... she's... she's goddamned *ovulating.*"

I frown, what the hell is he talking about? *Ovulating?*

"She's fuckin' what?" Bones asks, looking at me for clarification. I can't help him, my head is down and my shoulders are shaking from my laughter.

"She preggos?" Brock asks, bewildered.

Hutch barks out a grunt.

Bones is banging on the table with both his fists now he understands, takes him a second.

Gunner has no idea what's going on. "What's she doing?" he asks across the table.

"I don't fuckin' know, dude," I reply, "but it don't sound good."

"Don't get me wrong, the sex is fantastic, but it's morning, noon, and night. Surely you can't be fertile every fuckin' day," he goes on like we really wanna hear it. *We don't.* "A man needs a little alone time, a little time to himself, you know, to gather yourself, to get shit done; I don't know how much more I can take, she's like a woman possessed."

It's no secret they've been trying for a baby for a long time, but I'm not sure we need all the gory details.

Brock has his head in his hands on the table as his shoulders shake.

"Jesus fuckin' Christ." Hutch actually pinches the bridge of his nose, "This is what happens when your woman gets too big for her boots, boys."

"Yeah, you need to put her back in line," Gunner agrees, smirking, "you know you could start by asking her for your balls back."

Little Lucy has him by the shorts, that much is for sure because Rubble is not joining in with the laughter, oh no, he seems quite serious about his dilemma.

"You idiot," says Hutch, "you had us all fuckin' worried then about Lucy and you're complaining like a little bitch? Come see me when you hit fifty and over, son, then we can have a deep and meaningful conversation about how much sex you won't be gettin', Jesus Christ."

"Oh," Gunner says like he's just realized what's going on, "but wait, I don't get it, you're actually complaining that you're getting it *too much?*" He glances at us all again one by one, confounded, "Is he actually being serious right now?"

Bones slaps him on the back. "Some have all the luck."

Gunner shakes his head in dismay. "Quit complaining! Your ol' ladies hot, maybe you need a break, big boy, from shooting blanks, need me to go on over, help her out?"

Here we go, least he's focusing on Rubble now instead of me.

"You keep talkin', brother, and you'll be drinking out of a straw for the next six months," Rubble replies, dead-pan.

Everyone is so used to Gunner's sick sense of humor that nobody actually takes anything he says seriously, he's probably the only one of us that can get away with that kind of shit without getting his face punched in because we know he'd never do it. He talks trash and brags about his conquests, but out of all of us, he's the most respectful to the women of the club, just not around the table. He's even nice to the sweet butts, probably why they hang off him so much. He needs to be firm, as does Rubble, Lucy has had his balls in a sling for quite some time, we all know it, as much as he tries to deflect and pretend that ain't the case.

Gunner laughs, then adds quite seriously, "Just trying to be supportive, bro."

When everyone is finished laughing, Rubble looks up at us.

"So, yeah, anyone got any jobs that can get me out of the workshop, just for a couple of hours a day? It would be most appreciated."

Brock barks out more laughter. "So much for layin' down the law."

"Suck it up, sunshine," I snort, "some of us have real shit to do, like organizing a ride one of these days."

Everyone nods and grunts yeah's around the table. I look

pointedly at Bones, the Road Captain. "Now the weather is warmer, we should organize somethin' soon."

"Yeah, weather is clearing up nice next weekend," he agrees, "can sort somethin' for Sunday week, everyone in?"

"Yeah," Hutch barks. "Get the girls to call Rusty and we can do a spit roast or something… make a night of it."

I imagine Sienna on the back of my sled and I momentarily stop breathing. Like the time she had my cut on that night, I keep thinkin' about that too. It hits me that I might ask her to come, and if I do, that's gonna send an even bigger message to the boys. One I'm not sure Sienna will appreciate. They'll think I intend to claim her, which is ridiculous. I've only known her a week, she's made it clear she ain't sticking around once Max's house sells and she doesn't want to be 'someone's property'. I hope Max's house drags on forever and a day. Maybe I do want her around, *shit,* maybe havin' a woman in my life ain't as bad as I thought it was gonna be. It seems pretty sweet so far, but then again, these things always are three days in.

"You hear about Gunner's new venture?" I ask Hutch, time for a little payback of my own.

Everyone groans. I've been dying to bring this up in front of everyone. But Gunner's not ashamed, oh no, he'll do anything for a buck, pretty little pussy boy.

"I fuckin' have, and I've got my reservations, I mean, *Sizzle* magazine?" Hutch looks at Gunner with obvious distaste. "Only thing makin' me think it's a good idea is the coin."

"And all the chicks that are gonna be queuing up for a slice of this," he grabs his junk under the table. "I'm gonna be up to my elbows in pussy, read it and weep, bitches."

I shake my head. "We don't need visuals, thanks very much," I bark out, "we've all seen enough profanity at the workshop. Speaking of which, how about you keep your paws to yourself from now on and not grope the office staff."

186

"Ooh, here we go, touchy subject when it comes to a certain little blonde, anyway, she liked it, didn't see her shrugging me off."

"That's because she's too polite."

"Probably gonna buy Sizzle magazine for those nights when she's all alone," he winks while I try not to lean over the table and choke him with one hand.

"Watch it." I point at him.

He laughs out loud.

"You got it bad, bro?" Brock cocks an eye at me.

I huff out loud again. "What are we in high school?"

"He can't answer the question," Gunner cajoles, "which means yes, he doesn't want any of us sniffing around, that's for damn sure."

"That's because I need her to fuckin' sort my shit out at the office." It's such a lie, while I do appreciate that part as well, I much prefer her mouth moaning my name when I pump her hard, the office shit is just an added bonus. Thinking about what I did to her in the kitchen just makes me want to go over there right now, order everybody out, and do her on my desk this time. *Jesus.* Maybe Brock is right… maybe I do have it bad.

"If you ladies are all done talking about your rags and what you're having for afternoon tea, I've just about had enough of today, we're adjourned here unless anyone's got anything actually important or intelligent to say, which is highly doubtful."

'No, boss' rings out from all of us unanimously.

"Good. Steel, go relieve Colt of his duties with Lil if he's gonna help at the Crow tonight. Gunner, make sure one of the girls gets them rooms clean for the boys, and Rubble, for pity's sakes will you pick your chin up off the ground and grow a set, you got married and this is what chicks eventually want… babies. You gotta learn to deal with it and quit nagging."

Once again, Hutch brings us all to heel. He's a good man, a father figure to most of us, somebody we respect. He's done everything for this club and for us as individuals, he gave me a chance when nobody else would, he took Gunner in after all the shit that went down with him and Summer as kids, that crap was bad; enough to make a grown man cry, don't get me wrong, Hutch is a badass too if you get on the wrong side of him, but he's not someone you wanna disappoint. Not ever.

Hutch slams the gavel on the wooden table and we disperse out of the room. First thing I gotta do is go find Colt but Hutch calls me back just as I get up. He waits until the others have left and the door closes again.

"Tell Sienna I expect her there tomorrow night, no excuses."

"You think that's a good idea?"

I know it's not, it's too early for all of that, she'll take one look at us party animals and run a mile.

He cocks a brow. "Worried she'll head for the hills?"

I grunt. "You know what it's like when they're new to the club."

"You want her to stick around?"

I stare down at him, unable to lie but not able to articulate it very well, that's who I am.

"Thinkin' about it."

"She's good for you, a little too pure, but good, she'd make a good ol' lady but she's got a whole lotta spirit, boy."

"Nothin' wrong with that, she just needs to learn."

He nods over to the door. "Right, ask Rubble, he knows all about women with spirit, look where it got him, look where it got me with my ol' lady."

The man has got a point. I can't help a chuckle.

Yeah, that may be true but Hutch and Kirst have made it last and I've also never seen Rubble so content. He was fucked up on drugs when I first came to the club, he got clean with help from Hutch and with Lucy. She put up with a whole array of shit anybody else would have walked away from long ago, it says a lot about a person when they see you at your worst and they don't run away. Whenever something scares Lucy, she just runs right toward it so it doesn't scare her no more. Gotta respect the shit outta that. She's a good woman.

"Get gone, I got shit to do."

I leave, cursing under my breath, I mean I want Sienna to come, but I want her to want it. I want nothing more than to sling my arm around her and make sure everyone knows she's mine while she's in town—nobody else can have her. But I don't want to scare her off; she's already gone off just on what Lily's said about sweet butts. I'm at a crossroads. She needs to know what she'll be getting herself into if things pan out… *pan out? What the fuck?*

Even my own thoughts shock me. Maybe I've been alone too long. But I know that getting my little spitfire here tomorrow might be easier said than done.

16

STEEL

I MAKE an unannounced visit to Lily's salon to relieve Colt of his babysitting duties and also to have a word with my sister since she's been nagging me all week about being followed around, let it be a lesson to her.

I stride through the front door and she frowns when she sees me.

I raise an eyebrow, walking toward the back, ignoring the interested looks I get from some of the older ladies in the salon chairs having girlie shit done to them. I feel out of place in here so there's no need to linger.

Definitely not the place for a biker to be seen.

"Hey, Steel," says one of the girls standing behind a woman with tin foil all through her hair, I think she's called Jessica, I'm not good with names. I hope I haven't slept with her.

I nod as I pass and point with two fingers at Lily, indicating toward the back of the salon so we can talk in private. She rounds the counter and follows behind me.

"What gives?" she barks when we're out of earshot of the customers and staff.

I turn to look down at her. "Nice to see you too."

"Cut the crap, Steel, why is Colt still hanging around?"

I lean against the bench in the small kitchenette staff room. "He's helping," I shrug.

"Helping my ass, I need him gone, he's scaring the customers. Speaking of which, why are you paying me a visit? You usually only come here to lecture me and tell me off."

My little sister is so annoying, she might be cute as a button but no man on earth could put up with her and her never-ending array of shit, of that I am sure. She'd drive them around the bend. And she's pushing it talking to me like that.

"That's insulting, are you saying I'm scaring them too?"

She puts her hands on her hips like she's ready to fight me and I laugh. It's hard to take her seriously but she gets her temper from me.

"It's not funny," she says in an annoyed whisper, "tattooed bikers are bad for business."

I raise a brow and cross my arms over my chest. "Everyone in this town knows you are part of the M.C., so why would they care, and anyway, isn't Gunner going to be doing some piercing here or some shit? How come he's allowed?"

"It's just an idea, and he won't be wearing his cut, and he's pretty to look at and nice, *unlike you,* and not everyone in town wants to walk into Angel's Ink for an ear piercing, this is considered more respectable."

There she went with all her fancy words.

"I'm sure Gunner knows how to pierce a lot of things," I mutter.

She punches me on the shoulder which has no effect. Lily is twenty-two going on forty. She runs this place as her own business and lives in the apartment above. She came straight out of beauty school knowing what she wanted to do and did it, I'm proud of her for that, she works hard but she has a lot of responsibility.

"As long as he's hanging around in club colors, it affects business, no respectable lady wants to come in and get their bits waxed with tattooed, leather-clad dudes looking over their shoulders. Him wandering in and out is making my life difficult."

"Ah, there you go, making *your* life difficult; well, you should have thought about that before going on Tinder lookin' out for strange."

She stares at me agog, then lowers her voice even more. "I wasn't looking for strange!"

"What is it you're looking for, Lily?"

She bites her lip and looks away. "I don't know."

"Well, until you find out, you'll be staying where I can see you. What if that guy *had* raped you, Lil, what then? That was his sole objective; do you know he had ties to human trafficking?"

She shudders and tears form in her eyes. I pull her arm out of the open staff room and move into the storeroom next door where I can shut the door.

I don't know why she's making me out to be the bad guy, I'm the one protecting her because, clearly, she can't look after herself.

"That was hurtful," she says, wiping a tear.

I pull her into an awkward one-armed hug. "You know that if anything really did happen to you, I'd end up in a concrete box, don't you? Because I'd kill them with my bare hands," my tone is softer, I hate seeing her upset.

She sniffles into my shoulder. I don't like making her cry but she has to realize that there's bad people out there, this ain't Kansas.

"It could have happened to anybody," she mumbles into my cut, "I didn't ask for it."

"But it didn't happen to anybody, it happened to you, and you're goddamned lucky you got out of it alive. He had plans for you, Lil, and they weren't pretty, you gotta be smarter than that, you hear me?"

She nods and pulls away from me. "You've ruined my makeup now."

I roll my eyes. "What I do for you, for *all* the girls, is because I know what some assholes out there are like, I do it because I care. You wanna party, you come to Church, you don't go to the Crow anymore, got me?"

She shakes her head. "Not even if my friends are there?"

"Lily," I warn.

She huffs. "You won't let me see anybody at the club though."

"That's because you're better than that."

She narrows her eyes, her trauma suddenly forgotten.

"That doesn't say much for you lot then, does it?"

"What's that supposed to mean?" I balk.

She folds her arms over her chest. "You're saying Sienna is just a hang-around then?"

"You're getting a bit lippy," I warn.

"It's true though, you don't want her hanging around the club, do you?"

"Not without me, no."

"That's exactly my point!" she says with a humorless laugh. "How am I meant to meet somebody when I can't go out, and when I do go out, it's at Church where I can't even talk to anybody without you having a fit."

"You *can* talk to people, long as that's all that happens."

I know she used to have this big crush on Gunner—what teenager around here didn't? I made sure he knew that wasn't gonna happen in this lifetime or the next, and it seemed to have fizzled out, thank God. He's slept with more women than I've had hot dinners and my baby sister wasn't going to be another notch on his belt. I love Gunner like a brother but he ain't for Lily.

"You can't rule my life, Steel, I'm almost twenty-three."

I roll my eyes. "Yeah, and it's a wild world out there, haven't you heard the song? There's a lot of bad everywhere, Lil, even here."

I stare at her and I know I'm being a dick, but deep down, I love her. I held her in my hands when I was thirteen when she was born. I helped my mom out a lot being single and on her own; our dad died just after Lily was born, he'd been part of the club but wasn't a good man. It's not something I like to remember fondly, and I've made sure that as I got older, Lily had the best education and didn't miss out on anything, going to a private boarding school, getting out of Bracken Ridge, but she was a Rebel girl through and through, it was in her veins.

"I'll do you a deal," I say, letting her think she has the upper hand. It's the only way to get some peace.

She brightens momentarily. "Yeah, what?"

"If you meet a nice respectable boy in a nice respectable place, then you can bring him to Church, that way, you're safe and I can keep an eye on you, or more importantly, *on him*."

"Steel, I don't need a babysitter."

Even she knows I can make her life hell if I want to. I'm already doing a good enough job of that.

"And I'll get rid of Colt."

She looks swiftly up at me. "He'll be gone?"

"Yes, if you stop acting like you have no brain when I know you do have one, then I'll take him right now, but don't let me down this time, I have enough shit to do without worrying about you twenty-four-seven."

She doesn't need to think about it. "Done."

That was a bit too quick. I cock a brow again. "You got a date already?"

"No," she says, "but I wanna hear about Sienna, is she coming to the party tomorrow?"

I don't want to discuss Sienna with my little sister.

"Don't know yet, haven't decided."

"You and her getting it on?" She jiggles her eyebrows.

I shake my head. "That isn't something I'm going to discuss with you, Lil, and while we're on the subject, no more club talk either, I don't need you filling Sienna's head with shit."

She has the good grace to look shocked. "I don't know what you mean."

I shake my head. "I mean it, don't go scaring her off and telling her shit about the club or me or whatever it is you did the other day. We've got a good thing going, all you chicks do is bitch and moan when you get together, so just give it a rest. Now, don't you got work to do?"

The women in my life always give me grief. My mind wanders to Sienna and her back-chatting, yeah, that's something we'll have to remedy. I smile at the thought. I do like a little bit of 'spirit' as Hutch calls it, nothing wrong with the chase.

"You gotta give me something!" she wails, ignoring my warning.

I turn her by the shoulders and march her out the door. "I'll give you a biker-free salon, now move your ass."

She shakes her head but I can tell she's happy again. "Love you, Steel," she says quietly, nudging me in the ribs with her elbow.

"Right back at ya, kid."

I find Colt out the back, lugging boxes in. At least he's not slacking off somewhere like Jaxon and Lee tend to do, he's cleaned up all of the area behind the salon too and the car park where all the boxes just get dumped and forgotten about. He's no idea this is his last day as a shit-kicker. He'll make a good brother; I've never had to do anything that bad to him or reprimand him too much, which is a first.

I nod over to Colt as his eyes meet mine. "Hey, prospect. I got a new job for you," I say, walking towards him.

He looks up, ready for action, though anything had to be better than hanging around here all day listening to women moan and groan and gossip.

"Sup, Steel?"

"Stefanie needs some extra hands at the Stone Crow tonight, could be a permanent thing, security detail for a while until things calm down with the cops and the whole saga with Lily, the Crows got a target on their backs."

He looks like he may jump for joy.

"Great," he says. "I'm on it."

I side glance at him. "We'll go by later and I'll show you around, gonna get Jett from New Orleans chapter to set up some new security, got a few jobs comin' up, might make a go of turning one of the rooms at Rubble's into a business. Play your cards right, this could lead to something down the track in your favor."

I wasn't gonna hand no prospect anything today, but tomorrow will be a different story.

"Gotcha, boss, sounds good. Appreciate it."

He seems a little too eager to be out of the salon and I refrain from a smirk at cutting him loose. I can't blame him one bit.

"Finish up with whatever you're doing, we'll meet at the Crow at four."

He looks like he just won the lottery, which prompts me to ask, "Did my sister drive you insane?"

"No, but she certainly likes to talk."

"All women do, stay out of that shit if you know what's good for you."

He dares not say anything too much in case I knock him out. I grunt, then look at him sharply.

"You do anything with any of those girls working in the salon, including Lily?"

He looks like a deer caught in headlights, suddenly panicked. He's fairly wide-set, he pumps iron but isn't tall, he'd challenge me in an arm wrestle but not a fist-fight. And he knows his place, if only all prospects were like him.

"No," he says quickly.

"You thinkin' about it?"

"No, I mean the red-head is cute, but not with Lily… I wouldn't dream of it and not on work time, I didn't even look at her."

I can't help it, I have to play with him for just a little bit longer while he can't talk back, I always fuck with their heads just a little bit.

"She not pretty enough for you?"

His eyes go wide. "No, I mean, she's *very* pretty, obviously, but I'm a prospect, she's a club sister, and I don't want to be castrated and then fed to wolves. I like my nuts where they are."

I'm glad somebody came to work today. This time, I do smirk.

"That's right," I lean in and jab him in the chest. "Just remember that, got me? If you even think about sticking it to any club sister or look at any of them sideways, especially my sister, I'll bury you."

"I wouldn't," he maintains, standing his ground. I know he's telling the truth, he wouldn't dare.

I glare at him and then give him a nod.

"Glad to hear it, now quit your yabbing and get back to it. I'll see you later."

I walk back up the hallway through to the front door.

"Thanks for stopping by," Lily says with a little snicker that I ignore.

"Bye, Steel," calls Jessica, I ignore that too.

Goddamn women.

IT'S LATE when I pull up to Oak park cemetery.

I gun the engine and kick the stand down, Gunner's sled is parked on the gravel by the entry gates. I just got a very upset phone call from Summer, she said today is the anniversary of their mom's death and Gunner's chosen to go on another bender. She doesn't know where he is but I do, I can always find him.

The full moon is high in the sky and it casts a bright glimmer across the graveyard. I find him easily, at his mom's headstone. I've been here before, usually once a year to pull his sorry ass home.

"Gunner," I call out.

I hear him before I see him because he's clattering around noisily, talking to himself in the dark.

"Steel, my man!" he hollers when I approach.

Well, he is *usually* a happy drunk, but I know by now he'll go from that to emotional. Angry? No, he's never angry, I've never even seen him in a bad mood, even when he probably should be. It might even do him some good to get some of that shit out, but then I squint in the dark and realize what he's doing and my heart accelerates. He's loading a gun.

"Gunner, what the fuck are you doing?"

He points toward the headstone; I see there are bottles lined up all along the top. He loads the last cartridge and spins the barrel, then swings the gun up and aims. I immediately duck for cover, he's drunk and out of his mind, aiming at the bottles. Crazy bastard.

BAM. BAM. BAM. BAM. BAM.

Then he lets out a howl when he hits one, it smashes everywhere. He's a crazy motherfucker, he could easily hit the headstone and it could ricochet anywhere. I've seen him do some super crazy shit before, but this takes the biscuit.

When it's over, I look up to him, still crouched down as he laughs.

"You see that, Steel? I got one."

"Gunner," I say slowly. "What the shittin' hell are you doing?"

"Shooting," he says like it's obvious, and then he opens the barrel and proceeds to load it again.

"Hand me the gun," I bark.

He's unperturbed. "What if I don't want to? Come on, Steel, have a go."

I stand as he deliberates his next move. I can get the gun off him without a problem but it may still be loaded.

"I know what I'm doing," he slurs groggily. Even drunk, he looks like a goddamned fallen angel.

"Gunner, hand me the fuckin' gun before you kill somebody."

He gives me an exaggerated eye roll and then reluctantly hands it over. I make sure it's definitely *not* loaded, turn the safety on, and shove it down the back of my jeans.

"Taking you home."

He ignores me, goes toward the headstone, and retrieves one of the bottles, I realize it's full of Tequila; he grabs it and takes a couple of chugs, coughing as it runs down his chin.

Jesus.

"You know why I'm shooting her?" he sneers. Man, I've not seen him this wasted for a long time, he could be high too, he smells like weed.

"Yeah, kid, I know why."

"She did nothing," he states, "she did absolutely nothing!"

Here we go.

I was fifteen when he, at eight years old, and Summer, at seven, came to stay with us temporarily in foster care. It turned out they'd both suffered horrendous emotional, physical, and sexual abuse by their stepfather. When the dude got caught, he put a gun down his throat, their mom committed suicide shortly after by overdose. It's some pretty fucked up shit. Now and again, the trauma rears its ugly head.

"She knew and she did nothing, what kind of person does something like that?"

"She's gone now," I say. "Nobody can hurt you anymore, you know that."

I've always had a soft spot for Gunner, even though we rib each other and fight like cats and dogs, he's literally like my little brother. I taught him how to fight, how to be tough, how to shoot his first bow and arrow, hell, how to talk to girls. I shake my head at the memory.

"Summer still suffers, you know," he goes on, ignoring me. "You'd never know it but she does. I tried my best, I'd hide her in the cupboard and told her not to come out until it was over. He always preferred me anyway."

A cold shiver runs through me. I don't want to hear this, it turns my stomach. I've heard it all before and it never gets any easier. You'd never know by looking at either of them what they'd gone through. They ended up being adopted by a wonderful lady called Gloria, she lives down in Florida now. Gunner came back to prospect for the club the minute he was old enough. Hutch knew, Kirsty and my mom too, but nobody else, not even the brothers. The club saved his life, without Hutch, he'd be in the gutter strung out on drugs, probably follow in his old lady's footsteps.

He looks up at me. "You're the brother I should have had," he tells me with watery eyes.

He looks so broken. A lump forms in my throat as I take in his sorry state.

"The club did more for me than my own flesh and blood, I owe you. I owe Hutch."

He's also always had self-esteem issues, not that you'd think it the way he carries on with the chicks, but it's all bravado. I know him better than anyone.

"You owe us nothing."

"That's not true and you know it."

"We're your family, you know we'd do anything for each other, now quit this shit and let's go home. I'm freezing my nuts off out here."

While he's going off on his next tangent, I try and call my mom but she doesn't pick up, *shit*, she's on night shift all night. I dial Liliana.

"Hey, Steel."

"Hey," I say, stepping away. "I need you at Mom's, Gunner is going through a... *situation.* Mom is on night shift, you okay to watch him? He's been hittin' the bottle pretty bad this time."

It's risky, he may blab to Lily but I know him well enough to know he'll pass out soon and I don't want Summer to see him like this. It'll only bring up bad memories and upset her too.

"Jesus, is he okay?"

"Just meet me at Mom's, okay?"

"Okay, see you soon."

I hang up and dial Colt.

"Hey, Steel."

"Hey, I need you to bring your cage to Oak Park cemetery pronto."

He pauses. "Everything okay, Steel?"

"Yeah, I've got a small situation that I'm handling, just bring the cage and I'll take it from there but I need you to take my sled back to the club."

"Okay, I'm en route in five."

"Thanks."

I text my mom that Gunner is under the weather and he's gonna be in the spare room tonight, Lily's gonna look after him. I then text Sienna and tell her I need a rain check tonight. That sucks big time, I've been looking forward to being with her all day, but the brotherhood comes first.

I press send and turn back to Gunner.

He's sitting on his knees, quiet. Faze two has kicked in.

"Come on, we're gonna get out of here, I'll take you to my mom's." He likes it there.

He doesn't move.

"Gunner?"

"I hate her," he says quietly. "I fuckin' hate her."

I close my eyes. "I know, Guns, I know."

"I'm glad she's dead."

I don't say a word.

"Is that an awful thing to say? Am I an awful person, Steel?"

I pinch the bridge of my nose. "No."

"Where do you think people that hurt children go? In the afterlife?"

I let out a silent breath of air. "I don't know, definitely not to heaven."

He snorts. "Yeah, maybe she's in hell with him, maybe they're burning together, gettin' what they deserve."

I take the bottle away that's resting by his side and tip it out onto the grass. He doesn't need any more tonight.

"I'm sure they are, Guns."

He nods. "Yeah, and when I get there, I'll kill them both all over again."

My eyes go wide. I don't believe in heaven or hell… I don't even really believe in God, I don't think, but now isn't the time for a debate. "You won't go to hell, brother, that I know for sure."

He grunts a snort again. "You think?"

"Nah, Guns, *I know.*"

He laughs out loud, then he stills.

Faze three.

"She just didn't do anything," he whispers. He holds his head in his hands and starts to hunch his shoulders over. It's weird, he never cried as a kid, not once, but I've seen him cry before as a man and it's some heavy shit. He's as badass as they come in everyday life, but like this, he's a different person. Like this, he's just a kid fighting his demons and maybe he'll be fighting them for a long time to come.

He starts to sob. It's a horrible, horrible sound listening to a man do that, I'm not good with this kind of stuff, I can't even handle Lily crying.

What a fuckin' day it has been. I run a hand down my face, I suddenly feel very tired. I want nothing more than to go and snuggle in bed with Sienna… yes, snuggle, because she's warm and soft and she feels like home. Not for the first time today I realize I'm fucked. I want her.

I know Gunner will regret this display tomorrow, he'll try to make it up to me, not that he has to, I understand. I get it. I'm his person. I won't judge him, I never have. But I let him get it all out, he needs this. I stand there with my hand on the back of his cut and let him sob.

17

SIENNA

I'VE SPENT all day deliberating whether to come to the clubhouse tonight, but Steel made it clear he wants me there to meet everyone. I don't know if that's a good idea, it probably isn't, but they are celebrating and I guess I am too in a way—a new beginning. Plus, I would be lying to myself if I said I'm not curious about the club.

I'm starting to feel things for Steel and I don't quite know what to do about it, it's ridiculous, but I don't regret sleeping with him, and not seeing him last night reminded me of how much I've come to suddenly enjoy being here, largely due to him which is stupid, very stupid. And it's not just between the sheets, there's something about him that makes me feel safe, something I haven't known before.

I hitch a ride with Colt after my shift ends and text Steel when we're on our way. I wear some ripped jeans, my thigh-high boots, a bodysuit, and a short faux leather cropped jacket. I keep my hair loose and wavy. I hope he likes what I'm wearing. I don't have to wait long to find out; he's waiting for me when we pull up. I don't even get to the handle and he's there at the door. He pulls me out and into his arms, kissing me hard before I even know what's happening. He smells his usual musky scent mixed with bourbon and cigarette smoke.

Colt quickly disappears.

"What have you done to me, woman?" he says in my ear, his voice is low and husky when he breaks apart from me.

I'm breathless, I feel his hard length press into my stomach. *Holy Hannah.*

"I should spend a night away from you more often," I laugh. He shuts the door and pushes me against it, his lips on my neck.

"Christ, you look good, you wearin' those fuck-me boots just for me, angel?"

So romantic.

"Yes, funnily enough, an M.C. bonfire is the first place I've had the guts to wear them."

I feel him smile into my skin, he's awfully affectionate tonight.

"I like them."

"So, you approve?"

"Didn't say that, said I like them."

I shake my head. "Are we going to make it into the party?"

"My old room is upstairs if you prefer that, or there's always the backseat."

"Steel!" I chastise. "I came here to enjoy the party and mingle, remember? It won't look very good if we just take off upstairs."

He presses his boner into me and I close my eyes, my hands in his hair. "I don't care how it looks, and I don't like the sound of you mingling."

"Chest pounding again," I giggle.

"Luckily for you, I've got some club business to tend to with Colt, otherwise, I would be hauling your ass upstairs and you wouldn't have a say in it."

I bite my lip; I know he likes it when I do that. "Sounds awfully barbaric."

"You don't know the half of it, babe."

I smile and reach up, pulling him back in for a kiss just to tease him because he has to go. "That back seat is looking good right about now," he grumbles.

"Hey, Steel, pull your dick out and get in here!" comes a yell from the clubhouse doors.

I shriek and try to push him off, he doesn't budge and he just ignores the hollering.

"Fuckin' Brock," he mutters.

"Now they think we're going at it in the car park."

"Who cares?" He keeps kissing my neck, nibbling me gently.

"I care!" I stammer.

He snorts. "You worry way too much."

He pulls himself off me, adjusts himself in his jeans, and shakes his head at me.

"I need a cold shower," he mutters. "Get gone inside, Lily and Deanna are at the bar, get yourself a drink with the girls and I'll be there in a little bit."

"Is it safe in there?" I ask as we begin to walk.

"Of course, it's safe," he says like I'm delusional.

"What if they're not at the bar?" I don't want to be wandering around by myself.

"They are, they're waiting for you, and anyway, everyone knows you're with me so you won't get any trouble."

I stop, narrow my eyes, and consider that for a second but we're already through the doors and the pounding music deafens out anything I'm about to say.

Steel looks down at me. He's big and beautiful and, to be honest, I'd love to skip the party and go somewhere with him, anywhere, even if it is up to his old room upstairs which is probably not somewhere I want to be, especially because he's been with other girls up there. But all coherent thoughts go out the window when he looks at me like that. He leans down to my ear.

"We don't bite."

I try and fail to keep my head held high. "That doesn't sound reassuring," I say nervously.

He glances up and nods towards the bar, I follow his eyes and see Lily and the girl who must be Deanna sitting there on high stools, they're trying to get my attention. The main floor is packed; everyone has turned to stare at us, or namely *me*. That's uncomfortable. You can't hear yourself think over the music which is set up outside on a stage behind the bonfire, all the doors are open so the music floods through. Thank God there are no neighbors out here, the speakers are as big as Buicks.

"Can't wait to get you naked," he says in my ear, then he gives my ass a squeeze, pushes me gently toward the bar, and goes the opposite way as I snake through the crowd.

STEEL

I grab an unsuspecting Colt by the scruff of the neck and haul his ass back outside.

Once outside, I let him loose and he looks bewildered.

"What's up, Steel?" he says as I stare at him. I don't say anything for a long time, letting him sweat it.

"I think you know."

He visibly swallows and is immediately on the defensive. "I didn't touch her... you said to bring her here, Steel, I swear to God that's all I did."

I try not to laugh.

Okay, he wants to go there, good, I pretend to take the bait.

"You think about it?"

"No, I swear to God."

"Why, she not hot enough for you now either? Seems like nobody around here is. You think you're something special, prospect?"

"No, I know I'm not special, I didn't touch her, didn't even help her into the car."

"That wasn't very chivalrous of you," I bark. "She's a lady, not that I would expect you to know the meaning of that word."

I want to die laughing, like I've ever been chivalrous in my life.

I hear the boys behind me and Cole's face pales somewhat, he really has no idea how much he's proved himself, and yeah, I am just screwing with him, but it will be my last opportunity to do so after tonight. Nobody will be able to treat him like shit anymore, namely me.

I move so fast that he doesn't even see me coming, I grab onto his shirt and haul him closer to me.

"You gonna put up a fight, pretty boy?"

He steels himself, he wants to, but he won't. I'm a patched member, and he's a prospect, he won't fight me.

"You want me to hit you, what the fuck for? I don't have a death wish, I don't know what this is about, I swear to God, Steel…"

The boys surround us.

I slog him in the face with my fist and he jerks backward, he takes it like a man at least.

I stand over him and haul the lapels of his prospect cut then I yank it toward me.

"You think you deserve this?" I hold my arm out then

208

glance up at Hutch. He's holding Colt's new cut, the club colors facing us. When Colt sees it, his eyes widen, then a slow grin spreads across his face. His jaw is starting to swell already but he seems to have forgotten all about that temporarily.

"Oh, man. Oh, fuck!" he says, running his hands through his hair. "You're shittin' me, right?"

"So, I'll ask you again, brother, you gonna hit me, or you just gonna stand there like a limp dick?"

He shoves me off and I grin wickedly, that's my boy. I know he's a good fighter, a boxer, he has the moves, but he's never been able to use them on any of us. Now is his big chance. He'd better make it good and not show me up in front of the brothers.

"This is the happiest day of my life," he says, circling me, his fists coming up as I jab toward him. If he gets a punch in, I'll buy him a beer, but it's unlikely, I'm a very good fighter, it's why I'm the club's enforcer.

"Better than when you got your cherry popped?" I taunt.

"Oh, yeah."

"There's gonna be plenty of pussy in there for you tonight," I hear Bones shout, laughing ensues, "that's if you don't die first."

"Not if I fuck his face up," I holler.

"Oh, come on, not like he's gonna rival me," Gunner puts in. "I hold the crown for the most pussy around here, he's still wet behind the ears."

Yeah, as suspected, Gunner is over his breakdown from last night and we haven't really spoken about it since.

"I don't know," Brock calls. "The girls like fixing up the broken ones, you might be in luck after all, Colt, plenty of willing and able snatch in there tonight with your name all over it."

I snort as Colt jabs, and I smack him around the back of

the head. "Keep your focus on me, not on them or that cut," I tell him.

He swings again and I pull back, I plow both fists towards him in a fury and he puts his guard up as I pound into him, making contact, but my full weight isn't behind it, I don't want to break his nose and ruin his night, I back off and he swings just as I do and clips me on the chin.

Well, I'll be damned.

I rub my jaw as the boys laugh and yell out, I can hear the unmistakable hoot of Rubble clapping at his attempt, and Colt has a grin on his face that shows me all I need to know about how proud of him I am… how we all are. He's not only proved his loyalty to the club, but he's never mumbled, groaned, or complained once, and there's been some pretty shitty jobs over the last year.

"I've had worse slaps from my mother," I tell him, rolling my eyes then sock him in the side of the face, one more won't hurt.

The boys then join in, Bones punches him in the gut and he's winded for several moments, but that's where the fighting ends, we don't wanna fuck him up too much. Hutch holds the cut out and Colt shrugs into it as he slaps him on the back. I've never seen the kid so happy, he can actually smile now without being questioned why. He can have his way with any of the sweet butts and the blow-ins without fear of being beaten to death.

Hutch brings him in for a man hug. "You're one of us now, brother, we'll swear you in properly later, Steel wanted to get one more punch in while he could."

He looks happy. "I wasn't expecting it, I don't know what to say."

"Well, tongues aren't always made for talking, brother," Gunner puts in, "there's coupla hotties in there waiting to tend to your wounds." He slaps his arm around his shoulders and ruffles his hair.

"Bunch of pansies," I mutter.

Colt looks at me. "You do have one fine-looking woman though."

I go to slap him upside the head again but he moves faster this time. "Watch it or I'll make your right side match your left."

"Shit, gonna need an ice pack on that," Brock observes as we begin walking to the clubhouse doors. "Nothing a coupla sweet butts won't fix for ya, I wasn't kidding when I said they love fixing up a brother, the more fucked up you are, the more attention you get." He gives Colt a shove.

"Yeehaw!" Colt screams out into the night and we all laugh in unison.

"You deserve it, son," Hutch slaps him on the back of his cut again. "I'm proud of you, we all are. Gunner will sort your dues out, and we need to discuss ongoing employment with the security biz we're tryin' to carve out, you think that's somethin' you wanna do long-term?"

Now he's patched in, he'll have to secure full-time employment and contribute to the club coffers as a fully patched member, which means monthly fees, contributions based on earnings, and a gig that will benefit not just him but also the club. He's a free agent now he's not a prospect.

"Absolutely, I'm likin' it."

He's so happy he'd probably agree to be the local Cabana boy if he was asked.

"We'll talk," says Hutch with a grin.

We step inside and Hutch clicks his fingers to two sweet butts who have been waiting in the wings for our arrival.

"Take this newly-patched member upstairs and see to it that he is well looked after," Hutch says as the girls eagerly embrace him and lead him off through the crowded room. On his way through, he gets roars of cheers, more back slaps, and head ruffles as he passes by. I've never seen a man so elated.

"Someone get him a drink first!" I bellow after them. Jesus, he's gonna need it.

I make my way toward the bar, Sienna is sitting with Deanna and Lily, she doesn't see me as her back is to me, so I sidle up and place my large hands on her tiny waist and kiss the top of her head.

Deanna looks at me curiously, I give her a chin lift. The music is blaring so there's no need to converse, and I've done enough talking for one night. I want to take Sienna upstairs, but quite frankly, she isn't the sort of girl that I would usually take up there to my old quarters, but I don't really see any other way around it, I need her. I haven't had sex in almost twenty-four hours and she's goddamn asking for it in those boots.

Before I get the chance, Deanna squeals and says her favorite song is being played. She grabs Sienna by the arm and Lily's too and they all go off to dance. I can see Sienna has had some kind of cocktail as the glass is empty, I've only been gone less than twenty minutes and she's probably hammered already, this won't do, I don't want her drunk.

Watching Sienna in her boots is driving me wild and now I have to watch her dancing as well. I nod for Summer to pour me a whiskey and she gives me a small smile of thanks, I know it's for the other night with Gunner. I wink back at her.

I down the shot in one go and she pours another. "Thanks, sweetheart."

I turn to lean against the bar so I can watch Sienna dance when one of the sweet butts, Jaqueline, sidles up to me. She slings her arms around my neck in an unexpected move. *Shit, what the hell is she doing?* I mean, we've hooked up before but not for ages.

"Hey, big boy, haven't seen you in forever," she purrs in my ear.

I look down at her, she's pretty but nothing special, she has huge big fake tits which are barely contained in the midriff halter she may as well not be wearing. I definitely don't need Sienna seeing other women draping themselves over me and being flirty right under her nose.

Instead of pushing Jaqueline off, which is what I should do immediately, I glance over at Sienna. She's bumping and grinding with Deanna and they are both laughing, they seem to have hit it off. Deanna is definitely a bad influence if I've ever seen one.

"Rumor has it you've got yourself a permanent?" She pouts and leans around to whisper in my ear.

I don't answer.

"I need a good lay, Steel, what can I say? Don't be a stranger now."

My eyebrows shoot up, my eyes still on Sienna.

As if I've called her name, her gaze moves to me from across the room, I watch as her expression changes from happy to, well, slightly pissed off when she sees Jaqueline's arms around me. I watch as Lily, seeing what's going down, gallantly comes to the rescue. She takes Sienna by the wrist, leans, and says something in her ear. Sienna's eyes move to her, some kind of understanding passes between the two.

What the fuck is that all about?

When I don't respond, Jaqueline pulls back and looks at me, she glances down at my mouth but she knows better than to try and kiss me, that is reserved for private only. I never kiss in front of anyone, with one exception… and I broke that rule today.

"Babe?" she murmurs, pressing her breasts and her hips into my body, just in case I'm not getting what she's saying.

In actual fact, I've been so consumed with the exchange going on across the room that I didn't even hear anything she said.

"What?" I huff.

She glances over her shoulder toward where I'm looking.

"You hookin' up with that out of town bitch?"

I look at her sharply. Then I lean down to her ear so she hears me clearly over the throng of music. "I hear you say that again, you'll have something more to worry about like what you're gonna do on Friday nights from now on."

She doesn't release her grasp, and it doesn't put her off, she's a tough chick. She's heard worse. In her eyes, she'll just see it as some 'friendly' competition. But I'm not joking around. I don't want her, I want Sienna.

I've been hard since last night missing her, and now watching her dancing and giving me an evil look is turning me on big time.

"Feels like your mouth is saying one thing, and your dick is saying another." She presses her hips into mine again, I wish she'd stop doing that.

"That ain't for you, sweetheart, now go somewhere else before you embarrass yourself any further, I mean it!"

She pulls back, the smile gone from her face. "What the hell, Steel?"

I don't want to put her in her place in front of people but I will if I have to. I shoot her the death stare and she steps back.

I'm still leaning against the bar when Sienna's eyes flash at me again.

She gives me a cold, un-moving glare. Oh yeah, she's pissed off alright, which I like because it tells me she's jealous. I watch as Deanna takes her hand and they link fingers and dance together, ignoring anyone else around them. I slide the rest of my drink down which Summer has kindly refilled again as I watch them move and groove, ignoring me, laughing and carrying on as Lily bumps her ass into Sienna's, sloshing her drink all over the floor as they laugh. At least she fits in with the girls, that's a relief. They seem to like her and have welcomed her into the sisterhood.

Bones slumps down noisily next to me on the vacant stool, making it wobble. His mohawk is freshly shaved, he's chuffing on a cigarette as he zones in on where I'm looking.

"You still tappin' that, brother?" he nods in their general direction.

I'm sick of everyone sticking their nose in where it's not wanted, but I'm also sick of being coy. *She's mine.*

"Yeah, I'm tappin'. On top, underneath, behind, all over it, brother."

That'll shut him up for five seconds.

He whistles through his teeth. "Fine piece of ass," he observes, "lucky son-of-a-bitch."

I curl one hand into a fist, the other one is still clutching my glass, it's instinctive, I'm not actually going to hit him, the protective urge I have over the women in my life is something that is almost out of my control, it runs through my blood. I roll my head from side to side to distract myself. I watch Sienna's hot little body grooving and shaking, her tits look fucking fine in that top, it's very tight.

"Not just that, she's fuckin' smart too."

He glances at me and I wonder why the hell I blurted that out.

"You goin' soft, brother?"

I snort. "Definitely not." I adjust myself in my jeans just to prove a point and he laughs, almost choking on his beer.

"Every dude in here is checking her out, you gonna stake a claim?"

I glance at him. "I thought I already did."

I don't like the fact that guys are all eyeing her, but I have to expect it with her being new—as long as nobody approaches, we'll all be good.

Wisely, Bones doesn't say anything else but we both watch as Lee approaches the girls, he doesn't know I'm with Sienna but he shouldn't be approaching Lily or Deanna anyway. Oh, this should be good. I flex my knuckles.

"Here we go," I hear Bones mutter with a laugh just as I push off the bar to pay them a little visit. After the look Sienna just gave me and my pent-up frustration, I'm ready to sock somebody in the face, and Lee is my new target.

18

STEEL

SIENNA LOOKS down to stare at the back of the leather jacket that says 'Prospect' as Lee lies face-down on the floor, then her eyes dart back up to mine.

Lee moves around like he may need oxygen, but wisely, nobody goes to help him—serves him right. I contemplate if knocking him out might shock her, but the fact is, we're at Church and he has to be shown his place; there is no way around it.

"Steel!" she yells at me.

I bend down to her ear. "He was askin' for it, trust me."

She stares at me wordlessly. "That wasn't nice."

"You're right, it wasn't." I flex my hands, feeling a lot better now his paws are off her body.

"And neither was that girl wrapped around you at the bar," she says, hands on her hips.

I raise a brow and we have a few moments of silence as we stare at each other before I pull her by the hand off the dance floor, heading toward the back that leads upstairs. I need her alone right now. She can't answer back in front of the boys.

"Why did you do that?" she says as she shrugs out of my hold when we're away from the fray.

"Do what?"

"Punch that guy."

"He's a prospect and he should be working, not trying to hump your leg, he's no right to touch you."

She actually rolls her eyes at me; I move closer to her so she's pressed up against the wall.

"Wasn't that a little bit harsh?" She definitely isn't understanding the whole prospect thing, he's lucky he's still breathing. "To just go around punching everyone?"

I realize I have to tread semi-careful, she'd been involved in some pretty heavy shit since she had that restraining order against her ex, and he did, at some point, laid his hands on her.

But I'm not him.

"It's actually a respect thing, he isn't allowed near you girls and it's my job in this club to make sure that nobody is bothering you or, more importantly, safe, and you shouldn't be mouthin' off at me."

"Oh, right," she laughs without humor, "because it's okay for miss fake tits to put her hands all over you though and whisper sweet nothings in your ear? But not okay for me, right?"

She shouldn't be speaking to me like this and I'm glad we're out of earshot.

I lean in closer. "I got rid of her, didn't I?"

I brush her hair back off her face as she watches me. "I didn't like her touching you, Steel."

I should reprimand her, tell her she can't tell me what to do or who can put their hands on me, but I don't, I don't say any of those things because I don't like it either.

"I've been hard for you for over twenty-four hours," I mutter, my lips close to hers as I close my eyes. "And for the record, I don't want her, told you that before, you shouldn't question me, not gonna lie about it."

"Then why is she coming up to you and throwing herself at you? Have you slept with her before?"

I know from experience not to answer that question, not from a very pissed off female I actually want to be with, not to mention I still wanna get laid tonight… in a few minutes if possible, so jeopardizing that is not high on my priority list.

"Shut up and kiss me."

"Answer me!" she demands, clearly not happy.

"You don't get to demand nothin', sweetheart, you forgettin' you're in my club now? My rules, remember?"

I stare down at her as she glares at me. I smirk then quickly bend and haul her ass over my shoulder and proceed up the stairs, she bangs on my back and shouts wildly at me, *scream all you want, princess, nobody's gonna hear you.*

"Let me go, you Neanderthal!" I hear her yell into my back. She's outraged and I grin because there ain't nothin' she can do about it.

We get to the top of the stairs and I make my way down the corridor to my old room, I find the key on my keyring and unlock it, dumping her on the other side of the door. She's not happy I hauled her up here. Not one little bit.

She folds her arms across her chest as I try not to laugh at her face. She's so cute when she's mad, and boy, she's fired up now.

"You got me, babe," I say, shutting the door and sliding the lock home.

"*Wh-what?*" *she says*, confusion taking over her anger for a second. "You can't just drag me up here and expect me to just fall at your feet."

Here we go again, she always seems to think the worst of me.

I fold my arms against my chest and lean back into the

door. "I don't, that's why you can have me any way you want me."

She stutters again for a second. "What do you mean?"

Her eyes drop to my throat, I know she wants my mouth on her, well, she can beg me for it.

"You wanna be in charge? Then you're in charge."

Her eyes go wide. "You want me to…"

I nod. "Yeah, since I'm just a Neanderthal, right? A dirty low-down biker? You wanna boss me around, babe, boss me here, let's see what you got." I smirk at her wide eyes.

"You threw me over your shoulder!" she cries.

"You barked at me like a junkyard dog, I'm not used to that, princess, can't have it, you got some fire inside you that's for sure."

"Yeah?" she says, I can see she has a whole boatload of liquid courage in the form of Ginger's cocktails. "Well, better get used to it."

I shake my head. "Don't think so, babe, the only way you're gonna be in charge is in the bedroom and when I say so, like right now."

"Not in front of your *brothers* though, right? Wouldn't want to ruin your reputation and all," she fires back.

Oh, she has a bit to learn with the lip, and I want to be the one to teach her smart mouth, *yeah, that could be fun.*

"Yeah, that's how us cavemen work, haven't you heard?"

"If the shoe fits."

"How many drinks did you have?"

She bites her lip. "Two."

I bet they were double strength, she's definitely got some gumption from somewhere.

I come toward her. "You can be a spitfire in here, babe, but not down there."

"What if I don't want to?"

I look down at her, she's so goddamn beautiful, my chest

lurches at the sight of her and the tent in my pants ain't getting' any smaller.

I cock my head to one side. "You don't want to?"

"I didn't say that, it's just hypothetical."

"You can walk out that door, babe, but I don't think you really want that, do you?"

Her eyes drop to my lips but I'm not gonna cave, she can show me she wants this.

After a few moments, she shakes her head. "I don't want to go."

I refrain from a smug expression, she might just wipe it off.

"Show me."

She gulps. "I don't know how."

I can't help it, I brush a hand down the side of her face gently. "Just do what you want to me," I tell her in a low voice, "I won't stop you."

"You have to do what I say?" she questions in a whisper.

I grin. "In here? Yeah, babe, I do. I want you bad, so come on and stop teasin' me, tell me what you want and I'll do it, take what you want, princess, make me yours."

I'm so turned on and excited by this that I'm amazed at my willpower. I normally would be on top of her going to town by now. Instead, I stand, hard as a rock, hoping she'll take me up on the challenge. Oh, I don't mind these kinds of games at all, not one bit.

"Where do you want me?" I ask with a lopsided half-smile, and then I wait.

❦

SIENNA

I stare at the brute towering over me, submitting to me, and I can barely breathe. He's standing there waiting for me to direct him, and he's not touching me. *I want him to touch me.*

"Is this where you bring other girls?" I say.

His eyebrows crease in response.

"Hasn't been that many lately."

"Thought you said three weeks was the longest."

One side of his mouth turns up. "I may have under exaggerated on that."

Well, this could be interesting if I let it.

He's willing to do anything I say. Hmm, I could work this to my advantage.

I glance down his entire length, he's a God. "Take your cut off," I say.

"Yes, ma'am."

He proceeds to do so and hangs his jacket on the back of the chair. His eyes are dark as he watches me.

I lick my lips. "Pull your shirt off too." He does the same and lays it over the top of his cut. I take a good long hard look at his body from his face to belt buckle. My, my, he's a sight. His tatts are so badass, I think he knows it as he looks up at me with sexy eyes.

"You likin' this a little too much, babe?"

"Boots," I say, ignoring him.

He makes a snorting sound but complies, kicking them off, then ultimately bends to straighten them up neatly—the neat freak that he is.

"Undo your jeans."

He does.

My heart accelerates, he's turned on too. I'm so glad I had two cocktails or I'd never have the gall to do this.

With our eyes locked, I shrug out of my jacket and pull

the bodysuit open at the front. My black lacy bra comes into view and I watch as he swallows hard, looking down at me.

"Pull them off, boxers too."

I watch as he follows my orders, hoping he'll just take over and put his mouth on me, but he doesn't, once they're folded up too, his gaze is back on me.

I look down at his wood and shake my head at his length; he's hard as a rock and ready to go, his dick hangs heavily between his legs.

"Somebody did miss me," I breathe.

"Oh, yeah."

"Touch yourself."

He grabs his dick and starts to pull on it, his eyes still on me. I bite my lip and proceed to reach around to my clasp and undo my bra. I fling it at him and he catches it in his other hand. His eyes shift down to my breasts as I touch them, pushing them together like he likes.

"You getting off on watching me?" I purr, being in charge is fun, I think I like it.

"Fuck yeah, pull on them."

"Shoosh," I say, his eyes flick to mine and they crinkle from his half-smile. "I'm in charge, remember? Pull on it harder."

He does and the sight of him jacking himself off while watching me is such a beautiful thing that it may be ingrained into my brain forevermore. His tight torso flexes with every move.

"Come here," I say, "put your mouth on me."

He smirks, still holding himself, and stalks toward me. "Where do you want my mouth?"

I motion to my breasts as he drops to his knees and takes them in his hands. He rubs his thumbs over my hard peaks and I close my eyes as he takes one into his mouth and sucks, then repeats the motion on the other side. I'm lost when he does this.

"Take your pants off," he tells me.

"You don't get to decide that, lover boy," I say sweetly, taking my job a little too seriously. I reach down and grasp his length in my hand and he shudders. He's so hard it's ridiculous.

"I think I like you bossy," he tells me in between sucks.

"Put your hand in my pants."

He moves his mouth down my torso and pushes me back toward the bed, he follows me on his knees, he reaches and undoes my top button as he shrugs my jeans to my knees and I sit down on the edge of the mattress.

He pulls my lace panties aside and rubs two fingers through my heat. His eyes dance with mischief.

"Very wet, babe, you sure you don't want my mouth there?"

I don't get time to answer, he rubs my sweet spot back and forth lightly with his fingertips, then he circles around and around until my breathing hitches and I know I'm going to lose it.

"*Jayson...*" I wail. "Oh, God, *yes, yes, yes!*" I throw myself back onto the bed as the convulsions run through me and he dips a finger inside and pumps me slowly in and out, curling his fingers, his pace is maddening. I feel him unzipping my boots and then he pulls them and my jeans off as well as my panties. He replaces his fingers with his mouth as he lifts my legs and plants my feet on the bed so I'm open to him. His tongue licking me and sucking is my undoing and it doesn't take long before I'm there again, bucking off the bed like a mad woman, especially when he curls his fingers up inside me again, taking me to new heights that I've never experienced before. I'm so lost in all the sensations going on, I forget where I am.

"You like that, princess?"

I have no words, literally, I'm shaking. He kisses my thigh, his beard scorching my skin on every single touch.

"Where you want me now?"

"Standing," I pant.

"You on the pill?" he asks suddenly. My eyes go wide. I shake my head.

"That's something we might have to remedy, babe, feels better without a wrap, for you and for me. I'm clean. I've always worn one."

"Shut up and put one on," I say. His chest rumbles from his laugh as I watch his naked ass go over to the chair and he fishes out his wallet. He rolls one on by the time he gets back.

"Kiss me first." I reach for him.

He comes over the top of me and we kiss almost violently, I can feel his hard length pressing against my thigh, his tongue commands mine, I clutch onto his neck like I may never let go and moan into his mouth.

"I want you standing," I manage before he smirks into my skin again, pulling back to look at me.

"You're kind of enjoying this, aren't you, my little spitfire?"

I shrug. "Me being in charge may not happen again, so better make the most of it."

"Oh, it'll be happening, tie me up for all I care."

My brows rise in surprise. "Now you're giving me ideas."

He stands and pulls me back down the bed, holds my ankles with my legs resting against his chest, and slowly slides into me. It's a different position but it feels oh so good. He takes it slow—in, out, in, out—he closes his eyes.

"Look at me," I say, suddenly I'm hell and ready. Thank you, Tequila Sunrise.

"Can't, babe," he says, his eyes squeezed shut. "I'll lose it if I do."

"Better not, I'm not done yet... *oh, God! Oh, God!*" He adjusts his hips just as I say the words and gives me a thrust at the end; I want him to quicken the pace because this is maddening. I come hard and when I open my eyes, I see he's looking down at where we're joined as he continues his torture.

"Jesus, fuck," he mutters. "You look so good, babe, this is mine, you hear me? *Mine.* I want you so bad and I'm gonna have you."

I watch with satisfaction at his undoing. It's a glorious thing to witness.

"Flip me over," I say breathlessly. *Who am I?*

He pulls out, flips me over, and pulls my hips back then pushes my head into the duvet, my ass is in the air, then sinks back in, I hear him let out a hiss. "You're killin' me, babe."

He slides in and out as my hands clutch the duvet and hang on. Ah, God, it feels so good, he's big but he always makes sure I'm ready for him before he devours me. He's such an unselfish lover.

"I want you, Steel, harder."

He grunts and picks up the pace, his hands grip my hips firmly. "What's my name, babe?"

"Ahhh... *Jayson.*" It comes out like a never-ending moan.

"Tell me."

"Harder, I need you harder, baby, give it to me."

He complies, grunting, thrusting hard, so hard the bed begins to bang against the wall.

"So tight, Sienna, so beautiful, you're a naughty girl turnin' me on like this, you in those boots, goddamn, I want you naked wearin' only those next time."

I cry out again as he reaches under my torso and flicks my clit with his fingers. I convulse like I've never done before; I'm seeing stars for several seconds in the aftermath.

"Tell me I'm yours," he moans.

"Jayson..."

"Tell me I'm yours, I'm gonna come so hard."

"I'm yours!" I pant.

He grunts once, twice, then stills as I feel him let go as he convulses with a shudder ripping through him, he moans the most beautiful sound I've ever heard.

He squashes my butt down to the bed and collapses on top of me. We're so hot and sweaty, and thank God for the music or they'd have heard us on the other side of town.

I don't think I've ever climaxed so hard. Sweat covers my entire body.

"That was so hot," I say, my words mumbled into the duvet. He lifts up and then pulls out and rolls off me, landing at my side.

"You're gonna give me a heart attack," he says, completely out of breath. I've given him a workout then, good.

"I like being yours," I say before I can help it. He rolls on his side as I put my head up, still face-down.

"This is a thing," he tells me, brushing my wet hair off my face.

I let out a slow breath. "Maybe it is."

He kisses me chastely. "Don't make me wait for sex for twenty-four hours again."

I poke him in the arm. "Technically, you were the one who stood me up, remember?"

He smiles softly, he looks... *happy.*

"Never wanted anything so bad," he mutters as his lips hover over mine. "What spell have you put on me, Sienna Morgan?"

"The same one you put on me?" I breathe.

He smirks, runs a hand down my arm, and cups one cheek of my ass. "Think about stayin'."

I look at him with wide eyes. "Steel... I-I don't know."

"Think about it, that's all I'm sayin'." He kisses me quickly and gets up wandering into the bathroom, I hear the toilet flush a few moments later and the faucet run.

What is happening here? This is more than just sex, even I can admit that. We have a connection, he feels it too. *He's asking me to stay.*

What have I realistically got waiting for me back home? The thought of leaving him and being without his warmth makes me shudder. *I'm falling for him.* It hits me with full force.

I mean, how does that even happen after such a short space of time? I have no fricking clue but I know how I feel, or maybe I'm just still in the throes of the orgasm after-shocks and I'll agree to anything. That's a possibility, the man can move. But he's very sweet too, he takes his time, makes sure I'm satisfied, and in his own gruff way, he seems to enjoy himself.

He wants me to think about staying.

For the first time in my life, I'm at a crossroads and I have no idea what to do.

19

STEEL

Days turn into weeks and things just seem to get better and better. My office shit is getting cleared, there's overdue money rolling in and I've got a hot little office girl bossing me around, well, in the bedroom anyway. Life couldn't be sweeter. Rocky has turned into a little dude, he's put on weight and even lets us pat him, Sienna has been taking him and Lola for walks to the park and she takes photos of them nonstop.

I don't know when this happened, this aching need that I have for her that's taken over me. She's even been upstairs into my apartment, which she likes, and I've fucked her in my bed too, I let that sink in for a few days before I did it again. She's not needy like other girls are, she doesn't expect anything from me but I find myself wanting to give her it all. I wasn't looking for anyone permanent but it seems I was looking for so much more, I just didn't know it. I don't know where it leaves us but at least she hasn't run away.

It's Wednesday night and I'm locking up the garage after another crazy day. Sienna's finishing up too, my little pocket-rocket has everything filed nicely and my office doesn't represent a bomb exploding anymore. She hasn't said anything more about staying and I haven't asked her again, I don't want to pressure her.

"I've got something to show you, if you're up for a drive," I say, leaning on the side of the door jam, watching her.

She wears these glasses when she's on the computer for a long time, I can't get enough of her in office attire. She's had to stop wearing anything low-cut because I don't want anyone looking at her tits except me, and I've been paying them good attention for the last two weeks, we haven't spent one night apart.

"Oh yeah, big guy? Better be something I haven't seen before."

I purse my lips and move in, leaning over the desk, she lifts off the chair and we kiss over the top of it. It's mushy and pathetic but if I start, I'm not gonna be able to stop so I pull back.

"I gotta get the dogs ready though."

"We're going out?" she seems disappointed.

"Don't worry, it'll be worth it." I give her a wink and disappear.

I haven't shown her my cage yet—a fully restored 1951 GMC 100 black pick-up, it's basically a hard-on on wheels. I restored it myself painstakingly and it took me over a year in between jobs. I can't wait to take her on the hood.

"This is your ride?" she says when I switch the lights on next door in the second garage that we use for storage.

"Yep." I'm just a little bit proud.

"Wow, this is so cool, it's very you, very badass."

I snort. "Well, it took me over a year and a lot of coin, but it came up good."

She turns to look at me. "You did all of this?"

"Everything except the paint job."

She looks bewildered. "No wonder you like restoring if this is how old things can look with a bit of TLC."

Speaking of which, the cars from Max's are in storage until an auction comes up, I want her to get the best price possible, and right now isn't a great time for selling but things will turn around.

"If you have the patience, time, and money, yeah."

"Could you do up Max's cars?"

I shrug. "It would take a lot of time, I don't have the resources right now or the guys to work on restoration full-time."

"But could you expand? If you did this, you clearly have a talent."

One day, I'll show her my portfolio of cars and bikes I've done up, I'm pretty proud of it, but time is of the essence at the moment and we need to get on the road.

I shake my head, pick up Rocky, and put him on the front seat, Lola jumps up all by herself. They both have little woolly onesie outfits on, the nights can get chilly where we're going.

"One day," I shrug, "get in."

I drive us up to the ridge near the Canyon, it's off a dirt road, it's got one of the best views in Bracken Ridge and as being in a state park, there's a lot of places to stop and look at the view. People come in the summer time with picnics and to hike the gorges. This time of year, there aren't many tourists or campers, so when we get to one of my favorite lookouts, I'm happy to see it's deserted. I reverse park so the boot is facing the edge of the Canyon and I shut off the engine.

"Wow," Sienna says as I turn to her.

"Yeah, babe."

The sunset is gonna be a beauty tonight; it's already a

mish-mash of orange and pink as the sun slowly makes its way toward the horizon.

I jump out and come around the back to her door as she climbs out. She doesn't get far as I push her back into the closed door and claim her mouth.

"What was that for?" she says when I eventually pull back, she's breathless.

"Do I need a reason?"

She puts her arms around my neck and smiles. "Never."

I yank her hand and pull her to the back of my cage, I move to the cab and pop the back ledge down and unhook a double swag. I roll it out in the back as I turn to her; she's assessing me with a smug smile.

Without words, I lift her up by the hips and plop her on the edge, her legs swing off the side. We have a perfect view from our position, and a comfy place to sit and lie when we make out while the sun sets.

It's beautiful up here with nothing but the desert for company. Next to riding, this is my other guilty pleasure, the thing that I enjoy the most. Despite appearances, I feel more like myself when I'm out in nature, at one with the landscape and the fresh air. There's nothing like feeling the wind in your hair, on your face, and the smell of the earth up in the ranges. I feel totally free here, like all my stresses or worries can just melt away.

Up here, you can do anything, be anything, but most importantly, you don't have to do anything at all, just live in the moment, and I've been flying by the seat of my pants for a while now. I push the back window down so the dogs can pop their heads out if they want, which Rocky does, I give him a big scruff around his face, Lola is already asleep, she's seen too many sunsets to care.

I jump up next to Sienna and the whole car rocks, she

giggles. I set the bag I'm clutching, with the burritos I bought on the way, next to us.

She's looking straight ahead and I see Bracken Ridge Gorge has turned on another skyline of absolute magic. It's stunning tonight.

The sky before us is turning from the brightest of orange as the sun slowly disappears to a smoky peach streak across the horizon that will almost always turn into the most delicious shade of pink. Colors no painting could ever capture.

I glance at Sienna. She's prettier than any sunset and she seems pleased by my impulsive surprise.

"Like it, princess?"

She nods. "Yes," she's still looking in awe at the show nature has put on, it's a beauty, "it's the most beautiful thing I ever saw."

I rest my forehead on the side of her head. "No, you're the most beautiful thing *I* ever saw."

I feel her smile; she moves her hand to my leg. "Flattery will get you everywhere."

"I certainly hope so."

I lift off and swing an arm around her as we sit in companionable silence for a while, just watching, listening, the crickets are out in full force and it feels for the first time in a long time like I've not got a care in the world.

"Thank you," she whispers, it's barely audible.

I move my head sideways. "What for?" I lift my chin.

I brush a hand over her cheek.

"For this, it's better than anything I could ever imagine."

I pull down and lean back on one elbow and look up at her. "You sure about that, angel?" I can't keep the insinuation out of my voice.

She laughs. "Well, *almost* everything."

I know right then and there that I'm in love with her. It fucking hits me in the face like a runaway freight train. I don't even push the feelings down, I'm done with that. I'm Jayson Fucking Steelman and I take what I want.

They say that's how it happens, you just know, and I always thought the guys that said that were pussies. Now, as the realization hits me, I am completely at her mercy. It's a dangerous place to be—vulnerable. Somewhere deep inside me, I know it's right though, we fit.

"Come here and give me some sugar," I say to distract myself.

She leans down and presses her lips to mine. She has the lips of an angel.

I hold her closer, not letting her escape, my tongue is in her mouth and I hear her breath hitch as we kiss like teenagers. I pull her down so she's on top of me; my hands are greedily pulling the back of her shirt out of her jeans and there is no mistaking my hard-on pressed into her stomach.

"Steel, we're gonna miss the sunset." She bites her lip which just about sends me over the edge.

"You feel that, babe?" I say, ignoring her, bucking my hips up into hers.

"I always feel it."

I kiss her nose then look up at her, the smile reflecting back at me is better than any sunset, greater than any masterpiece. She's the vision.

"Then I'd better make it my best, hadn't I, baby?"

WE LAY in bed as I lie and stare at the ceiling, it's late. We made out in the back of my car for a while, kissing, touching, and rubbing and came back here to finish things off, several times. She likes my place and the bed is bigger here, plus she can also cook which is great because I can't. The sheet rides low as I take in her body; she sleeps naked now because I don't allow clothes in my bed. I trace her bare skin with my finger, her skin is so soft. She stirs under my movement and blinks a couple of times then smiles, snuggling up closer to me. She takes my breath away.

"Never knew you'd be a snuggler when I first laid eyes on you," she says, stifling a yawn.

"Never knew you'd be a giant pain in my ass either," I chuckle and kiss her on top of her head as she rests it on my chest.

"You don't seem to be complaining."

"That's because I'm usually busy shuttin' your mouth up."

"Did anyone ever tell you how romantic you are?"

I kiss her hair. "Go to sleep."

She rubs her hand down to my abdomen, she seems to like that area, she spent a lot of time in that vicinity tonight in the back of my pick-up. I stir at the memory.

"You're the one who woke me up," she reminds me.

I grunt into her hair. "Not my fault you're a light sleeper."

"I sleep just fine; you take up all the bed."

"You just can't keep your hands off me, it's alright, babe, you're only human."

We both look down as my appendage moves on its own accord against her leg and she giggles.

I roll over her and shut her up with my mouth, then settle between her thighs.

"How do you expect me to keep my hands off you when you have a body like that?"

I kiss her and she still tries to giggle while I'm doing it. "No, seriously, have you always been such a smooth operator? Do you say this to all the girls?"

"Shut up."

"That's a no then."

I buck her with my hips. "You remember what happens to lippy girls, they get punished."

She pushes against me with her hips. "I think I like your form of punishment."

I snuggle into her neck then come back to her face.

"What?" she says, pushing my hair back out of my face. "Something on your mind?"

My heart races a little. "I want you to come on the run with me on the weekend," I blurt out.

"I came last weekend, didn't I?"

That she did and it was a surprise to everyone. Not claiming her yet, but for damn sure I'm thinkin' about it, she just has to get used to the idea of being on the back of my sled and being my woman. Things have changed rapidly in a short space of time.

I love her like this, underneath me, looking up with those big blue eyes. She's no idea how sexy she is.

"You think about what I said at the bonfire, 'bout staying?"

She's got nowhere to go right now pinned beneath me, so she has to give me some sort of answer.

"Steel," she whispers. "You said you'd give me time." She runs her hands down my back and I move my face to her neck and kiss it lightly.

"You know I'm not a very patient man."

I know she just rolled her eyes at me. "This is hard for me."

"That's because you don't let me in," I say, kissing her pulse point as her hands still. She knows what I'm referring to; every time I bring it up, she shuts me down. I have to know. I *need* to know, and I can't exactly tell her I know about the battery and assault charges. *Why won't she tell me?*

"It's not something that I really like bringing up, it's in the past."

I murmur into her neck. "But it's stopping you from goin' forwards, babe, you know it is."

She bites her bottom lip and then lightly begins to stroke my back again.

"I don't want us to have any secrets, so if I tell you something secret of mine, will you tell me about what happened to you?"

All she's given me is that small piece of information the day we were out at Max's garage, but it's not enough to really know what went down.

She looks like she's considering it. "What's your secret?" she asks quietly.

I brush one knuckle over her cheekbone.

"I did bad things when I was deployed in the Middle East," I say, watching her eyes go wide. "Really bad, awful things, probably not going to heaven kind of things."

She blinks a few times, her voice low. "What kind of things do you mean?"

"I hurt people."

"Did you kill them?"

"Yes," I say. I never talk about my deployment; some things are just too raw.

"By accident?"

I shake my head. "No, but if it makes it any easier to digest, they were the bad guys, they deserved it and I don't want to get into details about all of that because it'll just dampen the mood, but shit like that sticks with you forever. I came back after I was discharged but I split with my ex shortly after."

"Why?"

"She was cheating on me, the only reason we got married was because I knocked her up, she lost the baby but I doubt there even was one, she just wanted to trap me and have the life of a military wife until it didn't suit her anymore."

Her lips part but she doesn't say anything.

"But her leaving was the best thing that could have

happened to me, I started prospecting, went back to my trade, worked all the shitty shifts I could to save up coin for my first ride, then I did it up real nice, that's when I got the love of restoration in my veins, makin' something new again after it's been beaten up."

"Do you miss it, the military?" she asks.

"No, though I miss some of my brothers, we had some tough times, things that scar you for life, I told you about the PTSD and I got night tremors for a long time, it's not a life I want to go back to."

"Did your ex scare you off relationships for good?"

I smirk. "Yeah, until you came along."

She kisses me but it's gentle, not demanding like it was earlier.

"What about you?" I say, lifting up again.

She sighs. "Can't we just get down and dirty?"

There she goes, deflecting again. "I think my dick can wait a little bit longer, princess."

She sighs. Her eyes look away and cloud over. "I met him at work." She stills her hands again. "He was really nice at first, good-looking, well to do, very smooth, he had a way with women... knew how to talk."

Already, I want to punch him in the face.

"We dated for a year and then I moved in with him, things were good for a while, then over the course of time, he began to change. He'd work longer hours, drink a lot, I think he started using cocaine, when he was like that, he'd be insulting and say some horrible things but it was just verbal stuff, I could never do anything right in his eyes."

Her body shakes underneath me. She's afraid of him, it's like all the warmth has left her body.

"Did he hurt you physically, princess?" Of course, I know the answer to that.

She swallows hard. "He grabbed me once, really hard, it

left a mark, and then another time when I answered him back in an argument, he slapped me, then he'd do it a few times as if enjoying the sound it made, it got worse after he'd been on the booze. The next day, he'd be so sorry, he'd cry afterwards. I told myself it was a slap, not a punch, he didn't beat me, so I was okay, he was sorry, he didn't mean it…"

She pushes up off the bed so she's sitting up slightly, resting back on her hands; I lift off a little but remain over her. She's shaking again; I pull the sheet up over us.

"You're afraid of him," I say, my fury is palpable. I really wanna find this son-of-a-bitch and cut his nuts off.

"I was for a long time, it was like living with a monster, never knowing who you'd get, walking on eggshells every day and an outsider looking in would think we were the perfect couple, he drove all my friends away so I had nobody to turn to, nobody to talk to, just him. On the last day, I saw something just snapped in him, that night, I'd had enough of his lying and his violent mood swings, that's when he hit me, punched me this time, he…" she trails off and I rub my hands down her arms.

"It's alright, princess, nobody's ever going to hurt you again."

She nods, wiping a tear before it falls. "He went crazy, throwing things, breaking shit, it was terrifying, the neighbors heard and called the cops. I was lucky, I got out. I have a restraining order against him and he got charged for battery and assault, spent six months in jail, lost his job, his friends, respect from his peers, it ruined his life."

I feel so much anger I have to hold back in fear that she'll think it's directed at her. I want to kill that crazy bastard. "Have you heard from him since? Has he tried to contact you?"

She looks down and averts my eyes. *Shit, she has then.*

"He's found my number a couple of times, I don't know

how but he always seems to find me, and when he does, I get a mouthful of abuse about what he's going to do to me when he finds me, I think he's all talk, just trying to scare me."

I realize I have to get Linc onto this crazy son-of-a-bitch and fast. I have to track him down and shut him down. I wish she'd told me about this sooner.

"So, you're living in fear?"

"Not since I came here, he doesn't know anything about Max because I never spoke about him, he was dead to me even back then."

I look at her sad face and I want to take all of that away from her so she doesn't feel it anymore.

"Sienna, it doesn't have to be that way, it wouldn't be that way with me, I would never hurt you, you know that, don't you?" I think back to some of the situations she's seen me in and they were pretty violent.

She nods. "Yes, I know, Steel, you're a good man, you protect the women in your life, I know that."

She clutches onto my arms for dear life and I want to take it all away, I really do.

"Let me make you forget," I whisper. I kiss her stomach as her eyes drop to mine.

"Then do it, make me forget, *please*," she says as she slides back down underneath me, her hands in my hair as her lips find mine and I settle back into her hips.

And I do make her forget, all of it, until the light of morning comes.

20

SIENNA

Cocktail Tuesday is somebody's genius invention. I'm meeting the girls tonight for happy hour, it's the most fun thing I've done with a group of girls in as long as I can remember. It's been almost a month now and things have been going from strength to strength, there's even been a couple of people looking through Max's house.

Jett, from another club, has been helping show him and Colt the basics for the new shop.

Rocky's settled in and that makes me happy, I can't say for sure but I'm certain that he's gonna be a foster fail. The little guy has really come out of his shell and shown his funny little personality.

It really is so normal. We work, I'll make dinner, we hang out watching a movie or drive out to the Canyon, and the sex has not slowed down—oh no, it hasn't. The man is a God. I've never been with anyone so good in the sack, he can be so tender when he wants to be and so rough and ready too, depending on the mood.

I step into Zee Bar which is the classiest bar in Bracken Ridge. Lily waves me over to her table and I see Lucy,

Deanna, Kirsty, Angel, Summer, and a couple of other girls I don't know.

"Sienna!" Lily hugs me. "You seriously have to get some of these cocktails in you."

"Hi! I reply. "Hey, girls."

"Hi," they say in unison.

"Sienna, this is my friend, Katy, and this is Jessica from the salon," Lily says as she sits back down. They seem nice, we say hi and I take a seat in between her and Angel.

"What are we celebrating?" I ask as Lily hands me a blue cocktail and clinks my glass.

"Tuesday," Lily shrugs.

Ting, ting, ting. "Well, actually, speaking of celebrations," Lucy begins, dinging the side of her glass with a fork, "I do have some news, now that everyone's here."

That statement alone warms my insides, I've not had a group of friends like this in a very long time, it's kind of comforting.

"Ooh? Do tell," Deanna says, rubbing her hands together, settling herself in for some juicy gossip.

"Wait," Kirsty says, holding her palm up, "this isn't another one of those kinky sex stories again, is it? If so, please pass me a bucket now."

"Yeah," Katy chimes in, "I so do not need another visual of Rubble in handcuffs."

Lucy rolls her eyes as everyone makes puking noises.

"Shut up, the lot of you," she chastises, "you're ruining my moment here, ya'll."

Angel snickers next to me. "Get on with it then, happy hour is *one* hour you know."

She smiles widely and then shouts out, "We're having a baby!"

Everyone gasps, which is swiftly followed by shrieking, gushing, and claps and then hugs all around the table. I feel joy flourish my chest that Lucy's waited to include me in her happy news, that is so sweet of her. We've been getting along well and she stops by once or twice a week to see how I'm going with everything.

"I'm so happy for you," I say when I get in line to hug her, Lucy's in her element; she's beaming like the cat who got the cream, dabbing her eyes with a tissue. I know from what she's shared with me that they've been trying for a while.

"How far are you along?" Summer asks.

"Not far, just past the six-week mark but I couldn't wait to tell you girls, Rubble's freaking out but he'll be alright, just as long as it's not a girl."

We all laugh.

"Not sure he gets a say in that," I reply with a smirk.

Kirsty orders more of the same from a passing waiter, these really are nice and I have no idea what's in it. "That's such great news, sweetheart, you've waited so long for this, I'm so happy for you."

Lucy's eyes well up with tears.

"Our first official club baby in what, twenty years?" She laughs.

We all hoot and clink drinks.

"Wait, does that mean Rubble's going to be without sex while your preggos?" Deanna asks.

Lucy looks at her strangely. "Why would it mean that?"

"Don't guys go off you when you're like up the duff?" she goes on. "Like I've heard some guys get weird about it, don't want to touch you."

"He better not," Lucy replies very matter-of-factly, "it'll be his funeral if he does."

"Hutch didn't," Kirsty says with a sigh. I have to say, for a fifty-something-year-old woman, she's one hot mama. "In fact, he couldn't get enough of me."

"Eww, Mom," Deanna grumbles. "Shut the hell up, that's disgusting."

"What, sweetheart? Your father is one very hands-on, very sexual man... what can I say."

Deanna makes puking noises behind her as we all laugh. "That's just wrong," she moans, trying to block her ears but it's too late. "Stop talking please before I have to bleach my brain."

Kirsty laughs with the rest of us and shrugs like it's no big deal.

"Have you got any names picked out?" Angel asks. "I have a cool kids' name book I can lend you, I got it given when Rawlings was born, it really helped, though everyone ribs me about her name every frickin' day."

"Thanks, Angel, haven't got anything picked out yet but I like tons of girls' names, nothing for a boy yet," Lucy says excitedly.

"Are you going to find out the sex?" Summer asks.

Lucy shrugs. "Rubs wants to, I don't know, I don't care what it is, I just want to get through this one with a healthy baby at the end."

The table falls quiet.

Deanna pats her arm. "It's going to be okay, we're all on board to help whichever way we can."

Everyone murmurs and nods and looks at Lucy hopefully. She hasn't gone into details with me as I hardly know her, but I can see how much she wants this.

"You won't be needing this then," Deanna laughs, dragging the cocktail from under Lucy's nose, she hasn't had a sip of it, and Deanna asks the waiter for a double shot of lemonade for the pregnant lady.

We fall into easy conversation and nibbles arrive for the center of the table, I guess a little bit of food should be consumed so we don't get too merry.

It's nice inside, quite classy, there's jazz music playing but not too loudly, though nobody is making half as much noise as our table. It's a pretty upmarket bar; the clientele are dressed in suits and business attire, like they've left work for the day, all except Gunner. He's unmistakable. He breezes through the door and grins as he sees us, if not a little bashfully, he wanders over to our table now he's been spotted. I wonder what he's doing here, it isn't exactly your typical biker hangout bar.

He's dressed in his usual cut and has a long-sleeved black tight top on underneath, his hair is slicked back off his face like he's made an effort. Heads turn his way; he's got the whole bad-boy biker look down pat, and the swagger to go with it. Lily's right, he is too pretty to be a biker. He stops at the end of the table next to Kirsty.

"Hi, ladies," he grins, "Jesus, I've never seen so many beautiful women at one table, have I died and gone to heaven?"

He leans and kisses Kirsty on the cheek. "Hey, mama."

She laughs as the girls say hi and offer him a cocktail.

"Hi yourself, are you lost?"

"No, but I'm flattered," he says, holding his hand to his chest, "that you'd let me join your little girls only soiree."

"It is *girls only,* get it?" Summer pipes up, accentuating the *girls* part with exasperation. "Meaning, *no boys allowed*, it's cocktail night, don't you have somewhere to be?"

He rolls his eyes. "That's hurtful, if I let you girls in on a secret maybe, you'll let me stay?"

He bats his eyelashes at us as Summer rolls her eyes.

"Oh, yeah, what secret's that?" Lily pipes up smiling broadly, waiting for him to let the cat out of the bag.

He leans closer to the table. "I'm in touch with my feminine side."

We burst out laughing; Kirsty slaps him on the chest.

"Honestly, Gunner."

"You douche bag," says Summer.

"What?" He pretends to be hurt. "I *am*, I'm totally down."

"Next you're going to say your dick fell off," Angel says, flinging a pretzel at his head.

He dodges the flying cracker and grins some more. "Maybe I did, maybe I should check it's still attached." He goes to his belt buckle and pretends to unfasten it.

"Ewww," Summer groans as Deanna grabs onto his arms to stop him. "Keep it in your pants, this isn't Church, it's a respectable establishment, you'll get us kicked out."

"I seriously doubt that." He laughs, looking around. Sure enough, nobody cares.

"Gunner!" Kirsty laughs, pretending to put her hand over her eyes so she can't see what he's doing.

He bends down to her ear but we can all still hear. "You are fuckin' smokin' hot, Mrs. Hutchinson, why does your old man let you out lookin' so damn fine?"

She cups his face and squeezes his cheeks like a mother would do to a son.

"You kiss your mama with that mouth?" She laughs, shaking her head. He kisses her cheek again and looks up at Lily. It's then I notice her beam at him when he turns his attention on her. *What's this?*

He gives her a wink as Summer addresses him again, quite impatiently. "What are you actually doing here, in case you didn't realize, it's also *ladies* night?"

"Ladies night, huh." His eyebrows shoot up. "Just as well, I've got a date."

I see Lily's face fall but she recovers faster than the blink of any eye.

"What kind of date meets a biker in a wine bar?" Katy laughs.

"A classy one," Gunner replies, waving the now empty cocktail glass around. "Hey, are there any more of these?"

"They're *girl's* drinks," Summer complains again, he's seriously cramping her style, "now get gone, this is a private gathering."

He ignores her and swipes one from the middle of the table.

"Gotta go anyway, ladies, don't drink too much, tonight's a school night," he gives us a wink and takes off with a cocktail in his hand.

"Urgh, he's so annoying," Summer whines as he disappears. No one seems to mind except her, in fact, most of us follow his very fine ass all the way across the room until he's disappeared from view.

"Is he really going to be piercing ears at the salon?" Deanna asks, turning her head back to the table.

"You should see him with kids," Lily just about swoons, "problem is, all the moms want a piece of the action and the high school girls, God, they are the worst, all batting their eyelashes and trying to talk to him. I hope I was never like that."

"That's only because he encourages it," Summer interjects, "which he shouldn't."

"He's always been an outrageous flirt," Kirsty agrees, "but he means no harm, and the ladies love him, you're gonna be busy, baby girl."

I get up to go to the bathroom and Lily comes with me. I can't help but notice her looking around, I wonder if she's searching for Gunner.

"So, how long you had the hots for him?" I say with a smirk.

She glances at me sharply. "Who?"

I roll my eyes. "Gunner."

She glances around. "What? Whatever makes you think that?"

I tap my nose. "A woman knows these things."

She rolls her eyes. "Well, it doesn't matter; he doesn't even know I'm alive."

I nudge her on the shoulder with mine. "Why's that?"

She huffs loudly. "I've liked him since I was a little kid, but that's all I am to him, a little kid, no more than a kid sister, so it's nothing… it never will be."

"How do you know though, you're a beautiful girl, Lily, you could have anybody."

She smiles kindly at me. "Thanks, Sienna, but with a brother like mine, I can't date anybody, much less somebody from the club *and* a brother."

"Yeah, Steel is a little overbearing with that kind of thing."

She shakes her head. "You have no idea."

"Still," I maintain, "you're your own woman, you are strong and independent, maybe you have to take charge."

I feel her look at me. "You mean, *ask him?* I'd rather die."

I frown at her. "Well, it seems like a waste if you really like him."

She turns to me as we push through the bathroom door. "You've got no idea what the guys can be like and me being the youngest, they're all very protective, they'd not only kill me but they'd kill Gunner too, it's just not done, he can't make it with a club sister and live to tell the tale, it's like some unspoken rule."

I roll my eyes. "Whose rules are those?"

She snorts. "Bikers."

"Well, that sounds really dumb to me. They may mean well but they can't tell you who you can and can't date, Steel included."

She smiles in a bit of a wicked way. "You mean, I have an alibi?"

I smile back. "You think you need one?"

"Where my brother is concerned? Oh, hell yeah."

I nudge her again. "You got it, babe."

She laughs. "Spoken like a true biker babe."

My head hurts a little as I wake from the sounds of my phone going off; it's on silent but I hear the vibration on the side table. *Ouch, those cocktails were good.*

I glance up, Steel is wrapped around me and the dogs are both on the bottom of the bed. I smile watching them for a second.

I turn and glance at the phone; I've several missed calls from Cassidy, my cousin. My heart lurches, oh no, something must be wrong. We don't speak all that much and she's down in Miami, or at least that's where she was last time we talked. I hope she isn't in trouble again.

I peel myself out from under Steel's arm and take my phone with me, tiptoeing out into the lounge.

I dial and wait for her to pick up, except she doesn't pick up, somebody else does.

"Hello, gorgeous," says a male voice.

I freeze from my pacing.

"Miss me, Sienna?"

I pull the phone away and stare at the number, it's definitely Cassidy's mobile.

"W-what... *who is this?*"

He sneers a laugh. "I think you know who, pretty girl."

Oh, holy shit. It's him; Ewan, my ex, but what's he doing with my cousin's phone? A sinking feeling shoots through my body like ice.

"Don't hang up," he warns, "just listen up good and nobody will get hurt."

I sit on the end of the couch, dumbstruck.

"I've missed you, pumpkin," he says in that voice I hate,

"you know what you do to me, what you've always done to me."

Bile rises in my throat.

"What are you doing with Cassidy's phone?" I whisper.

"Well," he snaps, "I couldn't reach you any other way, so I had to pretend to be an old friend in order to get your number from her, then I realized that you'd never come back to me unless I had leverage."

"Leverage as in what?" I stammer, my heart hammers in my chest. I know where this is going.

"Cassidy," he says brightly like I'm dumb. "Oh, I'm sending a screenshot of her now, so don't even think about alerting anyone about this like the cops."

A lump forms in my throat and I feel like I can't breathe.

My phone buzzes in my ear.

"Take a look," he sneers.

I pull the phone away and a photo pops up from a text on the screen. My eyes widen as I see the picture before me. It's Cassidy, she's tied up to a chair, her clothes are torn and she's all messed up with a gag around her mouth. I stare at it, shocked, this can't be happening. *This is not happening right now.*

"You there, my darling?" I hear him as I bring the phone back to my ear.

"Yes," I stammer again, I close my eyes trying to think, "why do you have Cassidy?"

"You've left me no choice, Sienna, you've brought me to this point, it's the only way we can be together."

Tears form in my eyes. "What do you want?"

"What I've always wanted," he laughs without humor. *"You."*

There's a long, uncomfortable silence.

"You still there, Si Si?"

His voice makes me sick and I always hated that nickname.

"Yes."

"So, we're going to make a deal."

"I'm listening. Just tell me where you are and I'll come to you, you can let her go, she has nothing to do with this."

"You're in no position to bargain with me," he snaps. "None at all."

"She's no use to you," I plead, "I won't make any trouble, I promise."

I wait for what feels like an eternity for him to answer. He thinks I'm weak so I don't doubt he'll think I'm also a pushover.

"What are you doing in Bracken Ridge?"

Shit, he knows where I am. I wonder if he knows about Steel.

"I'm sorting out my dead father's will."

"Ahh," he says, "well, we will get to that because you owe me, you fuckin' little bitch, you owe me big time."

"I'll do whatever you say," I whisper. My hand is shaking uncontrollably. He has my sweet, innocent cousin and I know he will hurt her, he's a mad man.

"I'll send you the details, meet me tonight, I'll text you the address. Come alone, Sienna, you of all people know what happens when you double-cross me or try to lie to me, that won't turn out good for you, or for your little cousin here, you know what I'm capable of."

"Can I talk to Cassidy, how do I know she's alright?"

"No, you can't," he barks.

"Please," I beg. "I just need to know she's alright… then I'll do whatever you say, I'll meet you."

I hear him huff then there's some shuffling; a muffled voice comes into the speaker.

"*Sienna?*" comes Cassidy's haunted voice down the line,

she's crying and stammering my name, she can barely get the words out.

"Oh, Cass," I say, closing my eyes.

"Please—" She gets cut off.

"She's alive, *for now*, do as I say and it might stay that way, you bring anyone or alert the cops and she's dead, you understand me?" he barks again. "Don't be a stupid fuck, Sienna, don't be a hero or she'll pay for it."

"Okay," I whisper, but it doesn't even seem like my own voice.

"I mean it, you stuck up little bitch, you owe me, I lost you once but I don't intend on that happening again, you double-cross me and I'll kill her, then I'll do the same to you, only this time, I'll do it very slowly."

"I'll be there," I tell him. "Just don't hurt her."

The phone clicks off. I stare at it with unblinking eyes, I can't cry, it's like no tears will come out.

I dart down to the bathroom and lock myself in.

I have no clue what I am going to do, but I can't tell Steel, if he finds out, he'll go in guns blazing and that could mean Ewan will follow through and kill Cassidy. He's probably high on drugs so that makes things even more unpredictable.

Shit.

I sob into my arm and shake with terror; my nightmare has finally come true. He's found me, he's found my weakness, and now I'm going to pay for leaving him.

I knew it was too good to be true, this happy new life I am about to create for myself, I may as well wish it all away down the toilet because he has my cousin, and there isn't anything I can do about it until she's safe.

I can't slip away without telling Steel, I mean, what am I supposed to say? That I'm going away for a few days, yeah, I could say that, but he'd never believe me. I could say my mom is sick and I need to go home, yeah, I could. But then he'd insist on coming with me.

Or I could leave, that way, he'll never follow me. That way, I won't put him in danger too.

My chest constricts; that means I have to hurt him. I can't have him following me; I don't want to put anyone else in danger, this is my mess.

A rational part of my brain tells me this is a matter for the police, that I should go to them right now, but he slipped away from them once, that's what he does, he'll do it again.

I wash my face, gather myself, and hope to God I can get out of here without hurting Steel too much.

I just don't know how I'm going to do that and make him believe it.

21

STEEL

I WALK into my office and instantly know something's up because Sienna is hurriedly packing shit up all over the place in a kind of frenzy. I lean against the door frame and watch her.

"What's up?" I say, my brow furrowing. She's been acting weird all morning, avoiding me. Maybe it's that time of the month or something.

"I got a call from my mom," she says, I realize she's been crying, "I have to go back home urgently."

"Shit, babe, is everything okay?"

She can't look at me.

"Sienna?" I say, moving toward her, "what's the matter?"

"I…" she begins. "I just don't know, I might not be coming back for a while."

I stare at her, perplexed, almost like she's joking, but we're definitely not role-playing anymore.

"What?"

"Steel, I have to get back… I'm sorry this is so rushed, but my mom needs me."

"Okay, I can come with you if you want, nothin' pressing here that can't wait."

"No," she says firmly, "this is something I should do alone."

I scratch my head. "Babe?"

"This realization has brought some things to the forefront, I thought I could do it but I can't right now, I'm rushing in too fast, this is all going *too* fast, I need some time to breathe." She tells me.

We made love like less than five hours ago and she enjoyed every fucking minute of it, she begged me not to stop, that I remember well, to say I'm as confused as hell is an understatement.

"Just calm down," I tell her, "we can talk this through; you don't have to go for good."

She turns to look at me. "The truth is, I don't know if I can do this, Steel," her voice shakes.

I stare at her unseeing.

"But what about your job, what about… *us?*"

It sounds like she's never coming back. *Shit, is she never coming back?*

I'm actually speechless; I don't understand what's happening.

"I have to go," she says eventually, her eyes on the floor. She can't even answer a simple question.

I stare at her, dumbfounded, as she tries to get around me.

"What do you mean?"

She breathes a long, low sigh, tears in her eyes. "*Us,* I can't, I'm sorry, it's bringing up some shit I have to deal with and I can't do this right now."

"What's changed all of a sudden?" I ask her quietly. "Why are you shaking?"

I have suspicion in my gut and that's never good.

She doesn't answer; she just stares at her feet. Her

behavior is so strange, it's like a different person has over-taken her body. This isn't the girl I've been getting to know for over a month and it's scaring the hell out of me.

"First signs of trouble back home and off you run?"

"It's not like that."

"Then explain to me exactly how it is, Sienna."

"It's complicated…"

"I don't understand, do you need more time? We can take things slower."

"It's not that."

"You just said it was exactly that, we're going too fast," I laugh without humor, "is your mom even sick?"

She stares at the floor as I rake my hands through my hair, and again, she doesn't answer. It's a lie.

What the hell has happened in the last few hours?

Maybe she has actually realized she's slumming it with me.

"I'm sorry, Steel, I thought I could do this but I just can't, I need some time. I'm homesick."

"Homesick?" I scoff. She doesn't even like home. "You never even talk about 'home'."

She knows that's true. She pushes past me.

"So, that's it?" I say after her. "You're going? No discussion, no nothing? You're just gonna walk out?"

"I need to think," she yells back. She's frantic to get away from me.

"Answer me!" I bark at her.

She dashes off, her hand over her mouth, stifling a sob.

I watch as she makes it out to the driveway, gets in her car, and takes off gunning the engine. I stand there in disbelief.

What the actual fuck?

I stare after her in complete shock. *What the hell just happened?*

I don't waste any time, I jump on my sled in the garage and race off after her. Yeah, it's probably not what she wants but who cares. I ride fast and take the shortcut but she's already parked in the car park behind the Stone Crow when I pull up, I make my way to the back door which she hasn't even bothered locking.

I take the stairs two at a time and barge into her room without knocking.

She turns to look at me, but then turns right back to what she's doing—packing. Her mascara has run down her face from crying.

There's stuff strewn all over the bed, I stare at her clothes trying to make sense of what she's doing.

I watch her, unsure of what's really going on. Has she just lost her mind or is she in actual trouble?

"What are you doing?" I ask in a low voice.

"What does it look like?"

I move closer to her but still keep some distance. "What did I do?" I ask quietly. "Why are you doing this?"

She laughs without humor. "You did nothing, Steel, nothing at all," she stops and turns to face me, "you're perfect, you're a good man, a decent man, I'm falling for you… I *am* and I don't want that, it's not your fault, none of it is."

I stand behind her. "We made love last night; everything was great, you were happy…"

"I thought I was alright," she says, her words are careful, "but getting that call from my mom has brought it all into reality. She needs me, Steel, and I can't be here and be there as well, at least not right now."

"I need you too."

Fuck. She's always made me weak but this is an all-time low for me, does she want me to get down on my knees and beg?

"Steel, I'm sorry…"

I let out a low breath. "You know you can tell me anything."

She turns back to her task, just throwing stuff in the suitcase with no care. I stare at her back, the adrenaline coursing through me.

"There's nothing to tell."

"Fuck that, there are things to say, you can't just go." I fling my arms out to nowhere, is she gonna actually go through with this nonsense? Running away, this is what she's good at. This is what she knows, but it doesn't have to be like that with me. I know I can make her happy.

"I have to…"

"You're running, Sienna, just admit it."

My mind ticks to the last few days, hell, the last few weeks, of absolute bliss we've shared, laughing, joking, cuddling, kissing, the sex… no, something is not right, she's acting like a crazy person.

"If it's time you need…" I go on, I know I sound pathetic.

"Please, Steel," she says, her words are strangled, "don't make this any harder than it already is."

I glare at her back. "This is fucked," I mutter, "and you know it."

She spins on me. "I'm sorry, I don't know what to say, please try to understand." She even sounds like she genuinely means it, the tears well in her eyes.

She doesn't want me, why doesn't she just come out and say it?

I'm not good enough. I could have told her that.

"Yeah, you keep saying that but something just doesn't add up. One minute, you're all over me like a rash, telling me sweet nothing's makin' it seem like you wanna stay here and make a life together, then the next, your tellin' me you have to go and you don't want me anymore and are packing your bags, excuse me if I'm just a little bit fuckin' confused about it."

Tears leak from her eyes and she doesn't even bother to wipe them.

"Just know this, I'll never forget you, please don't come looking for me, I need some time to get my head right, I don't deserve you, I don't deserve anything good."

I glare at her. *What the fuck is she talking about?* She's rambling and making no sense.

My anger takes over.

"The old 'it's not you, it's me' trick, hey, was that your plan all along? Just have a good time and then take off? You could have told me that before I got too invested, I would have been happy to oblige with no strings attached, have a few wild nights and then say sayonara; now what am I supposed to do?"

My anger is palpable. I want to throw something, namely her suitcase, across the room.

There. You've fucking hurt me. She sees it on my face as her eyes drop again. *Why can't she look at me?*

Her face is completely ashen. "I'll call you when I get there."

"Bullshit," I say. "You're doing what you always do, Sienna."

She doesn't even question me.

"Fucking this up on purpose, running away instead of facing things head-on, you know I can't help you if I don't know what the problem is, so screw me for even tryin'."

Her eyes plead with me and it lurches at my gut.

"Tell me you don't want me and I'll believe you."

I wait.

She looks at her feet again then back at my face. "*Please*, please just let me go."

She can't say it but I still step back like she's burnt me. I was smart to be single all this time, why did I ever let her get this far under my skin? *Why did I trust her?*

Now I'm fucked.

"Well, I hope it was worth it," I sneer. "The next time you plan on coming into someone's life to just screw them over, maybe let the schmuck know first so he can prepare himself for the fallout before he develops feelings for you. Who knows, you may hold onto this long enough to destroy your next relationship. I thought I knew you, Sienna, but it turns out I don't know anything about you, nothing at all."

I can't even look at her; this pain in my chest feels like I might have a heart attack. I turn as she calls my name, sobbing, but I can't, she's done enough, I slam the door behind me and head out downstairs without a backward glance.

SIENNA

And just like that, he's gone. I flop onto my bed and sob like there is no tomorrow, letting the tears and the pain flow freely. I may never be able to come up for air. Oh, God, it hurts.

I don't know how long I do that for but when I'm done and I'm sure there's nothing left, I curl up into a ball and rock myself for a while silently, I feel broken, like something inside of me has snapped and I'll never get it back. *He hates me now.*

I should have told him, he could have helped, but I can't, Ewan's watching me, he has Cassidy. Oh, poor Cassidy, she's tied up and he's hurt her. I cry some more but I realize that is not going to help anybody, I have to get going. Even though the meeting isn't until tonight, I have to get there as soon as possible, figure this out on the way. Sitting here feeling sorry for myself isn't going to get Cassidy back.

I scoop up my toiletries, leaving half of it strewn across the floor and zip my case up in a flurry. In reality, I've no idea what I'm doing, I'm on autopilot.

I haven't even told Stef. Jesus, what a mess. When I get to Cassidy, it will all be okay, I keep telling myself that but when I think about her tied up, I run back into the messy bathroom, open the toilet and throw up, heaving and crying and gasping for air.

Holy shit, I'm in some deep trouble.

I don't know what to do but I have to do what he says. As long as he lets Cassidy go, I don't care.

I clean myself up, shut the door and drag my case down the stairs, I half expect, or hope, Steel to be down there waiting and I can have an excuse to blurt it all out, but he isn't.

No, I've hurt him enough, and now he never wants to see me again. I deserve to feel this pain after what I've put him through. His face, oh my God, his face will haunt me forever, seeing the confusion and the pain I just inflicted on him.

Just know I love you, Steel, I'm doing this so nobody else gets hurt. I have to fix this myself.

I hate myself but I have to be strong, I have to do what Ewan says and she won't be hurt. He'll let her go; I'll reason with him, I know how he works.

I start the car, I need to get going. I stuff my case in the back seat and take off, leaving Bracken Ridge and everything else good in my life behind.

22

STEEL

I CAN'T BELIEVE she's left me.

I drive home in a blur, unable to think rationally as a million thoughts fly through my brain.

I drag myself upstairs to my apartment and take out the top-shelf whiskey, I unscrew the cap and take a large swig, then another, the sting momentarily soothes me, but I know it won't last.

She left me.

She actually fucking left me.

What the actual fuck?

What have I missed? Weren't we just in here hours ago, happy, worshipping one another? We told each other stuff, private stuff, things I've never told anybody. Yeah, I'm pretty sure that all happened and I didn't imagine it.

Maybe she's one of those crazies, women that get too attached then turn into some kind of nightmare for no apparent reason. If this morning's display is anything to go by then maybe I've dodged a bullet. Who knows, next she might be boiling bunnies on the stove for Christ's sakes.

Oh, who am I kidding?

I'm devastated, dumbstruck, goddamned confused, yeah all of the above. I sit at the breakfast bar and stare into space, letting the pound in my chest slowly simmer. I've never felt this pain in a long time and I don't like it. I don't like feeling weak. Only a fucking woman could bring me to my knees.

And not just any woman. *Her.*

I knew she was trouble when I first laid eyes on her, but did I listen to my own instincts? No, I goddamn didn't. I just carried on like a love-sick puppy thinking this time it would be different.

Lola comes up next to me and I reach down to stroke her head. Rocky is asleep on the couch, unaware of my life falling spectacularly apart.

"It's alright, girl," I say to her, "it's all gonna be okay, baby." She nuzzles into my hand and whimpers, I can't hide from her.

But it's not gonna be okay. Sienna's gone, she's driving out of town now probably as we speak and I don't even get a proper explanation. Here one minute, gone the next, like none of this even happened, like I meant nothing to her.

A thought hits me suddenly; I go with my gut and pull my phone out.

I dial Linc.

"Yo."

"Do you ever sleep?" I mutter.

"Rarely," he admits.

"I need a favor, a trace on this number," I reel off Sienna's mobile, "I need to see her last day or two's phone call log as well as text messages sent to and from her, pronto."

"Slick, that's gonna take some doing."

"Can it be done?"

"Of course, I just need a bit of time."

"It's urgent, bro, someone I care about could be in trouble."

Hell, I don't know what to think, this is just a hunch, but I trust my gut.

"Okay, man, I'm on it, I'll get back to you in a few."

"Appreciate it. I owe you."

I end the call.

I sit and think and push the bottle away. Linc has always been able to trace anything, that's what happens when you've got friends in low places.

Something is just not adding up though, I feel it in my bones.

Sienna went from looking at me adoringly to suddenly wanting to have nothing to do with me in five seconds flat, that's not normal behavior, and if she really was so calculating, why was she so upset? Why did she have tears in her eyes and couldn't look at me, that isn't the normal response from someone who has no feelings or isn't sure. She almost seemed heartbroken.

I run my hand through my hair in frustration. *She couldn't tell me she didn't want me.*

I flip my phone out and dial her number. It goes straight to message, I hang up.

There's nothing else to do, she doesn't want to see me, I have to let her go. Whatever her reasoning is, none of it makes any sense. If she wanted my help, she would have asked for it, not ran at the first sign of trouble.

I don't know how long I sit there, and I don't remember draining the rest of the bottle, but I crawl back into bed and hope that I wake and this is all a dream, it's still early after all.

I have no idea what I'm gonna do now and there's nobody here but the silence around me to give a shit.

∽

THE PHONE JOLTS me out of my thoughts; I'm still clutching it as it vibrates in my hand.

Linc's name lights up the screen.

"Hey, bro."

"Linc," I murmur, lifting my head.

"Got a bead, brother, brace yourself though; you're not gonna like it."

I scratch my head, not liking this already. "Shit."

"Sending now."

I wait as he sends through a series of text messages, and one is a photo.

I scroll through, quickly scanning the messages, then open the photo.

It's of a girl, she's tied up with rope around a chair, a bandana seals her mouth shut and she looks terrified.

What the fuck is this?

I gape at it then read the messages properly; my heart begins to thud in my chest.

Oh, holy shit.

I read quickly.

This must be him. *The ex-boyfriend.* He's threatening Sienna and he's got this girl, Cassidy, as a hostage, and there's an address.

I sit upright, suddenly more alert than I've ever been. Shit, she's in some big-time trouble and I mean way over her head, now she's heading there alone to some address in the wilderness? This guy is a psychopath.

I put my phone back to my ear.

"That's some heavy shit," I breathe, my mind is going a million miles an hour.

"Yeah, it's pretty fucked up," he agrees. "I'm tracking the number now, will try and get a trace, but you've got an address, brother."

"Thanks, man, I'll call you back in a few."

I close my phone and shut my eyes.

I can't believe he's threatened her, and instead of coming to me, she's running off to go and deal with this maniac by herself. *Why would she do that?*

I shake my head. I'm annoyed beyond belief that she's done this, I feel the surge of anger rise up in me about her putting herself in danger to that madman, but also relieved that she didn't *want* to do it, she didn't want to go. It explains the weird behavior, why she was lying and couldn't look at me. As if I can't deal with this little motherfucker once and for all by myself. I could do it in my sleep. He has no idea who the fuck he's messing with now.

I jump off the bed, go to the bathroom quickly, and all the while, hatch a plan as I'm moving around the apartment.

I need all of the boys on this.

I dial Sienna's number again, this time, I leave a message.

"Sienna," I say, my hand is shaking, "it's me, call me back as soon as you get this. I know everything, you don't have to do this alone, we can work this out together, you're forgetting I'm ex-military and I can handle this pussy. You don't need to do this, please, for God's sake turn around when you get this message, I'm coming to get you, do not, *I repeat,* do not go in there alone, I'm begging you."

I need to call Brock in a second and get everyone I can on this so we can get on the road.

I go downstairs into the workshop and down to the safe; I grab my duffel bag and pull out my large blade and a couple of guns and ammunition. I'm gonna need it.

Who knows what this crazy bastard is really capable of. I can't wait to get my hands on the prick. I think about Sienna going there alone and curse out loud. *How could she be so stupid?*

I start putting everything in the back of my truck; it's

then that I notice a car parked in the driveway—a dark blue Datsun.

My heart accelerates. Sienna's car.

I move fast to unlock the side door and swing it open as I quickly cross the driveway to the drivers' side, she's in there, in the driver's seat, her head is down against her hands on the wheel, she's slumped forward, lifeless. My heart hammers in my chest.

I tap on the window and she jumps. I hold my hands up.

"It's me," I say, tapping on the window, I go to open the door but it's locked. "Open up."

She gazes at me for a second, her eyes are red and blood-shot, her face is completely white and devoid of emotion. She looks like she's been to hell and back. Suddenly, she unlocks the door with a shaky hand, and when I reach in for her, she falls into my arms.

"Oh, Steel," she sobs.

I hold her for a moment then pick her up and carry her across the driveway in my arms and into the garage, shutting and locking the door behind us.

I prop her up on the bench facing me and let her sob into my shoulder, her body convulses uncontrollably.

She cries and cries and cries. I let her take as long as she needs; she's no use to me in this state so I let her have it out.

This isn't my strong point; dealing with emotional women, but I'm not a barbarian. I try to soothe her by stroking her hair and tell her it's gonna be okay, she's safe now, I'm here.

I don't know how long we stay like that but when she slows her sobbing down slightly, I reach to the bench and grab a clean rag and wipe her tears away.

"It's alright," I tell her, "I'm here now and we're gonna work this out."

"*It's him...*" she sobs, trying to get the words out. Pain stabs at my heart knowing she went through this alone, that she thought she had to.

"I know," I tell her.

"He's got Cassidy, my cousin."

She falls into my chest and I hold her there. Seeing her like this breaks me, this is some fucked up shit.

"It's alright, just calm down, we're gonna get to the bottom of it," I tell her gently.

She gathers herself enough to look up at me. "I couldn't do it," she says, she fists my shirt in her hands, her eyes look wild, there's my little spitfire.

"I tried, I drove for an hour but I couldn't do it, I got your missed call and I turned back, leaving you like that, you thinking that I didn't want you…" She cries again, I lift her chin so she's looking at me, tears roll freely down her cheeks. "It broke me, Steel… you don't deserve that."

I peck her lightly on the lips. "Sweetheart, you need to calm down," I tell her gently, "just breathe and hold onto me, you're in shock and none of that matters now."

She glances up suddenly, her body goes stiff.

"He can't know I'm here," she looks around the darkened workshop frantically; she's like a wild animal. I have to get control of this situation and fast, "I don't know if he knows about you, I don't think so but I can't be sure. He means business, Steel, if I don't do as he says, he'll kill her."

I brush her hair back off her face and cup her with both my hands and meet her eyes. I hate how scared she is of this jerk face and she almost came this close to tackling him alone. I try not to shudder at the thought, or what I'm going to do to him as payback.

No, I need to concentrate on her now, without all the information, I'm going in blind.

"He won't because I won't let him, you should have come to me, you should've told me," I say softly, I don't want to set her off again by being mad, even though I want to scream my lungs out, but that won't help her, she's scared, I have to be patient while she's in this state. It takes all my might not to fly off the handle. "But I'm here now and none of that matters, I'm here and I'm not going anywhere."

She sags with absolute relief at my words, falling into me again.

"Steel, I need you."

"I know," I say, kissing her hair, "I need you too, baby. Don't ever do that to me again, you hear me?"

She nods on my shoulder.

"How'd you find out?" she snivels.

"I know a guy." I shrug.

She looks up and gives me a watery smile. "Of course you do."

I kiss her again. "We're in this together, babe, you hear me, you don't ever have to run away no matter how big or small the problem is, you come to me first."

She nods. "I'm sorry to drag you into all of this…"

I silence her lips with my finger. "Stop it, this is what I do, babe, I'm not afraid of this piece of shit, and I have a whole team of brothers behind me, he's just one deluded guy who probably has no game plan whatsoever, we'll get her back, you have to trust me."

"I do, Steel."

"Good, let me handle this."

She still clings to me.

"What if he's working with other people?" she whispers.

"That doesn't matter," I tell her.

"I don't want you to get hurt." She's still clutching my shirt. Fear runs through her eyes as I rub my hands along her arms up and down. She's cold. I need to get her warm and get the rest of my stuff together.

"I need to get you upstairs and then you're gonna tell me everything I need to know, sweetheart, alright?"

She nods, total trust in her eyes, her belief that I can get her out of this tightens in my chest. I need her compliance; I need to know everything she knows about this piece of garbage so I know what I'm dealing with.

I'm not very happy that she chose to run off and put herself in danger, but I leave that for the moment, we don't have time and I don't need another meltdown. I have to get her upstairs, call the M.C., and make a plan with my brothers.

My eyes come back to her.

"Can you ever forgive me?" she pleads; her beautiful eyes watery like she might go again at any given moment. "Can you, Steel?"

"There's nothing to forgive," I tell her honestly. I kiss her gently again, she needs Jayson now, not Steel. I've never been this gentle with anybody before, but I know I have to. Screaming at her for being so reckless will only scare her even more.

"I love you," she says, it's barely audible but I heard it loud and clear.

I smile, my chin resting on her head as she pushes her face into my chest, inhaling my scent.

"I love you too," I say into her hair and kiss the top of her head. "And nothing and nobody is gonna ever hurt you again."

23

SIENNA

He places me down on the bed, and the minute he leaves me, I feel cold without him, he returns from the closet with one of his hoodies and pulls it over my head and I'm glad to feel the warmth. I'm shaking uncontrollably and I can't stop.

Imagining poor, sweet Cassidy and what she's going through—tied up and terrified—anger boils in my blood. I know I have to pull myself together but I just don't know how; all of those awful feelings have come rushing back. I know what he's capable of but I never thought he'd do something as crazy as this.

Steel comes back to the bed after disappearing for a few moments; he's holding a small tumbler filled with amber liquid.

"Drink this." He hands it to me and perches on the end of the bed, he's acting as if I'm made of glass.

"What is it?"

"Brandy, just take a sip, it'll warm you up and hopefully calm you down a bit."

He watches me and I've no idea what he's thinking, he was so nice downstairs, so patient and caring, telling me it was going to be alright. God, I've never hoped for anything more.

I reach for him. "I'm sorry," I whisper.

He smiles and brushes my hair off my face.

"You've nothing to be sorry or be worried about; you made the right decision to come back, to let me help you and I'm going to do that."

Hope blooms in my chest but it's quickly replaced by the gloom when I think about Cassidy.

"I need to get to her…"

"You need to take a beat and calm down, I'm going to take care of this my way and you have to trust me, that's how this is gonna work from now on, do you trust me, princess?" He gives me a lopsided but serious look.

I nod, I do trust him, but I'm scared. I'm scared of what he's doing to her right now and scared that I'm too far away to help her, but I do need to trust that he knows what he's doing.

"I need you to be strong, so you're going to rest for a little bit while I make some phone calls."

I watch him as he studies me.

"I'm sorry for what I said," I blurt out; I take the glass he's still holding and take a sip, still looking at him. I wince as it stings the back of my throat.

"Stop apologizing."

"I need to, it was wrong. *I* was wrong."

"You panicked and were under duress; the important thing is, you came back, now stop it."

I clutch the glass with both hands, isn't that the truth.

"You don't hate me?"

He smiles again. "I could never hate you."

"I love you, Steel, I don't want you to get hurt." The thought sends every nerve into overdrive.

He traces a knuckle over my cheek gently and I lean into his touch.

"I'm not going to get hurt, and I'm going to get Cassidy back just like I said, alright?"

I nod; I'm at his mercy now.

"I'm afraid," I tell him.

He grips my chin lightly with his hand and kisses me chastely.

"You don't have to be afraid, I won't let anything happen to you, that you can be sure of."

He rises from the bed.

"*Wh*-where are you going?" I stammer, reaching for him.

"I'm going to run you a bath; your lips are just about blue."

"I can't be sitting around here drinking brandy and having baths and a good old time when Cassidy's out there, terrified out of her mind…" I wail as I try to sit up.

He looks down at me and holds my shoulders to prevent me from moving.

"Listen to me," he says as I kneel on the bed and he pulls me to his body, "we've got hours of time, I need to call the brothers and work out a game plan, and I need you to warm up, calm yourself down by about a thousand notches, and let me handle this. Getting hysterical on me won't help matters."

His tone is final, there is no arguing with him, his eyes are fierce as he looks at me and I realize I want him to take over, I want him to take charge, I'm totally out of my depth here. "Shouldn't we call the police?" I murmur into his chest.

"No cops," he says.

"*Steel…*"

"Babe, quit."

He pulls back and tilts my chin to look up at him. "You freaking out isn't going to help Cassidy and it isn't going to help me think and get prepared for what I have to do and how to handle this so nobody gets hurt. I went into an Afghanistan war zone, I'm pretty certain I can handle this little piece of shit."

He's not like anybody else, any other person on the planet would be involving the police, the S.W.A.T, and whoever else you call in a hostage situation. Christ, I don't know.

"He's slippery, and he's smart," I breathe.

"Yeah, well, I'm smarter."

He kisses the top of my head and pulls away and walks down the hall, he comes back a few moments later and I can hear the bathwater running.

He stands over me and pulls the sweater over my head along with my t-shirt and unhooks my bra, he kisses me but it's not like normal, it's tentative, soft, like nothing I've experienced with him before this moment. He's being careful with me. Maybe he thinks I'll break, maybe I will. It could go one way or the other right now.

I cling to him as he unbuttons my jeans and press my body into his strong hold as I look up at him.

His eyes flash to me. "Babe…"

"I want you, Steel," I say, I can't get close enough to him. I nuzzle my face into his neck and he groans, his arms come around my body and I feel his heartbeat racing in his chest. He's so warm, so very warm, big and beautiful.

"You've plenty of time to make it up to me later," he whispers, and yanks my jeans and panties down in one fell swoop; he lays them over the end of the bed.

I turn and kiss him, trying to deepen the kiss but he pulls back, a smirk on his lips. He's always in control, *always*.

"*Steel…*" I murmur. "Don't."

"You're in shock and not thinking clearly," he tells me, against my lips. "I'm gonna carry you to the bath, babe, and you need to stop trying to get into my pants, so hold on."

He doesn't wait for me to reply, he picks me up and I

wrap around him, still trying to coax a deeper kiss out of him but he won't reciprocate, I need him so, so much.

"Why don't you kiss me back properly?" I moan as his chest rumbles with a laugh.

"Because I've got to keep my head in the game, princess, you trying to bed me is a distraction."

"I need a distraction."

He kisses me again and I slide down his body, he leans over the bath and turns the water off, there are bubbles everywhere.

"I didn't have bubble bath, so I used my shower gel."

I can't help but giggle, the bubbles are overflowing. He tests the water and then turns back to me, wiping his bubble-covered hand and forearm on the nearby towel. He holds me by the hips and lifts me over the bath so I'm standing calf-deep in the water.

"That temperature okay, babe?"

"Yes, thank you." I nod, I sit down and he pulls the shower curtain aside and sits on the top of the toilet with the lid down and watches me.

I sink and sit back into the warm suds and sigh. It feels good, and it smells like him.

"You scared me today," he says eventually, my eyes pop open and I look at him.

"I know."

"This relationship thing is a two-way street in case you didn't know."

I nod, feeling like the worst person in the world.

"And it won't work unless we're completely honest with each other, like I've said from the start—good or bad."

"Ok." I nod.

"From now on, we have no secrets, big or small, it doesn't matter if you think it'll make me mad or vice versa. I'll be madder if you pull a stunt like this again and don't tell me and then I'm going out of my mind with worry."

Oh no, his wrath is legendary, but his eyes soften as I stare at him.

"I'm a little rusty at this," I admit.

"Well, I'm not, babe, I've been around the block a time or two, and we have something special and I know you feel it too. The only way we can be stronger is if we work together, communicate, and not run away from problems."

I know he's right, and I need to lighten the mood.

"You ever think about going on Dr. Phil?"

He rolls his eyes.

"Can you be serious for three minutes?"

"Sorry," I mutter.

"I was so mad at you for leaving," he drops his head, "promise me you won't ever do that again and without an explanation, without us talking about it."

"I won't leave again," I tell him.

"Good because I will find you."

I smirk. "What will you do to me?"

He looks back up at me. "I know what you're doing."

"What's that?"

"Trying to distract me with dirty talk, well, it's not gonna work."

I smile. "I'm so happy I found you."

He rolls his eyes. "You didn't find me, I found you."

"Are we really going to argue about that?"

"Only if you continue to defy me." His eyes dance with mischief; I love it when he's like this.

"Now, I need you to tell me everything about your ex-loser boyfriend from the very beginning so I know who I'm dealing with, then what he said to you on the phone, exactly what he said, can you do that for me, angel?"

I stare at him wide-eyed but I nod. "Yes, I can do it."

He smiles gently, encouraging me, resting his forearms on his knees. There are so many pages to Steel, so many layers.

My heart races at having to talk about *him* though, I don't want to. He's my past, Steel is my future.

"Everything," he says with a nod as if sensing my hesitation.

I gulp. *"Everything?"*

"Everything."

IT'S A LONG DRIVE, longer than it should be because, no matter what Steel says about it being okay, I can't help but feel like this should have included calling the police.

Steel thinks it's unlikely Cassidy will be hurt if it's me he's after, he also assures me that Ewan has one chip he didn't count on; me asserting myself and having an entire M.C behind me. He won't be expecting it, so it will be to our advantage.

It's no shocker Steel doesn't want me tagging along but there is no way he's leaving me behind, besides, Cassidy will be scared enough without a bunch of bikers coming to her rescue, she'll need me when we get her back.

We drive to the location with what seems the entire club behind us—some on bikes, some in vehicles, there must be at least eight. Steel doesn't do anything by halves, plus if Ewan is wired on drugs, he could be unpredictable, making it far more dangerous.

I wonder how Steel is going to manage this when he goes in instead of me, *what if Ewan just shoots him?* I remind myself that Steel and the club are all armed. Steel is also ex-military, he knows how to handle these kinds of situations. Situations I don't really want to think about.

We pull up onto the side of the road a few miles out from the address.

I turn to Steel; he's been pretty quiet this whole way here. "What's happening?"

He glances in the rearview mirror. "The boys are going to hide their bikes in the shrub and get into the other cars and follow, couple of prospects will stay back here and keep tabs on the road out of town, we also don't want the sleds alerting him to our arrival."

"Oh." I realize.

Cassidy, hang on. Please just hang on, we're coming.

The passenger door opens and I jump out of my skin.

It's Gunner.

"Jesus," I say, holding my hand over my heart that just jolted out of my chest.

"Going my way?" he says holding his thumb up as if hitch-hiking, typical Gunner, always making a joke. "Scooch over," he tells me.

I move closer to Steel as he jumps in beside me. A few moments later, Steel begins talking.

"We move, follow my lead."

I stare at him, then I realize he has an earpiece in. *Who's he talking to?*

"Well, Sienna," Gunner momentarily distracts me, "I think this classifies as the most dangerous thing I've done in quite a long time, nothing like a perilous drive out to the country-side to seek out a crazy stalker to get the juices flowing."

"Gunner," warns Steel.

"First time for everything." I shrug, trying to keep calm.

Then he leans forward so he can see Steel. "She's quite the firecracker, my man, keepin' you on your toes."

I feel Steel gaze across at him but he doesn't speak.

"Yeah, this firecracker may go off any second," I warn.

"And to think he thought you were as pure as the driven

278

snow when he first laid eyes on you, probably couldn't imagine you'd get yourself into this kind of predicament," he muses, then whispers, "it's always the quiet ones you gotta worry about."

"Knock it off," Steel growls.

Of course, Gunner ignores him and glances at me with a wink.

"Told us all to stay away from you or he'd kill us, very vocal about it, some of the things he threatened to do were quite violent, that's when I knew," he taps his nose.

I look at him sideways. "Knew what?"

"Shut up, asshole," Steel barks.

"He's got it bad," Gunner replies, "despite what he says otherwise."

I can't help the smile that spreads across my face; I know Gunner is trying to take my mind off of this whole situation. God bless him. Maybe I do need a distraction like his babbling.

"You're gonna have it bad in a minute when I knock you out, sunshine."

Gunner rolls his eyes then whispers to me, "He's been saying that since I was a kid, still hasn't happened, all talk no action."

I can't help but giggle. "You like playing with fire, don't you?"

He just laughs.

"Don't you encourage him," Steel balks.

Steel turns the headlights off as he slows down for our approach and we pull up into a driveway. We're here. I can't help but feel like I'm living in a dream, or more like a nightmare.

A few moments later, I see a couple of figures in the dark pass us on foot and run around the side of the house. I learned earlier that Brock and Bones have already staked the house out and reported back.

"What are they doing?" I can't help the shake in my tone.

"Surrounding the place, seein' who's in there." Then he looks over my shoulder. "Gunner..." he says as they do that silent nod thing. I guess the next stage of the plan is kicking in, a plan I'm not privy to because Steel has told me nothing.

Then he turns to face me. "You're waiting here with Gunner, he's going to keep you safe while I go take care of this."

"No," I stammer.

I glance at Gunner; he's discreetly turned his head to look out of the passenger window.

"I need to be there," I whisper.

He leans toward me, the leather crunches under his body weight.

"No, you don't, you're staying here with Gunner until I say, this is my way of protecting you, not that you should even be here, so let me. We discussed this, so don't argue with me, princess, not now, do as you're told for once and stay put. No more lip, just do as I say."

His tone is short and deliberate, he definitely isn't kidding around. He grabs my chin and kisses me, forcing his tongue into my mouth. I clutch him, and when we break away, I'm breathless. His eyes flick across at Gunner then back to me.

"No funny business," he mutters in my ear.

I hold onto the lapels of his jacket. "I love you," I whisper.

He nods once.

"Keep watch," he barks at Gunner as he turns his head, "don't let her leave this truck."

"Gotcha, boss."

Without warning, he jumps out of the car and walks toward the house, he's holding a gun and I know he has more on him, plus his favorite knife and a couple of others he's hidden on his body.

I stare after him, my hands are shaking.

"This is all wrong," I say out loud, "I shouldn't have involved the club…"

Gunner turns his body sideways to face me.

"Why'd you say that?"

"I'm worried about him, about you all putting yourselves in danger."

He laughs out loud. "Honey, please."

"This isn't funny," I say, glaring at him.

"Come on, you're dealing with an entire M.C. and he's ex-fucking re-con, Sienna, this is what we do. Colt's a boxer, Brocks a tank, Bones can shoot a man clean at a hundred yards, we're hustlers, everyone here has skills. We're not freakin' pencil pushers."

"What about you?" I raise a brow sarcastically.

"*Me?* Babe, I'm just here to decorate."

"And babysit?"

"Yeah, because I'm the only one who can use my powers of persuasion," he winks. "Your ex is what, though? An investment banker? Ooh, so scary, probably can't fight his way out of a paper bag, probably good at scaring females and those weaker than him because that's what bullies and assholes do, but he's met his match, honey bun. Honestly, it's insulting to our intelligence, he's outmatched, don't worry your pretty little head over it."

I notice he has a gun tucked into the waistband of his jeans and I don't want to think about that too closely.

"You don't know him," I splutter, getting back to the point, "he's a loose cannon, especially now. I've never heard him like this."

"It's going to be okay, you just need to stop panicking,

we've got the place surrounded, even if he's not working alone, it won't be difficult. Just trust us, babe."

He sounds so calm, like Steel. I wish I was calm.

"You sound so sure but people do strange and unpredictable things when they're not in their right minds and he's probably high to boot, if something goes wrong, it'll be my fault."

He gives me a shove in the ribs with his elbow. "Thanks for the moral support," he sobers for a moment then adds; "nothing is your fault, he chose to do this and hurt somebody you care about, and Steel knows what he's doing. He's a machine, especially when someone messes with what's his, and with backup? Unstoppable, babe, we got this, he doesn't know how to fail."

I only focus on one part of that sentence.

"I'm his?"

He smirks. "Technically, he'll have to make you his ol' lady, but it's obvious, I've never seen him like this, you've put a spell on him."

I consider that for a moment. "How long have you known him?"

"Since I was eight."

Oh, that's a good sign, I think.

"Cassidy is not strong," I say after a while. "I don't know if she's going to get through this."

"If she's got your blood, then I'm sure she's gonna be fine."

I glance at him; he's so handsome, it really is a crime. Despite all his innuendos, I do see what Lily sees in him.

"Are you sure you're not just here to pep talk me so I don't go out of my mind?"

He smirks again. "Well, it's that or we make out and I know I definitely want my nuts attached to the rest of my body, so let's go with that."

"Such a smooth talker," I say, sounding more confident than I feel.

He raises both eyebrows. "My motives are questionable in most things, I admit."

I can't help but smirk. "What's your best line that works?"

"That's classified, babe, can't give you all my moves," he gives me a shit-eating grin, "and I never kiss and tell."

"Don't you mean *club business?*" I put on my deepest possible biker voice and he laughs out loud.

"That as well."

I roll my eyes. "Oh, here we go."

"And for the record, your biker voice sucks."

We sit for a while in companionable silence and my mind wanders to Lily. I don't know if it's the dire situation of life and death that we're in or the fact that Gunner is so easy going, but I doubt he'd take offense to what I'm about to say and I feel compelled to enlighten him.

"Do me one favor if we make this out alive?" I start bravely.

"Anything for you, sweetheart." He gives me a lopsided cheeky grin.

"Ask Liliana out on a fucking date."

His eyes go round. "What?" he splutters.

I turn back to peer out of the windscreen, showing no emotion. "You heard me."

He shifts nervously in his seat. "That's ancient history, not that it was ever anything…"

I laugh without humor. "Trust me when I say it's not ancient history for some people."

"Did she say something?" I can't help but note the interest in his voice, mixed with a little bit of panic.

I turn back to him. "It's not really for me to stick my nose in, but like I say, if we make it out of here alive, that's my one wish. Put a girl out of her misery, for God's sake."

He stares at me seriously for a second then he rubs his chin like he's deep in thought. He's finally putting two and two together and I'm not sure if he likes the answer, it's hard to tell.

"Steel would kill me," he says eventually.

"Let me handle Steel."

He chuckles. "Listen to you all high and mighty, got your man in his place in a few short weeks, better be handin' me his man card when he gets back here, his balls must be sore from the beating."

I roll my eyes. "Trust me, he's not complaining, but it isn't up to him, she's a grown woman and you're a grown man. If you don't feel the same, then stop leading her on."

I know I sound rude but what the hell... this is a life or death situation so maybe it's called for, and Lily for one can't go on like this, she needs to move on if he isn't interested.

I feel his eyes on me again. "I'm like that with everyone," he murmurs, "it's just how I am."

"Yeah, well, with some people, *some people* who care about you, that is..." I turn to face him. "It means something different."

Guys are such dummies; even badass bikers who've been around the block and have probably seen and done it all. He's finally realizing something he should have known a long time ago about Lily. What he chooses to do with it is up to him. I've no idea if he has the same feelings for her but now he knows. I hope Lily doesn't kill me when she finds out, or Steel for that matter.

He turns back to the front. "I hope to God we get out of here alive," he says after a long few moments.

I turn to him and we both grin at each other in the dark.

24

STEEL

THE PLAN IS in place as I make my way silently around the abandoned building. The lighting is dim and I peer through the gaps of the warped timber. Bones asks me through the headpiece if I have a visual. He's ex-military too and very good with a sniper rifle, not that I hope it'll come to that, but this psycho needs to be stood down, no matter what it takes.

I don't even want Sienna being here, but somebody has to be here to comfort Cassidy when I retrieve her, and it's a long drive back to Bracken Ridge with a terrified woman on my hands. One thing is for sure, Sienna will never have to see him again, that's my promise to her. Even if she wants to be involved, there is no way I'll let that happen, he won't get near her, I'll kill him with my bare hands if he even tries.

I think about the night she told me about what he did to her, the way her body shook beneath me from fear as she retold the story. No woman should ever have to feel fear like that, and it makes my blood boil, it makes me want to hurt him all the more and give him some payback; see how he likes hitting me in the face. Adrenaline threatens to over-rule my emotions but I push it back down and reel myself in. I can't let emotions get in the way of what needs to be done, there will be plenty of time for me to unleash that side of my nature after Cassidy is safe and out of harm's way.

I peek through the timber again and I catch a glimpse of the girl tied to the chair, at least she's where he said they'd be, which is another thing; I very much doubt he thinks Sienna will double-cross him, he seems to think she'll do anything he says.

I take another glance, then I wait and watch. I need him to come into sight so I know where the fucker is, the boys said he seems to be working alone, that makes life easier and a lot less complicated. I look up to the far side of the shed; I see Colt and Brock waiting for my instruction, both with guns drawn.

I hold the earpiece down. "I'm going in, wait for my signal."

"Roger," Bones says back through the earpiece, "I've got a visual."

Colt and Brock nod, the other guys are scattered around the building and at the front in case anybody should interrupt.

None of them want me to go in alone but it's the only way, if he shoots me dead at first sight, then yeah, that will be a problem, but he's not a soldier, he's a pussy boy who preys on innocent women.

I catch sight of movement behind the chair, it seems he's pacing around, agitated, he keeps running his hands through his hair. It's close to the time she's meant to be here.

I make my way to the makeshift door and take a collective breath, this is it, I need to put all of my military training into gear and get Cassidy out unharmed, and I need to not under-estimate this guy, especially if he's high.

I call through the rackety door instead of just breaking it

down like I want to, he may just shoot at the sudden impact and I don't need wayward bullets spilling everywhere.

"Hey, Ewan," I holler. "My name is Steel, I'm here because of Sienna, seems she got herself in a jam."

I hear shuffling from inside, I can't see him now that I'm in front of the door.

"I'm coming in and I'm unarmed."

I kick the door in, my first instinct is to duck, so I do and move to the left of the room behind a wooden beam, it's dark inside so I can use this to my advantage.

"Who the fuck are you?" he screams as I see him through the rafters. He's holding a gun, *shit, shit, shit,* and he's waving it around.

"Don't shoot," I say calmly, keeping well and truly behind the beam. I take in the surroundings quickly in this old dilapidated building, "Sienna's outside, I have her but we need to talk first, this isn't what it looks like."

"I said to come alone!" he barks. Yeah, he's definitely on something, without a doubt, he paces back and forth, agitated.

I hold my hands where he can see them. "Just hear me out, we both want the same thing in all of this, I want to help you." I'm lucky he isn't just firing bullets everywhere.

What did she ever see in this guy? He looks like he's been on a week-long bender that may never quit.

"I want to see her now, go fucking get her or I'll shoot you and the girl, I told her to come alone, clearly the stupid bitch has learned nothing since she ruined my life."

Hearing him say that only ignites the fire inside me.

"Think about this," I say calmly. "I have a proposition for you where we both win and you'll get what you want; believe me, you'll want to hear what I have to say."

I have to make him think that maybe it will be possible and I'm not the enemy.

He laughs coldly. He looks like shit, his sallow and ruddy complexion tells me he's on some serious smack, he's sweaty and unstable like he hasn't slept in days, his clothes are grimy like the rest of him; rock bottom is what they call that.

"The time for talking was a year ago when that bitch ruined me."

I hold my hands up and move out of the shadows.

"Unfortunately, it ain't so easy, Sienna owes me too, you see, but since I'm done with her now, I wanna make a trade seen as the crazy bitch can't keep her mouth shut."

I glance at Cassidy as her eyes are wide with fear watching me.

He assesses me as if I'm the mad man. He circles Cassidy, tapping the gun every now and again up to his forehead as he mutters to himself. I hope the thing goes off, it'll save me a job. Cassidy sits crying and shaking but she can't make too much noise with her mouth gagged. I want to gut him right here, right now.

He paces back and forth. "Who are you?" he splutters. "Why are you here?"

"I was a friend, took her in when she had nowhere else to go," I retort, "*was* being the operative word, until the bitch double-crossed me because that's what she does, right? You know only too well what she's capable of; uses you, gets what she wants, then spits you out the minute she's done with you. Well, she picked the wrong guy this time."

He sneers like he agrees. "She does that, she'll suck the life right out of you, stupid whore got fucked over because she never listens, started telling me what I can and can't do, where have I been? Who've I been seeing? She doesn't know her place, so I shut her up good the last time, pity the pigs got there before I could teach her to shut her pie hole for good."

God, and I thought I was a misogynistic asshole. I

imagine me tearing out his vocal chords so I don't have to hear his voice ever again. I want to hurt him permanently.

"Hear ya on that," I manage to spit.

"What do you want?" He narrows his eyes suspiciously as he kicks Cassidy's chair and she flinches; my gut tightens even more.

"To make Sienna suffer, I double-crossed her; said I'd get her cousin back unharmed when she came askin' me for help, but what I really wanna do is make her watch," I smile slyly as he smirks, *oh yeah*, he likes that idea, stupid fuck.

Cassidy's eyes go round like saucers. Ewan smiles like he actually believes it. This is going much better than I thought.

"We have a common denominator here," I go on since I've got his attention, "and I have a clubhouse full of brothers who like to take turns if you get my drift, you get Sienna, I get this new little whore and nobody has to know anything. It'll be our little secret, we're done with that thieving little bitch anyway, she's too much trouble."

"I want my money," he stammers. *Shit, what money?* "She owes me for what she did to me, I lost my job, my house, my car, respect... I lost everything!"

I think of a story for a split second.

"She has money from the sale of her dead fuck-wit father's house where she's been shacked up the last few months; suppose she never told you about that, did she?" I say like we're old chums. "I can get the cash out of her, she ain't got much choice, there's at least a hundred grand in it, could be quite lucrative for you, scratch like that don't grow on trees."

His eyes light up like Christmas. I really want to cut him. I'm glad I sharpened my knife before we left; I want to see him bleed.

Cassidy shakes in the chair as I physically restrain myself

from rushing at him and choking him to death, at least he has relaxed the gun.

"But in order for that to happen, we make an exchange," I go on. "I want her," I point at Cassidy menacingly; I need him to think I intend to hurt her as this is what this sicko gets off on. The thought of him with my beautiful, sweet, innocent Sienna curdles my blood cold. *How did she even get with this guy?* I mean, I know I'm no oil painting, but seriously.

"How do I know this isn't a trap?" he splutters, he moves from one side of the room to the other. "How do I know you won't double-cross me the minute I give her up?" He's getting more agitated by the second, going from calm to erratic in the blink of any eye, he even turns his back on me.

"You don't," I say flatly, "the fact that I'm here alone says it all though, I take her back and my brothers are happy—fresh meat. She's sweet as pie, they'll forget all about Sienna and what she's done, they're off my back, it's a win-win."

It feels like poison coming out of my mouth but he's starting to trust me, I can tell by the idiotic look on his face that he's considering it. We're not comrades, stupid fucker.

"I want her now," he yells out, wiping his elbow sleeve across his forehead in a panic, switching tact. "You go get her and we'll make the exchange."

I shake my head as I step closer, my hands still up, it's a daring move getting closer but I try to make out I'm just trying to be a nice guy by surrendering and appearing like I just want to be buddies. "I have no assurance that you won't shoot me and keep the girls for yourself; think about it, for me, it ain't a smart move."

"How do I know there are no others out there?" He nods behind me, if only he knew there's a sniper rifle pointed at his head right now. I really don't want Bones to shoot him because he deserves to suffer like what poor Cassidy has as well as reap the repercussions for the trauma he's put Sienna through.

I scoff like that's ridiculous. "Do you honestly think my club would be in on this? They've no idea I'm even here, I have to save face on this, I've risked a lot by even being here."

I hope he doesn't ask me why I haven't thought about taking the so-called money myself instead of just handing it all to him, but he's too wasted to think that intelligently, thank God.

He smirks like the devil. "She fucks with your mind," he says, tapping his head again with the gun. "This is what she does, she screws you so far into the ground that you can't get back up again, she destroyed me and everyone I've ever known, turned against me too."

That's what happens when you beat up women, asshole.

I nod sagely. "I know, she has to pay and she will, let this bitch go and I'll go get Sienna."

I need that fucking gun.

He paces again, running his other hand through his hair. *"I don't know, I don't know..."* he mutters over and over.

"Come on, man, I want to get out of here," I say, I've moved a couple more steps towards him and if he shoots me now, I'll have to be quick to get a shot out of my own, yeah, I'm packed. I really need no shots to be fired because I intend to make whatever is about to happen look like an accident—bullets are harder to hide than blades.

"Go get her!" he screams.

I hold my hands up again. "Alright, alright," I say, "but at least untie her, that way I know you intend on letting her go. Do that and I'll go and get what you want and Sienna is yours."

He thinks for a second, then, to my surprise, he complies, muttering under his breath.

Cassidy whimpers as I look at her, I close my eyes and breathe deeply. I just need him distracted for a few seconds.

"You won't try anything?" he says which just goes to show how delusional he actually is.

I sigh impatiently. "Why would I? We're in this together, bro, you can keep the gun, it's only fair you untie her for reassurance. Sienna is bound and gagged in my car, she's all yours."

That piece of information should please him, his eyes go wide and he smiles.

Cassidy starts to whimper again. *Please, for the love of God, hold it together.*

He thinks about it then nods. "Fine, but stay back."

He moves toward Cassidy and bends down, his eyes totally off me now and goes to untie the back of her hands, he's obviously tied the knots good because he can't undo them with one hand, I watch as he goes to rest the gun down on the floor, then changes his mind and shoves it in the front of his pants. He now has no hands on the gun and is untying her wrists. I take no time at all to rush at him. It's so fast, he shrieks as I come toward him, and in a few short steps, I lunge on him with all my weight. I pound his face with my fists and then go for the ribs like he's my personal punching bag. I hit him so hard, I hear bones crack.

"You think you can treat fucking women like this?" I scream in his face. He's bleeding profusely from his nose and I'm sure I just broke his jaw. "You're a piece of shit, I'm gonna enjoy gutting you, but maybe I'll let Sienna do it instead." His eyes go wide as I push him back so he doesn't get his blood on me, he stumbles backward and loses balance. I watch as he falls hard back on the concrete floor. I hear the crack as he goes down. Shit.

Suddenly, I hear noise behind me as Brock and Colt crash through the door, guns blazing as I stand over him and kick his leg with my boot. He ain't moving and he's bleeding like a pig.

I grab the gun from his pants, flick the safety on, and shove it down the back of my jeans, then I check his pulse. He ain't breathing. I can't help but feel disappointed that I only got a couple of hits in, he deserved to suffer.

I turn as I see Brock and Colt standing around me, followed by Dalton and Lee. Bones comes running in a moment later and Colt keeps untying Cassidy's wrists from behind the chair. He rips her gag off as I move in front of her and crouch down.

"Cassidy, I'm Steel, I'm a friend of Sienna's. I'm here to help you, honey, none of what I said to him is true." I hold my hands up as Colt finally releases her bounded wrists and she sits staring at me, dumbfounded. Her wrists are badly bruised and almost purple, she doesn't even go to rub them. I glance up at Colt as he looks at me worriedly.

"You hurt?" I check her over quickly but she doesn't move or answer me. "Sienna's here, she's safe outside, everything's gonna be alright now, okay, sweetie?"

She doesn't respond, she just stares at me blankly.

"What's wrong with her?" Colt mutters quietly.

"Shock," I state with a long breath. I've seen it enough times to know. This isn't good.

"Shall I go get Sienna?" Brock asks as I stand up and run a hand through my hair.

"No," I bark. God, she doesn't need to see this. "Lee and Dalton get back out front, secure the area, we've gotta clean this up pronto."

As they go to leave, a sudden movement at the doorway has me turning in that direction. To my astonishment, I see Gunner appear.

"What the fuck are you doing?" I yell at him.

He's holding Sienna by the elbow, she seems out of

breath. I give Gunner an expression that says he's got two seconds to answer but he doesn't get a chance.

"Cassidy!" Sienna shrieks as she breaks free and runs toward us, I catch her mid-run and swing her into my arms against my body, effectively pulling her back. She begins to wail and fight against me.

"I told you to stay in the car," I say between gritted teeth. I already have one catatonic woman on my hands right now, I don't need Sienna hysterical, that won't help.

She looks up at me as I glare at Gunner. "It's not his fault, I pretended I had to pee."

I give Gunner a pointed look and he holds both hands up.

Then she notices Ewan's body slumped on the ground, blood is oozing out of his head.

"Oh my God. *Is he...*"

I look down at her and nod.

Her eyes go wide.

"She needs you," I say, nodding to Cassidy. I let go of her and she darts onto her knees, and as she does, her cousin falls into her arms and shakes uncontrollably. I'm concerned there's no sobbing or any sound at all but at least this is some kind of progress.

Gunner hangs around nervously in the doorway. "We need to get out of here," he says, looking toward the open door, "like yesterday."

"No shit, Sherlock, but now we've got a dead body on our hands."

"Could call it in," says Bones, "we have proof she was being blackmailed, its self-defense, it'll stick."

"Or we make it look like an accident," Colt suggests. I like that idea better.

"No need to involve 5-0, got a better idea," I say.

"Can't trust the pigs," says Gunner, moving towards me to get a better look.

I point at Brock. "Get his car around the front, there's a bridge about a mile up; a terribly tragic car accident will clear all of this up quite nicely and leave nobody implicated."

Sienna continues to cry as Cassidy sits there limply staring into space, she looks up at me.

"You killed him?" she looks horrified.

I press my lips together. "Luckily for him, it was quick. He fell after I slugged him and cracked his skull, trust me when I say what I wanted to do to him involved him being very much alive."

"He had a gun?" she stammers.

"Yes, and he was gonna use it."

She gulps and looks back at her cousin. They look alike, except Cassidy has darker hair and she's paler, maybe that's because all the blood is drained from her face.

"Shit, is she gonna be okay?" Colt waves a hand in front of Cassidy's face, she doesn't even blink, it's definitely shock, I need to get her out of here.

"She might need a doctor," Sienna whimpers. She looks down at her ex's body and buries her head into Cassidy's shoulder. "Oh, God, what a mess."

"We need to get the fuck out of here," I say to the boys, I kneel down next to Sienna.

"We need to go, babe, I'm gonna take care of all of this but I need you to do this last little thing for me and get her out of here so we can clean this up, you got me?"

Sienna looks at me with tear-stained eyes and my heart lurches, she's been through so much.

"Thank you," she whispers. "Thank you, all of you, for being here, I don't know what I would have done…" She begins to cry again.

I run my hand down the side of her jaw and cup her face with both hands, then kiss her gently. "There's time for all of that later, I need you safe and away from here and we have to get Cassidy out, can you do that for me, sweetheart?"

She nods, completely trusting that I'll fix this. Nobody will be implicated because I've hatched a plan and I'm gonna stick with it. Accidental death by car crash. Such a pity.

Brock returns from through the doorway. "Ready."

I turn back to Sienna. "She's not moving," she cries, looking helpless as she gives her cousin a shake, "Cassidy, are you alright? Speak to me!"

I go to move but Colt steps in front of me. "I've got this," he bends down and takes Cassidy by the hands.

We watch as he scoops her out of the chair and into his arms, all the while, she just hangs there limply and lets him take her; I guess it's better than kicking and screaming, but still, this isn't good.

"It's alright, darlin', we're going to take good care of you," he whispers. "Nobody's gonna hurt you anymore."

I frown, not knowing Colt had this side to him, but I waste no time in pulling Sienna up off the floor and lead her behind Colt to the door.

"You go with Colt now to the car. Me, Brock, and Gunner won't be far behind."

"No," Sienna stammers. "I want to stay with you."

Now isn't the time for her stubborn shit. I pull her close to me and whisper in her ear. "Be a good girl and do as I say; your cousin needs you and only you can help her right now, I need you to be strong while I take care of this. You wanna be a good ol' lady?"

I pull back and she stares up at me.

"Yes," she whispers surprising me. "I do, Steel."

My heart hammers at her words.

"Then go with Colt and keep Cassidy warm while you wait for us, that's not a request, now go."

"What if we need a doctor?" she stammers.

"Then we'll go and find one." I hope she doesn't, if we do need to see someone, she might blurt out what just happened and I can't have that.

She clutches onto my cut. "I love you, Steel," she whispers. I wipe away her tears with my thumbs and kiss her on the forehead, I'm just glad this is over.

Bones' and Brock's eyes meet mine over the top of her head; they aren't used to seeing this side of me, including public displays of affection like the one in progress, so I need to get this moving along.

"I'll love you a whole lot more if we can get the hell out of here," I say in her ear.

I kiss her gently once and turn her by the shoulders to follow Bones and Colt out the door with Cassidy in his arms.

The plan is, we'll lay low once we're beyond the outskirts of the city tonight and bunker down, we'll get some rest and get back to Bracken Ridge tomorrow, but right now, me, Brock, and Gunner have an 'accident' to go and take care of.

"I'll get something out of the truck for the body," Brock nods toward the corpse on the floor, there's a pool of blood around his head.

"You carry body bags, dude?" Gunner says, giving him a sideways glance.

"If only," Brock says, jogging out of the shed to go and get whatever he's got.

I turn to Gunner.

"You had one job to do," I point at him, "you can't even keep one pint-sized girl in a locked truck for fuck's sake."

He rolls his eyes. "She said she was gonna pee herself, I was thinkin' about your leather seats, dude, sue me."

I shake my head. "You're just lucky I had this under control when I did, otherwise, things could have gone down a whole lot differently if she'd barged in here a minute earlier."

"Don't blame me, she's got a temper and she's sneaky, a bit too clever if you ask me, think you got your hands full with that one, champ."

"Don't I know it, but that's no excuse, thought you had a way with women?" I reply, annoyed, he needs to take this more seriously, that could have been so much worse.

"Don't you wanna know what we did the last half an hour?"

"I just killed someone, now's not the time to be cute."

"She's a good woman," he slaps me on the back, "think she'd make a good ol' lady, don't blame you for not wanting to let her go, she's got spunk."

I turn to stare at him. "You do, huh? Can I stop threatening to hurt you now?"

"Only if you bring it to the table," he smirks, "you got my vote."

Oh, yeah, Sienna's just gonna love that.

I rub my chin, best not to think about that right now.

We both look down at the body.

"Why are some people so fucked up?" I wonder.

He shakes his head. "Neglected as a kid, dropped on his head at birth, who knows? Fucker deserved all he got though."

"Yeah, and then some."

"Glad he can't hurt anyone else," Gunner agrees.

"Pity I didn't get to do what I really wanted, then he'd have known the meaning of pain and suffering," I grunt. I don't feel one inch of sympathy, assholes like him may get a couple of years in state pen and then get let out on good behavior, it would never end for Sienna, she'd always be living in fear. I only hope both the girls can get over this in time, especially poor Cassidy.

I turn to him. "You good?"

I sometimes forget I'm used to seeing dead bodies in my

previous line of work, and when it's wastes of space like this, I don't bat an eyelid, one less psycho out on the streets. Gunner, however, like most people, isn't.

"Yeah, it's just creepy."

I roll my eyes. "Come on, we've gotta move him into the car then torch the place, you up for some arson while we're at it?"

He looks at me with renewed interest. "Now you're talking, brother."

EPILOGUE

STEEL

THREE MONTHS LATER

ANGEL DIGS the needle into my skin like it's her mission in life to make me suffer. It's not her usual style.

"You take double your bitch pills this morning?" I gruff as she wipes my skin with a rag.

"You bet ya," she smirks without glancing up, "the more you whine like a little girl, the more it's going to hurt."

"It doesn't hurt," I say, rolling my eyes, that's a load of shit, ribs always hurt. I'm getting a new tattoo to fill the space on my abdomen; angel wings, I'm feeling kind of nostalgic.

Sienna giggles. I glance at her. "I don't know what you're laughing at, woman."

She pouts at me. "Well, you chose a monster tattoo, what do you expect?"

Angel grins. "Right on, maybe I could hire you to pep talk all my clients?"

"Pep talk them out of it," I mutter.

"What are you getting?" Angel asks Sienna in a teasing voice, she knows I won't allow it.

Sienna pretends to think it over. "I was thinking a butterfly across my shoulder, or a dolphin or something?"

"How original, *a butterfly*," I say sarcastically, "and you don't even like dolphins."

"How do you know I don't like dolphins?" she says, confused.

"Because you hate the water."

She ignores me. "Maybe something small then, like a heart and dagger, or a shooting star."

"You're not getting a tattoo," I bark.

Angel looks affronted. "Why the hell not? She'd look good with one."

"No, she fucking wouldn't," I say, annoyed, I don't know why but I like Sienna's skin perfect and natural and untouched. I don't want to see a tattoo on her body, it won't suit her.

"I like her how she is."

"But you're getting giant wings on your torso?" Sienna mimics as both the girls laugh at me. She'll pay for that later, even if it is only in the bedroom. She's never been afraid of me like so many are and I kind of like that about her, though it also means she knows exactly how to push my buttons.

"For your information, I've been planning this one for a long time, it finishes off the piece, and tattoos suit me."

"What about your name scrawled across me?" she says, raising an eyebrow. While I like the thought of that momentarily, I shake my head.

"Kiss of death," I tell her.

"What?"

"It's the kiss of death, right, Angel?"

Angel smirks again. "I do a lot of covers-ups," she admits. "In fact, I could just do cover-ups and stay in business for a looong time."

"So, you wouldn't get my name on your body?" Sienna

asks, raising her brow, she's so cute when she's pretending to be offended.

"I don't think Angel could fit 'Little-miss-pain-in-the-ass-who's-got-a-smart-answer-for-everything' on any part of my body, so that's a no."

"There is one part of your body that's long enough," she says and leans down to kiss me as I smirk.

"Eww, TMI! Gross," Angel says, affronted. "Get a room, guys."

When she pulls back, I hold my free hand with hers and we link fingers.

"Does it really hurt?" she asks more seriously, watching what Angel does with a wince.

"It hurts a lot less when you give me some sugar."

Angel wrinkles her nose. "Oh, God no, you two are not making out while I do this, uh-uh, no way. That's where I draw the line."

I chuckle then wince again, this hurts like a bitch and Angel is normally a lot gentler with me.

Sienna leans down to my ear. "I'll make it up to you later, I'll be your nurse," she whispers, "just use your imagination."

I grin into her hair liking the sound of that. "Oh, I know you will."

Angel stops and looks up at us. "My ears aren't painted on, you know," she shakes her head and gets back to work.

Sienna gazes at me lovingly. Things have been going strong for us ever since that night. Gunner and I took care of business and we made it back to Bracken Ridge without any further incident. We haven't spoken of it since that night. I killed him, in self-defense, but it still happened, and I think Sienna is still shocked by everything that took place.

Cassidy is still not in a good way, she's been staying with us, unable to practically leave Colt's side. Since he untied her and carried her out of the abandoned house, she's formed some kind of attachment to him which isn't exactly healthy, but at least she's eating now, and talking, though it may be some time before she's able to fully recover.

I don't think about that night very much, only the part where Sienna came back to me, that I will remember forever. We've been rock solid ever since. Sienna has quit the Stone Crow and moved in with me shortly after; she works in the office with me full-time. I was able to sell a couple of the old cars from Max's stash and get good money for them and she decided to start a new business with the money; car and bike restoration, a present for me. We've set up in the adjoining garage next to the workshop. I'll do up the Aston Martin first and then use the profits to keep buying and restoring more cars, without her help, this never would have been possible and I can now concentrate on that side of the business since Dalton is running the day to day mechanics at the garage. I've never been happier and I'm doing what I love.

Maybe this is just the honeymoon period, but it sure feels good. It's solid, stable, we have no secrets, life may not be roses every day but we're getting there. I can't get enough of her, her mind and her body, everything about her turns me on and I know I've hit the jackpot.

I know I'm a moody son of a bitch and I like things how I like them, but we're good together, she's an angel, *my* angel, it's why I got the wings.

It may not be perfect, and I know I'll fuck up a time or two, but she loves me, she tells me every other day. I never thought I needed to hear that until now, I guess there's a first time for everything and I'm not complaining. I'll never go back, I'm home. I'll never be sorry.

And I will make her happy. I'll spend the rest of my life trying.

SIENNA

The sun begins to set at our secret place on the ridge in the back of Steel's truck. I'm lying on a makeshift mattress on my stomach and he's lying on top of me, trying not to crush me. He's kissing my neck as I try to take pictures of the sunset with the new, flash camera Steel got me for my birthday a couple of months back, I've really enjoyed getting back into photography.

"Will you keep still?" I say, tutting him.

He grins into my neck. "You're the only ol' lady in the world who complains when her old man is trying to give her some action."

"Shh, not in front of the children," I joke.

Yeah, it went to the table. They did their chest-pounding thing and I'm now part of BRMC as his woman. While Steel maintains that it's just a formality, the whole "owning" me part, I couldn't care less, I've never felt happier.

I turn and look at Lola, she has her head propped up on the back seat watching us, but she's half-asleep, I look up higher and see Rocky curled up snoring next to her. Yes, we're foster fails. We've fostered two other dogs and adopted them out to new homes since Rocky, but we just couldn't let him go, he's such a goofy, funny little thing and we've both grown attached to him being around. He's a different dog now, no longer fearful and so loving, I don't know who he loves more; me, Steel, or Lola. We're one big happy family, dysfunctional, yes, but happy all the same.

My plan hatched, I smile to myself as he moves his hands down the sides of my body and I wince.

"What's the matter?" he says, pulling back from me.

"Umm… nothing," I reply. He continues to run his hands down to my hips, making suggestive noises as he nibbles my ear, and when he moves his hands back up, I wince out loud again.

"What the fuck, Sienna?" he says, pulling right back off me and pulling my tank top up from the hem.

My pretend tattoo is covered up with a bandage along the base of my spine across my entire back. "Oh, it's nothing, I cut myself on the..." I trail off as he rips the bandage off, *ouch,* and I can feel his stare glaring into my very core. Maybe this wasn't such a good idea? His temper is legendary.

"What the actual fuck is that?"

I bite my lip as he runs his fingers over the writing.

"Ouch!" I try not to laugh. "Be careful."

"You better not have," he growls.

"I did," I stammer, "it's a surprise."

I feel the heat of his anger radiate off him as he shakes his head. "What the fuck does that even say?"

"You don't like it?"

"Sienna Clare Morgan!" he chastises, oh, he sounds really mad.

Oh, shit. I didn't think this was a good idea at all but Angel thought payback was a good thing for all the abuse she's put up with over the years while she's tattooed his body.

"It was a birthday present."

I turn to look at him as he stares at me with thunderous eyes.

"A birthday present is a new cologne, or a pair of riding gloves, or a hot fucking night on the town with my girl, not... not *this!*"

I pretend to look affronted. "I thought you'd get a kick out of it?"

"You realize that is permanently on your body?" he barks. Oh shit, I haven't seen him this mad in a while.

"So are yours!"

"Mine are art, they mean something... this... this is some

kind of joke! *'Little-miss-pain-in-the-ass-who's-got-a-smart-answer-for-everything'?"*

He presses into my skin. "Owww," I groan, trying to slap him away, "careful."

He moves fully off me now to sit back on his hunches.

Angel and Deanna did a good job; they even put red ink around the whole thing and smudged it to make it look like my skin was sore. It's extremely juvenile but I do wish they could see the look on his face right now—priceless.

He starts digging around in his pocket.

"What are you doing?" I say, if he was any good as a special-ops guy, he'd be able to tell by now I'm lying my ass off, but he's in too much of a rage to see straight.

"Ringing fuckin' Angel, she tattooed this thing on you, she can get it off."

"It's permanent," I repeat like he's an idiot.

"Sienna," he says, and he actually looks really upset. I drop my head and begin to giggle.

He grabs my hips. "It's not real, is it?" He sounds desperate as if he really does want to believe it.

I don't answer.

"Is it real, Sienna?" He doesn't wait for an answer as he begins to rub my skin with one of his large hands and I no longer pretend it hurts, I feel him scratch away on the press-on tattoo and he exhales in what sounds like relief. I feel him peel some of the writing off my back and mutters a string of profanities as he does—something about teaching Angel a lesson and giving my ass a hiding. He gives my ass a smack while he's at it with the back of his hand.

"Not funny," he says as I continue to laugh. "So not funny."

"Oh my God, your face," I say, coming up for air. He digs his hands into my hips and flips me over so I'm on my back; I look up at him innocently.

"Don't give me that look."

"Admit it, pretty funny."

"Does it look like I'm laughing?" he repeats, he holds my wrists over my head and straddles me. "You almost gave me a heart attack."

"Oh, stop your moaning; you get me all the time."

"That's because you're as pure as the driven snow and I'd like to keep you that way."

"Correction, I *was* as pure as the driven snow... until I met you."

He smirks. "You're going to pay for that."

"Oh, yeah? Promises, promises, tough guy."

He comes down over me and I squeal at the heaviness of his body, he lets go of my wrists and settles between my legs as I wrap them around his waist.

"That's not a promise, princess, that's an all-night free pass to do what I want as punishment for trying to emasculate me."

I laugh out loud, as if that's possible. "Because it's your birthday?"

"No, because you're mine."

I grin up at him, still thinking I'm hilarious.

"I love you, Jayson Steelman."

"Yeah, you say that now but you might not be saying that when I don't let you come up for air for the next few hours."

I laugh again. "Oh, I'll be saying it, baby."

He grins and kisses me hard, his tongue in my mouth, possessing me, taking me, owning me, and it feels like the first time every time.

He comes to my ear as he presses his body into mine, his heat, his hardness ripples through my body, we were made for each other. Our bodies fit together so well, like we were always meant to be.

"I love you too, babe, but if you ever do that to me again, I'll make sure you can't sit down for a week."

"I'm faster than you, old man," I remind him as he cocks an eyebrow at my cheekiness. "Sure you can still keep up with me?"

"You're forgetting you're under me with no chance of escape."

"I'll get you again when you least expect it," I say as I gaze at him. I'll never ever grow tired of his beautiful face; a biker shouldn't be this handsome or taut and terrific, added to that he has a heart of gold, even if he is a grumpy son of a gun half the time.

"Goading me is never a good thing," he reminds me, pushing his hips into mine. "Lippy little thing with a smart mouth."

"You love it," I murmur.

I close my eyes at the friction, when he does this to me, I'm putty in his hands and he knows it.

"Sure you don't want to watch the sunset?" He laughs as his elbows come down to the side of my head and he kisses me like he's going to die. When we come up for air, I'm gasping.

"Hey," I say, trying to pull him back down, "come back."

"Maybe your punishment should be abstinence?"

I laugh out loud; we both know he can't abstain from sex for five minutes.

"That would be punishment for you, not me," I remind him.

"Is that so?" he says and lifts, pretending to get off me.

I wrap my legs around him like a ninja and pull him back down with my arms around his neck.

"Not so fast, big guy," I say reaching up as far as I can, "maybe I'll make an exception since it's your birthday and all."

He grins, falling back onto me. "Shut up and show me what that mouth is really made for."

I know now that I've found him, the man I'm going to spend the rest of my life with. He's everything a man should be—strong, dependable, capable, and he loves me to bits. I've never felt this liberated in all my life, he lets me be myself, and he even lets me play a few innings even when he likes to think he's in charge. We don't have it all figured out but taking it day by day and being totally honest only helps make us stronger. I'll never want anything else, how could I? Steel is more than enough man for me to handle.

"Getting bossy in your old age," I say as he moves down to cover my body. I love ribbing him about being older than me.

"You better believe it, princess."

"I'll never want anything more," I whisper. "Just you, all of you."

"You've got me," he mumbles as we kiss like long-lost lovers.

"Forever," I murmur back.

"Forever," he grips me tight, "I'll love you forever, princess."

I wrap my arms around him tightly as I give in to him, our bodies melting into one as his mouth moves to my neck and I shudder from his touch. Everything is as it should be. I open my eyes and watch the burnt orange sun as it sets on the horizon behind me, it's magical.

I love this place, our own private Idaho with nobody else around. I grin stupidly to myself, I'm free to be me, to be happy and that is the greatest gift of all. I close my eyes and revel in our own perfect piece of paradise.

ACKNOWLEDGMENTS

Thank you to all of the amazing people that have supported me in my journey, mainly my sister Kiki who's been a tower of strength, thank you! And my long-suffering hubby who keeps to himself (wise move!) Apologies to my fur babies Charlie and Bear for crying into your fur when it all got too much, love you to the moon and back, thank you for keeping me sane.

I'm forever grateful to YOU the reader for taking a chance on me as a new author, and hopefully you enjoyed Steel as much as I enjoyed writing it!

I have book #2 coming shortly in this same series which is Gunner's story (bring the tissues!) I loved every minute of bringing Gunner to life. He'll steal your heart…..AND…..I have a brand new Bad Boys of New York romance coming soon, book #1 is called Jaxon and it's an enemies to lovers hot read with a lot of turbulence, angst and (you guessed it!) hawt love scenes.

I've also co-written a stand-alone book with my sister Daktoah Fox with Jason Mamoa as our muse (cause why not?) it's being edited as we speak and is called 'Broken Wings – a New York love story' and is a contemporary romance. I can't wait to bring all these characters to life for you guys, it's going to be a crazy rest of the year!

Thank you to my amazing PA Savannah – check her out at @peachykeenas on Instagram and Peachykeenauthorservices@gmail.com - she's amazing and I could never have finished on time without you or got any decent teasers made. She also formatted my book (happy dance) and gave me lots of good advice and totally revamped my social media. Virtual hugs and kisses!

Thank you to Laura Wilkinson my amazing Editor (you can find her on Fiverr under: lmwilkinson)

Thank you to LJ from Mayhem Cover Creations for Steel's amazing cover and my website

Lastly thank you to all the bloggers, readers and kind people who have messaged me, encouraged me, shared my posts and just been AMAZING, I would have certainly not had the courage to finish if not for your support. I hope to continue on this journey with you for many moons to come!

Please take a few moments to leave an Amazon and Goodreads review if you enjoyed Steel, this helps me tremendously as a new indie author! Thanks in advance.

All my love xx

ABOUT THE AUTHOR

Mackenzy Fox is an author of contemporary and erotic themed romance novels. When she's not writing she loves vegan cooking, walking her beloved pooch's, reading books and is an expert on online shopping.

She's slightly obsessed with drinking tea, testing bubbly Moscato, watching home decorating shows and has a black belt in origami. She strives to live a quiet and introverted life in Western Australia's North West with her hubby, twin sister and her dogs.

Find me:

Facebook

Instagram

Goodreads

https://mackenzyfox.com

COMING SOON

Gunner – Book 2

EXCERPT......

LILIANA

7 YEARS EARLIER…………

Nothing's changed as I glance around the clubroom, except tonight it smells more like testosterone on steroids than stale beer. The usual Saturday night party is in full swing; loud music blares, some guys are playing pool, scantily clad women are strewn around here, there and everywhere, and Ginger's behind the bar serving drinks like nobodies business.

It's not the place for somebody like Steel's little sister, my brother being the Sergeant at Arms of the club, and it's definitely not the place for an underage girl, not that the brothers would do anything sinister, more like they'd send us packing out of here quick smart with an ass whooping.

I haven't seen Gunner since I was twelve, now he's back in Bracken Ridge prospecting for the club.

I guess you can take the boy out of the town but there was no taking the town out of this boy.

When Deanna, the club President's daughter, told me Gunner was back in town I knew I wanted to spend my

317

spring break back home to try and see him, secretly, just a glance, to see if he's just as I remember. He's always been sweet and kind to me, never treated me like a child, and he's drop dead gorgeous, or at least he was, I'm dying to see what he looks like now, it's been years.

Deanna's tugging on my arm, gabbling in my ear. I don't know how long we'll hold out before we get caught or someone realizes we shouldn't be there, everyone seems too absorbed in their Saturday night to notice us, but I don't care, just getting a look at him is worth the punishment.

Deanna walks in like she owns the place. I wish I had her confidence.

"We shouldn't really be doing this," I whisper, if I run into my brother then the night will be over instantly, he won't be happy. I glance here and there as we walk but I don't see him, *please don't let him be here.*

"Relax, nobody will question it if we look like we're invited," she says over her shoulder.

She's probably right. When you're the MC President's daughter nobody questions anything.

We get a couple of nods from a few of the guys who don't know any better, Ginger stops and gives us a pointed look as she pours a beer but we ignore it and pass by quickly before she can stop us.

"Crap Ginger saw us," I whisper worriedly, once we're past her hawk eyes.

"Just be cool," Deanna reassures me, she keeps walking unaffected.

Famous last words.

"What's the big plan anyway?" I wonder, hoping she has one.

"You wanna perve on Guns and I wanna see Amelia and party, hopefully somewhere in all of that we'll get some free beer too."

Urgh, I hate beer.

Amelia is Brock's younger sister, the Vice President of the club, she's been away at college and we rarely ever get to catch up unless it's spring break or Christmas.

We find Amelia pretty quickly; she's standing with a group of other older girls who are all done up to the nines.

I do not dare to think what will happen if Hutch, Deanna's father, catches us here, I shudder at the thought. The President of the club is many things, but he definitely won't approve of us hanging out partying underage, no definitely not, I don't like the thought of him telling us off, he's one of the few people scarier than my brother.

We get slipped a beer and try not to hide my disgust as I sip it, hoping to blend in.

The girls at my school don't party like these girls. I've made some good friends at boarding school and I know my mom is trying to give me the very best for my future, but my future's always belonged in Bracken Ridge. This is my home, these are my people, I don't know how I'm going to tell her I want to come home after I graduate. I don't want to go to university, I want to go to beauty school, but mom has big plans for me, as does Steel, plans they seem to want to make without my say-so.

"Don't look now…." Deanna says in my ear nudging me, I follow her subtle nod over to one of the tables behind me.

I turn and look over my shoulder. The first thing I see is the back of a Prospect cut and a mop of blonde shaggy hair. *Gunner.*

His cut's sleeveless and he's wearing a tight fitted henley underneath it. His hair's longer, still sunshine blonde but it's tied back, he moves around collecting empty glasses into a large container and he turns side on giving me a better look. Both sides of his head are shaved, so he has a Mohawk thing going on, his eyes still down concentrating on his job and my breath hitches in my chest as he turns to face us.

There he is, in all his glory. As gorgeous as ever if not more so, unlike me he's not sixteen anymore, he's grown from a boy to a man. His skin's slightly tanned from the outdoors, he's taller, broader, his arms fill out the tight sleeves of the henley well and he's got heavy, silver rings adorning his knuckles and chains and beads hanging all around his neck and up his arms. He is the epiphany of everything a man should be and everything I can't have.

I cannot keep my eyes in my head.

A biker shouldn't be that pretty, I think he's even trying to look bad ass with the Mohawk thing. He's got a small goatee thing happening too, I hope though he doesn't decide to grow it too long and cover up that beautiful face, my eyes linger and travel down his body…..*I can't even.*

I hear Deanna giggle next to me.

"You've got it bad," she says, nudging me with her shoulder.

I shove her back, my eyes still on him, "I do not."

"Uh huh, yeah you do."

"I haven't seen him in a while that's all, I'm allowed to look." I mutter.

Like a siren call, his eyes flick up toward me suddenly, he looks down and then immediately back up again quickly, momentarily stopping what he's doing.

Shit, shit, double shit.

He bites his lip and a slow smile spreads across his face as he gives me a chin lift followed by a cheeky wink. He doesn't wave though, or say hi, or come over and I have to admit I'm a little miffed; he's known me since I was three for god's sakes.

He's a prospect, I remind myself. That means he can't come over and socialize; he's working, and he won't do that until he's been dismissed from his duties, which may be never, tonight it looks like he's Gingers bitch and she's keeping him on his toes.

I look away, embarrassed to be caught openly staring and when I get the guts to look back he's moved on to another table and begins wiping that one down too with a cloth as he stacks more glasses up.

My heart hammers in my chest at the mere sight of him, his crystal blue eyes like sparkling topaz, full of promise. I know now why I'm not interested in any of the guys at school, because nobody compares to him.

Every now and again I get a glance at him passing by as he tidies up, moving around unnoticed, and every now and again our eyes meet and he smirks, each time I look away and I know I look like a loser but I don't care.

After a while the girls want to dance, Deanna and another girl Stacey drag me out onto the dance floor and we begin to shake our groove. It's dark and the music is blaring, some of the guys nearby watch us and whistle and cat call as we dance, it's probably good it's dark so we don't get too noticed.

I move to the beat as we dance and giggle and carry on like idiots, it feels good to let loose, this is a far cry from the afternoon tea parties I have at boarding school, if only my Headmistress could see me now.

I look up across the room and see that Gunner is staring at me. I keep moving as I watch him; I raise my arms up in the air and move my body to the beat. His eyes drop down and rake my body, they linger on my breasts in my tight tank top and move slowly down, he's checking me out, I feel a thrill run through me that warms my insides. He should not be looking at me like that.

Holy shit.

I break eye contact and I have to excuse myself to go to

the bathroom, I have to splash cold water on my face before I combust. When I come out of the ladies I run right into a brick wall, when I look up I realize I've run right into Gunner.

I gulp as he smirks to himself.

"You're beautiful," he shouts over the music as he stares down at me, "what's your name?"

I laugh and look down momentarily, then I meet his gaze as he's waiting reply a reply.

What the hell?

I think about it for a millisecond...*is there a chance he really doesn't know who I am?*

I mean, he's not looking at me like he knows me, if he knew it was me, he'd have hugged me by now and then probably marched me right on out of here back home.

I guess I was twelve the last time I saw him, I definitely don't resemble the kid I once was now at almost seventeen.

Suddenly a plan hatches in my brain. I want to applaud myself for my quick thinking.

He has no idea who I am....so I can be anybody, somebody he might want to make out with for example. If he finds out the truth, he won't touch me with a ten-foot pole, I'm practically his surrogate sister.... That's an awkwardly weird thought....

"Marie," I tell him before my brain catches up with my mouth, well, it is my middle name so it's only a little, teeny white lie.

He leans closer to me. "You're gorgeous, how old are you?"

My heart is beating so fast it could jump out of my chest right now.

"Nineteen," I lie, hoping he believes it.

His eyes graze down my body again and when he brings those blue eyes back up to mine I'm lost.

He leans to bend closer to my ear. "I'm on a break, you wanna go somewhere quiet?"

Say yes, say yes, say yes!

I nod, feeling like I'm in the twilight zone. My legs feel like jelly, I hope they don't give out on me, that would be embarrassing.

"What did you have in mind?" I say, looking up at him, if not a little nervously……..

Book 2 available soon, please check my social media for release date! xx

Printed in Great Britain
by Amazon

19277718R00190